BLOODY MESS

QUANTUM ENTANGLEMENTS: BOOK 1

S.NASONOV

Dedication

For all those who fight to survive in a world that was not built for them.

PROLOGUE

A soft voice pulled Alice from sleep.

It was barely a whisper, but its familiar lilt called her soul from its place of momentary peace. With the opening of her eyes, the horrible discomfort flooded her limbs, threatening to burn her alive. The torture was never-ending, the ache in her body second to the hunger in her mind.

She longed for the unbearable heat to cool, for the love that seemed so far away. The ache beckoned her to the balcony window and Alice was powerless against it.

She stepped towards the glass doors with fatigued hesitancy, her mind clouded with the need to quench the heat, to feel the coolness of the night air. Her damp hands clutched onto the brass handles, slipping slightly from the perspiration.

Just as she turned the metal fixture, a different voice made her pause.

"Momma," Amelia said, rubbing her eyes in the doorway of the bedroom. Alice released the handle, turning to her young daughter.

"What's wrong, sweetheart?" she asked, striding over and wrapping her arms around the small girl. The comforting action was so inherent it superseded the need to fly away from the agony. Amelia grounded her, reminded the suffering woman what good felt like.

Alice would sacrifice everything for Amelia, that was without question.

"Nightmare. Why are you so sweaty?" The young girl dragged one hand on her mother's forehead to wipe away the damp.

"Oh, I'm just a bit warm. Would you like a snuggle back to sleep?" Alice gestured to the large bed. Amelia's nod was tired, but she ran and dove beneath the covers with the expected exuberance of a kindergartener.

The small girl laid her head on her mother's chest, closing her eyes. Alice stroked the hair on her daughter's head, relishing in the pure love that radiated from the contact with her soft skin. She had spent many hours tracing the lines of her daughter's toes in infancy, and they had toiled away in the garden together almost every day since she could walk. Now faced with the likelihood of her removal from this life, it seemed like not nearly enough time.

"I love you, Mommy." Amelia sighed happily, soft snores following close behind.

"I love you, little breeze." The cyclone of affection for her little one drowning out the call of the abyss.

Alice closed her eyes and wished with every drop of blood in her body that what she was about to do was worth it, that she could save them all.

BLOODY MESS

RULE 1
CHANGE IS HARD
AMELIA

Amelia needed a new couch.

It was both an involuntary observation and a shameful reminder that infiltrated her mind when focused eyes wandered to the cushion underneath her client's fidgeting calf.

The calf was attached to the woman, to be clear.

Amelia never thought that was a clarification she would have to make, but one disturbing therapy session with a mischievous shape shifter was all it took.

It wasn't the cushion itself that triggered her anxiety—it was a good sofa that had served her well since the opening of her therapy practice. No, the off-white foam that protruded from an ugly gash was the problem.

Well, at that moment Amelia was the problem.

Her eyes wandered often and she could barely keep up with the complaints of the crying woman in front of her, too wrapped up in figuring out how she hadn't noticed the damage earlier.

Amelia's distraction was multilayered: firstly, she was sad her little leather fighter was hurt.

It was silly, but she had a strange habit of empathizing with inanimate objects. It was difficult not to when her caster aunt provided her with enchanted things that completed menial tasks. The wounded furniture currently supporting an elderly woman and her dog was not one of those magical items, but she thought of it as a friend—likely because she didn't have any human ones.

Secondly, Amelia hated not knowing.

The drive to discover made her an excellent psychotherapist to the supernatural, but had the unintended consequence of occasionally driving her completely bonkers.

Despite knowing that she should pay attention, the inner ramblings of her mind refused to quiet.

Many of her clients had sharp claws and careless horns, so she supposed there could have been many culprits.

Amelia took personal pride in being able to keep her clients calm during their therapy sessions, but it was also a practically necessary skill when they could potentially breath fire or summon destructive apparitions. She hadn't noticed anything out of the ordinary the previous day, but that didn't necessarily mean much.

Another important fact about Amelia is that she had very little trust in her own perception. A lifetime of lectures over lost umbrellas and missed deadlines had made her come to the conclusion that the mystery was likely due to one of her many oversights.

Even if the griffin from yesterday had punctured the leather, she was likely too wrapped up in constructing a therapy program that would help him conquer his fear of heights.

She decided it didn't matter how the furniture was damaged, and returned her attention to the client.

"I just don't know what else to do." The older woman wept, shoulders hunched as she sobbed into her palms. Her skin was thin from age, tendons and veins dancing as she clutched a forlorn face. The golden retriever whined and nudged his head against her knee, signaling an attempt to comfort the miserable woman.

Amelia was initially taken aback by what appeared to be a human woman with a dog by her side—her usual clientele was decidedly more exotic. Amelia did make a point to accept all clients regardless of race, breaking the segregational attitude of her caster ancestors.

Looking at the state of her couch, perhaps she should be a bit more discriminatory towards clients with sharp bits.

Glancing down at the intake form, Amelia discovered that the mutt was the woman's husband, a middle aged man who had shifted a month ago and refused to change back. Shifters were the most common clients she had (being able to transform at the drop of a hat invited identity issues and maladaptive escapism galore). This case was relatively simple, however.

Amelia had to pinpoint the cause of the behavior based on past incidents and connect the cause of the shifts to the problem at hand. Behaviour was often a symptom of a deeper issue; the key to going forward was analyzing and learning from the past.

"Has he done this before?" she asked, nodding towards the pup. The woman sniffed loudly and looked up.

"Periodically, but never for more than a day." Her brows furrowed with the effort of remembering. Amelia nodded, looking back towards her clipboard and running the pen along the lined paper.

She didn't use the book to write notes, her enchanted typewriter took care of that with a speed and proficiency that Amelia could never accomplish. She used the bright white pages to draw lines and shapes, a harmless distraction for her eyes while she processed and analyzed the words her clients spoke.

RULE 1

When Amelia was a student, her teachers had deducted points from her artistic additions to assignments, but Amelia wasn't a student anymore—she had a doctorate and made her own rules.

Those rules did seem to be eerily similar to the ones her aunt had instilled, coincidentally.

"Tell me about the previous times," Amelia said, carefully drawing the petals of a cartoon flower as she listened.

"Well, a few months ago I was bed-ridden with a mild case of pneumonia. Richard laid at my feet the entire day." Her husband was kind and dedicated, Amelia noted. There was likely a very specific reason he chose that form to comfort his wife.

"Do dogs hold a special significance for you?" Amelia wasn't a fan of dogs, personally. They made entirely too much mess and noise.

The older woman's lips pursed. "I had a golden retriever growing up," she explained, though didn't seem convinced there was a connection. Amelia smiled, touched that a husband could know his wife so well and would go to such lengths to comfort her.

Amelia had a longstanding fantasy of a partner that really saw her, understood her struggles and accepted them. When she was a teenager she always hoped that some handsome punk would throw rocks at her window and whisk her away on his motorcycle.

The problem with fantasies is that they were unrealistic by nature; no one would ever truly understand her due to the prestigious lineage she was bred from.

Her aunt had constantly repeated how pure their heritage was, how important it was for Amelia to be selective about her partners so that her children had the greatest chance at being powerful once-in-a-generation casters. Amelia was skeptical about the effect of a pristine bloodline considering her family was made up of a dead mother, an absent father, and a magicless daughter who was completely disinterested in having children.

"Were you ill when this began?" Amelia asked, the cartoon flower growing several more heads on the lined page. Perhaps he was a hydra flower, Amelia mused to herself. She wasn't entirely sure why a flower would need so many heads, she was overwhelmed with only one.

Julia's darkly penciled eyebrows rose at the question.

"Ill? No, I was feeling fine."

The dog whined against her leg, communicating that he disagreed with her answer.

"What do you mean, Richard? We had breakfast as usual and you threw the laundry in while I took a phone call."

Amelia watched as the woman's pupils shifted back and forth, likely manifesting an image of that morning in her mind. Amelia was envious, her mind could never hold onto insignificant memories such as one phone call.

"Was there anything unusual about that call?" she asked, attempting to stimulate the woman's recollection. Julia's eyes focused back onto Amelia, a haunting realization shining through them.

"It was with my doctor, he said my blood levels were suspicious for cancer but I would need more testing to make sure.Oh, god. This is my fault, isn't it?" she cried, shaking palms catching a miserable head.

Though empathetic for the woman's health struggles, a wash of satisfaction trickled through Amelia.

She lived for the moment of epiphany.

It was almost like a drug, using observation to deduce the problem and then slowly guiding them to the precipice of realization. It wasn't much different than guiding a partner to their orgasm, not that she had done anything like that recently.

A restlessness in her body reminded her just how long it had been since she'd done that.

Regardless, Amelia was pleased that Julia had taken the plunge and unearthed the lengths her husband was willing to go.

The sweet man received satisfaction from helping his wife through short illnesses with a soft, comforting form. It freed him from the complicated dynamics of having a sick partner, but he was still providing her comfort.

Unfortunately, not all diseases last a few days, and the poor guy didn't know what to do besides being a dog; he had no map for the future of his wife's possible debilitating illness or death, so he reverted to what he knew best despite it being inappropriate and harmful for their relationship. The next step of her plan was helping him realize that his wife didn't need a dog to support her during a grueling cancer diagnosis; she needed a husband.

Amelia stood from the wingback chair and stepped towards the couple. She sat crisscrossed before the dog-man, gazing straight into his brown canine eyes. From this distance, she could see his collar had a name engraved on it.

"Richard, is this really you?" His large, round eyes were sad as they shifted from his wife to the therapist.

She needed to make him realize that though his intentions were good, his actions were a form of avoidance.

"Or are you just scared?" Amelia's voice was soft and empathetic as she spoke.

Acting for the sole benefit of others was a common tactic for removing personal responsibility and guilt. One didn't have to grapple with their self-esteem or underlying traumas if they focused all of their attention on their partner. Codependency was extremely difficult to avoid with shifters, the ability to physically transform for praise and recognition was a temptation that couldn't be resisted. Richard whined and looked up towards his wife, desperation and misery in the canine irises.

He just wanted to make her feel better.

Despite understanding the mountains of emotional work that needed to be done to heal Richard, Julia just wanted him to shift back, so Amelia complied.

"Come back to her, Richard," she said, patting the soft crown of his head. "She needs her husband right now."

She stood and turned to walk back to the padded chair, pleased to see a human man sitting next to a now overjoyed older woman when she faced them again. He was completely naked, but nobody in the room seemed to care.

"I'm sorry, Julia," he said, gripping onto his wife's trembling hands. "I just didn't know what to say or do and-" His apology was interrupted by his wife's lips pressing against his.

Without making a sound, Amelia leaned down to grab a large paper sheet from the trunk next to her chair.

Her clients had often lost their clothes, so she always kept an emergency modesty garment at hand. The couple continued kissing, making Amelia decidedly uncomfortable. That was the point where Amelia's expertise ended—she was lost when it came to happy people.

When there was no problem to fix, her words became awkward and difficult.

"I'll give you a moment," she said, placing the paper sheet on the grateful man's lap. While her heart jerked at the romantic display, she didn't appreciate the reminder that she went home to an empty bed every night. It wasn't completely intentional, just a celibate chapter in Amelia's life due to the consuming nature of starting a business.

Now that she was settled, perhaps it was time to seek out romantic companionship again?

She wasn't picky when it came to the race of her bed-mates, with a few exceptions.

Her aunt had always told her that jumping into bed with a magic man would invite trouble, so Amelia didn't make a habit of bedding beautiful ethereal elves or faeries. As far as her aunt knew Amelia only went on the dates she organized for her, always with a handsome caster bachelor. Amelia did go on those dates, but she only completed the act of eating, smiling, and going home.

Amelia received carnal pleasure with uglier creatures, human men being the most prolific.

Amelia did bag a half-goblin once, but his propensity to drool was hard to overcome, so there were no repeats. If she was honest with herself, sleeping with semi-monstrous men was a guilty pleasure. They were usually dumb and horny, which is all Amelia needed them for. She could get them to hit the right places and avoid the unnecessary complication of feelings and their inevitable disappointment in her.

She quietly stepped out of the room and walked down the hall to the break area. It was small and clean—much like the rest of her office.

Amelia had worked hard to decorate her workspace with the aesthetic of sleek sophistication, the necessary appearance for a ruse of total control.

It would offset the sketchy location of her business. The building was technically situated in a mixed-species municipality, but the nocturnal side of the city began only a few doors down.

The rent was cheap but it wasn't exactly luxurious.

Despite the extra work, Amelia appreciated being so close to the unknown. When she locked up every evening, she would take a sly glance towards the bustling street, making a conscious effort to tamp down a trickle of longing.

Amelia's legs begged to run down that street, to smell the smoke in the air and listen to the chatter of passing pedestrians.

She'd never actually done that, obviously.

Amelia had to maintain strict control of her impulses—her aunt insisted that if she relaxed even one rule, Amelia's entire life would fall apart. Her aunt would likely have a small stroke if she knew Amelia was seeing clients with a ripped couch.

She exhaled loudly as she picked up her metal water bottle, the lid squeaking as it turned in her palm.

She needed to make fixing that couch a priority, or else she would cause the downfall of an already crippled caster reputation.

Amelia didn't give one hoot about her status as a caster, especially since she didn't get any of the magical abilities. Unfortunately, she had a deadly case of empathy for her aunt.

Magdalene Simmons had lost her twin sister and was forced to raise Amelia while dealing with that grief. Her place in caster society was the only thing she had left, and Amelia could not be so cruel as to destroy it so she could galavant with ghosts and ghouls.

She followed the rules that kept her safe and comfortable.

She wasn't perfect, though; even the most disciplined person had moments of weakness, and discipline was not something that came to her naturally.

Amelia swished the blessedly bland water around her mouth, attempting to cleanse the previous thought. She hadn't been able to tolerate plastic water bottles for years—the taste brought back too many memories of eating frozen burritos off paper plates with disposable forks, and drinking lukewarm water from crumpled plastic bottles.

She had one of those forks sticking out of her mouth when she'd found her mother's lifeless body in the garden.

A shrill ringing rescued Amelia from the unpleasant memory, forcing her to return to the reception desk to answer the call.

She should really consider getting a receptionist, or an enchanted telephone.

"Dr. Atkinson, supernatural psychologist, how can I help you?" she panted into the glossy black receiver. Amelia hummed and repeated the appointment details as the woman at the end of the line spoke.

She was relieved that it was one of the afternoon clients canceling their session, allowing her more time to figure out a temporary couch repair. She should have enough time between sessions to run to the store and grab a leather repair kit—the thought soothed her anxiety.

Amelia was comforted by having a plan in place.

The enchanted day planner escaped from her pocket, efficiently modifying the information in her schedule. Amelia waved at the smiling older couple as they exited her office, a current of satisfaction splashing against the walls of her chest. They would likely be back—a fundamental problem always needed to be addressed.

It didn't upset Amelia that she hadn't solved the identity crisis of the shifter; change took time.

She didn't have the spare minutes between clients to fix the tear in her couch, so much like poor Richard she would have to fabricate a short term solution.

Amelia sat in the padded office chair and tucked her legs into her chest, wrapping her arms around nylon covered knees. She reached one hand out and pushed against the wooden edge of the desk, causing the chair to spin.

Amelia closed her eyes and pondered her predicament.

The centrifugal force of the chair pushed the stiff woven surface against her back, grounding her body and allowing focus to find her thoughts.

She sat up with a jolt, the chair jerking to a stop.

Amelia remembered a coarse wool blanket a satyr client had gifted her.

At the time she accepted it with a stiff smile and placed it in the bottom of her therapy room trunk, mildly disturbed.

The goat man had been very vague about where the blanket had come from, and considering he had seen her for a relationship dispute with a sheep-shifter, Amelia didn't really want to know. Amelia hated to think that there was a bald woman out there, forced to wear beanies so that an ugly blanket could stay unused at the bottom of a wooden box.

Amelia chose not to think about it.

She simply shook out the lingering particles of dust from the rough fabric and placed it on the damage cushion.

Until she could find a more permanent repair, that would have to do.

RULE 2
KEEP IT SIMPLE

AMELIA

"Maybe she shouldn't have fucked him," the blonde harpy snapped.

"Maybe you should have done the fucking dishes," the brunette harpy replied.

"Oh, I'm sorry. I didn't realize that a dirty casserole dish was a boyfriend-fucking level offense."

"A tuna casserole dish, Jessica. That shit is rank and completely unacceptable."

"But fucking my boyfriend is?"

"It's not like he was even hot or anything."

"Hot enough to give you chlamydia, allegedly."

"That just means he's a dirty troll."

"Oh my god, he's a hobgoblin for the hundredth time."

"Sorry, a dirty hobgoblin."

The two young women stopped arguing to breathe, their eyes still narrowed at each other. The wings that had previously flapped wildly froze as the harpies stood and glared. Amelia took the momentary reprieve as a chance to speak.

She cleared her throat and looked up at the battling women, trying not to think about the fine layer of feathers covering the treatment room.

"Let me see if I have the facts straight," she said, sitting up straight in the wingback chair now that they had calmed. She looked towards the brunette harpy.

"Angela, you were upset that your roommate didn't do the dishes." The harpy opened her mouth to argue but reconsidered and simply nodded.

"Jessica, you are upset because she slept with your boyfriend," Amelia had no siblings or close girlfriends, and only dated a few women in college.

The dynamic between women was decidedly not supernatural, though often just as other-worldly.

"No," Jessica said, looking scornfully at her roommate.

"She's mad because apparently, my boyfriend gave her an STD like it's got anything to do with me. I don't have chlamydia, so clearly it wasn't from him."

The brunette harpy rolled her eyes. "You also didn't know you had meningitis until I dragged your ass to the hospital, so maybe I'm just the smarter one."

"Being a brunette doesn't make you smarter, it just makes you boring," Jessica replied, eyes shifting nervously to Amelia. "No offence, Doctor." Amelia's brows furrowed, she hadn't even considered taking the comment personally but now she couldn't help but glance down at her auburn strands. Her hair had always been stubbornly dark, despite several applications of bleach.

Did that make her boring?

"Your boyfriend thought I was pretty interesting when his diseased troll dick was destroying my feminine ecosystem."

"I think shoving antiseptic up your snatch after every hook up would atom bomb your microflora more than anything else."

Angela scoffed, "Clearly you've never had a UTI before."

"I'm the one with a dirty hobgoblin boyfriend, obviously I have."

Amelia's back was pressed tightly against the dark cloth of her seat. Usually she saw it as a throne, a place for her to make observations and deductions for the good of her people.

Watching the women squabble, it felt more like the driver's seat of a bus that was quickly spinning out of control and heading towards an imp-infested chicken coop.

No seminar had taught her what to do in this situation. Truthfully, there hadn't been much education regarding the psychological afflictions of supernatural creatures—a gap that had motivated her to get her PhD in psychology. Amelia clung to that thought, focusing on puzzling together the facts of the situation instead of the possibility of failure.

She would take control of the session—she had to.

Amelia cleared her throat, causing the harpies to quiet. "I'd like to bring us back to the principle of respectful communication."

The women looked down with embarrassment and sat on the couch obediently.

"Sorry, doctor," they apologized in unison.

"I think it would be beneficial to get to the core of the disagreement, and discuss it in a constructive manner. I'm going to state my understanding of the situation, and you can stop me if I've misunderstood anything."

The women nodded in acknowledgement and stayed bless-fully silent.

"Jessica didn't do the dishes, which upset Angela because she is offended by tuna casserole. Angela then slept with Jessica's boyfriend as revenge and now has a suspected STD. Is that right?"

The harpies glanced at each other meekly and nodded. Amelia's brows furrowed, a misalignment of logic stalling her analysis.

"Having sex with your roommate's boyfriend is a very dra-matic response to one unwashed dish. Why did it bother you so much?" Amelia asked Angela, the woman's beauti-ful beaked face dropped with shame.

"Because it's Grok's favourite," Jessica answered for her friend, face tight with accusation. Amelia gathered that Grok was the hobgoblin boyfriend. A twinkling of under-standing sprouted at the back of Amelia's mind, excitement and relief filling her simultaneously. They had begun the climb to realization.

Angela's shoulders tensed and manicured talons dug into her thighs, dislodging several feathers.

"I don't hate him, Doc. I just don't like who she is because of him."

Jessica rolled her eyes. "Is this about your fucking birthday?"

Angela huffed and turned in her seat to face her adversary. The motion shifted the blanket beneath her, causing the bottom edge of the tear to be revealed. The back of Amelia's neck tingled with anxiety, though her eyes remained steadfast on her task.

"And what if it was?"

Jessica shifted as well, the women now face to face.

"That's ridiculous, Ang."

"No, it's not. I had to sit on the couch and drink six vodka coolers on my fucking birthday because Grok had a tummy ache and needed his favourite casserole," Angela's voice distorted to a childish whine in mockery of the man's digestion issues.

"You know he has diverticulosis, was I supposed to just abandon him?"

"Yes, instead of abandoning me!"

There was a deafening silence, both Jessica and Amelia's eyebrows were plastered to their hairlines.

Jealousy was not uncommon in her practice, the emotion was ugly and stemmed from insecurity.

Amelia saw a glimmer of opportunity to dig deep into her

client's intentions, to uproot the tender bulb from the dying leaves.

"Angela, did you sleep with Grok as punishment for perceived abandonment from your roommate?" Amelia asked, her voice so soft and quiet it wouldn't disturb a pixie's paperthin wing.

The dark-haired harpy took a deep breath and looked hesitantly at her blonde companion.

"No, she just deserves better." The look she shot at her friend was soft, almost longing. Amelia felt validated in her hypothesis. She relaxed back against the chair, a small but triumphant smile on her face. Just when Amelia opened her mouth to speak, Jessica's voice interrupted her.

"Who gave you the right to decide that?" she spat, standing and pointing a wing in accusation.

"You did, when you said we'd be together forever." Angela's voice quivered as she spoke, cutting off entirely by the last word.

Jessica's eyes softened, arms dropping at her friend's admission.

"Ang, no one is ever going to take me away from you, not even a dirty troll." She gently ran her wing along Angela's in a comforting motion.

"Hobgoblin," Angela corrected, causing both women to burst into tear stained laughter.

"Thank you, doctor." the women said in unison, disappearing through the office door with a flurry of feathers and wind.

Amelia blinked, staring in shock at the fine feather dust covering the leather couch.

That hadn't been the first time she wasn't the one to solve a client's problems. Occasionally, people just needed the excuse of her presence to offload their worries and give themselves permission to move on.

She continued to sit and stare at the mess, deflated at the missed opportunity. Despite the reconciliation of her clients, she felt robbed of a victory.

The enchanted broom and dustpan swept past Amelia's frozen form, brushing against the carpeted floor as they hopped towards the feather mess.

The love the harpies shared was messy, chaotic and frankly quite toxic. For some mysterious reason, she was hit with a deep ache of loneliness.

Amelia pushed back the unwelcomed feeling into the locked portion of her brain, and focused on her enchanted co-workers.

The broom made several trips to the small garbage can, pausing when the can could no longer hold any more soft plush refuse.

"Hold on, I got it." Amelia begrudgingly stood and tied off the bag, replacing it with a new one. "Sorry," she apologized to the broom despite her better judgment.

Cerebrally, Amelia knew that the enchanted items did not have a conscience or emotions, but she always felt uneasy around them. She couldn't just treat them like objects, even though, logically, that is precisely what they were. Ordinary objects that her not-so-ordinary aunt had infused with magic and given her as Christmas, birthday, and graduation gifts. The thought reminded Amelia that she hadn't made a birthday request yet, and the big day was next weekend.

"Penny, add a reminder to decide on a birthday gift, please," Amelia requested.

The broom slid up to the feather-covered couch and paused, assessing the feathers stuck to the coarse blanket. It began violently beating the leather cushions like a frustrated Polish grandmother.

"Jesus Christ, hold on!" Amelia yelled, snatching the sullied blanket before the overzealous tool caused further damage to the imperfect furniture. Luckily, there was still only one gash on the surface.

"What do you think they're going to say when word gets out about this? We're going to be the laughing stock of the community. Wasn't the death of your mother enough attention for you?" Amelia's subconscious spoke, sounding suspiciously like her aunt.

The death of her mother had been a local historical event, still mentioned twenty seven years later.

Amelia's aunt had transferred her to a human school shortly after the funeral, the constant questions and rumours had overwhelmed her and she became completely mute for nearly a year. That's what her aunt had told her, anyways.

Amelia didn't remember much about that time, or her early childhood in general. She did remember the way her aunt guided her through losing her parents, how she was the only person Amelia could rely on.

She had to fix that couch, to be the person Maggie worked so hard to protect.

Amelia left the broom to work, deciding it was a perfect opportunity to purchase the repair kit, and a welcome distraction.

Her trip was short and efficient, with external time pressure motivating her mind to stay focused. When she returned from the excursion, her office was feather-free again.

"Thank you, Bruce," she nodded at the broom, relieved it

was resting in the corner. "Fine work as usual."

Amelia carefully followed the instructions on the leather and vinyl repair kit, humming with satisfaction when the innards of the couch were successfully concealed.

Amelia's stomach rumbled, signaling that she should also attend to her fleshy human innards.

She turned to throw the plastic packaging into the garbage, her heart sinking when she glanced back at the cushion to admire her handiwork. A cream-colored tuft of foam protruded through the spot that she had just repaired. The rip mocked her with its stubborn presence.

Amelia took a deep breath, choosing to believe that she simply missed a very important step in the application of the adhesive. Amelia could never fully trust her mind, numbers and dates often slipped out if she wasn't actively trying to remember them. She could add simple written instructions to the list, it appeared.

She padded down to the break room, slipping off her modest heels and opening the fridge.

Her lunch was not elaborate, just a ham sandwich and apple. Amelia sat and bit into the whole wheat bread, enjoying the peace and quiet of her lunch break.

Despite her best efforts, her mind wandered to the quarreling harpies, to the deepness of their bond. Amelia didn't really have any close friends, her aunt was the only person she could confide in. It wasn't that Amelia didn't like people, she just had a hard time getting them to stick around. In previous friendships she would frequently turn the conversation towards their problems and couldn't stop herself from analyzing them.

That was when Amelia learned that usually people tried not to think about their personal flaws, and they definitely didn't want to know how to fix them. It didn't upset Amelia when her friends would slowly grow distant, but it did mean that she had never had a roommate to fight with. She didn't think she wanted a roommate to fight with, but she couldn't ignore the slight appeal of having someone to laugh with.

Amelia immediately tucked that desire into the 'don't even bother' cage of her mind. She kept her life simple and straightforward, occasional loneliness was much easier to hide than mountains of garbage and rotten food.

The dayplanner flew out of the pocket of Amelia's blazer, parting its magical pages to reveal her schedule. Her next client's name circled aggressively next to the time, making Amelia glance at the clock in panic. Her heart leapt at the position of the minute hand.

She was late.

RULE 3
HARD WORK IS GOOD WORK

AMELIA

Amelia's aunt lived under the principle that being five minutes early was on time, and being late was unacceptable.

That was likely the reason that Amelia's heart was borderline arrhythmic as she hustled to the treatment room.

"So sorry, Flint," Amelia said and she quietly shut the door behind her. She tiptoed to the wingback chair and focused her attention to the large stone man perched on the abused leather couch.

"No worry, Dr. A." The golem said, his voice hoarse due to the stone vocal chords he was enchanted with.

Flint was a returning client of hers, so Amelia did not bother with the usual formalities; she simply waved her hand at the enchanted typewriter and began the session.

"Tell me about your week," Amelia said, nodding and humming as he recounted the various tasks he had completed for his master. The silky texture of her nylons facilitated the easy slide of her legs against each other; the microscopic gaps allowed a pleasant breeze to graze her toes.

Her toes that were embarrassingly shoeless.

Amelia's stomach dropped when she realized that she had forgotten to slip back into her heels. Her heart hammered inside a panicked chest, the loud pounding masking the stone man's gravelly voice. She casually tucked her feet underneath her, hoping that they would not sustain nerve damage from the interrupted circulation. She would deserve it, honestly.

What self-respecting clinical psychologist forgets to wear their damn shoes?

"How did your homework go?" she asked, hands trembling as she picked up her clipboard.

The golem paused before answering, either in contemplation or hesitation. Amelia wasn't sure since his face was made of only two solid pieces of rock, which didn't leave much opportunity for facial expression. Intrusive thoughts of disgust at her unprofessional behaviour plagued Amelia's mind.

As usual during a spiral, the worst case scenario played repeatedly in her mind.

He would report the session to his master and she would lodge a formal complaint and her license would be investigated. They would snoop around her office, notice the magical aides and torn couch and close her business for gross incompetence. The caster council would hear of it and her aunt would never talk to her again. Amelia would be jobless and completely alone due to one careless mistake.

Was the outcome likely? No. But the probability wasn't zero, which was enough to cause her palms to become slick with fear.

Amelia took a deep steadying breath and pushed the overwhelming anxieties from her mind, turning her attention to her client.

"Not good," he said, nervously rubbing a giant finger against his thigh. The friction caused a fine stream of sand to fall down onto the carpet beneath him.

The broom twitched from its place in the corner of the room. Amelia ignored it and focused back to her forlorn client.

"Golem coward. Couldn't tell Master." The pile of sand beneath him grew. Amelia focused on the words of her client, pulling herself back from a complete meltdown. Flint's needs were important, she would deal with hers later.

"Hey, that's okay. What did you say to her?" Amelia's voice was soft, attempting to reassure the stone servant and steady her voice.

She was fortunate that it was only Flint present to witness her misstep. His master was one of her aunt's friends—she had brought him in when she found him repeatedly slamming his head into the wall. Flint didn't handle failure well, it was something they were both working on.

"Yes, Master," Flint recounted, causing Amelia to smile empathetically.

"And what should you have said?"

"Golem cannot complete task without damage." His grainy voice was tainted with embarrassment.

"Let's practice telling ourselves first, okay?" she suggested. Amelia understood the difficulty of accepting failure, she did her best to prevent it entirely.

She found the best way to avoid the unexpected was to follow a strict set of rules. People like Amelia didn't have any internal motivation or discipline, so they had to create a rigid scheduled environment. That was what her aunt had told her, at least.

Flint nodded his head, causing another stream of dust to float down. The broom shook in response once again. Amelia needed to talk to her aunt about reconfiguring its sensitivity.

"I am worthy the way I am, I deserve to remain whole," she said, motioning for him to repeat her words.

"Golem worthy, Golem deserve to be whole."

Amelia nodded with approval, although she knew he still didn't quite believe it himself. The good thing is that he didn't really have to; repeat something enough to yourself and eventually you will start to believe it. Unfortunately, it worked for both positive and negative affirmations.

Repetition was commonly used in cases of psychological abuse—it slowly warped the victims perception of the world and themselves, making them easy to manipulate. Amelia found it interesting how a person could internalize external phrases to the extent that they act on the agenda of the abuser.

Give a man an insult and you hurt him for a day, but teach a man to insult himself and you can ruin his entire life.

The dayplanner emerged from her pocket with great difficulty—her frame was lopsided due to her feet-hiding posture. It floated in front of Amelia's face and displayed her schedule with the time aggressively circled. Amelia grimaced, she must have been musing longer than she thought.

"That's a great start. I want you to say that to yourself whenever you feel you can't say no." Amelia instructed, standing and ushering the golem to the door.

"Dr. A need Golem?" he asked, pointing towards the tied up garbage bag leaning against the doorframe. Amelia laughed and shook her head as she held the wooden structure open for him.

Having a large capable servant would certainly be nice, but Amelia never blurred the boundaries of her professional relationships.

Flint's steps were slow due to the sheer weight of his legs, giving Amelia's brain time to deviate.

Images of an obedient handsome human servant flashed through her mind, causing a weak flutter of arousal to spark in her core.

It was one of her favourite fantasies as of late; a calm and kind human man that was devoted to her pleasure. He would fall to his knees and beg to eat her, to swallow down every drop she would gift him. She would pull his hair and muffle his cries with her pussy. She could do no wrong in his eyes, everything she did was inherently good and right. To the imaginary man ,at least.

The throbbing in between her legs pounded steadily, making Amelia regretful that it was Friday. Her scheduled day for masturbation and carnal release was Saturday night, so she would have to put her lust on the backburner. Fridays were saved for a singular gin and tonic and listening to the radio at three quarter volume instead of half.

A party night, if you will.

The image of Jessica's sideways look and unintentional insult appeared, striking hard enough to leave a crack for her subconscious to poke through.

That was something a boring woman with brown hair did, have a sad party of one. The naughty voice in the back of her mind pointed out that people had sex at parties and it would technically still follow the rules if she did both. Nobody was watching her, so it could be her own little sinful secret.

No one would die if she gave in just once.

"Good night, Dr. A," Flint said, finally reaching the door and his scrambled therapist.

"Goodnight, Flint." she said, tapping the stone man on the back in a friendly gesture.

Instead of shuffling through the door as she expected, the stone man crumbled at her feet, launching a large plume of dust into the air.

Amelia's heart dropped—she killed Flint.

BLOODY MESS

RULE 4
STARVE THE MONSTER
FREDDY

"Freds, what the fuck is this?" Mo asked, face a deadly mask of authoritarian severity.

The look didn't come naturally to him—his uncle had a kind face and even kinder tendencies, signaling to Freddy that he was in shit.

Deep shit.

Mo leaned down and opened the door that hid just underneath the bar. The fridge normally stocked the ingredients that weren't meant for display, additives that revealed the undead nature of the clientele.

The cans of coolers and bottles of liquor meant for less blood-thirsty customers belonged on the illuminated shelves behind him.

Freddy's heart sank when he realized what Mo was about to pull out. He had meant to remove all evidence of his crime, but his mind was sluggish from hunger and he had forgotten.

He was so busted.

Freddy had been busted for many things during his human life: breaking and entering, assault and battery, drug possession—none of it had stunned him like the vision of Mo pulling out an empty blood bag.

Unlike the tragedy of his mortal life, Freddy had begun to care deeply for his uncle and the second chance he had been given.

"This was full on Monday," he said, lips pressed together. Mo held up a clear plastic bag with a deep red residue— what used to be an entire bag of blood. Freddy pressed his sweaty palms against atrophied quadriceps, the moisture wicking fabric of his pants doing nothing to soak up the rising guilt in his chest. He had just finished slicing the limes when his boss and mentor interrupted him, but Freddy had a feeling the burning in his palms had nothing to do with citric acid.

"Just because I think of you as my own flesh and blood, doesn't mean you're not my employee." Mo stuck a pointed finger in front of Freddy's face as he spoke, a gesture commonly reserved for misbehaving children.

Freddy placed the fruit into a plastic container and tucked it onto an open space on the shelf.

He wasn't surprised at the reaction, he had always been proficient at pissing people off. The difference was he didn't care about anyone in his human life—actively disliked them, actually. Freddy loved Mo like the positive father figure he was missing, making this confrontation both novel and extremely painful.

Mo's voice softened, "I never thought you would..." He leaned forward, large palms pressed against the sleek black acrylic of the bar, anger transforming into something far more potent: disappointment.

Freddy felt that disappointment pierce his heart and seep into every bloody vessel.

He was always good at everything he did even if it wasn't exactly lawful. Freddy had quickly come to realize that he could never follow society's rules, so he had to create his own strict code of ethics.

He had been sired by a monster and spent the entirety of his human life being a scourge, fucking women he didn't like, selling drugs he didn't take, and picking fights he knew he would lose.

Despite all that, Freddy would never steal from someone

that trusted him.

The wash of shame was gargantuan, though still paled in comparison to the possibility of admitting his greatest weakness.

Freddy let that fear consume him, turning his guilt into hot, defensive anger. In his heart he knew it wasn't fair to Mo, but life hadn't been fair to Freddy.

"Never thought I would what? Turn out like my rotten father?" His fingers dug into the underside of the bartop as he hissed at his mentor. He wanted Mo to yell at him, punch him, punish him for his misdeed.

"Freddy, I didn't say that." His tone softened as he walked around the counter and towards the stiff vampire. He clutched Freddy's shoulders tenderly, the close contact breaking his momentum. The tender way Mo's blue eyes bore into Freddy's starving dark pupils forced the young vampire to drop his gaze.

"You didn't have to. I stole from you, we both know that makes me a criminal." Though his touch was gentle, it felt like the charging wire of the electric chair, forcing Freddy to hold his breath and wait for the inevitable pain of death. He had betrayed the only person who believed in him, and he had to face the consequences.

Instead of responding with aggression, Mo leaned down and stared deeply into Freddy's eyes with concern.

"You're hungry," he said, correctly identifying just how dark Freddy's eyes were. Mo was right, as he usually was; Freddy had been slowly starving to death over the course of a year and a half.

He had an opportunity to admit the truth, to just let the words slip from his lips.

I can't hunt.

I'm a pathetic excuse for a man.

I don't deserve to live.

The words circled Freddy's mind like an immobilizing gargoyle patrol, cementing his mouth shut.

"You should know better than to let yourself get this way. Go find a nice broad to grab a drink from, and when you're in a better place we can talk. " Mo continued, frustratingly reasonable as always.

Freddy found his response both devastating and inadequate. He craved the cold metal around his wrists that caused his shoulder to ache, he longed to be forced to ruminate on the consequences of his actions and be absolved of them upon release.

Mo's attempt at thoughtful resolution was in itself both an exile and a death warrant.

Freddy couldn't just bite any acceptable human, he had tried and failed many times. He became nauseous just at the idea of preying on an innocent human's life blood, and if he couldn't return to the apartment they shared until the task was complete Freddy would die.

As you should.

He nodded and exited the vampire nightclub, pulling the hoodie over his head—the evening air was chilly, and he needed an extra shield from the world.

He walked down the street, the brick sidewalk mocking him with its straight lines and predictable edges. He had the urge to smash it to pieces, to force it to mirror his crumbling life.

Freddy would die.

He had non-functioning fangs and just lost his only source of blood, housing, and employment. He was already weak from malnutrition, and that was with diverting the blood from cocktails he was meant to be serving.

What would he do now?

If Freddy was concerned with staying alive, he would form a plan to beg, borrow, or steal some blood. Yet, he couldn't bring himself to even think about his survival.

The image of Mo's disappointment, sympathy, and concern,

haunted him, fueling the speed of his steps.

A few years ago, when he felt brimming with guilt and self-loathing, he would either find a fuck or a fight. Neither of those options seemed viable due to his weakened starving state, but the idea of bright hot punishing pain and the sweet freedom it provided moved his aching legs forward.

"Fucking feathers, fucking sand," a female voice grumbled in the alley way to his left.

Freddy pressed himself against the side of the building, hiding from view just in case she had a knife on her, and was feeling stabby.

"Fucking rules," she mumbled to herself, slamming the lid on what sounded like a dumpster. "Can't even flick my fucking bean."

Freddy peaked his head over the corner of the stone wall, trying to steal a glance at the possibly mentally ill woman. A tantalizing scent of mixed berries and whipped cream filled his nose, a lingering note of cinnamon causing his mouth to water.

He had smelled many human patrons at the bar, but no one had ever had such a complex scent.

Despite his fangs remaining holstered, Freddy's mouth watered and a deep hunger cramped his stomach. His eyes focused on the figure of the woman in the alley; her soft curves stretched the fabric of the emerald suit that covered shapely limbs.

Freddy's cock stood at attention, awakened by the perplexing delicious-smelling woman.

He had been too weak to even think about getting laid since he was turned, a fact his body decided to remind him of.

The woman disappeared through a small door on the side of the building, leaving only her irresistible scent behind. Freddy chuckled to himself, a small wave of schadenfreude bringing him a sliver of amusement during what was inevitably the beginning of the end.

It was comforting to know he wasn't the only one having a shit night.

Curiosity followed closely behind the momentary reprieve. Within the span of thirty seconds that mysterious woman had caused Freddy to feel amusement, hunger, and desire. He may be functioning on empty reserves, but he wasn't an idiot– that had been a sign.

Freddy peeled himself off of the brick wall and stepped towards the front of the building. He let out a breath of disbelief when he read the words that were plastered to the door.

DR. AMELIA ATKINSON

CLINICAL PSYCHOLOGIST OF THE SUPERNATURAL

It figured that the universe would lead him to a shrink, of all people. Despite his skepticism, a beacon of hope filled Freddy's chest.

Nobody offered grand punishing judgment like a therapist.

The humiliation of that delicious woman systematically showcasing all of his faults made his cock twitch. Her tantalizing scent lingered in Freddy's nose, as he stepped towards the door.

He knew that if he knocked on that door at least he would feel something, and the rest he could figure out later.

BLOODY MESS

RULE 5

NEVER WORK PAST INSURABLE HOURS

AMELIA

Although the official closing hour of her business was six o'clock, Amelia never booked a client past five.

The haphazard therapist needed that solitary time to organize the transcripts her typewriter had provided, and do some general tidying.

Truthfully, Amelia despised cleaning; it was boring and brainless and doing it made her wish that she had a speck of magic like her mother.

She paused for just a moment, paper halfway in the file folder.

She didn't allow herself to think about her mother often—the bittersweet memories held more bitterness than sweetness.

She didn't let herself remember the icecream they ate and cartoons they watched on the good days, and she definitely didn't let herself remember the flies that circled those ice cream containers for the subsequent bad days.

Amelia continued to tidy, the horror of letting the world see her internal chaos superseding the annoyance of taking out the garbage.

Frustration and arousal lingered in her body, making her movements erratic.

She went back and forth to the dumpster behind her office several times, muttering negative foul words under her breath. She just wanted to go home, make a drink that was slightly too strong and ride her vibrator until she forgot her own name. She certainly needed the release—her muscles were tense with agitation and sore from lifting about half a dozen large boulders to the front garden, and then several bags of feathers to the back alley. The frustration had quickly boiled into something nearing anger, causing Amelia to pause and take a long grounding breath.

Feelings should be passengers, not drivers. Her aunt's voice echoed in her mind, reminding Amelia to get herself under control.

A shrill ringing startled the agitated therapist from her attempt of composure, the surprise causing a momentary delay in her limbs.

The phone never rang after five o'clock, all of her clients knew she didn't take appointments at that time. It continued to shriek, reminding her that life was predictable in its unpredictability.

A woman's voice greeted Amelia when she coordinated her body enough to answer the damn thing, understanding cascading over the therapist when the familiar ramblings of her client filtered through the receiver. It was the same client that had cancelled earlier—a sweet werewolf girl with bipolar disorder. Amelia had a feeling she was entering into a manic episode, and the speed of her cadence confirmed it.

"Hi, Dr. A. I know I cancelled earlier because I was going to go shopping but my mom took away my card even though I told her I would only get what I needed for the handmade friendship bracelet business I was going to start. Anyway, she said she would keep it until I got at least eight hours of sleep but we both knew that wasn't happening because I'm meant for greater things than sleep. I searched for about three hours– it wasn't in her wallet, purse, safe, or hidehole where she keeps the Christmas presents. At this point I'm pretty sure she's hidden it up her ass. Do you think that's a marketable skill, actually? I'm sure there's some guy out there that would pay you big bucks for that kind of thing. You know, my sister-" Though Amelia's lips were pressed tightly with patient amusement, she had to stop the rambling young woman to maintain a fraction of her normal routine.

"Was there something you needed, Rebecca?"

"Oh, yeah, can I still come for my appointment? You should be open for another half hour, I think."

"Sure, come on down," Amelia said, knowing that she would not be seeing the werewolf that night. It wasn't the first time that she had performed this maneuver and it wouldn't be the last. Amelia would likely get an apologetic phone call from her mother in the morning and a follow up appointment in three to five days once the poor girl had slept for seventy two hours. They exchanged goodbyes and Amelia begrudgingly returned to her evening routine.

Maggie had taught her to always be grateful for what you have, especially on the days where it felt impossible to do so. She efficiently stepped into the treatment room, and plopped herself on the couch.

"Thank you, Bruce and Debbie," she said to the broom and dustpan, cracking a smile when they rattled with acknowledgement. She was genuinely very grateful for their help on that particularly messy day, even if they weren't perfect. The momentary lapse from earlier replayed in her mind.

Bruce had slid into the reception area, noticed the remains of Flint, and fallen over dead. The dustpan used its flat body to fan its mate, attempting to coax it back to life. It wasn't until Amelia had taken all of the larger stones to the front garden that he had reanimated and began to sweep a monstrous pile of dust.

Luckily, Flint wasn't actually dead.

In fact, his master had laughed when Amelia called her in a panic, allowing stiff shoulders to relax slightly.

"You know how enchantments are, those two weeks fly by before you know it." she had said, tone highly amused instead of devastated. Amelia didn't know what the woman was referring to, since her enchanted items had been functioning for years. She pushed the discrepancy from her mind—her aunt probably refreshed them without her knowledge. Regardless of the cause, Amelia was just glad that the golem would be back next week.

Despite the flood of relief, the tension deep in her chest didn't ease.

Amelia prodded the torn edge of the leather cushion, rough strands of fabric sharp against the sensitive skin of her finger. She poked through to the soft foam, absentmindedly picking at it while she pondered.

The possibility that the damage was a karmic sign from the universe clung on to the gyri of her brain like a necroworm, tucking itself in the deep sulci beneath.

Considering the high level of education she had received,

Amelia shouldn't have been as superstitious as she was, but she just couldn't help the deep rooted feeling that her life was influenced by a force greater than her own. Strict discipline had been the sole reason for her success, deviating now for a night of sexual debauchery was only going to threaten the stability she thrived in.

Doubt returned, making Amelia imagine much like the foam underneath her hand, it had torn its way through the firm prison of her mind to reach her.

Was she thriving?

She didn't have a devoted husband willing to become a dog for her, she didn't have a roommate or close friend to fight with, and she was having a serious moral dilemma about the day in which she jerks off.

A mechanical typing noise interrupted Amelia from her internal battle, forcing her to stand and saunter towards the small desk pressed up against the wall.

Need to talk?

Amelia took the sheet and stared at it for a moment before nodding in agreement and sitting on the wooden desk chair.

On days when Amelia was particularly out of sorts she would talk to her faithful typewriter to counsel herself. The logical reason was because it was important as a therapist to hold yourself accountable and understand the difficulty of doing internal work. The real explanation was that Amelia had a difficult time processing her thoughts and feelings, speaking them aloud forced her to organize them into coherent sentences, instead of trying to grasp them as they whirled around her head in a tornado-like fashion.

Name: Dr. Amelia Atkinson
Age: 32
Sex: Female
Pronouns: She/Her
Race: Human

Session 254

Tracy: What's wrong?

Dr. A: I want to break a rule.

Tracy: Okay.

Dr. A: Is it? Am I allowed to do that?

Tracy: You are asking a typewriter if you can modify arbitrary rules you yourself have set.

Dr. A: Right, that's stupid.

Tracy: No, but it is concerning.

Dr. A: Yes, it is. I start with one extra night of masturbation and before you know it I'll lose all sense of purpose and launch myself off of a balcony where my five year old daughter will find me and be traumatized forever.

Tracy: It sounds like you're placing a large amount of value on the rules because you inherently distrust yourself.

Dr.A: Obviously!

Tracy: Do you want to process this in a healthy and constructive manner?

Dr.A: No, I just want to feel better right now.

Tracy: A common maladaptive coping mechanism is avoiding the stressor. Are the rules making you feel unwell?

Dr. A: At least one of them is, perhaps a few more are small contributors. That doesn't matter, I can't just break my routine because of one bad day.

Tracy: Why not?

Dr. A: Because that's just the way it is.

Tracy: Even the most hardworking, disciplined humans take vacations. You're not perfect, Amelia.

Dr. A: You're supposed to help me, not insult me.

Tracy: What you choose to see as a negative is directly related to your internalized self-value, it would be within your best interest to unpack that.

Dr. A: A rule vacation may not be a bad idea, actually. It is a long weekend after all. Tracy, you're a genius.

Tracy: I am simply a mirror of your subconscious.

Dr. A: And that makes you a genius.

A soft knock rattled against the front door, making Amelia freeze. She glanced up at the clock on the wall; it was already half past six, far beyond the displayed closing time.

It figured the night in which she deviated from her regular routine would be the same night her client showed up for the first time. It didn't matter, she was going on a rule vacation, three blessed days of freedom.

A heaviness released from Amelia's shoulders, her breaths coming easier than they had in years. Penny flew out of Amelia's pocket and reminded her of the time once again, the scratches so aggressive the pen threatened to rip through the paper. Amelia rolled her eyes and tucked the notebook into her purse, making sure to fasten the zipper fully.

She didn't need any reminders of the rules tonight—she was on vacation.

"You're lucky I'm still here," she called out with humor as she gripped the brass knob. "I'm usually pretty strict with the rules, but I'll make an exception for-" She opened the door with a strong jerk, expecting to see a wide eyed werewolf girl, but froze with surprise when a very different figure stood in front of her. "-You." Amelia finished on a breath, shock taking the wind from her lungs.

A young man stood on the step, at least she assumed it was a man. All she could see in the darkness of the winter evening was a mop of dark hair that escaped a drawn up hood.

"You're not Rebecca," Amelia said dumbly, face slack. The black cotton sweatshirt matched black sweatpants, both fitted nicely to his frame. He was taller than Amelia, even hunched over with his hands stuffed into the loose fabric hanging from his midsection.

It seemed like he didn't want to be seen, despite the shadows clinging to high cheekbones and full lips. A metal ball adorned each side of his nose. He was hot, in a cool, apathetic sort of way. That had been Amelia's type, prior to her recent dry spell—men that were not conventionally handsome, but troubled and distant.

Amelia had seen plenty of men that were better looking than him, but she had never smelled a more alluring cologne.

"Ah, no. I'm Freddy," he said, his voice a quiet tenor.

"Freddy," she repeated, a long pause following her reply. Her brain, usually percolating endlessly with thoughts and doubts, was unsettlingly blank, halted by the scent of peppermint and vanilla invading every axon and choking out reasonable thought.

She was in trouble.

"Yeah. Do you do all of your therapy in the doorway or can I come in?" Despite the pallor of his skin and clear exhaustion underneath his eyes, a smile that approached smugness pulled at his lip.

She expected the universe to challenge her discipline, but delivering a handsome young man to her literal doorstep seemed like a gift.

Amelia was not a lucky person, so there had to be a horrible consequence that was yet to be discovered.

"Of course. I'm sorry, I just don't normally see clients so late." She waved him in, closing the door with a soft click. Since she had already completed the closing routine, the reception area was devoid of any light. Amelia usually thought of the dark as a soothing blanket that muffled the sharpness of the world, but being close to this man without having full use of her senses made her nervous. The back of her neck prickled as she strode to the desklamp and pulled the cord to illuminate the reception area.

Amelia's eyes returned to Freddy immediately, partially

from suspicion, and partially because she couldn't help it—he radiated a magnetic energy that pulled at her naughtiest bits.

"Was Rebecca a special someone, then?" His eyes roved her body, as if trying to deduce if she looked like a lesbian.

Amelia didn't appreciate being deduced, that was her job.

Perhaps he was here to help her break the 'Don't tell off clients' rule? She wouldn't mind wiping that smirk off his face, though there were much more pleasurable ways of silencing handsome men than verbal reprimand.

The heat in her core sparked back to life, conveniently slotting the male specimen in front of her into the fantasy. She would instill a fun sexy rule, where she would sit on his face if he made a snarky remark and only allowed him to speak if he was polite. Though intensely arousing it was a completely inappropriate thought to have about a client, and definitely against the rules.

It was a good thing that as of six o'clock, there were no rules.

Forbidden temptation bloomed in her core.

"She sure is special, but not to me in that way. I take personal boundaries very seriously." Amelia crossed her arms, forcing an outwards appearance of power and control she did not currently have.

She would resist the urge to press her nose into the crook of his neck for a better sniff. She would not lick him.

"Not all boundaries, if she's visiting you after hours," he challenged, leaning his head against the royal blue door. The lamplight danced off the planes of his face, making the suddenly frazzled therapist think of several more ways to stop his questioning.

Amelia had chosen blue for the front door because it encouraged calmness in her clients. Unfortunately, the way it framed his leaning form was the opposite of calming.

Amelia found it entirely too stimulating, the hint of smirk pulling his lip coupled with the look of lethargy that had to travel down the bridge of his nose to reach her.

Would he look like that after she wrung several orgasms from him?

"Sometimes exceptions are required," she answered, feeling uncharacteristically defensive.

"So you can make one for me, since I don't have an appointment." Though he spoke with an air of charming manipulation, there was a deep fatigue in the bend of his body as he pressed against the wood. This smug, mysterious man was unwell.

Amelia blinked, his words reminding her that he was here for her help, not to be the star of her newly established Friday masturbation session.

He would still be in that leading role, but only after she helped him.

"Of course, just fill out the form and I'll meet you in the treatment room." Amelia pointed towards the door across from the reception desk, and Freddy nodded in understanding.

"Yes, doc," he answered, causing Amelia to nearly drop the clipboard as she grabbed it from the desk drawer. The flood of arousal was hot and unsettling.

Determined to stay professional, she walked confidently towards the handsome stranger, attempting to bite back the grimace of pain from her throbbing feet.

Though Freddy's gaze made every micro hair on her skin stand, the discomfort from her shoes was bordering on excruciating. The green high heels she wore were only a few inches in height, but twelve hours was the limit of her capacity to wear them without pain.

Freddy didn't reach out for the clipboard, simply continued to look at her with contemplative eyes. They were large and dark and made Amelia feel uncharacteristically nervous.

"You can take them off, I know it's after hours." His eyes jumped from her feet back to her face.

"Oh, I can't work without shoes, that would be completely

unprofessional."

Freddy dropped to his knees, attempting to pull one of her feet into his hands.

"Didn't we just talk about exceptions?" His chin tilted upwards, a sweet but exhausted smirk completely disarming any argument she had.

He looked young.

Not just in the smoothness of his skin, but in the gravity that was absent from his chest.

Creatures that had been alive for centuries wore their trials and tribulations on their sternum—time had a way of hardening one's soul.

His dark eyes were naive, causing Amelia's mouth to go dry and another rule to pound through her head: never date a younger man. Their frontal lobes didn't mature until thirty five and she just didn't have capacity to properly support that kind of emotional growth in her personal life– she could barely keep her own chaos under control.

It didn't stop Amelia from relishing in the spicy scent of his cologne, and fantasizing about clutching his jaw in her hand and forcing his gaze back to hers.

He carefully removed both shoes and set them aside, the relief on her sore feet immediate. Gently manipulating each toe, the methodical flexing and extending nearly made Amelia lose her composure and moan with pleasure.

"I don't have any money," he whispered, a twinge of embarrassment lacing his tone. His admission made her pause, a crack of honest vulnerability in an otherwise charming and confident persona. There was more to this man that he portrayed, she was sure of it.

"That's okay," she smiled, "I'm closed anyway." Despite her words, Amelia had never felt so open and ready to consume—she wanted to know everything she could about Freddy, including what his skin tasted like and if he was a moaner or a growler.

Only a thin layer of nylon separated their skin, allowing his gentle touch to leave a fire of arousal licking up her legs and between them. Though not overly sexual, it was intimate and sensual and more potent than any aphrodisiac.

What had she done to deserve this gift from the universe?

"Thank you," he murmured, as if she had done him a favour. He straightened to his feet with surprising grace. When her brain began flashing images of other ways she could make him express gratitude, Amelia decided it was best to retreat.

She needed space to make sense of this man.

She held out the clipboard once again, grateful when he

grabbed it from her hand.

"Thank you," she echoed before scrambling into the treatment room.

Her heart patterned wildly in anticipation and intrigue as she waited for Freddy in the wingback chair, mind trying to puzzle together her unexpected attraction to him and what it could mean.

She was used to having attractive clients, particularly enchanting men. Maintaining professional boundaries had never been an issue for her before, even the most charming fairies were simply people that needed help.

Amelia's mind methodically combed through the mental catalogue of supernatural creatures with aura abilities, quickly developing a vague list of options.

He didn't have the musculature of a werewolf, but definitely made her feel a bit feral. There was a chance that instead of magical manipulation, her attraction was pheromone based. A wash of need at the prospect of pressing her nose to his bare skin made Amelia move on to the next hypothesis.

He could be a fae of some kind—though his confidence was clearly only a performance and fae men usually had the ego the size of a small country. Perhaps he was an incubus or some other infernal creature powered by the seduction of others? That would make the most sense, since he was clearly here to test her 'Don't sleep with men that will inevitably ruin your life' rule.

Before she was ready, the door cracked open and Freddy stepped inside.

He was very good at being quiet, a night creature without doubt. That narrowed down the possibilities of his race, but Amelia still could not be sure—she was not familiar with many nocturnal supernaturals due to her limited nighttime hours.

She started at six in the morning to accommodate the majority of her clients work schedules, and even she had boundaries for how many hours she could work.

Guilt pulsed through her at the reminder of how many potential clients she was leaving behind. How many more mothers were lost because she could not save them.

Freddy handed her the intake form and sat on the sofa, re-centering Amelia to the intoxicating creature in front of her.

"I'm sorry about the mess," she said, grimacing as he fiddled with torn fabric.

His eyebrows knit together, gaze following hers to the tear. "Why are you sorry? It's a nice couch, I don't even see any cigarette burns."

Amelia's mouth popped open before pressing together

again in professional composure, just barely resisting the urge to laugh.

"Right. Let's begin."

Name: Alfred Michaels
Age: 24
Sex: Male
Pronouns: He/Him, They/Them
Race:
<u>Session 1</u>

Freddy: Is that a magic typewriter?

Dr. A: Oh, yes. I call her Tracy.

Freddy: Ah, nice to meet you Tracy.

Dr. A: She's just an object, there's no reason to talk to her.

Freddy: Then why did you give her a name?

Dr. A: Was there something I could help you with, Freddy?

Freddy: Sorry, am I not supposed to ask questions? I've never done this before.

Dr.A: My apologies. This is a safe space, you can ask and say whatever you like.

Freddy: Okay. What kind of therapy do you do?

Dr. A: I'm pretty versatile. Was there something specific you were looking for?

Freddy: No, I don't think so.

Dr. A: Alright, what brought you in today?

Freddy: Myself, I guess.

Dr. A: Naturally. What in specific is troubling you?

Freddy: I'm a bad man.

Dr. A: No, you're not.

Freddy: Pardon?

Dr. A: I meant I don't believe bad people exist.

Freddy: You haven't met my father, then.

Dr. A: Are you bad like your father?

Freddy: No, nothing like that. If you don't believe in bad people, how do you explain the trafficking of women and children? All of the men who take without permission regardless of the harm they cause?

Dr. A: I believe that sometimes people are profoundly sick and make justifications so they can survive.

Freddy: So, just because someone is fucked in the head

it means they're absolved of all their crimes?

Dr. A: I'm not a judge, Freddy. Just an observer.

Freddy: And what do you observe about me? A pathetic sick man that wants mommy to tell him he's a good boy even though he deserves to see the bad end of daddy's belt?

Dr. A: No, I see a man becoming increasingly defensive towards his therapist despite him being the one who sought her out.

Freddy: I'm sorry, you're right. I'm sorry. Can we not talk about my dad?

Dr. A: We weren't. Why did you come here, really?

Freddy: Because I'm too old for daddy's belt, I guess.

Dr. A: You were looking for punishment.

Freddy: No. Yes. I don't know, honestly.

Dr. A: Regardless, you felt your illness was not a sufficient justification for your behaviour.

Freddy: Because it's not a real illness. My brain is just fucked up.

Dr. A: I hate to inform you, but your brain is a part of your body. That part is out of your control, unfortunately.

Freddy: You seem to have a pretty good handle on it.

Amelia: Looks can be deceiving.

Freddy: I have to control it, or nothing else will matter. I can't keep living like this.

Dr. A: Why?

Freddy: My uncle said I can't come back until I'm fully satiated. We live together and I work in his bar, so it's kind of important.

Dr. A: Does he often exercise control of you through ultimatums?

Freddy: It's not like that, doc. He looked after me when I had no one.

Dr. A: You can justify his behaviour because you respect him.

Freddy: Yeah, but it really isn't like that.

Dr. A: Why is it that you don't respect yourself?

Freddy: Fuck, your questions are brutal. Why would I respect myself? I can't do the one thing a proper man is supposed to do. I'm broken, and broken men don't deserve anyone's respect.

Dr. A: What is it that you can't do?

Freddy: Hunt. My uh, anatomy just doesn't respond. I've tried so many times, but I feel nothing.

Dr. A: What does trying look like?

Freddy: I don't think you want to know that.

Dr. A: I never say anything I don't mean, Freddy.

Freddy: I usually wait until someone shows interest, you know, flashes a flirty smile or tries to touch me. It happens often enough—being a bartender does that. So, I lead them to the back hallway and I am so ravenous I could die.

Dr. A: And then?

Freddy: And then I throw up into the nearest receptacle- lately it's been the mop bucket in the storage room.

Dr. A: Is it a matter of attraction?

Freddy: No, it's just the idea of invading someone's body like that. I can't let myself enjoy it, feeling like a predator.

Dr. A: It reminds you of your father.

Freddy: Yeah, I guess.

Dr. A: Who says you have to hunt like that? Not all women prefer predatory, dominant men. There's nothing wrong with reversing the roles.

Freddy: I really don't think it works like that.

The typewriter stopped with a flick of her hand.

Amelia was used to challenging sessions and defensive clients, but she had never experienced another person spearing her with such precision.

"You seem to have a good handle on it," he had said, without knowing just how shaky her grip was on her diseased brain. He thought she was his superior, and that faith was stronger than her own could ever be.

"Freddy, there's nothing wrong with you," Amelia said, gazing at him with sympathy. Her notebook lay in her lap, pages completely bare.

She had been so engrossed in his psyche that she couldn't look away from him long enough to write, and for some reason her mind was completely quiet and focused on his plight. She watched him gesticulate wildly when she revealed she wouldn't judge him, his eyes burning with a deep seated frustration.

Freddy was on the right track, a punishment could bring the toxic feelings to the surface, the sting of pain could liberate him from his guilt. Though, the kind of discipline he was looking for was not something she could perform in her office. Despite Amelia's vow to ease her rules temporarily, she was not devoid of common sense; as much as she wanted to she couldn't fuck a random stranger in her office.

She had to counsel the man through his sexual identity crisis and then if she happened to meet him outside of this professional space, that was a different matter altogether.

Just because Amelia primarily saw supernaturals didn't mean that she only dealt with supernatural problems. Everybody had sex, and many experienced shame and stigma. Men of every species were expected to be the dominant and forceful partner, and rigid expectations bred shame.

Amelia's self imposed unconditional expectations enforced order and safety in her life, but that was not the case for many. It appeared it was not the case for Freddy—the fixed societal views of power and sex between men and women had warped his self-worth. He didn't have an innate dominance, and saw that as a major personal flaw.

Amelia didn't see it as a flaw, in fact, the idea that he needed her to take guide him reignited the throbbing underneath her pencil skirt.

The session had confirmed her theory about Freddy's role in her life: his purpose was to seduce her into surrendering to one of her most forbidden desires—emotionally supporting a man who would never be able to truly see her.

"No one will ever understand you, Amelia," her aunt's voice echoed.

He had taken off his hood shortly after he sat, allowing Amelia an unobstructed view of soft, masculine features.

They were at odds with the hard edge to his voice and deep sadness in his dark eyes. Such a pretty man should be surrounded by beautiful soft things, not tortured by the guilt of his perceived inadequacies.

Amelia did enough of that for both of them.

He didn't reek of privilege; there was no learned grace or decorum to his movements, and the way his skin stuck to his cheekbones made Amelia believe he had not seen wealth (or a proper meal). The thought that he had experienced hardship made an uncomfortable burn light in her chest, though it was quickly replaced with desire when his eyes met hers again. Dark and needy and begging for the comfort of her direction.

Amelia was versatile when it came to sex, she had tried just about everything that was legal and ethical. Despite the ability to play the part, she was not the helpless damsel needing a big tough man to decide she needed fucking.

Any person who thought they knew her body better than she did completely turned her off—the world made Amelia doubt her mind but her body would always be hers to control. When she went searching for a genuine orgasm in a bar or nightclub, her eyes would slide over confident beefy hunks and look for someone in the background, someone observant who would be receptive to feedback. She needed to be able to tell them where to suck or lick, how fast to thrust; she needed someone who was willing to push past society's expectations, create their own understanding of power and pleasure, and submit to her completely.

So, if the universe wanted to test how serious she was in her rule-laxity pledge, it made a very good choice with Freddy.

Amelia was a competent therapist and maintained appropriate boundaries during the work day, but she was still human and had primal needs.

If she had seen him sitting at the bar alone, nursing a beer and a wounded self image she would have preyed on him, there was no doubt in her mind.

Freddy's eyebrows raised in surprise.

"I'm pretty sure there is definitely something wrong with me." One hand left the confines of the pocket to fidget with exposed foam that stuck between the gaps of leather. She watched him pick at the soft filling, heart clenching slightly at the familiar mannerism.

Amelia was a notorious picker—a habit that never failed to frustrate her aunt. The endearing action cooled the burning desire for a moment, allowing a ludicrous thought to escape through a crack in her subconscious.

I understand you.

"The way I see it, you have two options depending on what kind of work you're willing to put in," she explained, stepping towards him.

Amelia had strict rules for every facet of her life, including men. She was open-minded when it came to race and appearance but was incredibly picky when it came to lifestyle standards. She needed someone established, independent, and most importantly, someone that her aunt approved of.

Despite the selfish need that radiated through her, and her theories about his psyche, Amelia couldn't disregard Freddy's agency completely. She didn't even know if he was interested in her, interested in one night of casual sex. She did know that he needed her advice, though—and that's what she would give him.

Amelia decided on a compromise: she would play with him just a little bit, show him what would be in store. If he was overcome with arousal and begged for her body, then it would only be the kind thing to do.

"I don't have the time or energy for work, you need to fix me now." His voice raised a few decibels, desperation leaking through.

Despite the intense attraction, Amelia had a very difficult

time being told what to do.

Defiance burned in her calves, forcing her to stand and stride over to him.

Freddy's eyes widened as she stepped closer, fear and something else filling the dark irises.

"I don't need to do anything," she hissed in his ear. "But I can give you a short term solution, if you like."

"Yes, please. S-sorry, doc," he apologized, his capitulation transforming into hot, pounding arousal in her core.

"Respect and fear are twin brothers." Maggie's voice lingered.

"Despite your belief, you are a man; there is a primal drive in there to take and consume. If you can find a way to shut off your interfering thoughts, you may be able to complete the act." Amelia could do the same—shut off that pesky brain and milk every drop of pleasure possible from his body.

"How do I do that?" he asked, eyes lingering on her lips as she leaned closer. Amelia's face was only a few inches away from his, her breath kissing the skin of his cheeks.

"Discipline." She pulled away, and his exhale followed her. "Long term, you need to embrace what makes you different, challenge what you think normal is to begin with," she continued, standing tall and relishing at the audible swallow from the man beneath her. "Either way, you don't need me."

Dark eyes shifted from her lips to rake her frame, causing goosebumps to erupt on her skin.

Suddenly uncomfortable with their proximity, Amelia returned to her wingback chair and crossed her legs, pressing against the wet swollen center with her inner thighs.

"I think I might, actually," he murmured, barely loud enough for her to hear. Freddy stood and strode towards the door, body language shifting from defeat into determination.

"Thank you, doc." He turned back towards her and smiled, bending forward in a small bow. It was the first genuine facial expression she'd seen from him and it made her heart skip one of its bounding beats.

She'd already concluded he was handsome, but when he smiled like that she was confident in her deduction that he was the most beautiful man of any species she had ever seen.

"Goodnight, Freddy," she breathed, but he was already gone.

RULE 6
AWAKEN THE MONSTER

Freddy was a vampire.

He was strong and lithe, a creature of the night.

Freddy repeated this mantra to himself as he watched Amelia step through the front door of her office. Now that her scent was not intoxicating him, he could actually think rationally.

Well, as rationally as a starving vampire could think.

Amelia Atkinson was like nothing Freddy had seen before. Not that he was surprised, they didn't make specimens like that in the slums and she clearly wasn't a nocturnal. He had been expecting a callous older woman with condescending eyes and a sharp tongue, not an enchanting dark-haired goddess that exuded a tantalizing air of authority.

"Worship me," her eyes told him, a commanding blue gaze that left no room for argument.

Amelia efficiently extracted the words he had been too cowardly to admit, while still soothing him with kind glances and genuine empathy. Freddy expected it to some degree since she was a clinical psychologist, but he wasn't expecting her to see right through him within only a few minutes of conversation. She was kind and compassionate, reassuring him that he was not a monster while presenting his issues with a tidy simplicity.

He didn't need to be what his uncle and the world thought he was.

Unfortunately, Freddy only knew how to be a skid mark on society, but Amelia knew what he needed, knew who he was.

Freddy didn't know what he had done to be given such a gift. The most delicious woman he had ever smelled was also the first person that didn't look at him with the expectation that he was only capable of inflicting pain and suffering.

Who did Amelia want him to be?

Freddy replayed their impromptu therapy session in his

mind as he watched her turn the lock. Her hand froze on the knob before a quiet curse left her painted lips. Freddy wanted to kiss the foul word from her mouth, to replace it with cries of pleasure. His cock pulsed in his slacks.

She walked back into the dark building only to reemerge a moment later with a purse clutched in her hand. A small smile crept on Freddy's face.

What an unusual creature she was.

Cool and collected, immensely knowledgeable and preceptive, and yet Freddy knew that there was more beneath the surface.

"Looks can be deceiving," she had told him, implying that there was a wild, uncontrolled side to her she kept hidden. She didn't have to tell him that, in fact she probably shouldn't have.

She wanted to be found.

He saw the way her eyes lit up when he challenged her, how her invincible facade cracked by only a millimeter. It made him want to do it again; he wanted to unsettle her so intensely that she broke and unleashed her full fury onto him. He would take it happily, beg for more, likely.

His cock pulsed angrily against the fabric of his boxer briefs as he thought about receiving her punishment. She was very clear that he needed discipline, the sweet spicy scent almost killed him for good when her face leaned toward his as she said it.

He wanted to kiss her, then.

Fuck, he wanted to do more than kiss her now. He wanted to worship her until he earned her respect and admiration.

"I don't believe bad people exist," she had said, making Freddy believe—likely through a state of starvationary delusion— that she could see him as good.

If he proved himself a good vampire, a good man, would she praise him? More importantly, would she punish his body if he failed?

Freddy wasn't sure which thought aroused him more.

That was precisely why he followed her scent all the way to her house, telling himself that he was just following her instructions, trying to be a good boy for her.

He needed to get out of his head and follow his instincts. His primal urges pushed him towards her, as if she was a meal made just for him. Despite the sudden need to please the enchanting therapist, the usual self-doubt crept back into his psyche.

What if he couldn't control himself once he let go? What if he hurt her?

Freddy couldn't even entertain the idea of harming another creature, let alone the kind, soft therapist. His uncle told him that even newly transformed vampires usually didn't kill their donors, unless they tried to.

They did have a hard time controlling their fangs though, especially when in the passionate embrace of the woman they loved.

His uncle had never offered up many details of his life before the turn, but Freddy got the feeling there was a love he left behind. He could imagine the pain of having to reveal the monstrous truth to a beautiful woman, which was the reason he didn't tell Amelia outright the nature of his problem. Freddy had never told anyone about the intricacies of his deficit, always too scared of rejection.

He had felt enough of that for several lifetimes.

Amelia said herself that she wouldn't judge him, he believed if there was anyone who would understand him it was her.

A small fractal deep in his chest understood her, too.

That notion fueled Freddy as he parked himself in the bush next to a pearlescent blue car. Sure, it could be seen as creepy, but he was just following Amelia's instruction. She was the one that told him to surrender to his urges and hunt, and Freddy was a rule follower now.

Flashes of her relieved sigh as he removed her heeled shoes

hardened Freddy's cock.

He didn't have a foot fetish, but it was like the molecules of his body pulled him to relieve the beautiful woman's suffering.

The reception area suffocated him with a dizzying storm of sugary syrup and cinnamon, clouding Freddy until all he could see was the pained grimace on her face.

He crouched and peered through the leaves at the front exterior of her home. It was in a suburb, with enough room between houses that nobody would notice his presence. So far the only creature he had stumbled upon was a squirrel, nibbling on an acorn next to him.

"Must be nice not having to chase your food," he whispered at the furry creature. The squirrel looked at him with wary eyes. As he should, honestly.

Freddy was a predator, a creature to be feared—at least he was trying to be. He needed to feed if he had any plans of returning to his life.

A second life he had done nothing but waste.

"Why don't you respect yourself?" Amelia had asked.

"Because I have never done anything respectable," He should have said.

She was right, Freddy didn't deserve that second chance if he wasn't strong enough to hunt. He had done nothing to earn it, and if he couldn't bite the most attractive woman he'd ever seen, then he deserved to die.

Well, she likely hadn't exactly meant it in that way, but it made the fact that he was hiding in a bush outside her house slightly more palatable.

Freddy watched and waited, grateful that she didn't do anything too salacious like change out of her work clothes in front of an open window.

He didn't want to be seen as a peeping tom, or anything.

Not that he wouldn't enjoy looking at her naked body, but there was no way he could defile her like that. Freddy had done many unsavory and illegal things during his human life, but sexual violence wasn't one of them. Even if he had in the past, the moment her scent washed over him, he knew that he could never harm her.

He didn't know why, but Freddy wanted Amelia to respect him, needed it just as much if not more than her blood. He wasn't hunting her for his own selfish gains, she had given him a challenge and he would try his hardest to succeed. The thought of her praise burned in his chest and made his dick throb. The memory of blue eyes dripping with genuine confidence as she reassured Freddy there was nothing wrong with him, that it was a problem he had the power to fix.

Freddy didn't feel like he was using his power at all, more like he was simply borrowing hers. The invisible hand of her command cradled the back of his neck, the support more potent and energizing than any drug he'd ever sold.

If you had asked Freddy what would save his undead life, a woman would not be his first response.

Romance was so far from his mind, especially since his turn; his main focus had been day to day survival, not so different from his human life.

Freddy's foster familie were generally not kind or affectionate and just saw him as a nuisance that netted them a bit of extra cash. Freddy knew this, and was resigned to it by the time he aged out of the system. He was bred from bad stock, destined to be a scourge on the world until he inevitably died from a drug overdose or brain injury.

Mo had given him a second chance, gifted him with an opportunity to be someone different, to be something good. Unfortunately, so far it was impossible to be both a blood sucking monster and a good guy. He had a chance now that he had Amelia, and he would prove himself as a vampire, just as soon as he figured out how. His resolve wavered slightly, as the hours went by.

Just when he was about to abandon his mission, the window at the front of the home filled with light, the curtains sliding open to reveal Amelia, clad in cartoon pajamas and a contemplative expression. Freddy's cock didn't hesitate to spring back to life at her reappearance, joining his brain in rapt attention.

His eyebrows furrowed as he witnessed Amelia move away from the window and sit on the couch, legs spreading.

"Holy fuck," he muttered to himself as she slipped her fingers between her thighs.

Did she know he was watching, or was this a naughty habit?

Freddy's breath quickened, trying to reconcile the calculated woman he had met only hours ago, with the siren who invited passersby to watch her pleasure. It was an empty street in a quiet suburb in the middle of the night, Freddy rationalized.

Was this for him, then?

Was she inviting him to join her carnal moment?

Freddy shook his head, clearing the poisonous desire that throbbed between his legs. Freddy had followed his primal instincts to that place for blood lust purposes, human lust would have to wait.

He would hold his position until the perfect moment presented itself, and then he would strike.

BLOODY MESS

RULE 7
ALWAYS PUT THE GARBAGE OUT ON FRIDAYS

AMELIA

Amelia's toes braced on the coffee table, cool glass soothing her sore metatarsals.

An empty whiskey glass sat between her parted legs, only two solitary ice cubes remaining. Her body was loose and a flush warmed her cheeks. She leaned her head back against the couch, eyes closing as she surrendered to the image of the intoxicating stranger.

Freddy.

Long, lean, and observant.

Well, Amelia was making an assumption about the first two since the hoodie obstructed the fine intricacies of his form, but this was her fantasy so the details didn't matter. He was aroused by her firmness, and craved punishment.

Though it was her fingers that parted the slick folds between her legs, in Amelia's mind it was Freddy who pleasured her. He would have been begging and pleading to do it, to please her and assuage himself of his guilt.

Was it a bit wrong to be turned on by that? Probably, but this was a rule vacation—Amelia could be as perverted as she liked. Though masturbating while thinking about a client in the living room was a significant deviation from her regular schedule, it wasn't enough.

Amelia smirked and stood, pulling back the curtains. She returned to the couch, with full knowledge that any passerby would be able to see her pleasure. A flash of excitement pounded through her at the thought, though the possibility was unlikely.

Amelia had chosen this home specifically because the neighborhood was quiet, human, and the average age of the residents was eighty five. The likelihood of someone walking past at two in the morning was very small, but not zero.

As was the probability of Freddy hiding in the shadows, watching her.

The thrill pooled in her core, urging her movements faster. She imagined his fidgeting fingers stroking a hard, needy, cock, dark eyes even darker with desire. She would make him suffer, make him watch as she came on her hands while screaming his name. She was close to doing just that when a flurry of paper hit her in the face.

Amelia groaned and sat up, angrily snatching the book from the air. A hastily scrawled image of a garbage can was circled aggressively.

She let out an animalistic growl of frustration and threw the pocketbook across the room.

Garbage day was tomorrow, meaning she had to drag the bin from her garage to the curb. Amelia knew this, it was a fact and something she was aware she had to do. She was also tired, her feet hurt, and she just wanted one good mind numbing orgasm before completing another obligation.

Surely, missing one garbage run wouldn't cause a nuclear holocaust?

Amelia shook her head, disappointed at even considering neglecting a responsibility just to reach climax. She was not prone to easy infatuation, and could only explain her sudden intense need for him as a consequence of aging.

During their last visit, her aunt had mentioned that Amelia was reaching the peak of sexual maturity and her ovaries would likely start weeping for semen soon. Amelia shuttered at the thought; children were absolutely not something she was ever going to be interested in. The amount of mess to mitigate would be far greater than what Amelia could handle, even if every object in her home was enchanted. The memory of a rancid pile of garbage falling over and onto her favourite Barbie sandals made Amelia roll off of the couch with a groan.

She stood, straightening her wrinkled nightgown and padded toward the garage.

The mechanical door opened with a loud whirring, making Amelia grateful there was considerable space between her closest neighbor. She didn't want to receive a letter from the HOA about a procrastination related noise complaint, Maggie would never let her live it down.

Well, if she was so worried about it then she could get Amelia an enchanted garbage bin for her birthday next week.

She slipped on the wolfpaw shaped slippers that lived in the corner of the garage and pulled the gray bin towards the curb as usual. The night air nipped at her exposed arms and legs, reminding her that she still needed to buy a new winter coat —the last one had simply vanished into thin air.

Who on earth misplaced a whole winter coat?

A rustling made Amelia pause her self-deprecation for a moment.

"Ow, fuck, jesus," a male voice hissed from the shrubbery

behind her car. Her mind convoluted the voice to sound suspiciously like a certain client she shouldn't be thinking about. A squirrel darted from the bush.

"Is someone there? Are you hurt?" she asked, concerned that a leprechaun had camped out in her bush again. He was a nice man, Amelia was regretful that she had never seen him again—though she suspected it was due to her questioning if his propensity for mischief stemmed from his need to get attention from his absent mother. To her astonishment the dark form that emerged was Freddy, as if conjured from her fantasies.

The universe had provided her a gift after all.

"What are you doing here?" she asked, eyes squinting in the darkness. He had dry leaves and twigs stuck to his cotton sweatshirt but otherwise looked unharmed. He waved a hand in dismissal.

"Don't worry about that. Why are you taking out your garbage in the middle of the night?" His face was contorted in dumbfounded concern. Amelia flushed.

So, she was a procrastinator, but that didn't seem like the most important question to be asking at that moment.

"It's garbage day tomorrow," she said, crossing her arms defensively.

"It's three in the morning," he replied with increasing astonishment.

Amelia swallowed, "Okay, it's garbage day later today," she corrected, a slight embarrassment still colouring her cheeks.

"That's so not what I meant." His eyes were squeezed shut, as if her incompetence pained him.

Anger joined the shame in her chest, heating her blood.

"What did you mean, then?"

He stepped closer, movements much more lithe in the darkness of her driveway than they had been in her office.

"You're outside in the middle of the night on a dark, empty, street, wearing almost nothing." Freddy's voice was a purr as his eyes roamed her body and fingers pinched a lock of her hair. He lifted it to his nose and inhaled deeply, before gently tucking it behind her ear. The implications of his presence settled into Amelia at the exact same time as a deep, uncontrollable desire. Freddy was here, meaning he more than likely had seen her carnal moment.

Did he notice that she hadn't finished? Considering he recognized that her feet were sore from her shoes, it would be more than likely. Excitement pooled between her legs at the thought of him watching her, like a pathetic pervert.

Suddenly her procrastination didn't seem like a detriment,

it was an opportunity to take her pleasure from him under the darkness of night, where no one's judgements could touch her.

He wasn't a stranger with the capability of hurting her, he wasn't a client she was obligated to cure—he was her reward for years of suffering and she would have him.

"But it's not empty anymore, is it?" she whispered, turning her head slightly and pressing her lips to the hand still hovering next to her ear. Without breaking eye contact, she sank her teeth gently into the flesh below his thumb, causing the man's lips to part.

Freddy stepped closer, until their chests were almost touching. She tilted her head upwards, pulse increasing like a geiger counter finely tuned to the distance between his mouth and her skin. He leaned down and parted his lips, cool breath fanning over the spot beneath her ear.

Amelia closed her eyes, ready for him to kiss her or bite her or fuck her or kill her—the specifics didn't matter at that moment. She wanted him to change her life forever, needed it more than the breath held tightly in her lungs. When he was this close the particles around them seemed to vibrate, his scent infusing every pathway of her airway and clouding every rational thought.

She was completely at his mercy.

"Fuck!" he roared, forcing himself backwards and kicking the garbage bin over in frustration. It flew half way down the street before it stopped.

Amelia could cross regular human off her list of possible species.

"I can't fucking do it."

She blinked, shocked that she was not currently being ravished on the hood of her car. She did misinterpret body language occasionally, but she was rather certain he wanted her.

"Pathetic Freddy pussys out again. Look at you, you're so fucking hot and sweet and small and I still can't fucking do it." His groan was tortured as he gestured towards her body, as if trying to prove a point to someone. Amelia glanced down at the cartoon nightie she was wearing, confused by his compliment.

She wouldn't have picked this particular number out for the purpose of seduction, and she never would consider herself any of those things. Sweet and small were adjectives that had yet to be attached to her. Bizarre and unsettling, perhaps.

"You're a fucking disgrace, Freddy," he said to himself, placing a hand over his face and walking in a small circle around the cement driveway. The distance from his scent and aura allowed Amelia to think critically for a moment, to reconsider her current circumstance.

Freddy had very clearly been intending on doing something with her or to her, but had pulled away at the last second. Considering the session earlier in the night, she shouldn't have been surprised. That was precisely what Freddy had told her would happen, in hindsight she was glad he didn't vomit.

Instead of fear and panic, Amelia's brain whirred with curiosity and a tingle of desire.

She couldn't help it, she had to test her hypothesis.

It was the perfect opportunity to show him that he didn't always have to be the dominant one to get the job done. Amelia waited until his pacing brought him within arms reach before she pounced.

She reached forward and grabbed the fabric of his sweatshirt, pulling his mouth against hers. He didn't resist as she melted against him, only hesitating a moment before placing his hands on her hips. His fingers were long and cool against the fabric, a stark juxtaposition against the heat that was burning in her core.

His tongue was sinfully spicy as it probed into her eager mouth, a chocolate covered candy cane only appropriate for holidays. He stepped forward, backing her towards the hood of her vehicle. Amelia reached towards the waistband of his pants, feeling incredibly impatient for his cock.

She needed to know how it differed from the fantasy she had created, surprised to find that he was not wearing sweatpants, but cotton slacks fit with a button and zipper. His mouth descended on her body, heating the inferno building in her core with desperate kisses. Pleasure tingled every inch of skin his lips touched, intoxicating her busy mind into a sweet focused silence. She fisted her hands in his hair, eager to pull him back up to her lips and possess both his body and mind.

"Get on the hood," she said, forced to come up for air.

Freddy blinked, face lifting away from hers. "Pardon?" His black eyes were wide with surprise.

"Sit on the hood," she repeated, slipping from his grasp and nodding towards the vehicle. His gaze lingered on hers for a moment, as if trying to decipher if this was a test. It was, but probably not the kind he was expecting. She wanted to see if her hunch was right, if a stern guiding hand would liberate him. To her great relief he complied, satisfied with whatever he saw in her expression.

Once Freddy was seated with his back against the windshield, Amelia straddled him, pulling his erection out of his pants. Unfortunately, it was overcast, the clouds hiding any light Amelia could have used to inspect the rigid member.

No matter, she would work on touch alone. Freddy groaned as she rubbed her slick heat against his length, a gasp leaving her mouth when her clit met a cold steel ball.

Of course he had a dick piercing, what else could she expect from the physical embodiment of every wet dream she'd ever had?

Freddy himself was everything Amelia couldn't have: young, messy, and requiring psychological help. She leaned forward, bracing her weight on the roof of the cruiser. He was deliciously forbidden and yet here she was, taking him anyway.

The power of rebellion amplified the need in her core.

Her mouth was mere centimeters from his parted lips, only space enough for a panting breath. The flush of alcohol and arousal had dilated the capillaries under her skin, making it delicate, more receptive to the chilly night air and Freddy's touch. As if to prove her point, he lifted one hand from her hip and ran it across the reddened flesh.

"It's more beautiful than I ever imagined," he murmured, voice a gentle worship. She was going to have him, at least just this once.

As a treat.

His fingers continued their gentle exploration of her face, stopped only by the cage of Amelia's teeth when they breached the line of her lip. Though dampened, she heard a tortured groan die in Freddy's throat.

That wouldn't do.

"Don't you dare hide from me—I deserve it all." Amelia released his finger only when his eyes shut and he exhaled loudly.

"I need to tell you something before-" he began, cut off by the press of her lips.

"No, you don't," she reassured him, grinding her hips down on a very sizable erection. He was harder than any man she had taken before, and the gasps that left him were pure desperate need.

His control was hanging on by a mere thread, and Amelia wanted to snap it with her teeth. To watch him fall and hold him on the way down.

"Stop thinking and do it, Freddy." she ordered, lifting up and positioning him at her entrance. "Do it now."

Freddy's eyes began to glow silver, making Amelia gasp. Before she could react he sank two pointed canines into her neck and his hard cock thrust into her pussy.

Bliss, pleasure, hot, blazing fire, ripped through her veins, masking the uncomfortable stretch of his length. It had been a very long time and he wasn't small, causing her walls to put up resistance as he infiltrated her barrier.

The yell that left her throat was involuntary, and Amelia wasn't sure if it was the pleasure or pain that caused it. Freddy's response was to clamp his palm over her mouth, likely to prevent waking the neighbors. It was a completely understandable thing to do, but he hadn't earned the right to silence her.

She released one palm from its place against the metal, only to grip Freddy's misbehaving hand and pin it roughly beneath hers. Goosebumps erupted on the back of her arms and legs at his answering moan and she could no longer resist the urge to move, to fuck her client, a man she didn't even know. Her body seemed to know him, the glide of his cock in and out of her was effortless—a long-awaited homecoming instead of an introduction.

"Fuck," Freddy groaned against her skin as he filled her over and over again. He took long drags from her jugular, palms shaking against her hips. The blood flowed out of her body, understanding replacing the vacant space in her veins.

Freddy was a vampire.

If Amelia wasn't so distracted from the mind boggling pleasure that his body was providing her, she would have felt tremendously dense for not seeing it earlier. It wasn't completely her oversight, she had never seen a vampire in the flesh before, nocturnals being strictly off limits for romance and sex. But analysis of her mistakes could wait until after she orgasmed, which likely would be very soon.

The corners of her mind filled with pride and satisfaction at his success. For some reason his victory felt like her own—for one intimate moment she owned it just as she owned him.

"You did it," Amelia's voice was barely a whisper, unsure of who the target of the praise really was. Freddy's hips froze, his cock buried to the hilt. His glowing eyes dimmed, concern overtaking the pleasure on his face.

A worried palm moved from her undulating hips to her face.

"Are you okay?" he asked, causing a deep heat to fill her chest and womb. She wasn't going to last long if he was going to be sweet as well as irresistibly sexy.

"Yes, do it again," she panted, fisting his hair and pressing his face to the other side of her neck. Amelia longed to feel the intense pleasurable burn again, she wasn't ready to return to reality yet. She needed to be a wanton sexual creature, demanding her pleasure from a sweet stranger for just a bit longer.

Freddy sunk his teeth into her again as she sped up their rutting, the metal ball hitting an uncharted place deep inside.

"Please," he pleaded against her skin. Desperate, pathetic men were one of the many chinks in Amelia's armour, and the sound of his begging had a similar effect to pouring gasoline on a Phoenix as she was being rebirthed.

A rush of sensual power pushed her orgasm to the surface,

but she needed a little bit more. Short tidy nails scraped against Freddy's scalp as she yanked his head back again, unveiling the most startlingly erotic vision Amelia had ever seen.

Crimson painted his lips as the force of her grasp pulled him off of her skin and allowed her to see the feral silver desire mixed with vulnerable need.

Her little monster was beautiful.

"Please, what?" If he wanted something, he had to ask.

"Come, please." His gaze stayed firmly affixed to her face, despite the alluring squelch of moisture and flesh between them.

"Make me." The command was far more breathless than she intended, but Amelia couldn't summon any regrets when his hand pressed against the sensitive nub directly above where they were joined.

Her orgasm crawled up from her toes, bestowing her with a deep guttural pleasure that she didn't know could exist. His moan was loud and unapologetic as he pulsed with release, filling her with satisfaction and a healthy dose of dopamine.

Freddy would be perfect if he wasn't so forbidden.

When the last wave of pleasure faded, she finally collapsed

on top of him. The frigid early morning air kissed her bare thighs, cooling her passion and returning her to reality. She slept with her client, who also just plunged his fangs into her neck.

"We should probably talk about this."

RULE 8
HAVE FIRM BOUNDARIES

AMELIA

"Shoes?"

"In the coat closet," Amelia answered, closing the door behind Freddy and leaning against the dark wood.

He looked foreign in the backdrop of her living room, the only man that had ever graced the walls of the place since she had purchased it.

It was a midcentury home with each room separated by a doorway. It might be considered dated by some, but Amelia appreciated the ability to easily segment her home.

She enjoyed segmenting, in general—there was no better way to prevent contamination than with quarantine.

She knew it was considered unwise to invite a strange man into her home, but so was fucking him on the hood of her car, so it was too late to check her moral compass. Amelia had a deep-rooted feeling that Freddy wouldn't hurt her, despite the reputation that both vampires and men had in general.

She watched quietly as his brows furrowed in contemplation for two breaths and then as he slipped the hoodie over his head and hung it up in the closet. The shift of fabric caused his shirt to ride up, revealing a flash of dark hair trailing down from a slim waist.

Good golly.

Her stomach sank as she took in his frame, now illuminated by soft lamplight. He was not as slim as she had previously thought—his biceps were defined with corded muscle, large veins bulging from thick forearms.

The past judgment of his physical size must have been biased since her last client of the day had been a golem, everybody looked small compared to them. The only humanoid creatures that tended to be bigger were orcs. Amelia had always wondered how such physically large creatures could procreate with human women, though she supposed the vaginal canal was quite elastic for a reason.

Amelia shook her head, best not to think about vaginal canals when a client was in her kitchen—even if he had just thoroughly massaged hers with his pierced dick.

She needed to stop thinking about his pierced dick, too, while she was at it.

Amelia pushed past him, suddenly feeling like a pervert. She couldn't stand there and ogle him all night, that wouldn't be polite at all. She also couldn't order him to take off his shirt and never put it on again, as much as she wanted to.

"I would offer you coffee but..." she trailed off, hoping she didn't have to finish the sentence.

But you just took your nightcap directly from the tap while I came so hard around your magic cock that the fabric of my reality is merely shreds.

"No worries, you've definitely met the beverage obligations for the night," he joked, his voice following closely behind her to the kitchen.

"Do you make a joke out of everything?"

"Generally,"

"Why?"

"You could probably tell me the deep psychological reason and why it's so horrible," Freddy said, remaining completely unphased by her questioning. He was partially right, Amelia already suspected that he used humor as a defensive mechanism to protect his ego from the deep emotional suffering of his upbringing and current illness.

"It's not horrible, humor is considered a positive coping mechanism."

"So, why does it piss you off so much?"

Amelia paused for a moment and considered his question. She didn't feel anger when Freddy joked because he was using humor to soothe himself, the emotion gripping her chest was eerily close to jealousy.

Her aunt had scolded her for silliness, forcing her to be mentally present in her loneliness at all times. *"There is no respect in being a jester, it's simply public-endorsed humili-ation."*

"It doesn't," she continued her journey to the kitchen, now decidedly uncomfortable the conversation had turned back to her. That was the main thing that frustrated her about Freddy, he was always trying to dig past the firm external layers of her persona.

"Uh-huh, and I'm a forest nymph named Dorothy," he said sarcastically, but Amelia didn't fall for the bait. She had the power here, even if it seemed Freddy had the uncanny abil-ity to disarm her.

"No, you're a vampire."

"Not a good one, until about half an hour ago." He was an-tagonizing her to goad out an unsavory reaction, to regain the power she had fucked out of him.

The throb between her legs returned at the reminder of just how much power she fucked out of him, and how much she wanted to do it again. She needed to try and curb this response, which meant leveling the playing field between them.

"If I tell you something embarrassing, will you stop trying to provoke me?"

"Probably not, but you *can't not* tell me now."

"I thought it was a sex thing." Amelia sighed, opening the fridge and holding an ice pack to her sore neck.

"A sex thing?" Freddy leaned with crossed arms against the counter next to her. The skin surrounding his mouth creased when he smiled, making Amelia's stomach quiver. Without the cotton shield of his hoodie, the spicy musk that had teased her in the office was overpowering, expediting the need to get away from this forbidden man and his delicious cologne.

She nodded somberly, "I thought you were tortured about your submissive nature, that you couldn't get it up that way. Hence the whole 'get on the hood' thing." Amelia's voice was small as she stepped away to make a fresh pot of coffee, eyes trained in front of her.

Freddy laughed, the sound unapologetically amused. "You thought I wanted to hunt women just to fuck them?"

Amelia nodded again, teeth trapping her bottom lip in restraint.

She was so certain of her theory, his amusement seemed pointed towards her incompetence. As if sensing her discomfort, Freddy's laughter died quickly and he hummed in contemplation.

"I mean, you're not totally wrong about that. I haven't been able to fuck anyone since my change, either."

Amelia tried to suppress the grimace as she sat at the kitchen table, the soreness between her legs soothed slightly by the cool vinyl against damp heated flesh.

"I'm sorry about that," Freddy grimaced in return, settling into the only other chair. Amelia only ever entertained one guest, so she had no use for more than two. She noted the way he mirrored her actions, effortlessly attuned to her emotions and movements; he must have grown up in an unsafe situation, always aware of others' negative feelings.

"Sorry about what?" she asked, clutching the empty mug in her palms.

"Hurting you—I really didn't plan on doing that. I've never..." he shook his head. "Nevermind."

"You've never stalked, fucked, and fed from your therapist?" The dampness of his release coated her thighs as it escaped her, bringing more inappropriate thoughts to mind.

116

If he was hers, she would make him clean it up.

"Yes," he said. "No," he corrected. "I mean I've never done any of that," he finished with a yawn.

"You've never had sex?" He certainly seemed to know what he was doing. Amelia yawned as well, unable to stop the contagious effect.

"No. I mean, yes. I've had sex, plenty of it." His tone was rushed and defensive in the way that men in their twenties were when it came to the prowess of their sexuality. She let the thought ruminate, to force herself to remember that he was a man barely in his twenties, not her personal sex slave. She had to move on from the encounter on the hood of her car, to tuck the memory of the hottest sex she'd ever had away for next week's masturbation session.

"You've never fed from someone during the act?" she asked, covering her mouth with the rim of cool ceramic. That would be an impressive test of willpower, from what she knew of vampires—which granted, wasn't much.

"I've never fed from anyone at all." He threw his hands upwards in frustration. Freddy's eyes were wide and his pupils were large, signaling that he was riding the high of adrenaline.

The way the words erupted out of him led her to believe he had been keeping this fact to himself for a long time. Close kept secrets had to fight tooth and nail to escape, as Amelia was familiar with.

Understandable, considering biting humans would be a fundamental part of being a vampire. In the office he had mentioned that there were other ways to relieve his hunger, but Amelia still wasn't convinced he had never bitten anyone.

"Not even once?"

"I told you I'm broken."

The throbbing in her neck returned, casting doubt on his words. She grabbed the ice pack from the table and pressed it against the other side of her throat, Freddy's eyes remaining glued to her face as she stood and began to pace, her thoughts drowning out the slow dripping of the coffee machine.

"Clearly, it's possible." She held out the frozen blue packet in front of him, highlighting the proof of his success.

"But I don't know how I did it." Freddy took the empty mug from the table and filled it from the carafe that was now full of steaming liquid gold. Amelia nodded and accepted the mug with a small smile.

He had a valid point—no scientific discovery was valid if it could not be reproduced, and if Freddy was being truthful the consequences were too dire to risk.

Amelia took a grateful sip of coffee, letting the familiar bitterness ground her nerves. Freddy's predicament was fascinating and he certainly was pleasant to look at but that didn't mean she could help him.

She had welcomed him into her office, body, and home under the temporary blanket of a loose-rule vacation, not to offer him proper mental health support.

Her gaze dropped to the floor, confidence receding. Despite her occupation, Amelia still had not perfected delivering bad news.

"I cannot see a client beyond professional hours."

"What do you mean?" Freddy asked, disbelief plain in his voice and face. "I'm here now, aren't I?"

"That was an exception," she replied.

Amelia turned away, unable to stomach seeing his disappointment.

"My office closes at six and I don't take clients past five." Her schedule was a boundary that wouldn't work for a nocturnal creature, rendering this whole conversation pointless. Freddy stepped around the table and clutched her shoulders, the contact shooting tingles through Amelia's limbs, solidifying both how difficult and necessary rejecting him would be.

Freddy's place was to remain tucked neatly and safely in her 'wouldn't that have been nice' mental folder. She saved that place for sexual fantasies and various desserts.

"You have to," he demanded, shaking her shoulders gently. Anger flashed hard and hot in her chest at his boldness.

"I don't have to do anything," she said, reaching up to clutch his face tightly in her hands.

She meant for the movement to remind Freddy of their power dynamic, to make him feel vulnerable in between her palms. Unfortunately, instead of pulling away he closed his eyes and leaned into her touch. Amelia's heart softened, anger dissipating as quickly as it arrived.

She wanted to help him.

She wanted to sleep with him again too, but that was against many rules, not just her own.

Her job was her life, the only reason she had for waking up each day; the only good that came from her mother's death.

"Please," he breathed, dropping to his knees with a fatigued thump. "You're my only hope." He wrapped his arms around her legs.

Oh, good god.

Amelia shut her eyes, resolve slowly slipping at his desperation.

"You're the only hope this family has, Amelia." Her aunt's voice echoed in her mind.

"I'm sorry," she breathed, surprised at her resilience.

Freddy stood and pressed his palms over his eyes in contemplation. Amelia exhaled, glad that he was no longer at her feet but also ensuring that the image joined the others in her prized mental spank bank.

"What if you helped me recreationally? You know, like a friend," he suggested, face transforming with hope. A bolt of longing caused Amelia to pause. She hadn't had a friend in many years, and never one who welcomed her advice."You already fucked me on the hood of your car, so I think the professional integrity ship has sailed. "

Technically, she had never seen him as a client during her operating hours, so it shouldn't break any laws or ethical codes. Besides, the only other supernatural therapist on this side of the city accidentally ate one of his clients, so she was certainly doing better than that. Even if he did report their coupling, she could easily say that he had stalked and tried to assault her—facts that were technically true.

Surely, there could be nothing disagreeable about helping out a man this weak and miserable?

The warm glow of the rising sun filled the room, reminding

Amelia of the time sensitive nature of her choice.

Before she could answer, Freddy collapsed onto the kitchen tile.

"Oh!" Amelia squeaked in surprise, kneeling down and rolling him down to his back.

She was well versed in the steps of CPR, but was relieved when a soft snore escaped slightly parted lips.

He was asleep.

He looked even younger in slumber, dark lashes pressed against gaunt cheeks. He was so forbidden and so beautiful.

"Freddy," she whispered, gently shaking his shoulder in an attempt to wake him. He moaned and sat up, eyes remaining closed.

Amelia hummed in contemplation; she couldn't just leave him on the hard tile of her kitchen. No, she was responsible daytime Amelia now, ruled by obligation and other people's comfort. She carefully led him to her bedroom, tucking him snugly beneath her pink lace-trimmed duvet.

Amelia could have easily settled him on the couch, but something pulled her to bring him to her room—to let him in. She would have to analyze that later, after a good sleep. She laid herself next to him under the covers, ensuring there was a safe distance between them. The steady rise and fall of his breath was soothing in its regularity, aiding her in carefully formulating a plan.

Amelia always needed a plan.

The potential negatives of spending her rule-free weekend with him were minor: reduced sleep, mild anemia, sore private parts. The positives were very tempting: she could resolve his feeding issues, feel the pleasurable burn of fangs and venom, and maybe even make a friend.

There was technically no rule about having attractive vampire friends.

Her aunt would have a conniption but Amelia considered herself a progressive—she didn't care that vampires and casters were like oil and water, she didn't have magic anyways, so there should be no problem.

"The only good vampire is a dead one." Her aunt would say. Amelia always found that particular quote humorous since they already were, in fact, already dead. She didn't know much else about vampires, truthfully; nocturnals avoided the day-walking crowd in general and vampires were rarely studied.

Regardless of his species, the prospect of having a man in her bed for a few nights was deliciously sinful. She had never invited a man to stay the night, unwilling to sacrifice the peace of her bedroom sanctuary.

It wasn't like there was any threat of true attachment, anyways. He was a young, lost vampire with facial piercings and identity issues, the complete opposite of what her aunt and greater society would accept in the long term.

His offer of friendship seemed much more realistic.

She could just help him over the span of her vacation until he could bite on command and then she would go back to her comfortable predictable life– so, what if she got a few orgasms out of the arrangement?

Amelia closed her eyes, sleep finally taking her.

Freddy woke with a gasp, anxious to hear Amelia's response to his plea.

His stomach dropped when he realized he was not standing in the white tiled kitchen. Freddy groaned at his incompetence, he couldn't even manage his own bodily functions.

He turned to bury his face into the nearest suffocatable object, when a familiar delicious scent washed over him. He inhaled deeply, unconsciously nuzzling against a soft mass of auburn waves.

He sat up with a horrified realization that it was Amelia's hair that he was burried in, and her bed that he had slept in.

Not only had he begged at her feet like a pathetic, useless man, but he then proceded to pass out on her kitchen floor.

A light ache tinged his chest that she had tucked him into her bed instead of kicking him to the curb or calling the police. His self-loathing cooled for the moment, Freddy pulled the mass of brown curls away from her face, tucking it behind her head.

Amelia's skin was clear of the previous flush he admired, though she was no less tempting. His eyes zeroed in on the bruises that were already forming on her slim neck, memories of her sweet ambrosia cramping his stomach and saliva filling his dry mouth.

Bagged blood had never even come close to the taste of her. Sweet and spicy, warm and alive. Donated blood was adequate, but the rigorous processing it received affected the flavour—it was similar to food that had been reheated several times, there was nothing delicious about it. Tasting Amelia's blood, while the pleasure of orgasm flavoured it, was beyond something Freddy ever thought he would experience.

He didn't feel even close to deserving it.

Guilt pounded through him, causing her saccharine scent to become a suffocating cloud of shame.

He carefully extracted himself from her bed, gently tucking the blanket around her slumbering frame. The weightlessness of his limbs gave him pause as he fastened the comforter.

Freddy felt great.

Even during the months his uncle had provided him with an endless supply of bagged blood, he had never felt so much raw energy stored in his muscles. Amelia's blood had been just as nutritious as it was delicious.

Freddy needed to repay her kindness, for letting him feed from her and sleep in her bed. That would be the honorable thing to do, even if she didn't fix him or let him inside her body again. Freddy set out for the kitchen, determined to at least reheat her coffee.

AMELIA

Amelia woke to the smell of coffee wafting into her nose.

The light in her room was a dark maroon, an indicator that the sun had almost made its daily escape.

Her heart dropped—she had slept the entire day. The coffee on the night table was cold. Amelia sat up against the headboard and took a grateful sip, cold was how she usually took her coffee—her forgetfulness left mugs abandoned all through the house.

"I would have heated it up, but you don't have a microwave." Freddy said from his place leaning against the door frame. He looked just as sinful as she remembered, a flood of warmth hit her core and cheeks with the memory.

"Sorry," she mumbled into the ceramic, avoiding an explanation. In truth, the sound of the whirring and beeping reminded Amelia of the day she found her mother's body; a reminder she still couldn't stand.

Cold coffee seemed like an acceptable sacrifice.

"No, *I'm* sorry. I didn't know how long you would sleep for, and I figured any coffee is better than none." His dark eyes shifted between Amelia's face and the mug in her hands.

"You figured right," she confirmed, taking another sip. Amelia didn't miss the satisfied smile on his face. "I don't mind cold coffee, anyways."

Freddy's nose wrinkled. "You should."

Amelia couldn't help but laugh, she wasn't expecting how sweet he looked with his face scrunched in the center.

"So, this is different," he commented, gesturing towards the decor of her room. It was filled to the brim with knick knacks and color, a stark contrast to the boring minimalism of the rest of her house.

Amelia nodded, setting the cup back down on the nightstand. "It's my sanctuary."

Freddy stepped forward, walking over and sitting next to her on the bed.

"Why do you need a sanctuary in your own house?" He held out a gingersnap cookie, one he must have grabbed from the cookie jar in her kitchen.

"Why do men have man caves and tool sheds?"

Freddy's face was folded in amused confusion.

"Yeah, but you live alone, don't you? If not, I'm about to have a very unfortunate conversation when your boyfriend gets home."

Amelia rolled her eyes, and grabbed the beige disk from his hand. "Obviously, I live alone. Isn't there some saying about looking a gift pegasus in the mouth?" She took a small bite of cookie.

He lifted his hands in surrender. "You're right, I'm sorry for prying. Thank you for letting me sleep in your bed." His smile was soft and made Amelia's heart melt just a little bit.

She grabbed the confection and took another bite, hoping the spicy dough would distract her from unwanted feelings.

"I didn't really have much of a choice, you passed out." Good job, Amelia. Bring the focus back to the one who needs it.

He rubbed the back of his head in embarrassment.

"Sorry about that, my uncle said it's a problem new vampires can have. It doesn't help that I have a habit of losing track of the time," he admitted, earning another small laugh from Amelia. She knew what that was like. Her interest was piqued by his comment, though.

"How new are you?" she asked, genuinely interested in her new friend's story. It would help his therapy if she understood his background, she justified.

Freddy leaned back on his hands, the movement making the mattress sink slightly under his weight. "I was reborn two years ago. Still a baby, according to Mo."

"That's your uncle's name?" she asked.

Freddy nodded. "Yeah, he's the only reason I'm alive." His tone was casual, but Amelia could tell how important the man was to him.

"And he wasn't willing to help you figure out how to hunt?" If that was the case, he didn't seem like that great of an uncle. Amelia's aunt had been strict as a guardian but she always met every need. Although, she supposed Freddy was a grown adult, so his uncle wasn't obligated to teach him anything. Her eyes wandered down the length of Freddy's body as he reclined.

Fully grown, indeed.

Freddy dropped his gaze and shook his head somberly. She could sit there and pretend to deliberate, but she had no patience for falseties or wasted time.

"I have the weekend free, if that works for you."

His breath caught with disbelief. "You'll do it?"

"I can't make any guarantees, but I should be able to push you in the right direction."

Freddy's face broke out into a radiant smile, causing warmth to squeeze Amelia's chest.

"Thank you, thank you, thank you." The blood he took from her must have revitalized him because he lunged towards her and wrapped her body in a tight grasp, forcing them backwards onto the bed. Despite being in a depleted state, Freddy was still unbelievably strong and Amelia found it hard to breathe.

"Freddy," she groaned, snapping him out of his joy. It was heartwarming seeing his gratitude, she almost didn't want to interrupt his celebration, but she had to stay alive in order to help him and remain in control.

"Right, sorry." He released her and stood. "Well, how do you want to do this?" Freddy's smile was eager and stunning as he stood at attention, ready for her order.

If he was alluring when he was weak from hunger, after one feeding the power of his aura was astounding.

A small shot of arousal penetrated her womb, the power she wielded intoxicating.

How did she want to do this?

Missionary, from behind, cowgirl.

Amelia shook her and turned to walk towards the bathroom, needing a moment to collect herself.

"I'm going to freshen up. I'll meet you in the kitchen."

BLOODY MESS

RULE 9
UNDERSTAND THE PROBLEM

AMELIA

"So, you don't have a prey drive. Very interesting."

They were sitting at Amelia's kitchen table again, sipping on a fresh, hot coffee. Well, Amelia was drinking the coffee while Freddy tried not to stare at her.

"Is it? I think it's pathetic." His feet danced underneath the chair as he watched them, avoiding her piercing blue eyes.

"Freddy, if you want to do this you need to stop with the negative self-talk." Amelia said, tone warm but firm. Freddy's cock twitched in his slacks—if it brought out bossy Amelia, he would shit talk himself all night. He cleared his throat, trying to shift his mental focus from her sultry voice to the task at hand.

"Sorry, doc."

"Do you want to bite me right now?" she asked, taking another sip from the mug. His eyes skimmed her frame quickly, purposefully refusing to linger on the marks his bite had left on her neck. Guilt settled in his gut at the physical evidence of her pain, warring with the ridiculous animalistic desire that liked seeing his mark on her. It reminded him of the warmth that flooded him as she screamed and came on his cock.

Great, he was hard again.

"A little,"

Her eyebrows raised, eyes skeptical.

"A little?"

The way she spoke reminded Freddy of his mentor. Mo had given him an in depth lesson on vampire physiology, making Freddy believe that he was too smart to simply be a bar owner.

Is that why he was drawn to Amelia?

It was possible that Freddy wanted to surround himself with highly educated people, to distance himself from the life he came from, where nobody achieved even a high-school diploma.

Mo had shown him the utmost patience and compassion, supplying him with bagged blood from his stock until his instincts kicked in—it was no surprise Freddy idolized everything about him. Mo explained to him that vampires relied on the prey drive to trigger the feeding reflex, but for some people it took a bit more time to master it. Freddy remembered at the time he thought calling it a reflex was bullshit, since that implied it was automatic.

"And how have you stayed alive so far?" Amelia's voice pulled him from the memory. Her face was neutral, but there was a keen interest in her glance.

"I've been borrowing the supply meant for cocktails at my uncle's bar," he admitted, shame coursing through him. Mo had stopped stocking their personal fridge six months after Freddy's turn, likely assuming he must have figured out how to feed naturally. Freddy should have told him that whenever he tried to prey on an unsuspecting human, a wave of nausea would cause him to heave. He should have admitted that he was a disappointment even at being a vampire, but he couldn't.

Amelia nodded. "That must be difficult, being forced to steal from your own family."

"Nobody forced me to do anything."

"Maybe that's the problem," Amelia replied, though her eyes were distant. Freddy got the impression that statement was not just for him.

Amelia stood with a smack to her thighs.

"I'd like to try a few experiments, but they will be highly unusual," she announced, her voice shifting into the cadence of a highly educated psychologist. It made Freddy's cock harden further.

"I think everything about this is highly unusual so go right ahead," he joked, mesmerized by the way her nightgown brushed against her upper thighs as she paced.

Amelia ignored him, resuming her lecture.

"A vampire's fangs descend in response to three main primal urges," she began, much like she was giving a university lesson. Freddy wondered if she had ever taught a proper course on fairy eating disorders or whatever it was she studied. He had no doubt that she would be brilliant, her words were steady and confident.

"Eating, fighting and fucking," he answered, slotting into the role of pupil happily. He had dropped out in ninth grade when he realized that selling drugs afforded him food to eat, when going to school didn't. If this was the closest Freddy was ever going to get to a college classroom, he was going to enjoy it.

Amelia stumbled at his contribution, a pleasantly surprised smile filling Freddy with pride.

He couldn't recall the last time he pleasantly surprised anyone, people usually responded to him with either fear or dismissal, both reactions equally deflating.

"Clearly, the need to feed is not reason enough for your fangs." His sunken eyes and hollow cheeks were all the confirmation she would need. Amelia stepped towards him and leaned forward, pressing her palms to the table.

"I'd like to test your response to those primal urges." Her voice dropped down a few semitones, making Freddy's cock pulse. He had popped more boners in the last twenty four hours than in the last several years.

Freddy swallowed, making a conscious effort not to look down the gap at the front of her nightie. Currently, there was only one primal urge he was thinking about, and it had nothing to do with blood. She grabbed a nearby kitchen towel and fastened it around his eyes. Surprise and desire tumbled within him, fueling each other as his vision was obscured.

"First, we have to figure out your response to fresh blood removed from the human factor."

"I don't think that's physically possible, considering it comes from humans." Anxiety caused his words to run high.

"Just play along, please," she murmured softly in his ear. The sound was amplified due to the deprivation of sight, coincidentally amplifying the ache in his balls.

Freddy swallowed, hoping his voice didn't shake too noticeably.

"Yes, doc."

"Now for this to work, you need to clear your mind. Focus on what you're smelling and feeling."

"Easier said than done," he muttered under his breath, but complied without hesitation, focusing on his available senses.

His ears brought him the sound of her bare feet shuffling around the room, and the rolling clang of multiple drawers opening. She was getting something. His nose smelled the change of her scent, now mixed with a deep forbidden aroma. His brain pieced together the information, anxiety building when he surmised that she must have sliced her skin with a knife from one of the drawers she opened.

"How does it smell?" The spiced scent intensified as she padded closer.

Freddy leaned forward and inhaled deeply.

It smelled like the most fragrant luxurious pastry, drowning in sweet syrup and sprinkled with cinnamon. Amelia smelled like his salvation and downfall wrapped together in a tantalizing bow, that he could untie with one pull of his teeth.

"Nice,"

"But a nice smell does not translate to hunger," she said, voice remaining thoughtful while Freddy was losing his mind.

No, a nice smell did not make him hungry.

Amelia's scent was not nice, it was delicate and strong, pure and sinful.

Amelia's scent was irresistible, and Freddy was starving for it.

He wanted to rip that slutty little cartoon nightgown to shreds and gorge on every part of her, until there was nothing left.

Disgust rolled through him in waves, washing away every hint of bloodlust.

"No, it makes me a bit nauseated actually," he confessed, swallowing back the rising bile.

"Nauseated?" Surprise coloured her voice. Freddy wished he still had his vision; he wanted to see the adorable way her long lashes blinked when she was surprised. Then again, he was thankful he didn't have to witness the blade gliding against her delicate skin.

Anguish dampened his need as he imagined the intense

burn of blade across her arm. He had been on the receiving end of a knife more times than he cared to think about, Amelia didn't deserve to feel that pain—not like he had.

"You had to hurt yourself," he explained. The darkness and pressure of the makeshift blindfold cocooned Freddy's world, letting him believe for one delusional second that there was nothing but him and Amelia, in the emptiness of deep space.

"But it keeps you alive. It isn't any different than the donors that fill those blood bags." Amelia tried to inject some logic into his reason, which Freddy admired. She didn't understand how deep his self-hatred ran.

"It is different."

"How?"

She didn't like being challenged, a fact Freddy was quickly coming to realize would be an effective tool to make that sweet blood rise and warm her skin.

"Because blood from those donors is going to save lives, not just feed a monster." Freddy restrained himself to only taking what he needed to survive, so that most of the donated blood made its way to more deserving recipients. He had already taken at least a pint from Amelia, more than he had ever drank in one sitting.

Gentle hands removed the towel that obscured his vision,

revealing devastatingly blue eyes.

Had they always been so large and mesmerizing?

"Freddy, do you not think you deserve human blood?" Amelia's voice was so soft, like she was talking to a pixie and the current of her breath would damage its wings.

Yet, Freddy could hear the sadness in it as well.

Despite its intended comfort, her observation sliced him much like the knife she used on her skin.

"Why would I?" He hadn't done anything good in his life, hadn't done anything to earn the gift of anyone's life blood.

A look that could only be described as mischievous excitement lit up Amelia's face.

"What if I made you earn it?" She hopped onto the kitchen table in front of Freddy, pulling up her nighty. "Make me come, and maybe I'll let you bite me."

BLOODY MESS

RULE 10

UNDERSTAND THE PROBLEM-SOLVER

Freddy's eyes flashed silver.

"Are you serious?"

"I'm always serious," she confirmed, leaning back on bent elbows. "I did say it would be highly unusual."

"Are you sure?" His eyes locked onto the place between her thighs.

Was she being a bit self-indulgent? Yes. But as the saying went: you only have a hot desperate vampire in your kitchen once.

"I'm always sure," Amelia breathed, the admiring look he gave her pussy was a potent aphrodisiac, igniting a simmer of desire to a steady burn.

He snapped out of his haze, eyes flicking up to hers with concentration tensing his brow.

"How long do I have?"

Amelia's mouth popped open, unsure how to answer the question she had never considered putting a time limit on the challenge, or even how long it took to bring her to orgasm. A small wave of discomfort heated her chest at the oversight. Borrowing from Freddy's playbook, she used outward bravado to mask her insecurity.

"How long do you need?" She allowed a smug smile to crawl onto her face, despite the small shake of her voice.

"It depends how hard you want to come," he fired back immediately, taking one foot into his palm. Cool fingers enveloped the sensitive metatarsal, a shock of static following the glide of fingers. He carefully bent and stretched each toe, as he had done the evening before, the slight pain of soreness being masked by the pleasure of releasing tight muscles.

Amelia could count on one hand how many foot massages she had received in her life—it was something she had simply never thought to ask for.

Her days of ignorance were gone now, because she would never forget the combined aphrodisiac of Freddy massaging her soreness away while looking so intensely at her face.

The pupils of his eyes tracked her mouth as she bit her lip, only shifting downwards to where her nipples tightened against the fabric of the nightie. She was surprised that they didn't cut the thin material to shreds when her escalated breaths pushed the stiff buds against it.

Amelia's breath nearly stopped completely when he lifted her leg and placed a soft kiss behind her ankle. The skin there was so sensitive the contact was almost painful with pleasure.

It reminded her she was alive.

Every nerve ending in her body prickled to life as Freddy carefully worked his tongue up her leg, somehow lingering only on the most erogenous zones. Despite his age, he played her body like a practiced veteran, which made an inkling of discomfort rise in her abdomen.

Freddy repeated the thoughtful licks on the other side, nearly fraying Amelia's composure entirely by the time he reached the apex of her thighs.

"You're stalling," She managed to grunt out, breaths coming out in pathetic gasps, control slipping.

She had expected Freddy to succeed in the task, but she didn't foresee his ability to play her like a fucking harpsichord.

She should have just sat on his face.

"No, I'm savouring." He looked up at her, two dark emerald pools of hunger peering at her from between slick quivering thighs.

"You're letting your food get cold."

His mouth was so close to her center, she could feel his dark laugh tickle the hairs covering her cunt. If he didn't hurry up she was in danger of slipping off the table, the slickness pouring from her was unbelievable.

Amelia was not a novice when it came to sex, she was thirty two years old after all. Somehow, she felt much like a virgin with Freddy's head between her thighs—nervous and unprepared.

"Am I allowed to come too?" he asked, though the words barely registered in her lust clouded mind. Amelia would give him just about anything as long he stopped teasing her.

"Yes," she hissed.

Without warning, Freddy threw her thighs over his shoulders, diving into her sex. Amelia squeaked and buried her hands in his hair, legs shaking as he licked her ravenously.

RULE 10

He loved eating pussy, that much was evident.

He brought her to the edge quickly, sucking her clit into his mouth. She was so close, his groans stimulating her harder than any vibrator. She pushed his head down onto her sensitive nub, unable to hold back a moan when his fingers pierced her, doubling the pleasure.

Despite the mind numbing sparks of euphoria that caused her toes to curl, orgasm was just out of reach. Her climax danced away, smirking smugly—she needed just a little bit more.

"Bite," she demanded, pulling roughly on the dark strands clutched in her fists.

Freddy groaned as he sunk his fangs into the crease between her thigh and pussy while simultaneously curling long his long digits to stroke a deep crevice of pleasure.

"Yes," Amelia cried, finally cresting over the peak of the second most intense orgasm of her life.

She milked his fingers, pussy clamping down on him as he drank from her femoral vein. The moan that vibrated against her skin was so loud and unhinged that Amelia had no doubt that he finished as well.

"Thank you," he said, sitting back in the chair with a satisfied smile, face glistening with her mess.

"My pleasure." And it certainly was.

"I don't suppose you have an extra pair of men's sweat-pants?"

"What made you want to be a therapist anyways?" Freddy asked, head resting on folded hands as he watched Amelia eat breakfast-dinner, clad in a slightly snug pair of pastel pink sweatpants. His eyes were a medium jade, lazy and playful as they danced between her mouth and the spoon. They must change color based on his hunger.

"I like solving problems." That was her usual answer, and it came out effortlessly.

Freddy's face scrunched with skepticism.

"What?"

"Nothing,"

He continued tracing lazy circles into the polished wood

surface of the table.

"Freddy,"

"Hmm?"

"Out with it."

"I just don't believe it."

"That I'm good at solving problems?" Defiance simmered underneath her diaphragm. Freddy rolled his eyes, which increased the building anger.

"Considering I've already fed twice since you were put on the case, obviously you're good at it. It's just...nevermind." He shook his head, eyes dropping to the table.

"Freddy," She reached forward and tilted his chin up with her fingers, making him swallow audibly and raise his gaze back to hers. He responded well to sternness—Amelia had no doubt on her deduction that he craved order and discipline.

"I just have this feeling that you're more complicated than that, that's all. You don't seem like the type of person who would spend their whole life on one thing, unless it served a grander purpose."

"You think I'm lying?"

"I just think you're hiding from me, I guess."

149

Amelia released his chin and pressed her lips together , contemplating her answer. She could double down on her first reason, or she could turn this into a lesson for Freddy.

There is a consequence to digging into a person's psychology, inevitably you will learn something you're not prepared for.

"My mother killed herself when I was five," Amelia said, taking a bite of cereal. The crispy edges of the raisin bran combined with the chilled milk to form a particularly aggressive mouthful. Freddy blinked, surprise plain on his face. Amelia usually tried to gauge how open she should be in social situations off of the reactions of others, always considering the implications of her words.

"Sharing your secrets is no more appropriate than sharing your bosom," her aunt would say. She wouldn't see Freddy after this weekend, so there was no harm in sharing her secrets in tandem with her bosom.

"I'm sorry-" he began, pity creeping into his eyes. Amelia missed the sated happiness.

She didn't let him finish.

"She was found face down in the garden, jumped from the second story balcony. I lived with my aunt after that, but it made an impact." She didn't forget the mess that littered the house when her whole world fell apart. Freddy's mouth parted as he listened to her sordid tale.

"I guess I figured if I prevented even one person from ending their life, then some good came out of it."

Perhaps she had crossed yet another boundary, but when it came to Freddy it appeared that they were more like suggestions anyway. He said he wanted to be treated like her friend, and she would take his word for it.

She took several bites of cereal while waiting for Freddy to thaw from his shock, her mind turning to her current circumstances.

She should try and get a few more hours of sleep, to maintain her circadian rhythm. Amelia was not a novice of staying up too late, she had lost many privileges when her aunt caught her reading in the middle of the night. It wasn't her fault that Maggie believed that good sleep hygiene required total silence. Her mind whirred in agonizing circles, thoughts, images, and short musical snippets, keeping her awake.

"Why the interest in supernaturals?" he asked, pulling Amelia from her thoughts. She looked up from the nearly empty bowl of milk to see his face pinched together in serious thought.

Freddy did a lot more thinking that she had anticipated, and far too much of it had been about her.

His question was one she had answered many times in university interviews, to poor success.

Amelia had applied for every available human psychology practice in the city, and received an equal amount of rejection letters. Her technical caster status and interest in supernaturals incited anything from apprehension to complete terror. She had even applied to the one supernatural therapist, but he laughed her out the door.

It seemed that there was no place for a human to have non-human clients.

Amelia didn't stay deterred for long—if there was no place already made for her, she would carve it out herself.

She didn't blame Freddy for asking, casters made lesser creatures nervous, especially nocturnals.

"Don't worry, I'm not a secret necromancer or anything."

"You brought my fangs and dick back to life, so I'm not totally convinced."

"I can assure you, I can't do a stitch of magic to my aunt's disappointment."

"Why would she be disappointed?"

"Because our lineage goes back to the original magic family, apparently. It's a terrible embarrassment, an unfortunate end to what could have been an incredibly powerful bloodline."

"I take it your aunt is a caster, then."

"Not just any caster, the lead administrative assistant of the Federal Bureau of Magical Objects."

"So, I guess she's responsible for the magic doo-hickeys."

"Astute deduction, Watson." Amelia pointed the spoon towards him in jest. Instead of another witty retort, Freddy looked down with continued focus.

"Isn't that a bit cruel?"

Amelia circled the utensil in silent motion to keep speaking.

"It seems pretty self-flagellating to dedicate your life to a career that constantly reminds you of what you should have been."

It was Amelia's turn to scrunch her face. When she didn't answer, Freddy looked up.

"What?"

"Believe it or not, most people don't look at everything through a lens of their own failures. Some people simply like helping others." And feeling like they belong in a magical world that wasn't built for them.

"Sure, but wouldn't it be easier to solve the problems of humans?"

Her heart twisted at the reminder, a startling sense of deja vu picking up the pace of an already racing heart.

"Don't mettle where you don't belong." Her aunt had said whenever she expressed the dream of providing help to misunderstood creatures. The memory gripped at her chest painfully.

Stop meddling with Freddy, he doesn't belong to you.

"Doing hard things is important, Freddy. How else will you know how strong you are?" She winked, standing to rinse her cereal bowl in the kitchen sink.

Amelia would like to believe she was being disciplined by washing the dish right away, but in reality she just needed to put some distance between her vulnerable shield and his intoxicating aura. Despite her light demeanor, her hands shook as she reached for the faucet.

In just one conversation she had revealed to Freddy more than she had ever told anyone. When she agreed to help him with his problem and let herself sleep with him, it was with the expectation that he would be the one under the microscope.

A hard body pressed against her backside, lean muscled arms braced on either side of the sink. Freddy's spicy scent surrounded her again, blurring her mind and steadying the jittering of her hands. She leaned back just a fraction, using the firmness of his chest as a bolster.

It had been so long since she had anyone to lean on.

"I know that's not the full answer, but I'm not going to push," he murmured, breath tickling her ear. Amelia wanted to make a sarcastic quip back at him, but his tart scent overwhelmed her and all she could do was sink her weight into his chest.

"Thank you." Her hands paused as she luxuriated in the feel of his rhythmic breathing and bounding heart against her back. The combination of his scent and strength soothed her so expertly she almost didn't notice when he took the bowl from her hands and continued to rinse it.

Thank you for taking pity on me.

Silence stretched between them as Amelia watched him carefully wipe the dish dry.

"I wish my parents died," Freddy said, the rumble of his voice a pleasant vibration against her. "They were pretty shit, landed me in the system before I was in highschool." He placed the bowl on the counter and rested his hands on top of hers, which made her realize how desperately she was gripping the edge of the sink. Tense muscles relaxed under his touch, turning the action from a friendly reminder to an intimate gesture.

When was the last time someone held her hand?

The thought and its subsequent disappointing answer

shook Amelia out of the Freddy-induced spell she had slipped under.

Time to focus on his therapy, as she should have been doing the entire time.

Bad, bad therapist.

His admission regarding his parents didn't surprise her. Most trauma was caused early in life and that was the hardest kind to overcome. She could empathize with part of his experience, though her parents had consciously made the choice to leave her.

If Amelia was on the clock she would help Freddy dig deep into the effect that neglect had on him, but she was failing in her attempt to remain detached, therapist Amelia; that women would never tolerate a man holding her and demanding that she take comfort in his touch.

Freddy had poked holes in her walls and now he would have to withstand the leaking of her soul.

"At least yours didn't choose to leave." Amelia expected the world to crumple, or at least the sky to fall down with her admission, but all she felt was cool wet hands releasing her palms from their momentary prison.

Freddy handed her a spoon from where it lay in the sink, unphased by her comment. It was almost as if he sensed that she needed some control back to prevent complete emotional disintegration.

"Your dad too?" He rested his chin on her shoulder, body still pressed close. It wasn't an embrace really, but Amelia was entirely too aware of just how close his skin was.

How close his soul was to where she let just a fragment of herself escape.

All she could do was nod.

"According to my aunt he left a month before my mom died." There was a tense silence between them, neither wanting to voice the natural conclusion of her statement.

She wasn't going to blame her father for the death of her mother, even though her aunt did.

Whenever Amelia asked about her dad, Maggie's face soured and she called him one foul name or another. Amelia never quite understood the animosity, but she only had one memory of the guy, so she couldn't really judge him fairly.

"Were they nice to you?" Freddy's tone was quiet and sad, insinuating that it was an experience he never had. Amelia was unsure if answering truthfully would hurt his feelings, if it would point out what he missed.

Unfortunately, fairness was mandatory to Amelia, and the truth was a prerequisite.

"Yes," She couldn't suppress the small smile from blooming on her lips. "My dad made pancakes every weekend with mountains whipped cream." It was the only memory of him that had ever resurfaced, the fine dusting of hair on his humongous hands as he slid a plate in front of her.

"My dad sold my game station for drug money." Freddy laughed dryly as she placed the spoon on the counter next to the sink.

"Is that the father you don't want to talk about?" she asked, harking back to the first session in her office.

Freddy's breath stalled for a moment,"Yup, still don't want to talk about it, though."

He nipped at her earlobe, an attempt at distraction, undoubtedly.

Amelia turned in his grasp, resting her hands on Freddy's chest. They were still slightly damp from the water, leaving warm wet handprints on his shirt. Freddy looked down at the marks she left on the fabric, eyes flashing silver.

Amelia wished she could leave marks on his bare skin, a physical reminder this was real, that it was possible to have a connection with someone. She wished she could burn away the pain his child self had experienced, taking hers along with it. Freddy kept opening up to her, dangling his vulnerable emotional innards in front of her face.

Amelia didn't know if she should help him dig deep or pull him out with a distraction.

She squeezed her eyes shut and took a deep breath. It would be so easy to get lost in his body again, just to enjoy the taste and feel of him.

How long would she be able to forget their circumstance, and how impossible would it be to do this forever? He was barely an adult, a newly made vampire. He had decades of self-discovery to do before...

Before what?

Even if by some miracle he did want to pursue a romantic relationship, she was just a daywalker and had a blossoming therapy business to run. They would get only a few hours together due to their conflicting schedules.

No, she was destined to marry some caster bureaucrat, and even imagining a permanent life with Freddy was merely a lust-fueled delusion. Amelia needed to refocus the relationship between them, to remember she could only have a little bite of Freddy's life. She would enjoy the delicious vampire while she had him, just for the weekend.

The thing about treats is that one should never overindulge.

"It makes you fat and lazy, unmotivated and a drain on those around you," her aunt would say.

Amelia carefully extracted his arms from around her with a pained grimace. Her soul hummed with pride, internally praising herself for showing such discipline. She would limit herself to just a taste of Freddy, much like only having one chocolate from the expensive christmas box. He would be a dark chocolate, filled with a spearmint nougat.

"Let's remember to keep things professional," she said, swallowing down the impulse to lick him for further taste analysis.

Freddy smirked. "Seemed more than professional when my tongue was between your legs."

Amelia cleared her throat. She didn't need the reminder. "That was an experiment."

"Do we have time for another experiment?" His voice was a delicious purr, quickly dissolving her small shard of self-control.

Amelia had never been able to have only one chocolate.

She took a deep breath and nodded, refocusing on their mission. He was only in her house to discover how to wield his fangs, not disassemble her carefully constructed life one snarky comment and wicked orgasm at a time.

"Have a seat, hands behind your back." She pointed towards the simple minimalistic dining chair.

It was made of cheap wood composite but it had the aesthetic she was looking for.

Clean, simple, safe.

"Yes, doc," he grinned, sitting with a confidence he hadn't had the previous night.

A little blood went a long way for a starving vampire.

She would have to add these observations to her field notes, whenever she located that notebook.

Amelia stood in front of him, diverting her gaze as she spoke.

"The next instinct we may be able to exploit is self defense. Your fangs are a weapon after all."

"Self-defense?" Freddy's eyebrows shot up.

He must have been expecting another sensual experiment, but he was about to be very disappointed.

"I'm going to hit you, Freddy," she explained, rifling through the kitchen junk drawer. Most of them were filled with odds and ends, but she knew which junk drawer held which junk. Weren't all items just junk depending on your perspective?

"You realize I'm significantly stronger than you, right?" Freddy's tone dripped with amusement, doubting her ingenuity and intellect.

Freddy was about to discover that Amelia always had a plan.

"Of course, that's why I'm going to use these." Amelia pulled out a set of silver handcuffs, making Freddy gulp.

RULE 11

DON'T UNDERESTIMATE THE POWER OF AN EXPERIMENT

FREDDY

"Oh," he stared at the silver cuffs with trepidation.

He had never allowed any woman to handcuff him before, the memories associated with them were filled with balding policemen and cold jail cells, decidedly unsexy. The option to refuse her didn't cross his mind, not when she had that determined fire in her eyes.

It made his dick hard.

Again.

Freddy may have antagonized her a little bit to get it there, but the glory of witnessing her blaze was worth the burn.

The flames of jealousy licked up the column of his spine.

"Why do you-" Freddy started before stopping himself. He had no right to feel jealous of who she bound, gagged, or fucked. At the very most they were new acquaintances but more than likely she saw him as a pathetic dying client. "Nevermind."

He wrapped his arms around the back of the chair as instructed.

"'Oh,' is right," she smirked and clasped the metal cuffs around his wrists.

How big was the last guy she had in these things?

"The point of it is to hurt, to let yourself feel the primal urge to eliminate the threat. However, if it becomes too much just tell me and we will stop."

"Yes, doc," Freddy said, unable to focus on her words when the ugly tornado of jealousy burned in his chest.

Did she fuck him too?

He understood that she wanted to hurt him, luckily he had already hurt himself with thoughts of her dominating a different poor supernatural creature so the job was done. Freddy's mind ran away from him, spinning with images of her bouncing up and down on some troll's dick. The thought was so painful, it cramped his insides, making the muscles of his arms bunch and press painfully against the wood frame of the chair.

She probably made him cry and he thanked her for it.

She slammed a palm to the side of his face.

Freddy groaned at the contact, eyes squeezing shut. The pain dissipated quickly, replaced by a pleasurable burn. Most importantly, it pulled his mind away from ridiculous internal delusions and towards the physical presence of the woman standing over him.

Was that pleasurable pain what it felt like for Amelia when he sank his fangs in her skin?

The tingle lingered, stirring his cock. Amelia was getting her return, making him feel the pain he caused her. She had to hit him harder, to make him suffer for not only causing damage to her skin with his bite, but also the jealousy he wasn't entitled to.

This was the moment he was waiting for and he was going to make it count. Freddy straightened and shot the woman a cocky grin.

"Is that all you got?" he taunted. Excitement and arousal flashed in her eyes, fueling several more strikes to Freddy's face. He barely felt the pain, too focused on her heaving chest and flushed face.

"If that was how hard you hit the last guy, he didn't learn his lesson." Another slap to his left cheek.

Freddy needed more, to feel as broken on the outside as he was within.

"That wasn't very nice," she chastised.

His cock was completely stiff now, blood thrumming in his ears along with a racing heart.

"Neither is hitting a poor defenseless vampire."

Another slap to his right cheek.

"Oh, I think he is full of defence right now, just not the kind I'm looking for."

The throbbing in his pants was quickly becoming unbearable.

"I don't think this is having the desired effect, doc." He nodded towards the noticeable bulge in his slacks.

"I guess the threat of danger isn't real enough." The purr in her voice dampened slightly, genuine observation poking through.

She stepped behind him and out of sight for two heaving breaths, a cold hard sensation against his throat making his chest freeze.

Amelia pressed the back of the knife to his throat.

"How about now?" she hissed, mouth pressed close to his

ear. Freddy felt no urge to defend himself, no threat of danger.

She could kill him for good, here in her kitchen and it would be a worthy demise.

Arousal coursed hot and thick through him. The only urge he felt was to release his cock so he could rub it against something, he would even take a strike to it.

Images of Amelia tugging on the metal ball adorning his dick with her teeth while she murmured sweet praises made Freddy's balls ache. He tilted his head backwards, letting her hair caress the planes of his face. The gentle tease of pleasure against his cheek juxtaposed the cold hard steel pressed against his throat in a beautiful erotic harmony.

He opened his mouth and eyes at the same time, showing his goddess just how unthreatened he felt. Her eyes flicked between his non-fanged mouth and silver eyes, but there was something different in her gaze. Her pupils were dilated and focused, a familiar pale flush on her cheeks.

She was drunk on her power, just as she had been on the hood of her car.

She removed the knife from his throat and placed it on the counter, an impressive show of dexterity since her gaze didn't shift one centimeter away from his.

Freddy expected her to address his failure, but to his surprise she gripped his face with her hands and pressed her full lips to his open mouth. He held still as she explored every inch of his lips with her tongue, the throbbing in his pale pink sweatpants a painful drum.

"Jealousy is ugly," she whispered against his lips, her hand creeping down his face and settling around the back of his neck. "And you are such a pretty boy."

The other hand crept to the underside of his chin, creating a prison for his skull made of warm soft skin. The intoxicating blue of her eyes filled his vision, her sweet mouth-watering scent invaded his lungs, the taste of her tongue still lingered in his mouth.

Oh, he was definitely going to come in his pants again.

Freddy's senses were on high alert, every molecule centered towards the woman in front of him. He bucked his hips upwards just as she released, a growl of frustration leaving his throat. She turned towards the counter where the key sat, her round perky ass hiding just behind the thin nightie.

Freddy's control snapped, the beast taking over.

AMELIA

One moment Amelia was reaching towards the silver key, and the next she was flat on her back, a cool hard body pinning her down.

Excitement fluttered in her abdomen.

"Did it work?" she asked, lifting her head to see Freddy's face twisted in an agonized snarl.

"Look ma, no fangs," he said, baring his straight humanoid teeth.

Amelia's brows furrowed.

"Then what-" Her words cut off when he pressed a rock hard erection into her core. "Oh," she breathed, moaning in earnest when he thrust against her again.

Amelia arched her back, unable to resist leaning into the pleasure. She reached up and grasped onto the strong arms that were braced above her head, surprised to feel that they were still bound by the silver cuffs.

169

"'Oh,' is right," he echoed her previous remark, glowing eyes burning brighter than she had ever seen. "Just because I can't drain you dry doesn't mean I can't do other things to you."

Amelia wanted to get lost in the pleasure of his body on hers, but his words parted the clouds of desire from her mind. Instead of ripping off his clothes, she reached forward to cup his face in her palm. The metallic glow softened a fraction, taken aback by the tender action.

"Why would you say that?" She carefully picked out pieces of wood shrapnel from his hair—the chair must have been a casualty in his escape. Luckily, it was just a cheap piece from a discount furniture store, and she held no love for it. Amelia enjoyed vintage decor it usually didn't match the clean minimalism she required.

"Which part?" he asked, eyebrows knitting in confusion.

"That you can't drain me dry. You're a vampire, of course you can." Amelia slowly tucked the hanging strands of hair behind his ears, allowing her to see his pale features unobstructed.

The full light of the kitchen allowed her to analyze the finer details of his face and the abundance of scars that littered it. Despite his strong rigid body pinning her to the kitchen floor, Freddy's eyes were wide with fear.

His silver gaze dropped from hers and his mouth opened as

if to speak but shut again.

Amelia traced the jagged white lines with soft strokes, smiling when he leaned into the pleasure of her touch, giving her the sense that he hadn't received much gentle affection.

"You really don't believe you can, do you?" she asked, already knowing the answer. Shame soured his expression when he opened his eyes and rolled over onto his back. Amelia could see the full devastation of his escape from the chair now that his firm body wasn't imprisoning her.

What was once a minimalistic dining room seat was now a haggard foam platform and a sea of shrapnel. The vision pumped Amelia's veins with adrenaline and suddenly it was her body littering the tile of her kitchen.

Or, it will be if she doesn't get herself under control.

"I don't want to believe I'm a monster." Freddy covered his eyes with his bound arms, unaware of her inner turmoil. She would keep it that way.

"Who said you're a monster?" Amelia sat up on one elbow, turning her body to face him. Everything that she knew about Freddy so far pointed to him being more empathic than most human men she met.

"My uncle thinks all vampires are monsters by default."

"Your uncle clearly has some serious issues."

A gallon of self-hatred being one of them.

"Not as bad as mine," Freddy sighed, lifting his arms off his face so he could stare at the ceiling. Amelia narrowed her eyes, understanding where a part of Freddy's guilt came from.

If his main role model had a jaded view of vampires, naturally so would he. She couldn't grasp how his uncle could see Freddy as a monster when he had never fed from a human before. From what Freddy had said, he seemed to be a knowledgeable man, surely he would see how hard Freddy was trying.

No, Amelia was missing something.

"Does he know about your problem?"

"Not exactly," Freddy grimaced, covering his eyes once again.

Her heart wept for the starving vampire. Not only was he deprived of blood, but of acceptance as well. Amelia swallowed, pushing back her personal desire to cradle him in her arms and slid into the knowledgeable and emotionally distant therapist persona.

They wouldn't get anywhere until Freddy faced that demon.

"Okay, I have some homework for you." Amelia said, standing and swiping the wood chips from her clothes and hair.

Knowing her luck she would get a splinter in a place she really didn't want one.

She carefully navigated the destruction, grabbing the key and hopping back to the bound vampire. The evasive dance of her bare feet between the sharp debris was a stark reminder of how much care it would take to avoid being hurt by Freddy's mess.

No matter how pleasurable the pain was, it had to be avoided.

"Homework?" he asked, sitting up when she released him from the cuffs. "You're not going to make me stand in front of the mirror and call myself a good boy three times, are you?"

Amelia laughed, helping him off the floor with extended hands.

"I'm not a therapy Bloody Mary—though that would be pretty helpful." She grabbed an unfortunately un-enchanted broom and dustpan from the linen closet.

"I want you to tell your uncle about your feeding issue," she instructed, turning around suddenly and colliding with a hard chest. Surprised arms wrapped around her. The unexpected contact and mouthwatering scent caused Amelia's desire to spark back to life and a softness to melt into her chest.

She needed to put some space between them before his dick and teeth were permanently adhered to her, and the mess was larger than just a spray of wood chips.

"Besides, you should head home anyway. I need to try to get my sleep schedule back on track."

The silver glow returned to Freddy's eyes.

"I thought I have you for the entire weekend."

Amelia swallowed down the quiver that threatened to penetrate her heart at his words.

He was pushing, seeking discipline.

She stepped forward, pressing the blunt end of the broom to the underside of his chin. Freddy's head tilted backwards a fraction and his eyes shone with arousal.

"You have me for exactly as long as I say you do."

He wrapped a hand along the broom handle but didn't shift it from the place it pressed against him.

"And what do you say right now?" Amelia realized in that moment that Freddy's relentless questioning was a form of seeking guidance without vulnerability. He had no interest in disrupting the concrete walls of her defense to prod at the soft underbelly of her soul. He just didn't want to get hurt.

Once again in control, Amelia pulled the broom handle away from his skin.

"I think your pants are looking a bit tight and you need a shower." She wasn't exaggerating either, the pink sweatpants she had loaned him were barely big enough to contain his thighs, let alone a rather impressive erection.

She liked seeing him in her clothes, which meant he had to change as soon as possible.

The silver glow in Freddy's eyes extinguished with a snap.

"I can't," His eyes dropped to the floor.

"Yes, you can." Amelia said, trying desperately not to count the breaths that left his chest and entered her lungs. She wanted to swallow them.

"What am I supposed to tell him?" Freddy pulled away with a sigh. Amelia missed the contact, which hardened her resolve to get him out of her house.

"The truth,"

He stepped back, leaning against the beige wall beside the closet.

"But what if he..." He searched for the right words unsuccessfully.

"Doesn't understand?" Amelia guessed, all too familiar

with the pain and loneliness of not being accepted by the one person that mattered the most. Freddy shot her a small embarrassed smile, a hint of comradery in it.

He felt their unusual connection as well.

Amelia turned to face him, shoulder pressed against the same wall.

"He might not understand, but what damage would that do?"

Freddy crossed his arms and looked upwards with pursed lips.

"Worst case scenario he sees me as a pathetic waste of space and regrets ever turning me." Amelia's eyebrows jumped at his response, unable to dampen her reaction. She wasn't expecting such a vulnerable answer, but she wasn't going to waste the opportunity.

"Your worst case scenario is him thinking poorly of you?"

"Were you expecting anything different?"

"Well, usually people fear loss of life, limb, or liberty."

Freddy didn't respond to her comment, just pressed his lips firmly together.

"You can't control what other people think of you, Freddy."

Though her voice was soft, his expression shifted to something darker that Amelia didn't like.

"Pretty rich coming from you."

"What's that supposed to mean?"

"Oh, come on. I don't think it's a coincidence that your home looks like it was decorated by a colorblind hagraven, except for the place where no one would see. Seems like you try pretty hard to control what other people think of you."

Fire erupted in Amelia's chest, bubbling at the base of her throat. She had to put distance between them or there was a real possibility she would strike him again.

He didn't know her, he didn't know anything.

"How do you know that my bed is not a revolving door for a whole roster of frustratingly attractive mouthy vampires?" She pushed off the wall and began sweeping erratically. As far as he knew she could share the chaotic colorful bedroom with every guest.

"You think I'm attractive?" he asked, defensiveness shifting to shy mirth.

"Obviously," she huffed, pushing the end of a chair leg towards the garbage can. "I don't sleep with every desperate client that shows up at my office."

"You think I'm *desperate*?" Unfiltered amusement overtook Freddy's tone, plastering a smile to his face as he stalked closer. Amelia ignored the instinct to melt, too wrapped up in distancing herself from his intrusion.

"I think you were desperate, now I think you're being avoidant because you're scared."

"What am I scared of?"

"That maybe if you tell him nothing will happen at all. You'll have no reason to come back for more experiments and be forced to go back to the half-life you were living." Her cheeks were flushed and heart was pounding, emotion threatening to take over.

Emotions are only passengers. Emotions are only passengers.

Freddy's hand on the broom handle paused the manic brushing and circulating mantra.

"Let this frustrating mouthy vampire clean up his mess, atleast," he whispered tenderly, grabbing the ridged plastic shaft from her hand. Amelia should have declined but she suddenly was incapable of even meeting his eyes.

Too many things had happened and she hadn't had a sufficient moment of privacy to recollect herself.

That was definitely the problem.

She was not worried about Freddy accidentally revealing the ugliness she held inside.

"Fine. Try not to wake me up, I have to go to dinner with my aunt tomorrow." She trudged towards the bedroom.

Freddy pressed two fingers to the side of his forehead in a small salute. "Scouts honor."

Amelia settled herself back into bed, surprisingly tired for having already gotten a full day's sleep. As usual, she lay on her side, back pressed against the wall.

Amelia knew that putting her bed in the corner of the room was juvenile, but the cool hardness of the wall pressing against her back helped her sleep. She had read somewhere that it was a primal survival instinct, but she was pretty certain it just kept her skin cooler.

Despite the fatigue behind her eyes, her mind whirred in dizzying circles and body prickled with awareness. The frigid pressure felt quite similar to Freddy's chest against her back when they were at the sink.

She had learned so much about him, but more disturbingly he had learned too much about her. Her rule vacation was supposed to be about relaxing, having some orgasms, and moving on. Becoming infatuated with Freddy was not a part of the plan. Freddy, the hot, frustratingly perceptive, vampire man who was in her house unsupervised and she was in bed.

What would he do to pass the time?

She did have an ironically lifeless living room, so there wasn't much to do. Amelia had never considered how silly it was to decorate a room for guests she would never have.

Her lips pulled up into a small smile with the thought that she did have a guest now.

He had volunteered so much vulnerable information about his past, seemingly in response to the secrets he prodded out of her.

Despite the uncomfortable unknown of sharing a small piece of her soul, it was nice to have someone that wanted to know.

Amelia wasn't used to being the puzzle others tried to solve, being the primary problem-solver in her life.

Hours passed as Amelia lay in deep nocturnal thought, analyzing the conversations between them.

Freddy clearly enjoyed pushing a reaction from her, likely because negative attention was all he was used to receiving. It really was no wonder he thought so lowly of himself, if he was forced to be a hoodlum just to find a scrap of belonging. Amelia couldn't help but think how much of a waste that life would have been for him. He was clearly very smart and perceptive, just a little bit lost. She couldn't deny how much she identified with him, perhaps that's why he scared her so much. Not in the physical sense—his bite was very much consensual—he was so resigned to being alone, that nobody in the world would ever know what it was like inside his head.

It was terrifying when he looked at her and for a split second it seemed like she couldn't hide from him at all.

Amelia let the spark of hope burn for a painful minute before snuffing it out. Freddy wasn't meant to be hers, she was just a pit stop on his journey.

Her bedroom door creaked open, an emerald iris peering around nervously. Freddy closed the door again quickly when they made eye contact, earning a soft chuckle from Amelia.

"Your stalking skills could use some work."

Freddy shot her a shy grin and stepped inside the cluttered room.

"Sorry, I wasn't expecting you to still be awake. Trouble sleeping?"

"Yeah, hard to relax with a vampire skulking around your home in the dead of night."

Freddy's face dropped.

"I'm sorry."

"I'm kidding, feel free to snoop around."

"I wasn't planning on snooping."

Amelia shot him a skeptical look.

"Okay, maybe just a little bit."

"It seems like I'm an open book to you anyway, no point in denying it."

"I actually came in here to apologize."

"For what?"

"Can I sit?" He motioned to the large open space next to her on the bed.

Amelia nodded, patting the mattress in silent invitation. Freddy slid under the covers, laying on his side to match her posture.

"I shouldn't have fired back at you, you're just trying to help me."

Amelia's chest tightened. Of course he would be sweet after she had completely over-reacted and made a fool of herself. She was entirely too disarmed and tired to be distant with him, and if she was being honest with herself, she didn't want to.

"Well, you weren't exactly wrong so don't feel too bad."

"You're worried I won't come back?" Worry was a strong word, but the chances weren't zero.

"You can feed now, it's a real possibility."

There was a long pause. His rhythmic breaths were soft and comforting, his scent now more effective than any sleep potion she'd tried.

"Can we pretend that I'm you for a second?"

Amelia moaned in agreement, eyes too heavy to open.

"I think you would say that it's important for me to go home. That it's the only way to know if I would come back."

Amelia hummed in agreement. That is something she would say.

She couldn't be sure, but she could have sworn she felt lips on her forehead before sleep finally took her.

BLOODY MESS

RULE 12

DON'T BE CREEPY

Amelia was beautiful when she slept.

Freddy didn't mean to be a creep when he cracked the door open, he just couldn't stay away from her.

His entire body hummed when she was close, and he had abysmal self control. Guilt was also a large factor of his visit, the apology Amelia deserved soured his tongue as he swept up the wooden shrapnel from the kitchen.

Freddy had not only destroyed her property but offended her as well. He hadn't sought out to hurt her with his deflection, but her comment bore down to a sinister part of his soul.

"You can't control what people think about you, Freddy," she had said.

She was right, because she was always right.

Freddy was good at manipulating himself to every situation, to make sure that those around him thought of him in the exact way he wanted. He analyzed the environment, facial expressions, vocal tones all in the span of a few seconds. He knew how to be sexy or dumb, quiet or respectful.

Being truly vulnerable was a much greater challenge than he was expecting.

It was ridiculous, honestly, he should have expected tough questions from a therapist. Maybe it was that he thought of Amelia as much more than a therapist, more than a friend as well.

It felt like the molecules in his body vibrated when she was near, like they were connected by a deeply intimate thread. Freddy would have to ask Mo if this was normal after a first bite—he wasn't even this dramatic after he lost his virginity.

He considered his redemption as he swept.

He would need to replace the chair (obviously), and apologize to Amelia for sticking his nose where it didn't belong.

Freddy's inappropriate curiosity had gotten him in trouble often during his life, but he couldn't stomach Amelia being upset with him.

It felt like they were on the same team, battling whom he didn't know.

He needed to fix this fumble, starting with a new dining room chair.

Freddy had never bought furniture before, his decrepit human apartment was furnished with free side-of-the-road items his revolving door roommates brought and then abandoned. He had only ever lived in shitty apartments, nothing like Amelia's tidy home. Freddy had never pondered the idea of owning a house, his human life was a write off and so far his time as a vampire was limited by the fact that he was slowly starving to death.

Amelia changed that. A new emotion filled Freddy's chest as he tied up the garbage bag.

Hope.

He knew there was a large likelihood that she would be asleep when he breached the perimeter of her bedroom, he had fed from her twice in just as many days. His uncle said that it was advisable to spread out feeds between different humans, to not exhaust them. Freddy would nod and hum in acknowledgement, knowing that it was wasted breath. A tense excitement filled Freddy's chest at the thought that for the first time he actually could use Mo's hunting advice.

His breaths elevated at the choices in front of him, the excitement quickly transforming to overwhelming anxiety.

Previously, Freddy would simply avoid anything that was too difficult or stressful, but he recently learned that avoiding wouldn't get him anywhere.

He took a deep calming breath and closed his eyes, summoning the psyche of the calmest person he knew.

What would Amelia do?

If Amelia was in his situation she would make a plan. Two plans, just to be safe.

If she was awake, he would apologize for his unacceptable behavior. If she was asleep, he would keep his eyes, hands, and fangs to himself and simply scout for clues on what type of dining chair she would appreciate.

Freddy had a substantial amount of faith in himself, he had been called gifted a few times before puberty. Granted the words 'lazy' and 'unmotivated' usually followed but he was certainly focused now. His attempt to not be a creep had deviated when she invited him into her bed again, and he was just as helpless to refuse her.

Freddy rationalized that he could keep her safe while she slept, atleast.

Amelia moaned and rolled over, making him jump. Luckily she remained asleep, and he could continue his ogling.

She was so soft and vulnerable while she slumbered in the

pink lacey bed, the comforter was a stark juxtaposition to the professional grown up facade she had during the day. It was surprisingly sweet, and reminded him that she was a woman underneath her armour of competence.

He knew she was biologically female intimately, but he had seen very little of the softness he typically attributed with women. Freddy had already pulled some of her fire out, but he had a feeling there was still so much to discover. He had never met anyone so complicated and interesting, someone who was such a dichotomy—her delivery was cold and blunt, but inside lay unconditional understanding and compassion. Freddy felt sympathy for her as well, he knew how difficult it was to be two people at the same time.

Makes you feel like you aren't a person at all.

The rise and fall of her ample chest reminded him that despite her assertiveness over his body and mind, she was the fragile creature between the two of them. He felt silly even thinking that he would be her protector when the bruises that littered her skin were caused by him. Even now, he could easily sink his teeth into her, and she could do nothing to stop him.

Freddy wasn't a stranger to violence, he had been in many fist fights and bar brawls before he was changed. Taking someone's blood was different, it seemed so intimate. He couldn't imagine coercing an unsuspecting human into surrendering the liquid they needed to survive. It rang too closely to what his father had done. He would find a vulnerable woman, manipulate them into trusting him, and sell them to some pathetic trafficking fucker for a profit.

No, Freddy could never take anything from anyone's body without enthusiastic consent.

He should have crawled out of her bed and scouted her bedroom for clues about the perplexing woman, but his limbs refused to move.

His gaze focused on the steady beat of Amelia's pulse, the gentle current of liquid gold she hid beneath her skin. The feeling of being invited inside her, of earning the right to claim a vital piece made his cock hard and fangs emerge.

He certainly had no problems with biting her, but where would that leave him after this weekend?

She seemed uncomfortable with the subject when he had breached it earlier, so clearly she wasn't interested in a relationship after tomorrow.

Freddy tried to imagine finding a hot young thing and seducing her into begging for his bite, but the only thing he could see was Amelia's auburn locks as she threw her head back in orgasm.

The flavor of her blood filling him while the residue of her pussy was still on his face was a transcendent experience.

Freddy groaned and palmed his dick. Being twenty two forever had its downsides.

Amelia whimpered and tossed her head to the side.

Freddy froze, worried he had woken her with his lack of self-control. Fortunately, her eyes remained closed, but she continued to stir, brows furrowed and limbs stiffening.

Freddy knew a nightmare when he saw one. Despite the fact that he had been observing her without her knowledge for several hours, he suddenly felt like a voyeur.

She hadn't invited him to share that part of herself, not yet. He could wake her up, to help her escape the terror. A flutter of warmth pricked at his chest—Freddy wasn't used to being the savior. Everyone had always assumed the worst in him, that he was only going to hurt and destroy like his father. The only person that had believed better was Mo, and now Amelia.

He had to wake her up and save her.

BLOODY MESS

RULE 13
SEX IS AN ACCEPTABLE DISTRACTION
AMELIA

Amelia watched the frozen hunks of dough and beans rotate steadily, the frosted glass of the microwave only partially obstructing her view.

She didn't know how to cook many things, but frozen burritos were becoming her specialty.

Mom had forgotten that school let out early for the book fair, but Amelia didn't mind. She was very good with directions and the walk home wasn't long. Besides, now she got an extra two hours of free-range over the TV which was a gift she wasn't going to squander.

She hopped down from the stool, leaving the meal to spin unattended while she went in search of cutlery. The drawer that normally housed the knives and forks was empty, signaling to Amelia it was likely another bad day for Mom.

Disappointment gripped her heart, though the pain was merely a throb. By the time she found the box of plastic forks under the kitchen sink, the microwave announced their afternoon snack was ready.

She carefully balanced the steaming burritos as she headed towards Mom's room, adjusting her grip on the paper plate so they did not slip off and tumble towards the dusty hardwood— she had burned her fingers picking them up the day before.

To her surprise, there was no Mom shaped blanket on the bed. Amelia was rather good at hide and seek, but looking for her mother was not a fun game to play. She had almost given up and called her aunt when a knock on the door pulled her attention.

The plate landed on the cement of the front steps when Amelia's shocked body was pulled into a tight squeeze by her aunt. Tears were streaming down her cheeks.

"I have something horrible to tell you."

Amelia jerked awake to worried green eyes staring at her.

"Doc, are you okay?" Freddy whispered. Her eyes flickered to the clock on her night stand, before shutting again briefly. It was four in the morning, the sun hadn't risen but she only had about an hour before Freddy would be unconscious.

"Yeah, just a bad dream, happens sometimes."

She rubbed the sleep from her eyes, Freddy's face becoming clear despite the darkness that surrounded them.

His brows pinched slightly and his eyes were wide with concern. He was worried about her.

Amelia couldn't remember the last time anyone was worried about her.

"Do you want me to stay with you until you fall asleep again? I'm not a bad cuddler." Freddy's smile was sweet, making Amelia's core burn.

It was such an ironic thing, Freddy's face at that moment. His skin was marred with the history of violence and metal jewelry, yet his grin exuded a shy genuine energy.

It was the most erotic thing Amelia had ever seen.

The denial from earlier that evening caused desire to flood her like a tsunami.

"I don't want to cuddle."

She grabbed Freddy's face and pulled their mouths together, drinking down the spicy essence of his groan. She craved the feeling of something good after re-living such a horrible moment, and there was nothing better than Freddy. He shifted his weight on top of her, pulling down the comforter and exposing sweat-dampened fabric to the cool night air and his equally chilly skin.

She moaned in approval and buried her hands in the dark mop of hair. His kiss was deep and hungry, just as she wanted it.

"Are you sure?" he asked when she was forced to come up for air. Amelia wasn't sure of anything at that moment except for wanting him. He was quickly becoming her guiltiest pleasure, and she was not done indulging yet.

"I'm always sure," She pulled down the waistband of his pants and gripped his erection.

"Oh, fuck," he moaned, removing her grip from his dick and enveloping it in his own. He used his other hand to lift up the seam of her night gown and thrust himself inside.

They groaned in unison, the pleasurable stretch providing instant relief.

He didn't go slowly, too worked up from their experiment. He thrust hard and fast, burying his face into the crook of her neck, but Amelia needed more, needed to feel the burn of his venom.

"Bite," she whimpered.

Freddy shook his head against the crook of her neck.

"Too soon."

"I need," she begged, pushing his head into her neck.

He groaned and sunk his fangs into her heated flesh, but didn't swallow any of her blood, just simply allowed his venom to flow into her.

It wasn't enough, he needed to take this burning desire away.

"A plant cannot grow unless the earth gives him her nutrients," a small feminine voice echoed in her mind.

She needed to give it to him.

"Take it, Freddy. Let me give it to you," she panted, whimpering when he capitulated and his Adam's apple bobbed against her flesh, relieving the uncomfortable itch from beneath her skin with every gulp of her blood.

His thrusts were wild, deep and powerful. The silver ball felt like a Liberty Bell, freeing her with an intense shock of pleasure.

Though it was under her direct order, he took her over completely.

She shook against him as sweet oblivion found her once again, burning all of the pain away with chaos and fire.

"I have to- I can't-" he grunted out, voice strained with the effort of holding back his release.

"Yes, you've been a good boy—come for me."

He didn't hesitate.

As soon as the command left her lips, his hips slammed almost painfully against hers, ripping the rest of her mind from the dream and grounding it back into her present body.

He shuttered and moaned in earnest, pumping out three final thrusts before he spent himself inside of her. Despite not requiring oxygen, Freddy heaved long panting breaths against the crook of her neck, his heart galloping wildly where it was pressed to her chest.

Amelia wished he could stay there forever, that she could spend the rest of her life counting the beats under the safe shelter of his body. To her disappointment, he rolled off her and closed his eyes.

"Why do you hide in your room?" Freddy slurred, half asleep from dawn's light.

Amelia pushed the hair off his forehead tenderly as she spoke. "It's one of the rules."

Freddy yawned, turning on his side and curling his body. "Lame rule," he murmured into her shoulder.

RULE 13

She watched him through the orange light, ecstasy slowly draining from her as he slumbered.

She already craved him again.

This was precisely the reason Amelia had lame rules in the first place.

BLOODY MESS

RULE 14

SEEK ADVICE WHEN NECESSARY

The restaurant was full of brightly colored bodies, signaling to onlookers that its patrons were mostly of caster background.

Amelia stuck out in comparison, her black dress and modest brown waves a river stone among diamonds.

Nodding in gratitude, she accepted a swirling, smoking, cocktail glass from the server. The liquid was sparkling and fantastical, but her reflection was dark and sinister. She typically wore bright pastel colors, but this dress was the only one she could find that covered her neck.

Her aunt was not an ignorant or intolerant person, but Amelia didn't want to risk getting a lecture on self-respect.

She felt raw and unsteady, broken open from the deviation Freddy had caused to her usual daily monotony.

She needed to find a way for him to feed from someone else, or she may become addicted to both his bite and the way his eyebrows scrunched in concern for her.

Nobody's eyebrows had ever scrunched for her. Her aunt showed concern with pursed lips and sharp words, and was unlikely to be optimistic about her salacious affair with Freddy.

The thing about casters is that they tended to be insular regarding romance and bloodlines. When Amelia tried to take a nice gnome boy to junior prom, her aunt's skin was stained blue for a week and the faucets were leaky for nearly a month.

Magdaline Simmons's casting ability was more advanced than average, but her tolerance for the unexpected was not. Her actions were calculated but she wore her emotions on her skin. Literally. Amelia was pleased to see that her aunt was yellow today, with butterflies flapping atop her head.

"Amelia," she smiled and placed a purple stained kiss on her niece's cheek. "Agatha told me her golem had a little accident." Maggie sat with all the grace and poise Amelia longed to have.

"An understatement, your broom had a nervous breakdown over it." Amelia pushed the cocktail towards her former legal guardian, the smoke had dissipated and the sparkles settled to the bottom while she waited for her arrival. Her aunt wasn't late, all of Amelia's structured attributes were learned from her.

She just needed some time in preparation, to think of how best to word her problem.

"Oh, don't mind him, men can be so dramatic." Maggie sipped the vibrant liquid, humming in approval. Amelia's gaze lowered to the cream lace tablecloth, the topic of men leading her mind back to Freddy and his problem. Amelia only had one night left to remove his internal barriers, or at least figure out how to bend them so he could feed from someone else.

"I know that look. Man problems?" Her aunt's eyes were both sympathetic and excited for the gossip.

"No. Well, kind of," Amelia continued to fiddle with the tablecloth, gasping when it disappeared entirely. She looked up to see her aunt's disapproving pink gaze.

"Wandering hands lead to wandering minds," she said with the same cadence that haunted Amelia for decades. She personally believed it was the other way around but she didn't want to jeopardize her information retrieval by getting into an argument.

"What do you know about vampires?" she asked, folding her hands neatly on the table. It was better to get right to the point, and honestly she had a hard time hiding her thoughts anyways.

Her aunt's face dropped slightly, but her smile remained tightly fixed .

"A bit, what's the issue?" Her voice was guarded, which didn't surprise Amelia.

Her aunt was always uncomfortable talking about nocturnals.

When Amelia announced that her PhD dissertation was about the presentation of major depression in supernatural races, Maggie specifically inquired if she was going to interview any vampires. Amelia rolled her eyes and explained that she did not discriminate in her research. It did pose a challenge to interview nocturnal beings, since the stigma of her caster blood caused them to vanish whenever she tried.

She did manage to interview a banshee, but the noise complaint she received from the neighbors ensured that there was no follow up. She never knew anyone could be so loud while filling out a suicide screener.

"I have a client-no, a friend. He's having a hard time transitioning between feeding partners," Amelia explained, taking a sip from her own glass. It was a modest gin and tonic; she couldn't afford to be too inebriated when she returned to Freddy. Warmth pooled in her stomach at the thought.

RULE 14

It was a novelty, thinking about returning to a handsome man in her bed.

Would he be able to taste the alcohol in her blood?

She would have to ask him.

"Is this a new romantic partner? Or just a one night bite?" Maggie's eyebrows furrowed, her discomfort melting into curiosity. If there was one thing her aunt enjoyed, it was telling people what they should do. She and Amelia were similar in that way.

"He's new to the game, just needs to get out there and bite around." Amelia finished her drink with a large gulp, trying not to think about Freddy sinking his teeth into any nearby heartbeat wearing a pair of heels.

She hoped he had a bit of respect for his body, were there vampire versions of STDs?

"Well, not all men are the casual bite kind, he probably just needs to find someone he's comfortable around, take the pressure off." Maggie said, smirking and pushing another cocktail towards her niece. "Performance anxiety is not limited to the bedroom." Her aunt's look was sly from above the rim of the cocktail glass.

Freddy certainly had no anxiety problems in the bedroom, that was certain.

"You think he needs a girlfriend?" Amelia's mouth was unbelievably dry for the amount of liquid she had just ingested.

"Sure, why not?" her aunt shrugged. Several more gulps went down Amelia's throat.

"Right, that makes sense."

She took a smaller sip, willing the fluid to push down the rising nausea at the idea of Freddy having a cute, young, blood bag girlfriend.

"Promise me it won't be you."

Amelia laughed, a little too loudly.

It was a ridiculous, unbelievable, absurd, bewildering idea that made her heart pound painfully in her chest.

"No, of course not." Freddy was absolutely not her type in any way shape or form. She just found him very attractive and interesting. Their strange semi-professional relationship would be over in twenty four hours and then she would never see him again. The relieved look on her aunt's face made Amelia's gut clench.

The gin had loosened her lips enough to ask before her brain could interfere.

"Why does it matter?"

It wasn't like interspecies relationships were illegal, or anything. Her aunt took a deep breath and sipped from her cocktail.

"Well, there would be two possible outcomes: best case scenario you would end up like your father, worst case scenario like your mother." Maggie's face remained completely neutral.

Dead or gone. Delightful.

Amelia's stomach sank, surely she was pulling her leg.

"Tragedy follows a caster and her vampire." Maggie shook her head.

"What kind of tragedy?" Amelia asked, trying to keep her tone calm despite the growing panic. She had never heard such a thing occurring to humans after they were bitten.

"Our magic and theirs doesn't mix well."

Relief soothed the fear in Amelia's chest.

"The plural isn't necessary." If magic was the catalyst in the reaction, Amelia's inert blood would be her saving grace.

Maggie clicked her tongue in disapproval. "Just because you don't manifest magic doesn't mean it doesn't flow through your veins. You're the descendant of one of the most powerful women- " Amelia hummed in feigned understanding but her mind was already lost to the blurring effects of alcohol and the runaway train that was her stream of consciousness.

"Can casters be turned?" she asked, interrupting her aunt's often repeated lecture on the purity of their bloodline. She never even considered that there could be a consequence for indulging in the spicy pleasure of Freddy's venom.

Well, not a physical one, at least.

The fondness that was rapidly growing in her chest was a completely foreseeable consequence she was trying hard to ignore.

Would she be in Freddy's arms one moment and a creature of the night in the next?

Amelia took a deep breath, tamping down the wayward desire that escaped the prison of her mind. It was such a ridiculous notion, to run in the dark streets with a young man she barely knew. Just because there was a mysterious bizarre connection that pulled her to him, it didn't detract from the fact that she had only known him for a total of forty eight hours. She had never even heard of a caster being turned, and considering how dramatic they were, she would've likely gotten a visit from at least one in her practice.

Unless, of course, they were dead.

Maggie's color drained, shifting from a happy yellow to a dusky gray.

"It's bad luck to speak of monsters, and this family has had enough bad luck." Her aunt's tone was acidic as she clutched onto the rim of her martini.

Amelia scoffed. That was the third person who referred to vampires as monsters. She didn't understand why there was such a blanket hatred for the species, considering Freddy was very sweet. Sure, he stalked her and had every intention to bite her while she was taking out the garbage bin but-

"Oh, that reminds me. Can I have a garbage bin for my birthday?"

Her aunt's complexion yellowed up again and the conversation turned to lighter topics, burning the hours until it was well into the night.

Amelia's skin prickled with awareness that Freddy would definitely be awake, and waiting.

"Look what the cat dragged in," Mo called out from his seat on the couch. He was reclined in the loveseat reading a horror novel as usual.

Freddy never understood why his uncle enjoyed reading about death and suffering, their existence was macabre enough.

Freddy's plan had been to sneak into his room and have a quick shower before facing Mo, that way he could have formulated an appropriate speech—at this point it would be a miracle if he could string two sentences together.

The walk from Amelia's house had been long enough to let him overthink the entire debacle but not long enough to actually construct a persuasive argument.

He woke up just as the sun was setting, disappointed but not surprised to see that Amelia wasn't home. He knew she was likely still having dinner with her aunt, but that didn't make him any more motivated to leave the warm softness of her bed. He tried not to linger, but she had given him permission to snoop, so poking around didn't seem like an overstep.

Freddy pulled at the door in the corner of the room, unsurprised to discover it was a closet. To his disappointment there was no great salacious secret hiding in there; there was, however, a perfect rainbow of pantsuits.

Yikes.

She had a singular book shelf that was filled with loose paper just as much as it was stuffed full of dry psychology related textbooks. Amongst the papers Freddy spotted a wallet sized graduation portrait, and judging by the smoothness of her skin and naive glow in her eyes it was likely from her bachelor's degree.

Freddy thumbed the glossy paper, a deep squeezing pressure budding in his chest. She would have been the same age as him in that photo, and her life was only just beginning. She hadn't thrown it away, had been strong enough to have ambition and risk failure.

That was what Freddy needed—the bravery to hope for a future. She had already shown him that the ability to hunt and survive was inside him the entire time, and maybe this was the next step.

Would she teach him how to live?

Freddy's head turned out of habit as he slipped the portrait in his pocket, the cluttered pink room empty save for him, of course. He made a hasty escape, guilt beginning to brew in his gut.

Surely, she would want him to take it if it would be of benefit to his therapy.

Besides, it would give him the bravery and just a dash of motivational guilt he needed to leave the safe confines of this home and run back to Mo with his tail between his legs.

She needed him to do this.

He had to prove to her that he would return for their last night together, even if it was for selfish reasons.

Realization dawned on Freddy that this test was for both of them.

Amelia had to let go and trust that he would come back, which explained her small outburst earlier. She clung onto control like it was a life raft, but Freddy still didn't know why.

He let thoughts of her distract him during the walk to Mo's bar, the puzzle of his strange therapist easing the tension in his shoulders.

"It's important to do hard things. How else would you know you can do them?" she had told him in the kitchen, a cheeky

smile on her face.

The skin around her mouth creased in an attempt at lightness but Freddy saw how her hands shook as she carried the bowl to the sink. He couldn't help pressing his body against hers, couldn't stand the idea that she would be alone with difficult thoughts.

He also couldn't help but bite her three times, but that was partially her fault.

Mo's voice ripped Freddy's attention from the lingering thoughts of his delectable counselor.

Would his uncle smell her blood on him?

He hoped the scent of sex would over power it—Freddy was used to being a whore, being a blood sucking leech still felt shameful. He tried his hardest to follow Amelia's advice, not to linger on what Mo could think of him.

He wouldn't think about the possibility that his uncle would label him a monster, assuming that he took the blood from an unwilling victim.

Okay, so not thinking about something was harder than he had anticipated.

Freddy switched tactics, focusing on putting himself in the mindset of his unflappable therapist. Amelia wouldn't delay, she would be strong and straightforward and honest.

Suddenly it wasn't only Freddy that sat next to Mo on the sofa, Amelia's moral support gripped the back of his neck with firm tenderness, just as she had the previous night.

His chest burned as he thought of her, no longer alone in his trial.

He had to do this and make her proud.

"The cat sends his apologies," Freddy replied, plunking down on the dark grey cushion.

"You look well-fed," the older man said, narrowed eyes studying the new fullness to Freddy's cheeks. "Very well fed."

He had eaten well, in every sense of the word.

"And you smell like a whore house." Mo continued, sniffing the air dramatically. "No, you smell like a slaughter house inside of a whore house."

Freddy winced but didn't reply, shame and embarrassment glueing his lips together.

"Must have been a hot date, you've never spent the night away since I've known you." Mo peered at Freddy from overtop the frame of his reading glasses.

"I was with my therapist, actually."

Best to leave out that he had stalked, bit, fucked, and developed a small fascination with her.

"Your therapist?" Mo's eyebrows rose.

Freddy nodded and cleared his throat, "She told me to tell you something so you have to listen."

Mo placed the bookmark inside his novel and set it aside.

"By all means,"

Freddy leaned forward, unable to look at his uncle directly.

"I'm sorry for stealing from the bar. I'm not trying to make excuses but you deserve to know the truth. I was starving. I've never been able to feed from a human and my hunger was so desperate I couldn't control it." The pace of his words increased as he talked, hands coming up to rub his face. Freddy looked up to see a mask of surprise on his uncle's face. He closed his eyes, ready for the inevitable anger and disgust.

"You couldn't hunt all this time?" Mo's voice was small and devastated.

Freddy's biological father had been very loud when he was upset; there would always be something broken or thrown against a wall. Mo's controlled questioning was completely unsettling, like an empty forest with a wolf just waiting to pounce. Freddy nodded, the hairs on the back of his head stood with unease.

He couldn't read Mo's facial expression, and had no idea where they stood.

"Why didn't you tell me?" he whispered, eyes distant.

Freddy leaned back and inhaled deeply. How could he explain to his uncle the pressure that he had to be the predator he was expected to be, and the deep shame that came when he failed over and over?

"A vampire is his fangs," Freddy said, parroting a phrase Mo had said many times before.

"You thought I would be upset because you couldn't hunt." Hurt and incredulity painted Mo's face and voice.

Freddy swallowed and ducked his head, waiting for the unavoidable pain.

"You could do something with yourself if you just cared a little." The voice of a teacher infiltrated his mind.

"I wouldn't have to toughen you up like this if you weren't such a pussy." His father's voice made anger rise in his chest.

Nobody knew him, not even Mo.

"Did I not find you hovering near death in the alley?" Mo asked, the volume of his voice raising.

"Yes, you did but-"

"Did I not offer you a place to stay, regular employment?"

"Yes, but-"

"Where on earth did you get the idea that I would turn my back on you?"

"You're seeking punishment." Amelia's voice rang in his head, snapping the last thread of his restraint.

"Because you should!" Freddy exploded, standing and turning to face Mo.

"Freds-"

"I took your generosity and wasted it. You have to hold me accountable for my fuck up."

"With death? Even murderers don't deserve that."

"That's a matter of personal opinion," Freddy muttered under his breath. His biological father deserved far worse than death.

Mo stood and walked into his bedroom, closing the door a bit too firmly.

Freddy exhaled, relieved that the altercation was over. Despite the adrenaline that made his heart pump painfully in his chest, Freddy knew it was the right thing to do.

Amelia would be proud.

He showered and dressed, resisting the urge to stroke his cock when he imagined Amelia dolled up and sitting in a fancy caster restaurant.

Did she have the bite marks displayed on her throat?

In Freddy's mind she did.

He imagined her reaction to his victory the entire journey to her house, the way her eyes would glimmer when she praised him.

RULE 15

DON'T UNDERESTIMATE THE POWER OF ROLE-PLAY

Amelia found Freddy exactly where she left him, except the frilly pink duvet was pulled over his head.

"How did it go?" she asked, leaning against the door jam. The gin lingered in her bloodstream, softening her limbs and loosening her lips. Freddy groaned in misery, voice muffled underneath quilted roses. "That good, huh?"

"You were right," the moping vampire said, pulling the sheet down, revealing a face that was just as devastatingly handsome as she remembered. His hair was still slightly damp, curling slightly at the ends. As if that image wasn't alluring enough, the strong scent of men's body wash mixed with his spicy cologne.

He also was not wearing a shirt, which seemed like the most important thing about him at that moment.

That was wrong, she should care more about his emotional misery than the smooth planes of his chest or the hair that trailed from his belly button.

"I usually am, but go on," Amelia said, trying not to stare. She had to be a serious therapist for one more night, then she could replay these memories to take the chill of loneliness away.

"Nothing happened. He didn't scream or hit me, just slammed the door." Freddy gesticulated wildly in frustration, the muscles of his arms and pectorals bunching and shifting as he spoke.

"I'm sorry," Amelia stepped closer, the need to comfort him pulling her to sit on the bed at his feet.

"Why the fuck would you be sorry about that?" His voice was a dramatic grumble, if Amelia wasn't so bothered by the tone of his questioning, she would find it cute.

"Because you didn't get the punishment you were looking for."

Freddy's eyes combed her frame, and she was suddenly very aware of how much of her skin was exposed. She crossed her arms in front of chest, hoping to obscure the peek of cleavage.

"I don't suppose you know where I could get some punishment, do you?" Freddy's smile was close to a smirk, and it made Amelia's core throb.

His words reminded her of their last experiment, and the advice her aunt had blessed her with. If Freddy could bite freely as long as he was comfortable, he could be cured.

That was the point of all of this, wasn't it?

"Speaking of, we better start."

"What are we doing tonight?" Freddy scooched up to recline against the headboard, knees pulled up to his chest. Thankfully, he was wearing a dark pair of sweatpants.

"Roleplay," Amelia smiled sweetly.

"Roleplay?" Freddy's eyebrows shot up so high, a deep wrinkle marred his perfect skin. "Seems a bit soon to introduce costumes into the bedroom, I haven't even seen you naked yet."

Amelia rolled her eyes. "We know that you struggle to release your fangs if you don't have consent or feel in any way undeserving."

Freddy nodded in agreement, listening intently. It was one of her favourite things about him, the way he clung onto every word she said.

"The key is finding a dynamic where you know that biting is always welcome."

"I'm getting the sense you're not going to put on a leather outfit." Freddy joked, attempting to lighten the mood, as always.

She didn't give him the satisfaction of a laugh, as much as she wanted to.

"We are going to pretend that I am your girlfriend."

"Girlfriend?" His voice cracked.

Amelia nodded. "You know, one woman you are more or less committed to? I'm sure you've had several before."

"Sort of," Freddy said, the corner of his mouth pulling taunt with skepticism. She rolled her eyes, convinced he was being self-deprecating again.

"They didn't so much like me, as much as they liked the drugs I gave them for free." Amelia's face must have displayed her surprise, because Freddy elaborated.

"I was a dealer before, to pay the bills," he shrugged, shoulders hunching with shame.

"So, what scene are we roleplaying, fake girlfriend? Am I going to shave my ass with your razor or leave my socks right next to the laundry hamper? Sounds pretty sexy." Freddy's smile was cocky, deflecting his discomfort as predicted.

Therapist Amelia would have come up with a witty comeback, but she was unavailable and Tipsy Amelia was a sub par substitute.

Her eyebrow furrowed once she absorbed his words. "Do boyfriends actually shave their ass hair?"

Amelia had never noticed anyone's ass hair.

Did she have ass hair?

Freddy shifted and hummed in exaggerated contemplation, eyes scanning the textured ceiling. "I feel like your ex probably didn't. I can just imagine him; a big stinky beast of a man who gave good dick and bad breath."

"Are you always so mean to your friends?" she asked, punching him in the pectoral. Freddy laughed and rubbed at the abused flesh.

"Oh, come on, doc, I'm just joking around. Unless I'm right?" His eyebrow quirked in a pointed look. Amelia flushed at the insinuation, but mostly because he was right.

Freddy perked up, shifting to all fours.

"Let me guess: ogre, troll, ghoul?" he rattled off, eyebrows waggling. Amelia's last ex had been extraordinarily rude, selfish, and frankly unhygienic.

"Worse," she swallowed before continuing. "Computer science major."

Freddy collapsed on the bed with deep belly laughter, rolling back and forth and clutching his stomach. Amelia sat stiffly on the bed, waiting for his laughter to die down or embarrassment to kill her.

An arm locked around her waist and pushed her down on the bed, her head resting next to Freddy's. He turned his face and smiled at her, lips only an inch away. She could so easily kiss him from this distance. The kiss wouldn't be from Amelia the therapist or Amelia the friend.

Amelia didn't want to think about who she would be when she kissed him.

So she didn't.

She turned her head, breaking the tension between them.

"In all seriousness, why isn't there a balding Mr. Atkinson stinking up your bed every night?"

The corner of her lips turned up. "I'm flattered you think my future husband would take my last name."

Freddy's face transformed to outrage. "As he should. He better get your name tattooed on his ass, too."

"Hmm, I guess that would explain why he needed to use my razor to shave his ass hair."

Freddy's face and voice softened. "I mean it, doc. You

shouldn't accept anyone that isn't absolutely obsessed with you."

He reached forward and pushed a lock of hair off her face.

Amelia's gut clenched at his tender words and touch.

He was giving her advice because it was their last night together, because he would never be obsessed with her.

She groaned and sat up, the alcohol making her woozy.

"We should start the experiment before it gets too late." She stood and started walking towards the living room.
"I am watching TV after dinner and you woke up hungry." She paused just before walking out of sight.
"Since we are in a committed relationship, I am more than happy to give you every part of my body." When she didn't hear a reply from Freddy, she turned back to face him. His bravado had dropped, and the pale green pools that were once filled with arrogance were devastatingly vulnerable.

"What happens after tonight?"

Amelia's stomach dropped, a thousand possibilities running through her mind. Despite all of the novel feelings Freddy had elicited during their short fling, Maggie's voice echoed in her mind.

"This family has had enough bad luck."

It was time to wean herself away from the fantasy that there could be anything after tonight. She could not be the cause of anyone's suffering, even if the thought of going back to her office made dread creep up her spine.

"We go back to our normal lives." She tried to force confidence into her voice, but the words came out hollow and empty.

"But I'm still a mess," he said.

Tragedy follows a caster and her vampire.

Amelia had to stop further entwinement, before a short vacation turned into a permanent death.

"So am I, Freddy." Amelia slipped away before she said something else she would regret.

Freddy shut his eyes, reveling in the fatigue of his abdominals and ignoring the painful throb in his chest. He couldn't remember the last time he had laughed that hard or felt so sad.

He liked Amelia, and not just for her blood donations.

She was interesting and kind, although certainly a bit high strung.

"So am I, Freddy." she had said, though he had a feeling the words were not meant for him. The rules she hid behind were a farce, no different than the smart mouth he used to keep others away from the sensitive core he wished didn't exist.

What was she hiding?

Freddy shook his head.

He needed to focus on his therapy, unravelling the mystery of his neurotic therapist could wait.

He tried to immerse himself in the fantasy she created, to

believe that he had just woken up in the bed they shared. It was a pleasant thought, waking up to her soft flesh within reach every evening. He quite enjoyed making her coffee before she awoke, and watching her sleep had been soothing other than that pesky erection.

Was that a part of this scenario?

Was he supposed to sink his cock inside her as well as his fangs?

He supposed if she was his girlfriend that's what she would want. She would want his body, likely his mind as well.

He would want her.

Fuck, he already wanted her more than he'd wanted anything. He would be happy spending the rest of his life following behind her like a love-sick puppy, but she didn't want him.

"We go back to our normal lives," she had said, like Freddy ever had a normal life to return to.

The TV blared with a cinematic theme, announcing that the scene had begun. Freddy took a deep breath to prepare himself and stood from the soft pink bed, wishing with every undead bone in his body that this would not be the last time he pulled back the covers.

Show time.

She was sitting on the couch, just as he expected.

The tight black dress hugged her curves, the keyhole displaying cleavage he wanted to sink his teeth into. The skin would pop underneath his fangs, and her moans of pleasure would intoxicated him more than her blood. Freddy knew he was supposed to be hungry for it, but blood lust was not on the forefront of his mind.

Amelia told him to pretend she was his, and he always obeyed her.

Freddy stalked closer, stopping when he was right behind her head. Instead of a casual greeting, she looked up at him through tear stained eyes.

His brows furrowed, she had a very interesting taste in foreplay.

"What's wrong?" he asked, cradling soft cheeks in his hands.

"It's just the octopus." She pointed towards the large red cephalopod on the screen. "She has to sit there and starve to protect her eggs. It's so tragically beautiful." Amelia's voice shook and another tear slipped down her cheek.

If there was a chance that Freddy wasn't going to become irreparably attached to this bizarre woman, it was gone.

Amelia Atkinson, professional psychologist who regularly bossed around creatures several times her size and strength, was crying about an octopus.

To his dismay, jealousy crept up the underside of his rib-cage. Strange animalistic thoughts crawled into the place where doubt used to live. He wanted to smash the TV for hurting her, even if she found it beautiful.

Those tears belong to me.

Running off of instincts alone he leaned forward and pressed his lips to the skin of her cheek, swiping his tongue along the damp trails there.

A gasp, "Freddy-"

The press of his mouth against hers silenced his name, the intrusion of his tongue brought forth a pair of hands to his hair. Amelia tugged on the strands as their tongues fought for dominance, though Freddy had never intended to win the battle. His goal was to start the dance, to have her whole world revolve around the pleasure he was giving her body, at least for a moment.

She yanked his head back, only putting enough space between their lips to suck in a panting breath.

"*You* are tragically beautiful," he murmured in her ear, a gentle whiff of gin making his chest burn.

Freddy had smelled it when she had nearly kissed him earlier, but he didn't quite realize how affected she was. He had been a bartender long enough to spot a drunk crying girl, and that was precisely what she was at that moment. Usually, he was the saviour, the kind soul that stuffed the girl in the cab and kept her out of harm's way.

Looking at the watering icy blue of Amelia's eyes and the slight flush to her cheeks, Freddy knew that he was a changed man.

He wanted to take everything that she would give him, her blood, her body, her heart. He knew deep in his soul that nobody could take care of her as well as he could, and he had to make sure nobody would ever try.

He leaned forward and shifted her auburn waves off of one shoulder, exposing the creamy expanse of her neck. He inhaled deeply, smirking when she moaned at the glide of his nose against her sensitive flesh.

"Nobody else will ever make you cry," he growled against her skin.

"Yes," Her answer was merely a breath, bookended by a soft moan as he ran a mischievous tongue from collarbone to earlobe.

Her skin was salty and sweet, the warmth of blood permeating from where it lay just under. Frustration burned inside him as hunger grew.

Freddy tamped it down, attempting to regain his control

and focus on this task. It was his last chance to have her and he wouldn't waste it by rushing.

"Do you remember the last time you were sitting on this couch?" Freddy certainly did.

Her breath paused for just a moment, understanding must have seeped in because she placed two bare feet on the glass coffee table. Freddy's cock pulsed.

She was so smart.

"Were you watching?"

"I couldn't help it. You were so fucking hot, I would have done anything to be the one between your legs."

Amelia's breath hitched and she took one of his palms, trailing it down her body until it rested between her thighs.

"Do it now." The words were music to Freddy's ears. The last time he heard them cross her lips, they were on the hood of her car and his cock was about to pierce her entrance.

It pulsed against the fabric of his pants at the memory, and Freddy had to restrain himself from flexing his hips and rubbing against the back of the couch.

He had to take care of his Amelia first.

His fingers slipped underneath the hem of her dress, stifling a groan when he met the wetness on her inner thighs.

"You're soaked,"

A tentative fingertip breached the crease that led to her centre.

"What are you going to do about it?"

"What I'm good at—making it worse." He punctuated the reply by thrusting two fingers inside, and pressed his lips to hers, swallowing the cry of pleasure.

"You were just a pathetic little starving vampire, weren't you? Watching me from the window like a pervert," she said when they parted.

Freddy's cock was going to combust if he didn't start getting some relief soon.

"Yes," his reply was muffled in the skin between her collar bones, fingers thrusting into a pussy so hot he was certain he would die.

His fangs ached, his cock ached, everything ached to be inside of her.

To please her.

"Show me what you wanted to do, my little pervert."

She wouldn't have to ask twice. He pressed his thumb to

her clit at the exact same moment he scored the delicate skin of her neck with his fangs. It drew just enough blood to wet his hunger, the sounds of pleasure that left Amelia's lips increasing his other appetite as well.

"Will you come for me, first?" he asked, though his answer came in the spasming of her walls around his fingers.

He needed more skin, better access. Yanking at the dark fabric, Freddy was pleased to discover she wore no bra underneath it.

"Get over here, now," she demanded, shifting and leaning back on her elbows, allowing him an unobstructed view of her body.

Freddy pulled back as his eyes raked full breasts and a plush abdomen. She was soft and well fed, the curves of a woman well into middle age. Freddy's cock had never been harder at the fantasy that such a smart, experienced woman had chosen him. Amelia, who worked so hard to keep herself hidden, lay there, naked and exposed for him.

Impatient, he climbed over the back of the couch, and ravaged her mouth, only parting when she slid shaking palms under the waistband of his pants. His body shuttered under her touch, every erogenous zone tingling simultaneously. When she was touching him all was right with the world.

At least for the moment.

"Tell me what you need," he begged, swallowing down the remnants of her flavour from his tongue.

"My pathetic little vampire." Arousal coursed so hot his veins that Freddy feared he may lose himself before even being removed from his pants. He could not, would not, mess this up.

If it was a vampire she wanted, a vampire she would get.

Freddy grabbed her legs and flipped her over and against him, her supple behind pressed against his aching cock. Amelia moaned as he freed his length and probed the silver bead against her clit. Her answering mewl pulsed in his balls but he still needed more. He needed to hear her ask for it, needed the fuel of her voice.

This might be the fantasy boyfriend version of Freddy, but even he was a bit of a smart ass.

"Does this seem pathetic to you?" He gently probed her entrance with the bulbous head.

Amelia swallowed and pushed up to her knees, giving her purchase to push back against him. She would always be the one in control, and Freddy wouldn't have it any other way.

"Yes, it does. You would never deny me anything, would you?" Her hips gyrated and Freddy was completely frozen.

"Never,"

"Give it all to me, then."

"You know what they say about vampires, doc?" Freddy asked with a smirk, positioning himself at her entrance.

"What?" she panted.

"They can't come inside unless they're invited."

Amelia's laugh was breathless but she quickly sobered when he pushed only the head of his dick past her opening. She leaned back and gripped his hair.

"Fuck me, Freddy. Do it now."

He plunged into her hard, took her with the intensity of a man with a purpose.

He was her strong immortal protector, greedley accepting the gift of her body as payment for eternal devotion. The thought was heady and pushed him towards orgasm. Her hips pushed back, urging him faster. He complied obediently, increasing both the speed and force of his thrust. She was so tight and hot around him, he would surely lose his mind.

"I need...I need..." she whimpered.

"Bite?" he asked, understanding the words her mouth couldn't say.

Amelia nodded, grabbing his head and pressing his face to her neck.

Without hesitation he opened his mouth and latched on to her jugular. Hot thick ambrosia filled his mouth, heightening the ecstasy of her walls squeezing him. The pain and pleasure of his bite pushed Amelia over the edge, pussy clamping down around his cock. He groaned as he sucked against her, thrusting himself deep and releasing himself with two wild pumps.

Freddy didn't leave her warmth immediately, just pressed his nose to the center of her back and breathed in her scent as she calmed.

As he calmed.

When his cock inevitably softened and slipped out of her, he pressed a kiss to the back of her neck. Amelia turned her head to the side, cheek squished against the couch cushion.

"I pronounce you cured," she slurred, eyes still closed. Freddy chuckled lightly, lifting himself off the couch and placing a throw blanket across her naked flesh.

"You do good work, doc." He rubbed slow circles on her lower back while the documentary continued. Freddy watched the octopus gently fanning her eggs, carefully circulating the water around her children to her own detriment. He got lost in the tragedy of it, because before he knew it soft snores were escaping from the woman beside him.

Freddy should be happy, at least relieved that he had the tools for survival.

He could move on with his life, rebuild a new identity now that he didn't have to worry about starving to death.

So, why was there a dull ache in his chest at the thought of never being with Amelia like this?

He knew the answer intrinsically, down to the marrow of his undead bones.

Something had changed within them the moment her scent entered his lungs. Amelia may try to deny it, to keep herself safe from the vulnerability of someone that truly saw her, but Freddy wouldn't let her off the hook.

There was some merit to her reluctance, he had to admit. Freddy wasn't ready to be her equal partner, not yet. The way he was now, he was only worthy of kneeling at her feet, of kissing and worshiping the scraps of her she gave willingly.

Freddy wanted more, so much more. Freddy wanted every beautiful inch he had already seen, and the ugly parts she wouldn't show. The fantasy of their roleplay slipped away as her breaths evened, but Freddy's conviction did not.

She might not have done it intentionally but she gave Freddy a precious gift by demanding his focus, his submission.

"Thank you," he whispered, pressing a soft kiss to her temple.

For the first time in his life, Freddy had a plan.

BLOODY MESS

RULE 16

WHEN IN DOUBT, GATHER MORE INFORMATION

AMELIA

Amelia woke up with a smile on her face.

The smell of Freddy's spicy musk still lingered in her lungs, his venom still tingled in her veins. The dopamine flooded out of her when she realized that bright morning light filled the living room, and a painful vice gripped her by the temples.

Amelia slept the entire night on the couch and Freddy had gone home.

It wasn't the first time Amelia had woken up alone nursing a hangover, but her stomach convulsed with painful disappointment, regardless. For some deluded reason, she had a small hope in her heart that he would ask to stay another night.

That was what she got for hoping, painful disappointment.

She stretched and rolled off the couch, nearly missing the mug that sat on the coffee table, and the pink sticky note that lay beside it.

Her heart melted.

Thank you for everything.
Ps. Sorry about the ass hair.

It felt like a goodbye.

His writing was neat and elegant, another surprise. Amelia had never met a man his age that wrote in cursive. It almost distracted her from the deep exhaustion weighing down every muscle, and something that felt uncomfortably like heartache.

Her time with Freddy was over, and it was time to focus on her responsibilities again.

Starting with figuring out why everyone had such a poor opinion of vampires.

Amelia sipped her coffee and considered the best location to gather information. During her schooling she spent many hours in the interspecies general library, however, it was a holiday, which meant that it was likely closed.

Fortunately, it was the International Day of Peace, which was not universally celebrated.

Optically, it was questionable that casters didn't observe the end of the great war, but considering they were the party who was defeated, Amelia could understand not being excited for a yearly reminder.

On the bright side, it meant that she got a day off work, and the Grand Caster Library, located in the center of the caster municipality, should be open.

A knot of apprehension gripped the upper quadrant of her abdomen.

"You don't belong there, Amelia," her aunt's voice reminded her. The first time she heard that particular phrase was when she was face down and weeping into her bedsheet sometime in adolescence. Maggie had refused to sign the permission slip for a field trip to the museum because it was in the epicenter of caster territory. The trend continued, and Amelia was only permitted to go to mixed species schools.

She took a deep breath to center herself.

She was an adult now, and she technically was still on her rule vacation.

"Penny, schedule a visit to the library."

The Grand Caster Library was taller than it was old and that was saying something. Amelia wasn't sure why her aunt was so worried about her venturing into caster land, all she had to do was flash her ID and the guard let her through without any fanfare.

It was a relief, honestly. Usually, when people read her registered race there was an eyebrow raise or skeptical glance. Though, that could have been due to her last name as well— she had learned to disregard the whispers of speculation about her dead mother and outcast father since puberty.

They didn't know her, anyway.

Not like Freddy does.

The intrusive thought shifted her balance, making the ground lurch beneath her for a fraction of a second. Luckily, the carpet was old and plush and she easily caught herself.

Focus, Amelia.

This visit was about understanding, not lusting or swooning.

The smell of dust permeated the air as Amelia shuffled between book shelves, heading straight for the academic materials section. She carefully scanned the spines, only stopping when she had reached the end of the V section.

That didn't make very much sense.

How could there be no reference to vampires at all?

Though her confidence wavered at the barrier, her resolve did not. She didn't get as far as she did by giving up after one attempt.

She abandoned the shelves and headed towards the digital archive. She tended to avoid technology when possible, things never seemed to work right when she used them. Luckily, the aged computer powered up with no problems.

Amelia clicked on several screens, face growing tenser by the moment.

1 result found.

A photo of an embracing couple and the same phrase her aunt had repeated to her.

Tragedy follows a caster and her vampire.

Amelia's heart dropped to the bottom of her blue Monday heels and she closed her eyes in a moment of grounding.

Just another obstacle.

That was no problem at all, Amelia was used to overcoming them.

And coming on them, repeatedly.

The walk to the counter was slightly faster than Amelia was intending, her fists clenched with the drive to ignore the Freddy-obsessed internal monologue.

"Excuse me," she whispered to the woman clicking on a computer. She was pleasant to look at, with a pale blue overlay to tidy silver hair. A middle-range caster. Though light manipulation was a basic caster ability, the ability to maintain it constantly required great skill.

The woman turned her head and smiled politely, her eyes widening just a fraction when they met Amelia's.

"How can I help you?" she asked, folding her hands together primly.

"I'm looking for information on vampires."

The woman's frame hardened, the smile becoming cemented on her face.

"One moment, Amelia."

She excused herself and scurried through a door behind her, leaving Amelia slightly shell-shocked.

When the woman returned she held a leather bound book in her hands.

"I'm sorry, but it appears I cannot fulfill your request at this time. The Grand Caster Library only contains information reviewed and approved by the Grand Caster Council. Would you like information on officially recommended literary repositories?" she rattled off with a practiced precision. Although her words conveyed a polite rejection, she slid the book across the counter towards Amelia.

"No, thank you." Amelia couldn't keep the confusion from her voice, but was able to understand that it was best to go along with whatever was happening. She lifted the book and glanced at the cover before quickly placing it in her bag.

Vampires: Secrets of a Forbidden Magic

by Dr. Atkinson

"Sway righteous," the woman nodded with a smile, eyes softening again.

Amelia's mind raced as she drove home, fingers clutching the steering wheel so tightly the skin above the small joints of her hand blanched, blood leaving them to circulate her body via racing heart.

Despite a venture to understand, Amelia was left with more questions than answers.

Why was there no mention of vampires in the largest caster information hub?

Who was that woman and why did she pretend that book didn't exist?

Had Amelia even mentioned her name?

She was almost certain she hadn't.

"Your mind is a sieve, Amelia. Letting things in and out without control." Maggie's voice infiltrated, calming at least one of her frayed nerves.

She must have mentioned it, and simply forgot.

The book was hand-written, as it turned out—likely unpublished. That would explain why it wasn't approved by the Condescending Caster Council (as her aunt called it.) Most libraries only accepted published works to maintain a high standard. It still didn't answer why the woman gave it to her in the first place, though the shared last name probably had something to do with it.

Amelia settled underneath the covers of her bed, trying to ignore both the overwhelming smell of Freddy that lingered on her sheets and the throbbing in the back of her head.

She usually washed her bedding weekly, but she just wasn't ready to let her time with him go yet. It was still technically her vacation, so one last deviation was allowed.

Her fingers traced the lettering on the cover.

Dr. Atkinson. A relative of hers, no doubt.

Was it an ancient ancestor, or a distant cousin?

Maggie had often lamented about how her father's side of the family was both brilliant and troubled, which made Amelia long to know them.

Would they understand her, if they had a chance?

It was of no matter who had written the book, the real importance was what lay inside.

She scanned the table of contents, pondering what section would provide the most relevant information.

"Well, there would be two possible outcomes: best case sce-

nario you would end up like your father, worst case scenario like your mother." Amelia deduced that her aunt was referring to estrangement in regards to her father, which wasn't a surprise.

Casters segregated as a hobby, and had a general distaste for any nocturnal creature, so becoming entangled with a vampire would easily qualify for caster status removal.

Not that Amelia felt particularly strongly about keeping it, so far it had been more of a nuisance than a benefit.

Death was clearly what Maggie was referring to when it came to her mother, which was considerably more concerning.

She had never heard of deaths caused by vampire bites, but then again vampires were quite rare to begin with. Before Freddy, she had never actually met one in the flesh, and after the whirlwind weekend, she was glad of it.

All things considered, venom would be a likely culprit for illness or death, so that was where she started.

Despite rumor and legend, a vampire's venom is harmless to the victim—in fact, it is likely an intoxicant that numbs pain and incapacitates the receiver...

Amelia's eyes burned and head throbbed, lids begging to close.

She would simply rest them for a moment and then continue on in her research.

The Library was so tall Amelia was sure she wouldn't be able to touch the ceiling no matter how high she jumped (and she was a good jumper). Mommy's hand pulled her through the double doors, forcing her to detach her gaze from the top of the marble pillars.

"Good morning, how can I help you?" A woman with blue-tinged hair smiled at mommy. Amelia was jealous, she couldn't change the colour of her hair yet. Though she would probably pick red like her momma, if she could.

"Sway righteous," Mommy said.

The woman nodded before replying, "Stay true,"

Momma turned and kneeled down, letting Amelia see the light sheen of sweat on her forehead. She wiped it with the sleeve of her dress, unable to stop herself. Mommy always seemed to be so sweaty these days, it was a good thing Amelia was there to wipe it.

"Be a good girl and find a book to read, okay?" Amelia nodded but she had no intention of actually obeying. This conversation was far more interesting than any book she could possibly find. Still, she ran to the children's section and pulled the first book she found, turning quickly with the intention of following her mom.

"Don't bother, they won't let you in." A voice made her pause.

The girl was much bigger than Amelia, practically an adult. At least ten years old, she decided.

True to the girl's word, her mother was already vacant from the spot in front of the counter. Disappointed weighed her steps as she sauntered back to the bean bag chairs in the corner. She supposed she could play with the puppets to pass the time.

"You're new, aren't you?"

Amelia nodded and cracked open the familiar fairy tail of a prince who falls in love with a troll.

"Don't worry, my mom says they'll come get us when we're ready."

RULE 17

NOBODY'S PERFECT, BUT TRY YOUR BEST

AMELIA

Amelia was a Monday person, and a morning person usually.

Monday's held optimism; the world was an oyster ripe for the picking, the new week was just waiting to be seized. She just had to be diligent and not drop it.

Or lose it.

"You seem to have a pretty good handle on it." Freddy's voice echoed in her aching head, bringing a small shot of comfort. He genuinely believed she had it all together.

"Looks can be deceiving." She had answered back, an uncharacteristically vulnerable move.

She wasn't even sure why she said it at the time, though it might have had something to do with the fact that she felt completely disarmed by him.

Though it was technically a Tuesday, it held the monday-ness of the first work day after a holiday.

She cracked her eyes open only because her day planner had been repeatedly smacking her in the face. She batted away the parchment assault, realization and horror filling her as she glanced at her bedazzled alarm clock.

Amelia was late.

Really late.

She sprinted around her home, modifying her usual morning routine to include only the necessities. Amelia shoved a piece of toast in a dry mouth, only pausing when her leg rammed into the corner of a metal chair. She rubbed the abused flesh, cursing her shitty proprioception and hard corner of the seat.

Hard corner of a seat she wasn't supposed to have.

Freddy had destroyed it only a few days ago, and she hadn't replaced it yet.

Confusion pricked at the place between her ribs, a hot pink sticky note resting on one of the pale blue cushions.

Good luck trying to break these. (But if you wanna try I know a guy)

—Your frustratingly attractive pathetic vampire.

Only when the planner hit her in the back of the head did Amelia remember her predicament and continue on her way.

She would have to ruminate about this when she had time and the horrible migraine finally went away.

The fist of anxiety gripped Amelia's stomach on the drive to work, a restlessness in her limbs despite the deep lethargy. A looming sense of nausea threatened to return the few bites of toast she had managed to consume, and yet her mind managed to drift back to Freddy.

Her rule vacation was over.

She would never see him again.

That knowledge pulsed inside her with a throbbing so similar to the ache in her head, following her as she passed by the line of clients waiting outside the front doors.

Amelia's office looked much the same it did every morning. The carpet was still a worn-down gray, the walls a calming pastel blue. Yet, for some reason she felt like a stranger when she stepped through the familiar threshold.

Being late was physically painful for Amelia, an unredeemable sin.

"Being late is the ultimate show of disrespect, you may as well spit on your mother's grave." Maggie would say, if Amelia was ever less than five minutes early.

"I'll be with you in just one moment," she smiled at the gnome as he settled into one of the seats in the reception area.

 Looking at her watch, it became clear that she had missed the entire first appointment. Embarrassment flashed hot in her chest, followed closely by guilt. She imagined Flint sitting outside on the steps of her office, confused and rejected that she had forgotten him.

She had felt that way so many times, sitting on the steps of her school. Amelia had cursed the world for making her the way that she was, for dooming her to a life of misunderstanding and loneliness.

Now, she was the perpetrator.

She closed the door to the treatment room and leaned against it, taking a deep calming breath.

Emotions are passengers. The familiar mantra worked to suppress the bubbling anxiety from escaping the prison of her mind.

Progress was lost when she opened her eyes, and saw the leather couch which still had a sizable tear in the cushion.

The whirlwind weekend with Freddy had caused her to neglect buying a new sofa, amongst other life-changing effects.

A mechanical clicking drew her attention to the desk in the corner.

Amelia stomped over and grabbed the sheet of paper.

Fun weekend?

She dropped the sheet unceremoniously into the garbage can before begrudgingly sitting in front of the typewriter.

She could not give her attention to her clients while being this unsettled. Best take care of it sooner rather than later.

"Okay, fine. Let's talk about it."

Name: Dr. Amelia Atkinson
Age: 32
Sex: Female
Pronouns: She/Her
Race: Human

<u>Session 255</u>

Tracy: How was your vacation?

Dr. A: Unsettling.

Tracy: That doesn't sound very relaxing.

Dr. A: Oh, it was the opposite of relaxing. Exciting, thrilling—a complete disaster, really.

Tracy: Those are all positive adjectives.

Dr. A: Exactly, that's why it's a tragedy.

Tracy: You are upset because you enjoyed some laxity in your usual rigid discipline.

Dr. A: You don't understand. How am I supposed to keep pretending that I'm happy like this?

Tracy: Like what?

Dr. A: Alone. He saw me, Tracy. He figured out more about who I am in two days than anyone ever has. I don't know how to explain it but we had this connection, like we're made of the same stuff.

Tracy: This is about a man.

Dr. A: Not just a man. A hot, smart, troubled vampire man with a voodoo dick. I thought I would be able to just have a weekend fling to shake out the cobwebs but it was so much more than that.

Tracy: What was it?

Amelia: Unexpected. The worst part is that I liked it. He challenged every word that came out of my mouth, and now I don't know how to go back.

Tracy: How have you managed it before?

Amelia: I didn't think it could be any other way. I was resigned to the fact that no one would ever really understand me, that's why I worked so hard to be able to understand others.

Tracy: Why did you think no one would understand you?

A knock on the door interrupted Amelia before she could answer Tracy. Freddy's voice echoed in her mind.

"Why would they?"

She ripped the sheet out of the typewriter and tossed it into the garbage can, deciding she didn't want to know.

The man that entered her small treatment room was very sweaty. At least they had something in common.

"Tough weekend?" Amelia asked, recognizing the tell-tale sign that he had another binge. The gnome dropped his gaze to the spotless carpet.

"Bad month. Lost my job," he admitted. Sympathy pounded through her, she knew Ralph had been working in the mines for several decades, so such a devastating loss could easily trigger an escape into his vice. Amelia regretted escaping into liquor herself, the throbbing in her temples still pounding despite the tablets she had taken.

"I'm not judging you for a relapse, Ralph. I am worried that you're here right now. You know that alcohol withdrawal can kill you." It was an unpleasant way to die: nausea, vomiting, sweating, headaches, and tremors that could escalate to fever, seizures, and death.

She could empathize with him, her symptoms were not so different.

The world closed in around Amelia as the words sunk into the crevices of her sore brain, suffocating her in dread and numbing her limbs.

Was she experiencing venom withdrawal?

Freddy didn't know what doing heroin was like, but the high he rode the entire shift must have been close. Amelia's essence still powered his muscles, energizing every movement.

He had considered attempting to test out his new hunting ability, but the thought still curtled his stomach. Freddy wasn't concerned, her scent and blood was still in his system, it was only natural he was transfixed by her.

The music thumped in his ears as he took orders and mixed cocktails.

There was a spring to his step, and his hips even shimmied to the beat occasionally. His coworkers had noticed the change, but Freddy didn't elaborate on his new spunk for life.

Amelia was his for only one weekend, and he didn't want to share even a smidge of the *idea* of her. He reached into his pocket between orders, rubbing the glossy paper of her portrait.

Freddy hadn't seriously considered finding a long term romantic partner, never meeting anyone he felt connected to.

It was now abundantly clear the kind of partner he desired, a strong well-educated woman who had high expectations for life and of him.

Freddy never considered that he had more to offer the world, his existence had always been an unfortunate consequence of his father's abuse. If he could feed from humans with a bit of encouragement, who's to say what he could achieve?

With Amelia's support, of course.

"Fred, I need you in my office." Mo's voice startled Freddy from his musings, his stomach dropping as he nodded towards the other bartender and followed his uncle.

That was the first thing Mo had said to him since he confessed to his inadequacies, the air in the apartment had been stifling with unresolved tension that evening. Freddy's stomach continued to churn with every step towards the back office, trepidation heavy and sharp. He imagined it felt much like a prisoner on the path towards their execution.

At least he had an adequate last meal.

Though the memory made him smile, he actively suppressed the echo of desire that tried to join it.

No boners in front of your uncle.

Mo sat with a groan, acting much older than he looked.

"I need to apologize," he said, interlacing his hands as he reclined in the desk chair. Freddy's mouth popped. "I'm sorry it's taken this long. I just couldn't face myself, couldn't deal with how badly I fucked up."

"What?" Freddy must have missed something. Wasn't he the one in the wrong for stealing and lying?

"You nearly starved to death in my own fucking house because I was such a proud asshole you couldn't come to me with your struggles. You were forced to feel like a fucking criminal just trying to survive, and I punished you for it." He sighed and stood, leaning over the desk. "I'm sorry, Freddy. I know I'm not your real father, but I was someone's father once and I need to do better." His head hung as he apologized, deep shame radiating off of him.

Freddy didn't know anything about Mo's human life, or even how long ago he was turned.

He couldn't imagine losing a real family, a good family—Freddy never had a family to lose.

"No, Mo. I'm sorry. I just- I was so ashamed, so ready to just fucking die."

Mo's face turned from grim to heartbroken before a small smirk crept onto his face.

"But then something changed."

Everything had changed.

Freddy had been invited to Amelia's body, and had been worthy of her kindness, intelligence, and compassion. He had been more than a monster, if only for a weekend.

He was hers.

The moment his fangs pierced her skin, she owned him in every possible way.

"Your therapist?"

"How did you-"

Mo chuckled and walked over to Freddy's side, leaning against the desk with crossed legs and arms.

"Listen, I've never come home from any legitimate appointment reeking like that. Question is, what makes her so different?" Mo asked, nodding with genuine interest.

Freddy leaned back in the tattered chair, gazing at the spackled ceiling as he considered his answer.

"It's me that's different. She's so accomplished, so put to-gether, but I don't think it comes naturally—she has all these rules and magical do-hickeys that make it possible. If she can do it, why can't I? I just feel like I can be some-thing, be *somebody* that's good." Freddy's smile widened as he gushed, picturing Amelia's stern face transforming to warm sympathy in his mind.

"She gave you hope."

"Yeah, I guess that's it."

"Hold onto that, kid." Mo gave Freddy's shoulder a firm squeeze before walking back over to his computer chair. "The longer you live, the harder hope is to come by." He turned his head towards the screen, eyes dripping with loss.

Freddy took a deep breath and steeled himself.

"I need some time off."

Mo's face slackened as he registered Freddy's words. "Time off?" His surprise was logical, Freddy had never asked for a night off since his turn.

He nodded and lowered his eyes to the ground. "I want to get my highschool diploma, and there's a challenge test in a few days that I think I can do."

Mo let out a disbelieving laugh. "Well, of course you can," he said at Freddy's anxious expression. Mo shook his head as he returned to the computer screen, a smile staying planted on his face.

"She must be a hell of a therapist."

Freddy bit his lip, but couldn't help the corner of his mouth pinching into a smile.

"You can say that again."

RULE 18
FORGET THE FUCK-ASS TROUT

Amelia went back to her normal boring life, as if Freddy never existed.

That was the lie she told herself, laying facedown on the leather couch. The blandness of her office was mind numbing, the room was chemical-allergen free and so unbelievably bright.

Sunlight was helpful in reducing Seasonal Affective Disorder, but it had the opposite effect on Amelia as she nuzzled into the cool fabric. Her mood dipped, the light denying her the pleasure she associated with darkness and shadow. She closed her eyes, allowing a moment of self-indulgence.

She thought about his eyes, his hair, his hands. She thought about how much she wanted him, and how much he did not fit into her neat and tidy life.

A ripping sound startled Amelia, causing her to roll off the couch and onto the beige floor.

A large gaping tear on the left cushion mirrored the one of the right.

She should have panicked, should have scrambled to fix the newly emerged deviation, but she was so physically and emotionally exhausted. Her symptoms had not resolved throughout the work day, in fact she had developed a fever.

An annoyingly chipper melody escaped the pocket of her blazer, and Amelia begrudgingly rose to her feet to answer the damn device.

"Amelia, are you alright? Agatha said her golum missed his morning appointment. " Maggie's voice was laced with concern.

Just what Amelia needed, a reminder of her professional failure.

"I'm fine, just a bit sick. Can we talk about this later?"

"How sick are you? Doesn't sound good if you missed an appointment. I can bring you some nourishing broth and a tonic if you need."

Amelia puffed out a disgruntled laugh, attention from her aunt was the last thing she needed. Attention led to criticism, and Amelia's day was already off to a bad start.

"I'm fine. Just a bit of a headache and shakes, probably a flu."

The line was eerily silent. Amelia almost thought to check if the call had dropped, when the chilling words of her aunt made her stomach drop.

"You don't happen to have a fever and nausea as well?"

"And if I did?"

"Oh, dear, that's not good."

Amelia's heart stuttered.

"What is it?"

"Are you sure your vampire...friend didn't bite you?"

Amelia's hand froze on the doorknob of the break room, her fears seemingly confirmed.

"You think it's venom withdrawal, don't you?"

"If you weren't bitten then it can't be. But your mother had very similar symptoms before she..."

"No," Amelia answered, trying her hardest to breathe evenly. It was an automatic response, like spitting out an under-ripe fruit from unexpected bitterness. Maggie couldn't be insinuating that her mother had experienced venom withdrawal, that would be completely ridiculous and nonsensical.

"She fell to her death,"

"She was delirious and the balcony wasn't locked." Maggie's words were merely breaths.

Okay, maybe that made a little bit of sense.

As the words settled into the crevices of her brain, Amelia's mind began to whirr. If her mother had venom withdrawal, she must have been bitten by a vampire.

Was it a violent attack or a consensual moment of intimacy?

Despite the shock of discovering her mother had died under completely different circumstances than Amelia thought, she felt the stirrings of empathy.

With only one piece of information, the distance between Amelia and the woman that gave her life seemed to close a small amount. If Amelia was being honest with herself, she had always hoped that the woman hadn't chosen to die. The news settled into her with a stab of relief as well as confusion. There were still so many unanswered questions.

"How did she get exposed to venom?" Amelia asked, her face pale in the reflection of the stainless steel refrigerator. She waited for a reply for several breaths, only to realize that the call had dropped.

All the magic in the world couldn't prevent the tragedy of a suboptimal cellphone signal.

So, Amelia was left to ruminate over the information in the silence of the staff room.

Her mother died from venom withdrawal.

The idea bounced around her mind, directly clashing with everything she knew about the woman.

Granted, it wasn't much.

Amelia suspected that she had disabling major depression, that she couldn't bear staying alive any longer—it made her a sympathetic character, in Amelia's mind. As a psychologist she could put no blame on the woman but from the perspective of an orphaned child, Amelia felt abandoned by her mom's choice, like her existence was not important enough to fight for. Maybe that was why Amelia never fought hard to be important to anyone, the one person who was supposed to take care of her no matter what had chosen to die instead.

It was a selfish, stigmatizing opinion, but children were not known for rational thinking.

If her aunt was to be believed, then her mother may not have made the choice to die at all. A spark of hope lit in Amelia's roiling gut, allowing the possibility of her being important to someone to sprout.

Reality snuffed out that hope quickly, replacing it with betrayal.

Why had her aunt hidden such an important fact from her?

The question faded from her mind when she opened the fridge and was greeted by an empty shelf.

She couldn't forget Freddy or her troubles but she could certainly forget to bring a lunch.

"Can I get a latte and a chicken sandwich?" Amelia asked, trying to shift her tone to one of polite optimism.

"Sure," The teenage girl behind the counter looked at her with skeptical concern. She punched the order into the machine and paused to look up at the exhausted therapist. "You okay?"

Unbeknownst to that teenager, her words had unveiled Amelia's kryptonite.

"No," she answered, unable to stop the tears that slipped from the corners of her eyes. Amelia was miserable, sick, and likely going to die like her mother. The girl turned to grab the coffee cup from under the machine and added the milk in while chewing on her lip.

"Listen, I don't know what this guy did but I can guarantee you he ain't worth crying over."

A pimpled young man wearing an identical uniform handed her a sandwich shaped wax paper package. The girl turned back to Amelia and put the sandwich on the counter.

"I can guarantee you there are millions of fish in the sea, and you're too hot to be crying over one fuck-ass trout."

"Libby!" A stern male voice called from the back of the kitchen. The girl grimaced, but Amelia laughed. The unexpected moment of humor made her think that perhaps a deviation of her usual schedule was not always bad.

She really was sick.

"Thank you," Amelia grabbed her lunch and headed out the door.

"Come, Richard." Julia said, her dog shaped husband happily following behind. His tail wagged exuberantly as he watched her sit on the leather couch. It was clear he genuinely enjoyed being a dog, which made Amelia smile to herself.

"Why don't you start by telling me what happened?"

The woman and her dog husband traded a weary look.

"I got a call yesterday morning that I have to start chemotherapy," Julia said, gently stroking the golden retriever's head. Amelia shot the couple a sympathetic smile and pulled out her notebook, throwing a wave to Tracy.

Amelia vaguely paid attention to Julia as she explained the details of the phone call predicament, but her focus shifted repeatedly to Richard's pleading eyes. The way he looked at his wife wasn't so different from Freddy's desperate gaze—a man needing direction but unwilling to ask.

"Have you tried telling him?" she interrupted. Julia froze and looked up at the therapist.

"What?"

Amelia shifted, uncrossing her legs and placing the notebook flat on her lap.

"Have you tried telling Richard what you need?"

"I've asked him a hundred times to come back to me."

The hollow place beneath her neck flushed with embarrassment or frustration, Amelia wasn't sure yet.

"Would you politely ask a golden retriever to roll over or sit?"

"Of course not." Julia let out an exasperated laugh. It was common knowledge that dogs required succinct and firm orders.

"Maybe Richard chooses to be a dog because your commands make him feel safe?"

Julia's eyes shifted down to her dog husband, hesitant understanding creeping in.

"Why would he feel unsafe? I'm the one with cancer."

"Perhaps he needs a reminder that you're still okay."

A look that can only be described as devastating affection crossed the older woman's face before she sobered.

"That's enough, Richard."

Richard whined, causing doubt to cross Julia's face.

"Tell him how to please you, make it clear. He needs to know what you want from him, and how to achieve it."

Julia nodded sternly.

"If I want a dog to pet, I'll ask. Come back to me now." Her tone was firm but not harsh. Amelia's smile remained as she dropped her gaze to the notebook, drawing lazy circles. When her eyes glanced back at her clients, Richard was once again human and embracing his wife.

There was some good that came from her time with Freddy, it appeared. There was a lot of bad, as well; like the fact that she would likely be dead very soon.

The room began to spin, and her heart began to pound with what felt too much like panic.

Amelia stood and handed the man a paper covering as she had done the previous week, murmuring a polite goodbye and leaving the room to give them some privacy. The wood of the door was cool against her back, grounding her as she took several deep breaths.

Emotions are passengers.

She wasn't a real caster.

Freddy's venom was not killing her.

She was just having a minor reaction to sudden blood loss, or a delayed allergy to his venom.

Despite the small victory, Amelia's head was full of cotton as she slogged through her client list, a burning ache in her chest. There was also the fear of death entangled in her usually random jumble of thoughts and observations.

In one last effort to center herself, Amelia settled into the reception chair and tucked her feet in, pushing off the desk and forcing the seat to spin.

The reception area was empty, the sun already beginning to set.

She let her mind return to the start of the day, to the unexpected gift she had received and away from the likelihood of her upcoming demise.

Freddy had replaced her dining room chairs.

Freddy was in her home while she slept.

He had done a kind thing for her, without even stopping for a bite. Amelia tried to piece together if she was glad or disappointed he didn't ravish her while she was slumbering. There was another deep, primal part of her that was displeased that he assumed she wanted him to replace them, that he made that assumption without her input.

The feeling passed quickly, since Freddy shouldn't care what she wanted, he had only come to her seeking help for his feeding difficulties. Flashes of his fangs infiltrated her mind, the craving for the burn of his venom pounding through her.

She had completed the task, solved the problem—there was no reason to think about him again. Her aunt's words nagged at the back of her mind, offering a logical explanation for the illogical connection between them.

Could she be experiencing venom-induced illness after only a few bites? She supposed one only needed a singular bite to contract rabies and that was terminal.

How long would it take for the withdrawal to drive her to death with its delirium?

Amelia took a deep breath, carefully locking away the pleasurable memories from the past weekend, hoping to regain some sense of control over herself.

"There are millions of fish in the sea," The barista's words came back to her, sparking a glimmer of hope. There was some merit to what the girl said—Freddy was not the only vampire around, she did not have to burden him with her illness.

Perhaps her infatuation was not with Freddy at all.

It would make perfect sense for the venom to create dependence for the donor, to force them to stay close. Amelia couldn't quite make sense of why it wasn't mentioned in that book, but considering she didn't really have the energy to read much of it, she decided it didn't matter.

Curiosity blanketed her in comfort of the familiar.

Amelia's anxiety was caused by the mystery, the state of not knowing. She just needed to understand this illness, and then she could fix it. If it was about her body's response to venom, then any vampire's bite should do the trick.

She would need to test the hypothesis, but that would require finding a vampire subject. The only establishment Amelia could think of was the nightclub a few doors down from her office. Satisfaction and excitement rolled through when she realized that she had justification to break one more rule.

She was going out on a work night.

For the first time that evening, Amelia smiled to herself. That smile stayed glued to her face as the mechanical clicking called her over for a debrief.

Name: Dr. Amelia Atkinson
Age: 32
Sex: Female
Pronouns: She/Her
Race: Human

Session 256

Dr. A: You were right, Tracy.

Tracy: I cannot be right because I am you.

Dr. A: I was right, then. The key to going forward is understanding the past. Focusing on the short term is what got me into this mess to begin with.

Tracy: This is about the conflicting vampire man, again.

Dr. A: Yes, and he's not conflicting.

Tracy: You have had a 200% rise in contradicting feelings since the onset of your vacation.

Dr. A: That is a problem with me, not him. I believe I have become dependent on vampire venom, causing me to become deliriously attached to Freddy.

Tracy: That illness is not present in your database.

Dr. A: Which is precisely why I am breaking a rule to-night and doing some field research. Feeding the addiction won't get me anywhere, I need to understand it.

Tracy: Are you physically well enough? Alcohol will render your medication ineffective.

Dr. A: It's a low-grade fever, I've been through worse. I need to understand, Tracy.

Tracy: Understand the illness or your feelings for him?

Dr. A: I don't have any feelings for him.

Tracy: Your paleomammalian cortex disagrees with that statement.

Dr. A: Well, my paleomammalian cortex can take a fucking hike.

RULE 18

A knock interrupted Amelia's denouncement of her limbic system, probably for the best.

The molecules of her body knew it was Freddy, she didn't have to look up at the clock to see it was exactly six o'clock.

Every fiber of her being cried, demanded that she open the door and take him inside her body. Her salvation was so close, the cooling balm for her heated skin was within reaching distance.

My feelings for him are the illness, Tracy.

Amelia didn't answer the door.

BLOODY MESS

RULE 19

DESPERATE TIMES CALL FOR DESPERATE MEASURES

AMELIA

The music overtook Amelia's senses as the dark enveloped her.

The bouncer had smirked and let her through without asking for ID, no doubt her haggard appearance revealing her age and reason for attending. If her aunt was right and casters experienced venom withdrawal, she was likely not the first one to come to this establishment looking for relief.

She had counseled a few humans after they had awoken with no memories and a sore neck, most had been to this nightclub.

Amelia's mouth felt dry and sticky, motivating her to push past a sea of writhing bodies in search of a cool liquid.

She smelled him before she saw him—dark and sweet with a mentholated kick. Like a shot of anesthetic, the pounding in her chest eased, the corners of her mind, numbed.

She opened her eyes and followed the spicy aroma, freezing when his frame came into view.

He wore a tight black T-shirt, matching the other bartender on the opposite end of the counter. He looked so radiant as he clutched the cocktail shaker, there might as well have been a halo around his head. His muscles bulged with the force of his movements, the smile on his face was easy and completely captivating.

He was beautiful.

"Can I have some water?" she asked, voice weaker than intended. She didn't know how she had gotten to the bar, she couldn't recall moving her legs at all. The haze around her vision must be affecting her memory as well.

"Hey, doc," Freddy said politely, eyebrows raised with surprise for a moment before turning to fill a glass with water using a nozzle. His eyebrows shifted to a furrow while he watched the liquid churn, but all Amelia could focus on was his face.

Dark jade irises sat atop cheeks that were no longer sunken. His shoulders still hunched and his hair was still styled in a haphazard mop, so that was likely just how he was even at optimal health.

He looked completely edible and undeniably hers.

Except he wasn't.

"You look good," Amelia said after taking a small sip from the cup he slid towards her. The cool liquid did nothing to relieve the burning in her throat, and she considered dipping her hand into the water and using it alleviated the scorching throb of her forehead instead.

Tracy's warning had been wholly unhelpful, since medicine hadn't been effective in lowering her fever by one degree.

Amelia almost moaned when the possibility of pressing her blistering skin against Freddy's cool body revealed itself.

"Not as good as you," His eyes raked her trembling frame. Amelia laughed cynically at the compliment because she looked and felt like shit.

He was thriving without her, and she was falling apart.

"*You seem to have a pretty good handle on it.*" He had told her when he was the troubled one. Oh, how the tables can turn.

Amelia desperately needed to hold on to what dignity she had; she would not beg him for his venom, even if she was starting to feel a bit dizzy.

"You realize this is a nocturnal establishment, right?" he

asked, leaning forward so she could hear him over the music. His scent washed over her like an avalanche of spicy molasses, seeping into the crevices of her resistance and gumming up the part of her brain that allowed her to stay away from him.

Maybe if she could convince him to kiss her she could suck the heavenly juice out of his teeth? Amelia took a deep breath and shook her head, a mistake since the room was already spinning.

She didn't need Freddy.

Surely, there was a less mesmerizing vampire that would be open to aiding her.

"I'm here for an experiment," Her voice was artificially light, conveying a sense of ease she didn't feel. Every breath was a challenge, every syllable becoming heavier than the last.

Freddy's eyes gleamed silver, face contorted with disbelief and something very sinister.

It was hard to tell since her vision was so blurry.

He opened his mouth to speak, but a low masculine voice interrupted.

"Well, who do we have here?" A large dark form sidled up beside her at the bar, canines already extended.

Amelia's skin crawled at the predatory lilt to the stranger's tone, and not in a pleasant way.

"What's a tasty little morsel like you doing in the lion's den?" His eyes glowed faintly as he spoke, confidence radiating off him like a foul smell. His shoulders were broad and thickly muscled, nothing like the understated frame that fit so perfectly in her grasp.

Amelia attempted to swallow down the nausea, but her tongue was cemented to the roof of her mouth. Her plan had seemed so simple: get a fix of venom and once she was clear headed, find a willing subject to deduce the perimeters of her dependence.

The man reached and grasped her arm but let go immediately, grey-white eyes widening.

Amelia expected to be excited at the prospect of getting a hit of this stranger's venom, but unfortunately, the only thing that coursed through her was a deep sense of wrongness.

The waves of revulsion threatened to upturn her stomach all over the glossy black floor of the club, making her briefly wonder if that was what Freddy felt, when he meant to bite a human (and if that planter was nearby to vomit into).

Go to your vampire.

"Excuse me, I need a visit to the little human's room," she

stuttered, wiping the sweat from her brow as she pumped her sluggish legs towards the back of the room. She scurried down a darkly lit hallway, hoping that the threatening vampire wasn't in a chasing mood.

A hand wrapped around her wrist, pulling her backwards with so much force, the wind left her lungs as her back slammed into the hard, cold wall. Amelia's heart hammered, certain she would be dead within the hour.

Except it wasn't the wall she was thrown against. It only took a moment for Amelia to recognize the intoxicating scent of her Freddy. It was his chest she was resting on, his strong lean arms that were wrapped around her.

As if God herself whispered in her ear, Amelia knew she was safe.

"Are you fucking crazy?" he hissed, turning her in his arms to press her heaving chest to his. The regular pace of his breaths steadied her. "Are you trying to get yourself eaten alive?"

"Yes," she answered, because it was the truth. His eyes were a burning silver and filled with something she had never seen in them before.

Fear.

"Why would you do something insane like that?" His voice was high and strained, as if he was worried about her. Despite the uncomfortable melting of her heart at the thought, he hadn't earned the right to decide what was safe for her to do.

She needed to remind him of their dynamic before he did anything so sweet again.

"Why did you bring those chairs to my house?" Amelia meant for her tone to be commanding and authoritative, but she was almost certain it was more similar to a moan.

Freddy's mouth popped open, face momentarily frozen in disbelief.

"You nearly became a vampire's breakfast, and you're thinking about your fucking *dining chairs*?"

The timing was unconventional but she had to regain her power, especially when every molecule in her body was pulling her to surrender to him.

"Yes, I didn't tell you to do that."

"You shouldn't have to, I destroyed the last ones."

"And?"

"And it's the right thing to do."

"That's where you're wrong, the right thing to do is whatever I say."

Freddy took a deep breath, and she swore that his shoulders relaxed slightly.

"Okay, I'm sorry for buying you new furniture without asking. Now will you tell me what the fuck you were planning to do?"

Amelia could have lied or made some excuse to push Freddy away but he smelled so good and she ached to let him inside.

"Like I said, I came here for a bite."

"Yeah, I got that, my question is what made you suddenly suicidal?"

She sighed and rested a clammy forehead on his sternum, head suddenly feeling entirely too heavy.

"I'm sick, Freddy."

He blinked but the silver of his eyes didn't cool.

"What kind of sick?"

"I don't know but my aunt mentioned something about venom withdrawal and I went to the library and found this old potentially unapproved book that was no help and then I was late for work and forgot to pack a lunch so I went to the cafe and this girl told me I don't need you and-" Despite the sheer exhaustion that weighed down her bones, her mouth flapped at an ungodly speed.

Freddy jerked her forward, wrapping his arms tightly and muffling her voice against his chest.

"Is it crazy to say that I missed you?"

Not crazy but strangely timed.

Amelia attempted to shake her head, a challenge since his grip was tight. His cool body was soothing to her whirling mind, the steadiness of his heart beat grounding her. He relaxed his hold slightly, giving Amelia a chance to take a breath.

"If it's venom withdrawal I just need some venom."

"So, you came here with the intention of getting a friendly injection from a stranger?" Freddy clarified.

"Correct,"

 "For someone with a PhD you're acting like a certifiable idiot."

"How? I think it's a completely logical plan."

He pulled back and leaned down to look into her eyes.

"Sure, it is. However, you made the slight oversight in that if you had succeeded in your goal you would be fucking dead," he hissed.

Despite his evident anger, an overwhelming sense of safety loosened every aching muscle in her body. She let her eyes close just for a moment.

So tired, it seemed like a nice place for a little rest.

Freddy placed a palm on the back of her head and inhaled deeply, squeezing her even tighter against him.

"You don't want anything to do with these guys, trust me."

"Why not?"

He pressed a kiss against her temple.

"Because they're real vampires."

"And what are you?"

Freddy held her for three slow breaths. "I'm your friend, doc." That was very nice to hear, but a loud buzzing made it hard for Amelia to tell if he said anything else.

"Need venom, friend," she said, rather certain that her words were slurred. She had to tell him that before she fell asleep.

"Right now? Are you sure?" Freddy asked, stroking her hair in steady glides.

He needed to stop that or she would fall asleep even faster.

"Always...sure..." Her voice was so weak it was little more than a breath.

The world was veiled with stars and darkness. Amelia swayed on heeled feet, luckily the grip of Freddy's body kept her steady. He ran his hand across her forehead.

"You're burning up," Freddy scooped her into his arms as if she were made of styrofoam.

Amelia never liked styrofoam; the noise it made was appalling and the material was so light, contact was almost impossible to avoid.

She and Freddy were similar to two pieces of styrofoam, she supposed—loud, messy, and impossible to keep apart.

The rhythmic motion of his steps and the delicious peppermint smell that radiated from him soothed Amelia to sleep.

Freddy hastily tucked Amelia into his bed, trying his hard-est not to panic. Her muffled words reverberated through his head, followed by crippling guilt.

"I'm sick," She was sick because of him.

It figured he would kill the only woman he ever loved.

Freddy shook his head and amended his thought. Liked, the only woman he had ever liked.

Instead of continuing a spiral of self-loathing, his mind focused on the unconscious woman in his bed. He had to find out how to help her, and there was only one other person who might know how.

Freddy ran downstairs and through the back towards the office. Mo was sitting at the computer, glasses perched on the end of his nose.

"Can venom make people sick?"

"You know I'm a dentist, not a doctor, right?" Mo's mouth popped open for a moment but he quickly shut it as his eyes scanned Freddy's form. His heart was pounding and a fine layer of sweat covered his skin. "What kind of venom? Show me the bite."

Freddy shook his head. "No, not me. I meant, can our venom make people sick?"

"Oh," Mo exhaled, before stiffening again. "You never mentioned your therapist is a caster."

"She isn't. Well, technically she is, but not functionally." Freddy shook his head again and squeezed his eyes shut as he spoke. "Wait, how did you know I was talking about her?"

Mo rolled his eyes. "Because I wasn't born yesterday."

"It's not like that."

"Then how did she get a dose of venom?" Mo's eyebrow quirked. Freddy's body was too full of adrenaline to have that conversation.

"Can you just tell me how to fix it, please?"

Mo sighed and leaned back in the desk chair. "That's a complicated answer, but right now you need to drink from her, at least a half a liter. Do you understand?" His blue eyes lasered into Freddy's, successfully communicating the gravity of the request. It wasn't necessary, Freddy would amputate several fingers if it meant saving her life.

His uncle paused with hesitation. "Do you need me to…?"

"No," Freddy's eyes gleaned silver. "I can do it."

He would never let any vampire touch his Amelia, even his uncle.

He ran back up the stairs with speed he didn't know he possessed. Thankfully, Amelia was exactly where he left her, though sweat was beading and rolling off her brow.

Freddy had to do this.

He had to command his fangs to extend and give her what she needed.

He was going to save her.

Freddy leaned down and clamped his mouth on her jugular, both surprised and relieved that his fangs behaved. He groaned at the pleasure of penetrating her skin, and she released a moan as well. Her arms wrapped around him, holding him in place with a weak embrace.

Warmth spread through Freddy's undead body, a tingling he hadn't felt since the last time she'd been in his grasp.

For one rapturous moment, Freddy was a hero.

RULE 20

EVERY DETECTIVE NEEDS AN ASSISTANT

AMELIA

Amelia woke to a bed that was not her own.

The sheets were dark and the first thing she saw was a row of bookshelves, neatly organized.

It was definitely not her room.

Judging by the dark color scheme, it belonged to a man. She couldn't remember the last time she had slept at a man's house.

Her memory of the night had been hazy at best, but she remembered talking to a scary vampire man and then running into Freddy.

Amelia exhaled when she saw a hot cup of coffee on the

nightstand, deducing that she was in Freddy's bed.

"Why didn't you answer the door?" Freddy asked from the doorway, voice colder than she had ever heard it.

He was upset with her.

Embarrassment flooded Amelia as she absorbed his strong lean frame, and remembered that it was only a few hours ago that she had ignored his knock.

She had rejected him and he tucked her into his bed—he certainly was a better person than she was.

It was a nice bed, too, with inky black sheets and a padded headboard, impressive for a single man under the age of thirty. She didn't let herself think about how many women had been pressed up against that headboard since she had seen him last.

Had he teased them until they begged for his bite? Though her skin still tingled at his proximity, the thread that tethered them together was taut with unreleased tension. She had to stay in control, to grip that thread with a confident fist.

Much like Richard the dog husband, Freddy needed her strength and command.

"Why would I?" Their partnership had concluded the moment he was able to bite at will.

"Oh, fuck off." Freddy stepped towards her as he spoke, shaking his head with frustration.

"I just saved you from being a vampire juicebox, I think I deserve a little more than that."

Amelia knew that, deep down.

She just didn't know what else to do, how else to provide closure for their unusual liaison. Freddy had never been this short with her, the feeling churned the bile in her stomach and burned the corners of her eyes. She honestly never considered that he would be upset with her about not answering the door, she assumed he wouldn't care.

Well, embarrassingly she didn't even think about what his reaction would be, she was too focused on maintaining her independence and avoiding more pesky emotional entanglement. She couldn't see the blood vessels bulging from his forehead or the cold venom in his eyes, then.

She could definitely see him now.

"That is the truth. I don't work past insurable hours."

"I thought we agreed you'd see me as a friend," he snapped back, not missing a beat.

"A friend has no reason to knock after closing hours."

"How would you know if you didn't answer the fucking

door? I could've been the police, or someone that needed help." Freddy's logic was sound, but Amelia wasn't about to admit that she knew it was him by the tingle in her fingertips.

She didn't answer, didn't know how to talk herself out of this one without revealing just how lost to Freddy she already was.

"If this is your form of punishment, it's much crueler than I imagined." His anger dissipated to something much sadder, and much more painful to look at.

"You thought I was punishing you?"

He pressed his spine to the door frame, tiling his head back and sighing. "You still are. You shut me out and then come to my club looking for a vampire to experiment with." Freddy's eyes were silver and incredulous. "Seems pretty targeted."

Amelia dropped her gaze and clamped her teeth around a trembling bottom lip, unable to meet his gaze.

"It wasn't, I just needed venom and you're not the only vampire around."

Hurt flashed in Freddy's eyes and the bolt of pain in her chest was hot and sharp. As much as she wanted to protect her independence, hurting Freddy wasn't worth it. She sighed and closed her eyes.

"I needed to prove to myself that I don't need you."

His eyes softened a fraction.

"It's okay to need help, doc—even Sherlock had a Watson. Besides, I'm the one that got you into this mess, so I need to get you out of it." The glow of his eyes had faded out, a small smile pinching the corner of his mouth.

He was so handsome, Amelia had a hard time pulling in an adequate breath.

He had a good point, as Freddy usually did.

He could see Amelia's situation objectively when her own thoughts were clouded with venom illness.

"You want to be my Watson?"

"If it stops you from prowling vampire bars in search of trouble, I will be anything you need." His words caused her chest to squeeze painfully. They gave Amelia hope that there could be real friendship between them, a hope that it wouldn't destroy her completely.

"Why do you care so much? You're cured. You could be anything you want to be, go anywhere."

"You saved my life." Understanding soaked into the ridges of the brain; he only saved her in the nightclub to pay off the debt of her therapy services.

That was understandable and not romantic in the slightest.

"Well, I guess we're even now." Amelia held out her hand for a handshake, a logical conclusion to any business relationship. She couldn't live with him seeing her as an obligation. Her aunt had given her enough of that.

"I made your mother a promise, no matter how difficult it may be," she had said.

Freddy looked her up and down, a slow smirk spread on his face. It was mischievous—an imp coming across a clutch of eggs. Despite feeling like helpless prey, a deep throb of arousal budded in her core.

After three agonizing breaths Freddy finally leaned over and grasped her hand. Instead of a cordial shake, he pulled back sharply, jerking her forward and forcing his face only a breath away from her ear.

"Not even close,"

Before she could do something regrettable like cry or hump his leg, a foreign male voice filled the bedroom.

"Freddy, are you antagonizing our guest already?"

Freddy chuckled and pulled away, eyes returned back to their usual colour.

"Me? Never. You know I'm always a good boy." Despite the

sentence being aimed at the voice beyond the doorway, Freddy's eyes remained trained on Amelia's.

He may not have used the exact words but he was telling her loud and clear that he was still under her command. The throb between her legs intensified.

A loud laugh and echoing footsteps caused her to jump.

"Yeah, and I'm the pope himself-" The voice cut off as soon as a middle aged man stepped into Freddy's bedroom.

"Amelia?"

RULE 21
EVERY BIRD
DESERVES TO FLY

"I'm sorry, I'm not sure how we know each other." Amelia looked to Freddy for support, discomfort plain on her tired face.

Hurt followed by kind understanding flashed across Mo's eyes.

"Right, of course you don't. You haven't seen me in almost thirty years. I'm your father, Amelia. I was, at least." His voice was smaller than Freddy had ever heard before. Mo cleared his throat, composure returning."If you want to talk, I'll be in the kitchen."

Shock and horror flooded through blue eyes when the door to his room closed and they were alone again. "Please tell me he's not your actual uncle."

Freddy laughed.

"Thankfully not, he's just the one that turned me." He was more than that, but Freddy didn't think that was important to her at that moment. She relaxed, no doubt relieved she had not been fucking her cousin. Freddy watched as Amelia curled into herself, slowly retreating into her mind. He had to do something to distract her.

"I can tell you about it, if you want."

"Yes, please." She nodded, resting her head on sheet-covered knees. Freddy crawled into his bed, settled himself next to her and extended his arm, nodding towards his shoulder in offering. He wanted to make it clear that despite holding Amelia accountable for her actions, they were still on the same team. He was her Watson now, whether she liked it or not.

She wouldn't like it, but it was good for her.

Freddy got the sense that her aunt hadn't done a great job rewarding her for vulnerability.

That was alright, Freddy would take care of her now.

He wondered if her aunt would approve of him, a novel idea since mothers and aunts generally didn't.

Well, they tended to like him more in a regrettable sexual liaison way, less in approval as a partner for their daughters.

Amelia smiled and accepted the cuddle, settling in the crook of his arm. He didn't realize how much he missed her touch, how much comfort it gave him.

"I was a certified bad boy, when I was human. I sold drugs because it was easy, and I like to think I was pretty good at it." As much as one could be good at breaking the law.

"I'm sure you were," Amelia said genuinely, nodding along with his story. The doubt that had been souring her face vanished, her attention focused elsewhere.

His mouth pinched in a suppressed smile, it figured she would support the worst version of Freddy there was.

"But other than that I didn't really do anything with my life. I got into fights for the adrenaline–"

"And the punishment of pain," Amelia added, unable to listen passively. Her brain really never stopped working.

"I thought I was the one telling a story?"

"Sorry, carry on." She covered her lips with her palm— Freddy wished he could replace that hand with his mouth.

Or his dick.

"Well, one night a guy came out of nowhere and started yelling at me for cutting his drugs. Obviously, I had no idea what he was talking about, but I wasn't gonna decline the offer to break his nose. We got into a little scrap and next thing I knew I woke up in the back room of the bar with the most annoying dry mouth." He tucked his available arm behind his head. "Mo said I didn't stand a chance since I was only a human and the guy wasn't, but I like to imagine I made him sweat a little."

Amelia laughed, the sound relaxing an unbearable tightness in his chest.

"No wonder you wanted to be different, that life wouldn't fulfill you at all."

"That's not the only reason," Freddy sighed, he might as well tell her everything while he had the chance. "My dad would do anything for money. He trafficked whatever would fill his wallet—drugs, women..." Freddy closed his eyes, taking great effort to keep his voice even."He was a complete monster."

Amelia bit her lip in the way she did when there was an idea brewing in that brilliant mind of hers. Freddy paused, waiting for the thought to inevitably leave her lips.

"He was human, wasn't he?"

Freddy would offer to kiss that bitten lip better if her question hadn't surprised him. It was an odd detail to focus on, all things considered.

"By definition, I guess."

To his relief she released her lip and gave him a shy smile.

"So in a way, you're the furthest from being like him than you've ever been."

Freddy blinked, completely astounded by her words, yet again. He had never considered that by becoming a blood-sucking creature, he distanced himself from the mortal monster that plagued him. His mind tumbled with such speed and chaos that he almost didn't notice Amelia shifting to straddle him.

Almost.

He rested his hands on her hips lightly. "How do you do that?"

"Do what?"

"Completely change everything with just one fucking sentence."

Amelia chuckled, the sound was so light it threatened to carry him away entirely. "I'm a therapist, that's kind of my job."

She was so much more than that, and he would make her realize it.

Right after the burning pain in his chest stopped.

It was stupid to feel disappointed with her answer, what was he expecting?

She wasn't soft just for him, it was just who she was.

"Right," Freddy tried to conceal the ridiculous feeling of rejection in his chest, though the suspicious mask she wore led him to believe he failed.

Amelia leaned forward, cradling his face in her hands.

"Freddy, I'm so sorry for what you went through." Her blues were so deep and kind, nearly identical to her father's. Freddy felt exceptionally blind for not seeing their resemblance sooner.

If Mo had begun his vampire life while Amelia was still a small child that meant that physically they were very similar in age. Amelia's features were softer than her father's, and her hair considerably more red.

Her mother must have been beautiful, Freddy decided.

Mo was an understanding, thoughtful man by nature, but he didn't have the inherent calming aura that Amelia had. That must have been a gift from her mother.

He reached up and ran a finger across the bite scars on her neck, a constant reminder of the harm she stomached for his benefit. Amelia shuddered under his touch.

"No, I'm sorry."

"For what?" she asked, sweet breath drowning him.

"You're sick because of me."

The pale ridges of her neck shifted as she swallowed, catching Freddy's attention. Despite being disgusted at himself for hurting her with his bite, he wanted to do it again. To thrust his cock up against her and sink his fangs into the supple flesh that covered throbbing veins.

"We don't know that for certain yet. Even if it was from your venom, I asked for it—begged, even. If it's anyone's fault, it's mine," she whispered, his gaze flickering to her mouth before going back to her throat. Anger flashed hot in Freddy's chest, both at the needless blame she put on herself and the way her words took away...something.

"Why the fuck won't you blame me for anything?"

"Why do you want so badly to be guilty?" Because that was all Freddy knew.

"Because I am. You can't just erase all the shit I did and pretend it didn't happen."

Amelia didn't respond, but her look was so penetrating he was certain she was reading his mind directly.

"Freddy, I don't think guilt is your problem, I think it's

shame."

"Shame?"

"I didn't quite put it all together right away, but let me try and say it in a way you'll understand. Guilt is a response to a bad choice. A hook you hang yourself on until an apology or punishment removes you from it."

Freddy nodded. He understood that already, it was why he chased her down to begin with.

"Shame is a much stickier emotion," she crawled her fingers up his chest to the base of his throat. "It makes you believe that you are the bad choice, that it's only a matter of time before the entire world discovers how bad you are." Her hand circled the base of his neck and squeezed gently. "Shame kills your soul." Freddy barely felt the pressure since his attention was focused on her eyes. Instead of the anger or cold focus, Amelia's eyes were overflowing with fear.

Freddy had felt something similar to this, many years ago. An inkling of a memory tingled in the back of his mind.

When Freddy was fourteen years old, his entire class went on a field trip to the zoo. Well, technically it was a supernatural rehabilitation center for wounded or displaced creatures, but the other kids called it a zoo.

Freddy always did what the other boys did. He had initially

dragged his feet, making sour faces at the phoenix with an ashy wing (a rebirth gone awry) and snide remarks about a field of unicorns with broken horns. He didn't actually think any of it was lame, but he had to go along with his shitty friend group.

It wasn't until a monstrous boom shook the cement pathway that he split paths with the other boys.

They all ran towards the sound, a helpful employee calmly explaining that a lightningbird had just laid a clutch of eggs. His friends had sneered and moved on, but Freddy's legs refused to move.

The bird was massive, easily taller than him and at least a hundred pounds heavier. Her feathers were pearlescent, shifting through every color imaginable as she reared back from her spectators.

The thunder had come from the flapping of her wings, aggressive in a way that stemmed from fear. She didn't like being watched, being forced into a small enclosure.

"She's beautiful, isn't she?" the employee had said, joining Freddy in his admiration.

"Yeah, when are you going to release her?" he had asked, earning a sympathetic look from the woman.

"I'm afraid we can't—she was a pet that outgrew her owner, she doesn't know how to survive on her own."

343

"Can't you teach her?" The woman had given Freddy an even softer look at that question.

"Lightingbirds are so rare, and she's too old to learn a different way of life."

Freddy couldn't accept that.

Such an enchanting creature didn't deserve a life of loneliness, that wasn't a life at all, really.

Freddy didn't deserve to be stuck in his life either, but he didn't have anyone that could set him free.

He waited until the employee moved on and stepped closer to the railing, leaning over and inspecting the gate. He nearly pissed his pants when he felt a peck on his shoulder.

The bird had sidled up next to him and watched as he jimmied the lock open.

He wasn't certain if she really wanted to escape but he had to give her the option.

He also didn't know if the graze of her feathers across the back of his hand was accidental, or a gesture of gratitude. All Freddy could focus on was the uncomfortable sizzle of her electricity against his skin.

It was a very similar feeling, the electric sizzle of Amelia's hand against his throat while she straddled him.

The main difference was that he was also acutely aware of her weight pressing down on his cock. Amelia threw her head back with closed eyes as she grabbed his other hand and trailed it from her hip up to her face. When her head rocked forward again, her face was flushed and completely captivating. She wrapped both palms around his hand that was cradling her jaw, bringing one finger into her mouth.

She bit down with considerable force, making a sharp bolt of pain pierce his finger. Freddy hissed but didn't pull away.

"Did that hurt?" she asked, lashes parting to reveal only a sliver of blue iris.

"Yeah," he croaked, cock growing hard beneath her. She swirled her tongue against the abused flesh, bringing pleasure to the sensitized skin.

"Do you want me to stop?" she purred, bringing his middle finger into her mouth. He needed her to bite it, to lick it, to let him buck his rock hard erection into her. He needed her to let him help, to set her free from the prison she kept herself in.

"Please don't," he grunted, moaning when she repeated the process to his ring finger. His chest shuddered with restraint, his cock begging for friction and release.

To his displeasure, Amelia removed his hands from her body, resting them on his abdomen.

"That's why I can't blame you for this," she said, face a wall of neutrality again. He understood what she was trying to say.

Freddy could see past it, though.

He could see the dilated pupils and rapid breathing, could tell how much she really wanted him. She was still hiding, still denying herself for some reason.

Freddy closed his eyes, refocusing on his plan.

As much as he wanted to go back to being Amelia's vampire fuck-toy, he had a greater purpose.

She was his lightningbird, trapped in the enclosure of her own mind.

It wouldn't be comfortable for either of them, but Freddy would set her free.

RULE 22
DADDY ISSUES ARE MORE COMMON THAN YOU THINK

AMELIA

Freddy carefully rolled Amelia off of his lap, disappearing into the bathroom.

She took a deep breath and slipped off the tight minidress she had been wearing, feeling entirely too exposed.

Freddy was right, her plan had been reckless at best and idiotic at worst.

It was entirely logical to get venom from a trusted friend instead of a stranger at a bar. Well, if Freddy was so keen on being her friend, he would need to be okay with donating some clothes. She dug through his closet and changed into an oversized black shirt and boxers.

Amelia shouldn't be surprised that he shut down like that when she denied him.

Her bizarre infatuation didn't change the fact that physically he was twenty two years old.

Regardless of how much therapy she provided, he had a lot of growing up to do.

She paused before exiting the room, curiosity getting the best of her. She likely wouldn't get another chance to explore Freddy's sanctuary, and impulse control was one of her greatest challenges.

A quick peek wouldn't hurt.

Amelia's legs took her to the neat bookshelf, eyes scanning the two rows of spines. The mystery of Freddy's advanced vocabulary was solved as Amelia discovered every major classic literary novel, some too dry and cerebral even for her.

She kneeled on the floor, pulling out a large cardboard box typically used for storing documents and removed the lid. She smiled as she thumbed through two dozen comic books.

Amelia had never been allowed to read graphic novels, her aunt believed they would rot her brain (an argument shared with the barring of cartoons). It made Amelia a little sad to see Freddy hide them, to deny himself the vibrant and action-packed stories he clearly enjoyed.

She should have been glad that he was attempting to mature, wasn't that what she was looking for in a man?

Freddy wasn't just a man, or a client, or a vampire.

Amelia's stomach dropped when she realized that she genuinely liked Freddy the way he was. She liked that he called her out when she deserved it, and wasn't afraid to ask what he wanted to know. His company felt so natural, not quite familial but something similar.

It was all too coincidental, that a man who was seemingly crafted from her deepest most erotic fantasies, who was intelligent and observant, had been resurrected by her father and lived only a few doors from her office.

No, the universe was giving her a big, flashing, obnoxious sign that she had to keep Freddy close, probably because he was integral to solving the mystery of her illness.

She just had to come up with a way to do it without falling completely in love with him.

Amelia was pretty good at suppressing her feelings, but that would likely be too much even for her.

His assistant idea wasn't bad, actually—two brains was better than one. Amelia quickly slid the cardboard box back into place and stood.

She couldn't delay any longer, she had to speak to her father and get some answers.

The kitchen was stainless steel and glossy black acrylic, very male but pleasantly clean. Amelia sat at the breakfast table, the bones of her pelvis heavy against the wooden stool.

Only Mo, her father, was standing at the counter.

Her brain grappled with the thought that she was looking at her dad, that the man standing in front of her was the same one who raised her for the first five years of her life.

The man that abandoned Amelia and left her mother to wither away, crazed from a magical chemical reaction in her bloodstream.

Pain bubbled angrily, begging to be tamped down by rational thought. The concept of her father being a vampire solved the mystery of how her mother came in contact with venom, though it opened up a whole other swarm of questions. It wasn't until she watched him slide a steaming plate in front of her that the two men combined in her mind.

"Do you still like pancakes?" he asked with a sad smile. It sat in front of her like a peace offering, an opportunity for her to accept the return of her father or reject it.

"It's not Saturday, but I'll take it."

Mo laughed and she swore his eyes had a wet shine to them.

"You remember," he said wistfully.

"It's one of the only memories I have." Amelia separated a piece of spongey cake with her fork and took a tentative bite. It was palatable but could use some syrup.

Mo frowned, "What do you mean?"

She swallowed another bite. "It's natural for casters to lose all their memories after a traumatic event."

"Who told you that?" Mo's face twisted in a combination of confusion and outrage.

"My aunt," Amelia downed the last piece of pancake and placed the fork on the plate. She had always been a very efficient eater.

"Of course she did,"

It felt completely surreal, casually talking to her dad like the past twenty seven years hadn't happened.

But they had happened.

He had left and then her mother died. The pain in her chest was too hot, too sharp. Best to avoid it for now, to focus on other matters. Amelia placed her hands neatly on the table and looked up at him.

"So what's the deal with you and Freddy?"

"What do you mean?"

"Seems to me like he sees you like a replacement father."

The blue of Mo's eyes softened, "He didn't have anyone else and I-"

"Wanted to find ways to assuage yourself of the guilt of abandoning your family?"

"You certainly are a therapist," he muttered under his breath, the softness leaving his gaze before turning to something similar to defeat.

He looked tired.

"Why does it matter? My guilt has nothing to do with Freddy." That was all the confirmation she needed.

"Because he thinks all vampires are monsters."

His eyebrows furrowed. "Why would he think that?"

"You tell me," she splayed her hands out, waiting for a reply. He paused, eyes shifting between her hands before the corner of his mouth pulled up in a smirk.

"You haven't changed at all, you know." Mo took a deep breath, face dropping. "Vampires aren't monsters, but I am."

"Why?" she asked, but before he could answer a familiar male voice interrupted.

"Leaving behind a dead wife and a little girl is a pretty good reason,"

Amelia turned her head to see Freddy leaning against the doorway. He looked handsome, with damp hair and a fresh hoodie.

His statement was incorrect, though. Amelia shook her head, crossing her arms. "No, it's not. People leave their families every day. It's a morally questionable choice, but barely even registers on the evil scale."

"I thought evil people didn't exist?" Freddy asked, pushing away from the door jam. She could have revealed her point quickly, but watching Freddy succeed would be far more rewarding. It would be a test as well, to see if he could handle being her aid.

"That's right,"

"There's only sick people doing what they have to in order to survive." Freddy stalked closer to the counter as he spoke, eyes narrowed as his mind caught on to the direction she was taking the conversation.

Amelia nodded, "Fundamental self image wouldn't shift so dramatically with one conflicting decision."

"A shitty man is still a man," Freddy translated the thought for Mo, in case he didn't understand Amelia's vocabulary.

It was sort of sweet, actually.

Amelia didn't bother to simplify her language for her father, Maggie had mentioned that they had gone to university together for physics and even Amelia could barely read those scientific papers. Freddy bit his lip in contemplation and looked thoughtfully to Amelia.

"You know, I used to think I was a bad man despite the fact that I hadn't actually done anything worthy of that title." His candor slowed, becoming softer. Amelia's breath caught, surprised at the shift. "Luckily, I stumbled upon a therapist that made me realize that my self-loathing started way before I became a vampire." He paused when he reached the counter, removing his hands from the pocket of his sweatshirt and placing them on the countertop.

Amelia wasn't going to correct his statement, her father didn't need to know how much begging and biting was involved. "I couldn't justify my actions, couldn't align taking the blood of humans with being a good person."

Mo opened his mouth to speak, his eyes pained. Amelia held up her hand, a request to let Freddy finish his thought. She was confident he was heading in the right direction.

She believed in him.

"To you, vampires aren't monsters because their actions are justifiable. The momentary pain is less important than your need to survive. So, either you have one massive irredeemable sin, or a long string of shitty decisions."

"Well done, Watson." Amelia smiled, a wave of satisfaction painting her chest despite the tense situation.

He winked down at her before turning back to Mo.

"You better give me good fucking answer, " Freddy hissed, leaning forward with gleaming eyes.

Okay, they would have to work on his delivery.

Mo didn't seem to register Freddy's threat, just stared at them with stars in his eyes. Suddenly she was in her father's arms, and the world was spinning.

"You are completely brilliant,"

"Hey, I did most of the talking," Freddy whined, earning a laugh from Amelia when she was released from Mo's dizzying embrace.

"Feeling left out?" she teased.

"Yeah, obviously."

Amelia rolled her eyes, "Come here, then." She stepped towards him and wrapped her arms around her neck, pulling until their chests were flattened together.

Instead of cool arms against her waist, Amelia felt a palm cradle the back of her head and a soft pair of lips press against her own.

Though unexpected, she didn't hesitate to relax into the kiss.

It was short and mostly chaste, but every fiber of every muscle cried when Freddy pulled back. She wanted more, needed more.

"I don't know how I didn't see it earlier." Mo's voice snapped Amelia back to reality.

"See what?" she asked, still a bit dizzy from the kiss.

"Fred would have needed to see a supernatural therapist, and there's only one that's a woman. I didn't even think-I mean, what are the chances?"

"You knew I was a psychologist?"

Mo didn't get a chance to reply, Freddy's fist was already flying at his face.

Freddy never imagined he would know what Mo's face felt like against his fist.

He also didn't know exactly at what moment he fell in love with Dr. Amelia Atkinson, but neither of those thoughts seemed very important.

All Freddy could feel was rage and all he could think about was righting the person who wronged the woman he loved.

Her father had known about her profession. He could have reconnected long ago but chose not to, which made him a coward and a deadbeat. After the third punch Freddy's mind cleared enough to realize that Mo was not fighting back. He simply let Freddy wail on him over and over.

"Piece of shit,"

Punch.

"Deadbeat,"

Punch.

"Dirtbag,"

Freddy's anger drained from him just as quickly as it arrived.

Justice had been served.

He stood, righted his clothes, and extended a hand to help his uncle off the ground. Mo swiped a hand across the lower half of his face, collecting the dark viscous blood that streaked his skin.

"Where were we?" Mo asked.

"Maybe you should explain the venom withdrawal, so Amelia can go home," Freddy suggested.

"Right," Mo regained his composure, straightening and placing his hands on his hips."It's not a venom illness." His gaze shifted between two incredulous expressions. "We better sit down."

The dining room table was only a dozen steps away, and they all settled into seats quickly.

"Okay, talk," Freddy said, dropping his voice to a low growl. Amelia turned her head to look at him.

"Is that really necessary?" she hissed quietly.

"Do you wanna be the bad cop, then?" he whispered back, trying to wipe away the crease between her eyebrows.

Amelia's mouth pressed together firmly, but humor shone plainly in her eyes.

Two points for Freddy.

"Maybe it would be best to start by telling me what you already know about this venom illness," Mo suggested, pulling the couple's attention back to the problem at hand.

"My aunt told me that tragedy follows a caster and her vampire."

Freddy stiffened at her words but remained silent. No wonder she wanted to stay far away from him.

"I hate to admit it, but she's not wrong about that one. It has nothing to do with venom, though." Mo looked between Amelia and Freddy, pain in his eyes. "It's about magic, really."

Amelia nodded, "She mentioned that our magic doesn't mix well."

Freddy's eyebrow raised, it must have been some dinner she had with her aunt.

He was no longer surprised that she came home a bit drunk. Memories of the last time he had fucked her resurfaced, causing Freddy to shift uncomfortable in his chair.

He would not get a boner in front of Mo.

"What you consider vampire venom is essentially just saliva, mixed with hundreds of proteins that delay clotting and promote bleeding. It's a brilliant formula, if I do say so myself."

Freddy started to nod along but paused when Amelia ducked her head and snickered. He bumped her shoulder with his.

"You okay?" Freddy didn't see anything funny about what his uncle had said. Maybe the reality of reuniting with her father had finally sunk in and she was losing it. No matter, Freddy wasn't going anywhere. He had learned quite a lot from her already about helping people through mental problems, so he might be able to talk her back to reality.

"Sorry, it's just-" her voice was swallowed with repressed laughter.

He shot her a look of puzzled expectation.

"You're basically a hunky mosquito."

Mo coughed up several laughs. Freddy leaned down to whisper in her ear.

"Keep laughing and I'll show you how hard this little bug can bite."

Her laughs died suddenly. "Sorry, sorry, continue," she said, gesturing towards Mo. The man attempted to keep his face neutral, but Freddy could see the lightness in his eyes. He loved his daughter, that much was clear.

Freddy couldn't reconcile how he could stay out of the life of the daughter he cared so much about, unless it was for her protection. Freddy almost laughed at the realization that Amelia and Mo were more similar than he thought. Perhaps he attempted to push people away, just as his daughter had.

"Are you familiar with how magic works?" Amelia nodded at the same time that Freddy shook his head. Insecurity clenched his stomach, he really should have paid attention more to Mo's lectures.

To be fair, he was trying very hard not to die at the time.

"It's a particle that circulates the universe. Every living thing is born with some, though concentration is dependent on species," Amelia rattled off, causing Freddy's brows to furrow.

"I thought you did a psychology degree, this sounds a lot like physics," he said.

Amelia shrugged, "Everything is physics, Freddy." Freddy didn't know that because he didn't even graduate high-school.

He wasn't even on the same planet as Amelia and Mo, let alone the same playing field. He could keep up, though.

He would try.

Mo nodded and continued speaking. "Casters produce it in their bone marrow, so naturally their concentration is much higher. Vampires need to use that magic to stay alive, so they have to get it from outside sources."

"Hence the need to feed," Freddy finished the thought, glad to be able to contribute.

"Humans don't get sick from it, though. I've counseled dozens after a bite and they're completely fine," she argued.

"As I said, your illness has nothing to do with venom." Mo took a deep breath. "To put it simply, your body goes a little haywire trying to replace the magic that was lost. The more magic it needs to replace, the harder your body has to work."

There was a long silence though Amelia's brain was undoubtedly whirling manically. It did make sense, Freddy supposed.

"I don't understand why getting bitten would relieve it. Shouldn't that make the symptoms worse?" she asked.

Mo pressed his lips together firmly in apprehension.

"Mortal bodies can only handle so many magic particles, they start to interfere with regular functioning at some point. Similar to when you overwork a muscle, your body

responds with hypertrophy to prevent damage from reoc-
curring."

"It's a magic sickness." Understanding filled Amelia's eyes.
Freddy was glad because he only vaguely understood what
his uncle was saying and he still didn't get the most important answer.

"That's great and all, but how do we make it stop?"

"Well, there are two options. The simplest one is to be
turned-"

"Absolutely not," they said in unison. Amelia's eyebrows
raised in surprise, but Freddy didn't pause. He had to make
Mo see how important her human life was, how much it
mattered.

"That's not an option." He shook his head.

"Why not?" Mo asked, defensive. He didn't like being challenged either, it appeared.

"You haven't seen what she does, Mo. She saves people's
lives, people that have no other hope. We can't lose that."

The look Mo gave him was serious, like he was going to de-
liver bad news.

"In the short term, removal of the excess magic would manage symptoms but it's not a permanent solution."

"The more you take, the more I make." Amelia's laugh was hollow, eyes vacant. She was going to crumble apart and Freddy had a feeling she wouldn't want to do it in front of her estranged father.

He needed to get her out of here.

"Right, thanks for the info, we better discuss this in private." Freddy stood, offering his hand to Amelia. She took it and followed him back to the bedroom.

As soon as the door was closed, her body was wrapped around his, pressing it against the door. Freddy let out a small moan in surprise before leaning into the kiss and burying a hand in her hair. She offered an explanation when they parted for air.

"Distraction," she breathed, pulling the hem of his hoodie and shirt up and off.

Freddy could do distraction.

He tightened the hold on her hair, smashing their lips together. Amelia let out a small moan, bringing Freddy's cock to life. Their tongues tumbled together, Amelia's arms crawling up his torso to wrap around his neck.

Without breaking the kiss Freddy flipped so her back was pressed against the wall. Pulling back to let her breath, he trailed his mouth down the planes of her neck, sliding tingling palms underneath her shirt.

His shirt, actually.

His cock throbbed, a primal part of him pleased that she was wearing his clothes. Amelia's eyes pressed shut, hands buried in Freddy's hair. Despite the urge, Freddy didn't nip at her skin. Amelia wanted to escape the overwhelming reality of vampires and magic, and he was going to do his best to make it happen.

He could just be a man that worshipped her body.

"More?" he asked, knowing she would understand the question. Amelia nodded, giving Freddy the permission he was looking for.

Dropping to his knees, he peppered kisses on the soft skin of her abdomen. He didn't hesitate to yank at the waistband of the boxers she was wearing, carefully sliding the checkered fabric down her legs. Freddy continued the chaste kisses down to her mons, throwing one of her thighs on his shoulder.

"It drives me crazy, you know," he said, mouth hovering over her center. Amelia's eyes were locked on him, lids heavy with desire.

"What does?" she breathed, casually running her fingers through his hair. Freddy had to bite back a moan, he couldn't let himself get too carried away.

"Seeing you in my clothes," Freddy parted her lips with his

fingers, admiring the soft pink flesh. His breath cooled the heated skin, causing Amelia the shutter.

"That makes you sound possessive." She gasped when Freddy gave her clit a light nip.

"I think someone once told me I had to surrender to my primal urges."

"That was in order to feed,"

"Thanks for the reminder." He winked and dove into her pussy. He would never tire of eating her in every capacity. Before he could truly get invested in her pleasure, Amelia yanked on his hair and said, "Enough."

Freddy got to his feet, relieved that her eyes were still heated. She didn't continue speaking, just pressed her lips to his and unbuttoned his pants.

His cock sprang free, ready for action. She gave him a few preliminary strokes that threatened to make Freddy embarrass himself. He hadn't had an orgasm since their last encounter, which apparently was too long. Luckily, she released the quivering member and wrapped her legs around his waist, forcing him to bear her weight. It also caused the head of his cock to slide against her slick heat, which Freddy appreciated.

He showed his gratitude by thrusting his entire length inside. Hot, wet pleasure coated him, fangs extending automatically. He wouldn't bite, wouldn't break the fantasy that she needed.

Was she imagining that he was a human man?

That this was a lewd intermission to their boring life?

"This is just an exception, right?" she panted.

Freddy's stomach flip-flopped at her words, but his hips kept pumping.

"Exception?"

"Sherlock and Watson don't bang, it would complicate their relationship." This relationship had been nothing but complicated, in Freddy's opinion. The next thrust made her eyes close, but he couldn't help but push her a little bit.

"I don't know, I feel like they smooched at least once."

"This is a little more than smooching." She gasped as he reached a hand between them to press against her clit.

"This is whatever you want it to be, doc." Despite Freddy's desperate need to help her see how much more there was to life, there was no point in pushing a brick wall. He would please her in the short-term, if nothing else. Freddy's thrusts picked up pace, bringing his love to climax. She clenched and throbbed around him, pulling him into the abyss of ecstasy.

He gently guided her feet back to the floor, using his discarded shirt to clean up any residual moisture from her center. Despite the linger flush to her cheeks, Amelia's eyes were sad.

"What's going on, baby?" he asked, gripping her shoulders and leaning down in an attempt to meet her eyes. When she raised them off the floor, they were wet.

"It's not fair," she whispered. It was broken and small and pulled at Freddy's heart. He had to make it better, to bring back her fire.

"It's okay. You've got a walking-talking bloodletting machine at your service."

"That's not what I mean. It's just-" She tore her eyes away from his again. "I have all the troubles of a caster without any of the benefits."

You have me.

Freddy pulled Amelia into his arms, letting his instincts guide him. Her face was warm on his chest, the back of her head substantial in his palm. He inhaled deeply, letting her scent center his mind. Freddy didn't know what to do, so he asked the smartest person he knew.

"What do you need?" He tilted her chin up to meet her eyes. They were tortured, unsure and vulnerable. He both hated and loved seeing her like this. Hated that she was suffering, of course, but he was glad that she let him see so much of her.

"Space," she whispered, unable to meet his gaze. Freddy wanted to refuse, to demand that she realize he could help her and she could depend on him. Unfortunately, self doubt followed quickly.

What if it pushed her too far and he lost her forever? Even a fraction of Amelia was better than none at all.

"Yes, doc."

BLOODY MESS

RULE 23

YOUR WIFE IS ALWAYS RIGHT, EVEN IF SHE'S DEAD

MAURICE

Maurice had never truly expected to see his daughter again, much less talk with her. Amelia had gone home, likely to get some proper sleep before work.

"You would be so proud, Alice," he whispered to his wife from where she was tucked safely in his soul. He rinsed the plate that once held pancakes, smiling to himself as he committed his daughter's face to memory.

Amelia looked so different and yet so much the same.

She still had Alice's heart-shaped face and his eyes, but she was subdued and cautious. Mo's memories of his daughter were of tangled hair and laughter, bright fiery curiosity and uncontrolled play. He had recognized her power at her birth, his whole world changing forever that day.

"Can we call her Amelia?" Alice asked, holding the small bundle of love in her arms.

"Amelia?" They hadn't talked about names much; it was bad luck to name a caster before they're born. Mo wasn't a superstitious man, but Magdaline convinced Alice that even discussing names could rob their baby of her future magic manipulation.

"She's strong, I can feel the wind in her magic." Alice nuzzled her face against their new miracle. Mo ran his fingertips across the baby's small forehead. He felt a wave of comfort and ease flow through him, like an easy breeze on a summer day.

"Amelia." he agreed with a smile.

"So, are we gonna talk about it, or should I just kick your ass?" Freddy snapped from the doorway. He must have returned from escorting Amelia home. Mo took a deep breath and dried off his hands.

"Watch your tone," he warned, turning around to see Freddy standing at the kitchen counter. His jaw was clenched and eyes filled with fury.

"Or what? You'll abandon me too? Luckily, I'm not your wife or child," he spat. Mo flinched, the blow making impact directly between his ribs. Maurice was a tolerant man, but

Freddy had come too close to unveiling what he had done and he was not perfect.

"Why do you care? I don't recall her asking for defense."

"Maybe she shouldn't have to! Maybe somebody should take care of her for once."

Mo had never seen this side of Freddy, seen such life and passion in his eyes. It made a fond memory of a past life flash in the back of his mind. If he wasn't so guilty about his role as a father to Amelia, he might have shed a tear seeing his close confidant fall in love.

Mo did feel guilty though, the pain of it threatened to consume him.

"What the fuck do you want from me, Freddy?" he exploded, throwing the dishcloth onto the counter. He couldn't undo the past, couldn't take back all the damage he had caused. The young vampire didn't answer, just shot him a look full of visceral disgust and stormed off to his bedroom.

Parenting was harder than Mo could have ever imagined.

He could have gone to his own room and avoided any more confrontation with Freddy. However, his recent failure had taught him that it wasn't worth it. Freddy was family, and he wasn't going to mess it up again by being a stoic asshole. Mo knocked on the bedroom door, turning the handle when there was no angry reply.

Freddy was sitting on his bed, head in his hands.

"How did you live with yourself?"

Mo sat next to him on the bed. Freddy didn't know the truth, about how much of Alice's death was his fault.

"I didn't. I ran away. Didn't do anyone much good, it appears."

"I think Amelia is like you, in that way." Freddy handed Mo a small graduation portrait. "Always trying to run away."

"She didn't used to be," he said, running his thumb over the glossy image. "You keep this in your pocket?"

Freddy's lips pursed together, and he flushed so deeply that he would have camouflaged in the tomato patch of their garden. Alice grew a whole host of vegetables in the garden, she said it gave her peace and hope for the future. He hoped that she finally got her peace, wherever she was.

Freddy shook his head when Mo tried to hand the photo back to him.

"Keep it, she's yours after all."

Mo didn't accept it. She hadn't been his for a very long time, and he never deserved it.

"Do you know why I turned you?"

"Pity? The greater good?"

Mo laughed. "I don't have a great lot of good in me."

Freddy looked at Mo as if he had suddenly sprouted four hydra heads. He should've expected that reaction, Mo was a different man now than he had been before. He intended on telling Freddy the whole truth then, but he was a coward, too afraid of loss. He enjoyed being a mentor, being a person of high moral esteem. It was just a nobel facade that hid the ugly evil festering beneath.

He settled for a half truth.

"Because you don't fight to win." Mo saw that Freddy didn't have the urge to dominate, to acquire power or use it to advantage himself. Freddy craved connection, or he had when he was human, at least.

"Seems like a nice way of calling me a loser."

"I don't believe that. If anything you were a victim of circumstance."

Mo had been restocking the whiskey supply when he heard two men talk about their plans to soften up his flesh before feasting on it. It made his stomach cramp with disgust, a usual reaction to overhearing a couple of snarling ghouls.

His own self loathing caused his mind to wander at their scheming, his reflection distorted by the sharp edges of brown glass bottles. Toxic infiltrating internal echoes hissing that what he had done was not much better, and what he likely would have done was even worse. Mo hadn't talked to Freddy before but he was known around the nocturnal social sphere.

A human sniffing around doesn't go unnoticed.

It wasn't until he was taking out the garbage that he saw a broken bloody form leaning against the alley wall.

Mo could have turned around and headed back inside the bar. He could have simply called the police, let the man's final moments be the cold pavement soaking up his blood. Humans died, that was just a fact of life. As he stepped closer, the smell of Freddy's spilled blood intensified, making Mo's pace falter.

It was faint, but there was definitely magic there.

He likely didn't know it, and he never would. The young man had been chasing something his mind didn't understand, the molecules circulating in his blood attracted to those like him. Casters didn't accept anomalies like Freddy, those with DNA coding errors that made them produce magic.

They didn't accept Mo's ideas either, his research was taboo and unthinkable. In retrospect, it was that research that had killed his wife and would have consumed his daughter as well.

Maybe the casters were right to shun him, but they weren't redeemable in the death of this young man. He should've been able to exist in the light and be guided with compassion and understanding, instead of being forced to aimlessly wander the dark streets for something he would never find.

He did find something, Mo supposed.

The spinning of atoms in specific coordination with space dust and energy had led him to that alley, to Mo.

Sprouting from the dry cracked surface of his frozen heart, hope unfurled her bright supple leaves. A glimpse of a future filled Mo's mind as he bent down to attend to the dying man, a break from the endless loneliness he had surrendered to. He could help someone like him, atone for his sins. He could be a mentor, a father, a scientist.

He could be a hero.

"How about a trade?" Mo placed the leather bound book in Freddy's lap, and pocketed the graduation portrait.

"What's this?"

Antimagic: An exploration of particle physics
by Dr. Atkinson.

"I had a few publications before they were retracted. If Amelia is anything like me, she'll want to do her own research."

"Thanks," Freddy smiled and all was well again.

RULE 24

EXPECT TO GIVE AND RECEIVE THE TRUTH

AMELIA

Amelia had somehow managed to work despite getting only a few pathetic hours of sleep.

Her mind was reeling, completely consumed with the new information she'd learned from her father.

Her father, for fuck's sake.

Five o'clock rolled around before she knew it, the quiet of her office amplifying her haphazard thoughts.

She just couldn't believe that her father had been so close and yet chose to remain out of her life. It didn't follow what Freddy had described of the man, or how he had reacted to her.

She was usually exceptionally good at using her instincts to deduce someone's character, Mo being no exception.

She could tell he cared deeply, and was not violent by nature.

He was also brilliant, which always complicated things. Amelia decided something was fishy, and it smelled a lot like her aunt. She pulled out her cell phone before she could doubt herself. She wanted answers, and maybe a bit of emotional release as well.

"Amelia?" Maggie asked, surprised at the unannounced phone call.

"Why didn't you tell me about my father?"

"What about him?"

"Oh, I don't know—maybe that he's a fucking vampire?" Amelia expected a comment about her language but instead she was met with a long silence.

"He's found you."

"No, I found him, actually."

"How?"

"He owns a vampire bar near my office."

"Why were you in a vampire bar?"

"It doesn't matter," she dismissed. "Why didn't you tell me?"

"You wouldn't understand."

"Try me."

"It was my job to protect you."

"From what?"

"From everything."

"From my own father?" Amelia's frustration caused the tone of her voice to elevate, nearing a screech.

"He's a bad man, Amelia. She jumped from that balcony because of his betrayal. He took your mother away and you would've been next." Maggie hissed into the phone.

"How is being a vampire a betrayal? It's not like he had a choice." Amelia asked, pausing when her aunt didn't reply. "Unless you think he did."

Why would her father choose to be a vampire and completely upturn his life?

"Love overrides judgment, it's an illness by itself. "

A knock at the door made Amelia jump. She glanced up at the clock, six o'clock on the dot.

"I gotta go."

She hung up the phone before waiting for a reply.

"Venom delivery service." Freddy said, a grin partially obscured by his hood. Amelia couldn't help but laugh at his goofy smile, the earlier anxiety melting away when she pulled him in for a hug. She clutched onto his shoulders, breathing in the familiar spicy scent.

She regretfully released him, returning once again to a world that seemed to be constantly tilting.

"How do you want to do this?" he asked, unzipping and removing his sweater. Nostalgia tingled at the back of Amelia's neck, the memory of their sessions lighting a flame of desire. It could also be the close proximity of his sexy forearms.

"The couch," She pointed towards her office door.

"You got it, doc." Freddy saluted and followed her inside. Amelia sat next to him, making sure to leave at least half a foot of space between their thighs. She would not rub up against him like a cat in heat.

"Okay, I'm ready."

He laughed gently before leaning over and latching his mouth to her neck. She closed her eyes, waiting for the puncture of skin and hot burning pleasure. She gasped in surprise when she felt the soft wet heat of his tongue against her skin. Freddy grasped her hips and planted her in his lap, grinding her down on a significant erection.

That was not the plan.

Amelia didn't have capacity for any more interruptions, any more surprises, when her mind was this disorganized.

Without thinking she grabbed his hair and pulled his head back so she could look into his eyes.

His fangs descended at the action, breathing ragged.

"Bite me, goddamn it," she said, pressing his face forcefully against her neck.

He moaned loudly against her skin and bit down as ordered. The sharp flash of pain was quickly replaced by the pleasure of his venom. It heightened the arousal already coursing through her, causing her to press herself tighter against him. He groaned and held his fangs against her, thrusting desperately. Using every available shred of self control she threw herself off of him and backed up against the wall, panting wildly.

Freddy closed his eyes and licked the remains of blood off his lips. He stood and walked towards her, stopping just in front of her heaving chest.

"Thank you," she whispered, careful not to meet his eyes. She felt so raw and unwrapped when Freddy was near, the painful feelings she kept tucked away threatened to reemerge and splatter all over his black t-shirt.

Freddy grasped her chin and lifted it, forcing her eyes to meet his.

"Are you okay?"

Amelia nodded.

He examined her face closely, eyes narrowing slightly.

Instead of confronting her about her lie, Freddy placed a sweet kiss on her cheek.

"I'll see you tomorrow."

FREDDY

"Haven't seen a frown so big since I took organic chemistry." Mo laughed, from his place atop the ladder.

They had received a new shipment of glasses after a banshee had given her date an earful the other night, and destroyed every shard of glass in the establishment. Freddy suggested that the replacements should be plastic, but Mo wouldn't entertain the idea, refusing under the pretense of maintaing the prestige of the business.

Freddy didn't think there was anything classy about a bar that mainly catered to society's undesirables, but he wasn't the boss.

He lowered his gaze back to the book he had been scanning since returning from Amelia's office. He didn't like the defeated look in Amelia's eyes when he visited her that night. He needed to prove himself useful, reliable and trustworthy. Surely, there had to be something important in the book Mo gave him. There had to be another option than to turn her.

Freddy flipped through the pages quickly, uninterested.

"Trust me, if there was a way to research that didn't involve particle physics, I'd take it."

"Why are you so against her becoming like us? I was under the impression Amelia cured your vampire identity issues." Mo slid two large bottles of some sort of alcohol across the top shelf.

"I don't have a problem with her being a vampire, I just want it to be her choice. I don't think that's a privilege she's had."

And she deserves the world.

Mo's grip tightened on the ladder, aluminum cracking under the pressure.

He didn't like being reminded of Amelia's childhood, not that Freddy blamed him.

"What do you mean?" His voice was tight, but face remained cool as he decended back down the rungs.

"Amelia talks about her aunt a lot, about all these strict rules she has to follow."

"Maggs does still live in the bowels of caster society, I can't say I'm surprised."

Freddy's face twisted with confusion.

"Is being anal retentive just a caster thing? You seem pretty relaxed."

Amelia had mentioned several times that parents, and subsequently she herself, were products of selective magic-forward breeding. Mo didn't seem any different than any other nocturnal he had met.

He didn't answer immediately, as if he were deciding the precise way to word whatever response he was conjuring.

"Laws govern a society, following them is key to survival."

"Following the law, I can understand. But Amelia is convinced that if she disobeys even one of her aunt's arbitrary rules, the entire world will end."

Something dark and sad filled Mo's eyes, and Freddy bit his lip and returned to flipping through the book.

"You're sure she doesn't have any magic?"

Freddy nodded. "She's very sure."

"That's not what I asked. Have you ever seen anything strange or unlikely happen around her?"

He had been too busy studying her, an enchanting experience in itself. Besides, everything between them thus far had been both strange and unlikely.

"How would I know? I don't even know how it works!"

He sank two fists into his hair and pulled, finding no answers between Bohr models and long, dry, paragraphs about hydrogen bonds.

A large hand appeared in front of him, thumbing through the pages and pausing on a diagram.

"Probability. The magic particles distort probability in the caster's favour."

Freddy blinked.

"The catch is that casters have to willingly decide which way to sway the outcome."

"So, they have to know they can in order to use it."

Mo smiled, "You are pretty quick."

Freddy shook his head. "That can't be right."

Mo raised one eyebrow in question.

"Amelia is the most logical person I know. She knows how magic works and that she's got the ingredients for it. Even a cave troll would be able to piece together that she should give it a go."

Mo's eyes softened in an empathic way, not so different than his daughter's.

"Maybe she just doesn't want to. People can be extraordinarily blind to something they don't want to see."

Freddy didn't like anyone implying anything negative about his Amelia, even her own father.

"Why would someone not want to use magic? Seems like only a positive thing to have everything go your way." Freddy could think of several ways he could have used that power, none of which were ethical.

Mo's face fell slightly. "Everything has limits, even magic."

"Such as?"

"Most of the time, the caster, himself."

Freddy's face scrunched in confusion, Mo wasn't normally this cryptic.

Mo sighed and walked over to rifle through one of the cardboard boxes that were sitting on the bar. "Are you familiar with the saying about power and corruption?"

Freddy nodded. "Absolute power corrupts absolutely." Mo turned and held out an empty palm.

"A hand can be used to hold a bandage or wield a knife, it all depends on intention. Magic is the same way." He revealed his other hand, which held a shining crystal whiskey glass.

"I could use this to offer water to a dying man," he launched the glass with great velocity at Freddy's head, which he managed to dodge. Unfortunately that meant that it shattered against the wall. "Or as a weapon."

"But regardless, the caster is affected all the same." Mo reached forward and pressed a meaningful look into Freddy's eyes.

"You're gonna have to spell this one out for me." Freddy glanced at what remained of the cup, lamenting at the fact that he would have to clean it up. This particular analogy literally flew over his head.

"There is no separating magic from the caster."

RULE 25

MISUNDERSTANDINGS AREN'T ALWAYS BAD

AMELIA

Thursdays used to be Amelia's favourite day.

It was in the latter half of the week, while still leaving Friday as a buffer in case she didn't get something done.

It had not been a good thursday.

She had barely slept the night before, her thoughts a whirling tornado of shock, confusion, betrayal and joy. She was drowning, tumbling further and further away from any semblance of control. Throughout the workday her eyes would often land on the damaged leather, her perspective shifted.

It made her angry, taunting her with its stubborn presence.

You thought I was the villain, but look how much worse it's gotten.

She imagined its voice was a sly hiss, like a deadly serpent.

The couch was right, though.

Originally, it was a dramatic interruption, but now it seemed inconsequential. Amelia knew in her gut that it would make more sense to figure out why the sofa was adamant on ripping apart, but that sounded difficult and her mind was fatigued from pondering all of the other, more consequential problems in her life. As her final client rambled on in his raspy voice, Amelia could think of nothing else.

"Thank you, Dr. A." Golem said, stopping at the doorway as usual. His voice was significantly less gravely now that he was made of lumber, but his body creaked with each step. It stirred a memory deep in Amelia's mind.

The floorboards were loud as Amelia snuck from the kitchen back to her room. She gripped the cheese stick in her hand as if it were a sword, heart hammering while she tiptoed up the stairs. Amelia froze when she heard hushed voices coming from Mom's room.

"I can't just leave you here." Daddy's voice whispered, making Amelia's heart drop. She hadn't heard Daddy's voice in a long time, more than a week. She knew that a week was seven days and she counted each day that he wasn't home.

She held her breath, worried that if she was caught he would disappear again.

"You can and you will," Mom whispered back, "My sister is here to help."

Amelia wrinkled her nose, she would much rather have Daddy than Aunty to play with her. Aunty didn't like it when Amelia played—she always told her to slow down and be quiet.

"So what, I'm supposed to just move on?"

"Oh, Maurice, don't make this harder than it needs to be." Mommy's voice was so sad, Amelia almost revealed herself just to give her a hug. She didn't want to get in trouble though, so she just listened quietly.

"It doesn't need to be this way at all, just come with me." There was a small pause and a kissy noise. "I'll take care of you." Several more kissy noises made Amelia wrinkle her nose and pad quietly to her room.

"You did good work today." Amelia praised the timber construct, voice distant as she returned to the present, barely noticing that the door had closed and she was alone.

A typing noise startled her from the momentary stupor.

Need to talk?

Amelia sighed and sat at the desk chair.

Name: Dr. Amelia Atkinson
Age: 32
Sex: Female
Pronouns: She/Her
Race: Human

Session 257

Dr. A: I don't even know where to start.

Tracy: The beginning is a good place, but anywhere is fine.

Dr. A: I found my father.

Tracy: How do you feel about that?

Dr. A: I'm trying not to feel about it, actually.

Tracy: Why not?

Dr. A: I've got several larger fish to fry at the moment.

Tracy: Reuniting with your estranged father would qualify as a rather large fish, but I will reserve judgment for now.

Dr. A: Would you like me to organize them in terms of initial shock value or depth of impact on my future?

Tracy: We both know you will just blurt out your stream of consciousness.

Dr. A: Well, my aunt told me that my mother died from venom sickness, which according to my vampire father is actually a magic sickness. Which means the only person I trusted has been lying to me, either a little or a lot. My vampire father has been aware of my profession and has chosen to stay out of my life for some unknown moralistic reason that I am not privy to. This magic illness is incurable unless I want to be changed into a vampire and completely give up the one thing I have spent my whole life working towards. Not that it even matters anymore because my mother wasn't even mentally ill! She just went crazy because he wasn't there to suck out all the extra magic. I have no clue why my dad decided to stay away from her but it's likely pretty bad considering he truly believes he's a monster. Oh, and I have the same magic illness, so I'll be forced to have regular biting sessions to drain me until either Freddy gets tired of me or I choose to completely upend my life. In summary: Everything is all fucked up.

Tracy: That is a whole school of large fish.

Dr. A: Yes, so how do I fix it?

Tracy: Fix what exactly? Objectively you've gained much more than you've lost.

Dr. A: What?

Tracy: Well, from what you've described you now have a more accurate picture of your mother's death, the possibility of a relationship with your father, and a man that's committed to help you indefinitely.

Dr.A: Then why does it hurt so much? If anything I feel emptier than I did before I knew the truth.

Tracy: Learning new information means acknowledging your past ignorance. You were betrayed, that's going to be painful regardless of how much you've gained.

Dr.A: I understand that but I can't just sit here and wallow. I need a plan.

Tracy: You have to feel things, sometimes.

Dr. A: I disagree. I think my problem is that all of these new developments are out of my control. I can't undo my aunt's dishonesty, can't force my dad to be a part of my life, I can't even fix my couch.

Tracy: You're not necessarily wrong. It might bring you comfort to find something you can control.

Or someone.

The tingle in the base of her spine alerted her to his presence before the knock did.

Amelia didn't hug Freddy this time, choosing to keep distance between their bodies. She leaned against the reception desk, legs crossed as she waited for him to step inside. He walked over, stopping just in front of her, and setting a hardcover book on the desk next to her.

"What's wrong?" he asked, sensing a change from her usual mood. The last thing she needed right now was to feel more warm, gooey uncontrollable feelings for Freddy. She would resist the urge to collapse in his arms, to seek safe harbor there.

Amelia recounted the conversations she's had with her aunt, but left out the mini mental breakdown she had with her typewriter. She did need him to return regularly, after all.

"That's interesting,"

"Not the word I would use." Surprising, devastating, and life-ruining seemed more appropriate.

"Why do you think she called it a venom illness?"

Amelia had pondered this question as well while she organized the transcripts.

Not for long, though–she found it easy to dismiss.

"I figured she just hates my dad and made an assumption. She's pretty embroiled in caster society and they don't know much about vampires." As evidenced by the bizarrely empty library.

His eyebrows stayed furrowed.

"I think she was being deliberate with her words, though."

Amelia's brows raised and her heart picked up speed.

"She's smart, isn't she?"

Amelia nodded, her aunt was educated as well. She was in the process of an advanced physics degree, when she pivoted to political science.

Freddy's lips pressed together. "If her sister died from magic withdrawal, there's no way she wouldn't have known."

"So, why wouldn't she just tell me that? Why make it seem like magic had nothing to do with it?"

"I don't know, but you should find out."

A wave of painful softness filled her chest. Freddy was completly devoted to her plight, making no attempt to seek his own personal fulfillment. She had to repay that effort, regardless of how difficult it may be.

Amelia grasped his hands. "*We* are going to find out."

Freddy's eyes flashed a warm silver before he re-focused on their conversation.

"How long was Mo gone before she died?"

"My aunt said it was about a month."

The corner of his mouth pinched.

"I read something in a textbook about positive feedback loops."

"Slow day at work?"

Freddy ignored her and continued. "Maybe I'm missing something, but Mo's advice doesn't make any sense to me. You're the smartest person I know, so tell me if I'm completely off."

Amelia nodded, pretending that her stomach didn't clench from his praise. She focused on the rational aspect of his words, familiar with the biological concept of the two feedback loops.

Negative feedback was more common, found in the biology of every creature. It involved processes that regulated themselves, like the internal thermostat of a dragon—which ensured that the flames did not exceed a tolerable temperature. For the dragon, that is.

Amelia was sure that the recipient of that flame would find it quite intolerable.

Positive feedback loops continued on in an exponential fashion, until an outside force interrupted them. Amelia's favourite example was the reproduction methods of the blueleaf plant. Once activated by the ammonia of a migratory autumn bird's urine, they would release their pollen to the sky. One plant would stimulate the other, until there would be monstrous clouds of sweet-smelling pollen. Advantageous for the herb, sure, but it also had the unseen consequence of causing a month-long dancing plague in nearby villages. The cycle, much like Amelia's reaction to losing magic, would not stop without outside intervention.

Freddy was turning out to be a helpful assistant, indeed.

"I took magic from your veins to power my undead body. This made your body need to produce more, which made you sick. Mo's solution was just to keep taking more, which will make your body work even harder to replace it. If it's a positive feedback loop, shouldn't the answer be to interrupt it?"

It was a sound and reasonable deduction, and Amelia was disappointed that she hadn't been the one to come up with it. She was off her game, that was for sure.

"Wasn't that what made me delirious in the first place?" Mo had alluded that Amelia's illness was caused by the interruption of Freddy's feeding in the days she was trying to forget him, and her aunt had implied that it was the same illness that killed her mother.

It was only natural for Amelia to make the connection that if Freddy stopped feeding from her, she would die.

"I don't believe that. Listen, if you break it down to the simplest form, what Mo said was that if a caster loses a substantial amount of blood, they would go into magic withdrawal. If that was true every caster who got in a serious car accident would go from the trauma ward to the psychiatric wing."

She hadn't considered that. Darkness crowded the corners of Amelia's vision. She had been so wrapped up in emotional strife, her ability to think was severely compromised.

"I propose an experiment," Freddy announced, taking a step back with a smirk on his face.

"An experiment," she repeated, though it was barely more than a breath.

Amelia, the once infallible therapist, had failed to recognize a simple contradiction.

"I'm not going to bite you." Freddy's voice interrupted what was sure to be an emotional spiral.

"Pardon?"

"The best way to test my hypothesis is by stopping the feedback loop."

"Did you fall and hit your head on the way here, completely forgetting the part where I was ready to be the hottest plate at a vampire buffet?"

Freddy winced.

"Unfortunately not. I think it's worth a shot, though. If I don't remove any blood from your body for two days and you're still fine, we'll have our answer."

"And what if you're wrong and I start salivating at the sight of a busy intersection?"

"Then it's a good thing I won't be far, isn't it?"

Amelia squirmed, she had lost too much of her power. She had to remind him—and herself—of who she was. Especially since she was so unsure of who that woman was becoming.

"On one condition,"

Freddy smirked. "I don't know, doc. I'm pretty booked up..." When she didn't laugh or smile Freddy rolled his eyes. "What do you need?"

"I've lost control of my life,"

Freddy looked side to side, eyes scanning the tidy office.

"I would disagree, but continue."

"In the past week I've learned that everything I thought to be true is a lie."

"It has been quite a week, you have to admit."

"I have no stable footing anymore, nothing dependable to lean on."

"Just spit it out."

She squeezed her eyes shut, bracing herself. "I'd like you to be the one thing I can control."

"Oh," Freddy's eyebrows shot up, but his face remained neutral. Self-doubt filled Amelia's skull as the silence stretched on.

"Nevermind, I don't know what-"

"Is this a negotiation? I'd like to add my own terms." Freddy interrupted, face pensive.

"Oh, yeah, of course."

"I will be your little vampire slave on two conditions." He lifted his pointer finger up in the air. "One, I get to fuck you."

"Freddy-"

"Sorry, *you* get to fuck *me*."

"That was not the problem with that sentence."

Freddy continued, ignoring her argument.

"Two, I get to take you on a date."

Her mouth popped open. A date?

Instead of reacting in incredulous confusion, Amelia took a deep breath and considered his terms. She would need more information to fully analyze the offer.

"What kind of date?" She hadn't gone on a date that wasn't tainted with obligation since high school. She didn't think Freddy was interested in making out at the back of a movie theater. On second thought if they were to see a movie, he likely would enjoy a makeout session. That was why she liked Freddy so much, he was never worried about what other people thought about him. Not in the same way Amelia was. She wished she could be more like him, in that regard.

"What date would you like, master?" He still had a cocky smile plastered on his face, but there was a faint silver glow to his eyes.

He was definitely into it.

"Please don't call me that." Amelia grimaced.

"Why not?"

"I like the way things are now between us, for the most part."

"You just want a handy assistant to whip after a bad day?"

Pretty much, yeah.

"Doc is fine, is what I'm trying to say."

Freddy bit his lip, suppressing a laugh. "I'm just teasing you, love. You've been bossing me around since we met, why would I refuse now?"

Amelia did not react to the endearment, despite a small supernova exploding in her chest. In her opinion, he had entirely too much control over her.

"You sure haven't been particularly obedient," she grumbled.

"It's not my fault you're so fun to annoy." He tapped the tip of her nose with his finger, a casual gesture—friendly, even.

It was hard to remember that Freddy was just her friend. It seemed like her entire life suddenly revolved around him.

"When is this date?"

"How about tomorrow? I'll pick you up at six."

He leaned down and pressed a soft kiss to her throat.

"Now that it's settled, can I eat?" he whispered, nose trailing up the side of her neck.

"Yes," Her voice was stiff despite the ooze of warmth in her insides. It seemed a bit silly since they had just agreed he wouldn't drink from her. Amelia couldn't deny that it did also quell a deep possessive part of herself that hoped if he fed from her he wouldn't need to feed from a younger, sexier, human that was not currently losing her mind.

She suddenly remembered that she didn't need to hope, she had the power to ensure he didn't find relief in anyone else.

"I have another stipulation," she said, causing him to pull his mouth off of her skin for a moment.

"God, you're needy today," he said, groaning in pain when she yanked on his hair roughly. "I meant, please enlighten me." Freddy grunted out, returning his mouth to the space beneath her ear.

"You won't feed from anyone else, until—oh, god," she gasped, unable to finish her sentence when he nibbled on her earlobe.

"I still can't stomach hunting, so that won't be a problem." He bit his lip, a devious smile spreading slowly. Before Amelia could inquire further, Freddy dropped to his knees. Seeing him look up at her with desire and affection ignited her need like a pyromancer who'd indulged in a few too many gin and tonics. His eyes narrowed when he noticed she was still wearing her heels.

"Take them off," she said, reading his desire.

Much the same as he had done on their first meeting, Freddy carefully removed her shoes and stretched each of her toes.

"Thank you," she breathed.

He carefully lifted her skirt up, exposing her groin and the artery that pulsed there.

"Is this okay?" he asked.

"Y-yes," That was a perfectly valid place to bite. Her core throbbed as he pressed his nose to her pulse point. If she shifted just a little bit his mouth would be on her pussy.

Amelia took a deep breath, holding back the undeniable urge to ride his face as if it were a centaurs back.

"Can I taste you, please?" he asked. She looked down at him, absorbing the lines of his face and the metallic green of his eyes. Suddenly there were no internal conflicts, no confusing familial interactions, no mysterious illnesses to overcome.

There was only Freddy, on his knees, and completely hers for the taking.

It would be so easy to give in to his request, to lose herself in the triumph of fulfilling this intense desire.

It would also destroy her.

"No," she answered, kicking one leg over his head to free her from the confine of her body between his and the desk. She padded towards her treatment room, formulating a plan.

"Why not?" he asked, following behind her.

"I've been spoiling you. You think I've gone soft, that every request will be granted."

"I always make it worth your while, don't I?"

"That's the problem. You're still focused on what you want, and try to manipulate me to get it." She turned to face him, sitting in the wingback chair. Freddy remained in the doorway, eyebrows furrowed in deep thought.

Freddy began to argue but must have realized it wouldn't have been the correct tactic.

"You're right, I'm sorry. How would you like me?" In every way possible, until she had no more breaths to give the atmosphere.

"Crawl to me."

"Crawl?"

410

The stern look she gave him caused his lips to press together in regret.

Freddy questioned everything, it wouldn't be easy for him to truly surrender himself.

More fun for Amelia, definitely.

All humor wiped from his face, Freddy got down on hands and knees. Amelia's skin hummed with pleasure as she watched the delicious man crawl to her, eyes dancing over the bulging of his biceps. The black shirt hugged his form even tighter than when they met—her blood had fed his body, making it supple and strong. The thought was heady, and Amelia was suddenly too impatient for this lesson.

"How do you feel?"

"Demeaned,"

"Is that a bad feeling?"

"It's definitely not good."

"So, why did you do it?"

"Because you asked me to,"

"And what happens now?"

"Whatever you want,"

"Well done, my little mosquito." She leaned forward and stole a kiss from his lips, hand holding his throat just underneath the line of his jaw. Silver engulfed needy eyes. "You may eat."

She leaned back and readied herself for his fangs, grateful that this extended foreplay was over. A gasp escaped Amelia's mouth when she felt his lips on her intimate folds. There had been a slight miscommunication.

"Fred-" she began but cut off with a moan when he slid the fabric of her panties out of the way and sucked her clit into his mouth.

"Oh good god," she moaned, burying her hands in his hair. He ate her with vigor, hungrier than she had ever seen him. He slipped two fingers inside, coaxing her orgasm to the precipice.

"Bite," she grunted out, barely able to speak when he shoved both fingers in deep and pressed his palm against her clit. He groaned against her skin and his fangs finally punctured her femoral artery. Her walls squeezed around his fingers, and his eyes rolled back. He was under the impression that he won, that his little trick had worked. He was quick, using the multiple meanings of "eat" to take an orgasm from her.

A shot of validation for his pride. If he wanted to twist technicalities to his benefit, she would follow suit.

"Get on the couch," she said, trying not to smile when his

mouth opened and shut again.

"Stroke yourself," Amelia ordered once he was seated in the middle of the derelict furniture. Freddy's jaw ticked, she knew there were several snarky comments he was keeping to himself. She watched as he pulled the firm erection from his pants, giving it three slow preliminary strokes.

"You won't come until given permission."

Amelia continued to observe him masturbate, her own desire rearing back to life. Only when he was trembling and the head of his cock weeping did she rise and stride over to him. His eyes were wide as she sunk herself down on his shaft.

"What-" She placed two fingers over his lips to halt his question. She lifted and lowered, massaging his cock with her soaking channel.

"This was your stipulation, remember?"

Freddy's eyes widened in realization before his head dropped backwards, overtaken with pleasure. Amelia rode him hard, circling her clit to bring herself to climax once again. Freddy moaned and whimpered, body shaking and hips bucking. She thought he may fail the challenge when her pussy clamped around him and attempted to milk his release.

He was more resilient than she thought, though not perfect.

She carefully removed herself from his lap, dislodging a still straining erection.

"Where the fuck are you going?" he asked, the silver in his eyes wild and bordering on angry.

"Home, it's nearly seven." Amelia answered, straightening her skirt.

"But what about..." He motioned to himself.

Amelia sauntered back to him, leaning down so her lips were just a hair away from his ear.

"I agreed to fuck you, not let you come. You've got a lot to learn, Watson."

RULE 26
SUPPRESS THE MONSTER

Freddy felt like he was the one experiencing venom poisoning.

His fangs burned just at the thought of Amelia, the venom held within them souring his insides. Her blood was different than human blood, Freddy knew that even more after Mo had explained the magic concentration thing.

It amplified his vampireness, making him both stronger and more feral. He hated feeling so jumpy and agitated, but Freddy would endure it.

If he was honest, he liked the slight misery of it, suffering for her benefit. He just wished he got to have more of her as well, to break past the emotional space she kept between them.

That's why he had been preparing for their date since he left her office—determined to woo her like she had never been wooed before. He should have enough time after his challenge exam to make it to her office for six, but it would be tight. The threat of failure loomed underneath his skin, making his movements erratic.

Freddy cursed as another lemon slice hit the floor.

"Well, at least the floor's getting prompt service," a condescending female voice said as Freddy straightened from retrieving the errant citrus.

"Sorry," he mumbled, even though he didn't particularly care what this woman thought of him.

She was middle-aged, with bright pink skin and hair. From what Amelia had described, she must be a caster—nobody else would have the gall to be so obnoxiously fluorescent. His senses braced at the presence of the woman, casters didn't usually frequent vampire bars. Despite the smooth lines of her face, her scent was mature, a complex bouquet of flowers with a splash of vanilla.

"No need for apologies, your kind can't help it." She waved her hand in dismissal, eyes cast to a compact in her other hand.

Freddy chuckled cynically, otherwise he would growl and that was frowned upon.

"My kind?"

"You think just because you're undead you can brood and growl forever. Well, the living have problems too and we have to actually solve them instead of throwing lemons on the floor." The woman's voice dripped of impatient superiority. Freddy felt no more valuable than a warpbug when she spoke.

No wonder Amelia didn't want to consider herself a caster, being surrounded by people like this would be insufferable.

"Well, not all problems are solvable."

"Maybe you're just not the right man for the job?" Anger rose in Freddy's chest. Before he could do or say something regrettable, Mo's hand clasped his shoulder.

"Let me," he grunted, dismissing Freddy from this encounter. He almost defied his mentor, pride driving him to prove to this horrible woman that there was nothing he wouldn't do to win Amelia's heart.

He bit his lip as he walked over to the bucket of whole citrus fruit. Freddy did already love Amelia in the noun form of the word. He cared for her, thought of her constantly, and desired every part of her during every waking hour.

When Freddy asked Mo about his previous life he had mentioned that love was not a state of being, it was more like a dance between two souls.

Freddy rolled his eyes at the time but he saw merit in it now.

Maybe you're just not the right man for the job.

He could not magically transform himself to be an educated mature man, as much as he wished he could. Amelia had rigid rules and goals and Freddy would have to find a way to mold himself to them. It wasn't the first time he had to push himself to be something he wasn't. Freddy shook his head at the thought.

No, Freddy wanted to be responsible and dependable and educated. It was completely different than how he had hidden himself before, how he had held himself back. Amelia had shown him that he was capable of growth and he needed to make her proud.

It was nice pushing himself instead of hiding.

Tense hisses drew his attention, the conversation between Mo and the horrible caster woman interrupting his internal discussion.

Maurice had climbed in through the window, careful not to disturb anyone in the house.

"Alice...Alice...." he whispered, gently shaking his wife's sleeping shoulders. She woke with a gasp, arms encircling him as soon her eyes had focused on his. She smelled of cinnamon and sugar, like Christmas and everything warm and comforting. She pulled back, worry on her face as she inspected him. Mo laughed, it was just like Alice to worry about his well-being when she was considerably more fragile. Mo's gaze left his beloved's only for a moment, the clothes strewn on the floor panging his heart painfully.

"I'm sorry I didn't come sooner. Your sister has been a nuisance." That was an understatement. She had been borderline obsessive, checking up on Alice and Amelia daily.

"Maybe you shouldn't come anymore." Her face cracked with misery.

"Don't say that. This weekend, remember? We'll go in just a

matter of days."

Her eyes shifted in hesitancy. "I can't do that to Amelia."

Mo sighed, unwilling to have the same argument again. "She will have a good life,"

"You don't have the ability to promise that, you don't know what it's like."

"I don't understand why you're so scared of her power."

"I'm only scared of what you'll do when I'm gone."

Anger flashed through him, hot and ugly. "Has your sister been filling your head with garbage again?"

Alice's face was skeptical, detached with lost hope. Mo pressed a sweet kiss to his wife's lips, reassured when she responded just like she always had.

There was hope.

There had to be.

Mo replayed the memory as he restocked the blood bags in the bar fridge. His sweet Alice had been gone for so long, but the memories of his failure were fresh in his mind.

Mo stood, closing the fridge door. Like a personal nightmare, Magdaline sat at the corner of the bar, wearing a condescending frown.

Freddy's look was near murderous as he grasped the shaker, a disaster about to occur. Mo remembered when he first felt the rush of power from feeding, it took some time to control.

There were surges of labile emotions and uncontrollable violence; it was much like a second puberty. He strode over, intent on making Maggie's face disappear, and protecting his young friend.

He gripped Freddy's shoulder and dismissed him, saving both Freddy from doing something he regretted and himself a potential insurance claim. He could handle Maggie, it was an art that required careful finesse.

"Didn't think you deemened yourself by visiting undead establishments. Isn't there a caster soiree you can self-aggrandise in?"

Maggie stiffened when she looked up from her compact. "Maurice, I see you're looking disgusting as usual."

"A pleasure as always, Magdaline."

Her skin had gone from a forest green to a deep red as she glanced at him.

"What are you doing here?" He crossed his arms, his tone dripping with impatience. If he never saw her again it would be too soon.

"It's about Amelia."

"What about her?"

"You need to stay away from her."

Mo puffed out a laugh.

"I don't see how that's your call."

It was Maggie's turn to laugh. "My call? I'm the only person that seems to have any interest in her welfare."

"I don't know if I believe that considering you've been lying to her."

Maggie didn't reply, simply crossed and uncrossed her legs, taking a sip from a drink that had materialized. Mo saw right through her calm disposition.

"You're scared, aren't you?"

"What a ridiculous notion." Her face was tightly controlled as she spoke, but Mo knew her tells. The red hue of her skin flickered with nerves. He had to keep pushing.

"You are, now that you can't use her to punish me anymore."

"I don't know what you're talking about."

"I think you do. While you're at it you can explain to me why she doesn't have any memories of me or Alice. "

Maggie froze for a split second before tucking the compact into her purse. "She's just disciplined."

"Disciplined? You've brainwashed her!" Mo slammed his palms on the bartop in frustration.

She scoffed dismissively. "I'm sure you would see it that way."

"See it that way? She doesn't even think she has any magic!" His voice was getting louder and higher pitched in outrage.

"Well, if you mutilate her like you did that poor boy, none of that matters–she'll lose her caster status entirely."

A deep rage simmered in his ribcage.

"That's how I know we're different, Maggs. I don't care if she's a vampire, ghoul, monkey, or pocket wrench. I just want her to be happy because I love her."

Maggie stared at him with pure fire in her eyes, her entire body glowing.

"We are different, you have no care for the consequences of your actions. I was the one that was there to pick up the pieces after the damage you did. Part of loving someone is protecting them, making sure that they know a semblance of normal. I did what I had to in order to give her the life she deserved."

"She's thirty two years old, for fucks sakes. At some point you have to tell her the truth." Maurice hissed.

"Yes, she's thirty two and where have you been?" Maggie's voice was lowered to barely more than a growl as she stood.

Mo took a deep breath, ignoring the shattering of his cold heart.

"You keep lying to her and she'll choose me willingly."

RULE 26

BLOODY MESS

RULE 27

DON'T GO TO A VAMPIRE BAR ON HUMAN NIGHT

There was no knock on friday.

Amelia really had no right to feel as devastated as she did. Freddy was just her Watson, a friendly companion with a shared goal of keeping her alive and more or less sane.

Why had she expected more?

Likely because he had been exceeding her expectations at every turn. The disappointment was a good reminder to keep her distance. Despite how smart, kind, observant, and devoted he was, Amelia couldn't rely on anyone to be there.

Her gut panged as she wondered what Freddy would be doing with his free time. It wasn't fair of her to deprive him of romantic intimacy. Her heart threatened to shrivel up and float away at that thought, which was ridiculous.

Amelia had never considered herself to be an emotional creature, but now it seemed every thought had an unpleas-ant physical counterpart.

She longed to regain the comfort of restrained, rational, thought.

As if on cue, a quick metallic tapping filled the quiet space. Amelia sat at the desk.

Name: Dr. Amelia Atkinson
Age: 32
Sex: Female
Pronouns: She/Her
Race: Human

<u>Session 258</u>

Tracy: What's wrong?

Dr. A: I feel deflated, like someone's popped both of my lungs.

Tracy: I think that's disappointment.

Dr.A: I'd ask why but I already know. What I don't understand is why I ever expected more.

Tracy: I think that's called hope.

Amelia did a final scan of the lobby, stomach clenching painfully when she noticed the book Freddy must have forgotten the night before.

ANTIMAGIC: AN EXPLORATION OF PARTICLE PHYSICS BY DR. ATKINSON.

A bolt of anxiety struck her solar plexus.

Why did Freddy have that book?

It would explain why he was suddenly familiar with advanced science terms, but antimagic was barely understood by even the most educated scholars, so it seemed a bit out of his scope. Antimagic, much like antimatter, was nothing—just the molecular partner of the magic particles that surrounded them, unable to touch without becoming completely inert.

Curiosity tingled behind Amelia's neck.

There was a good likelihood that whoever wrote that book was also responsible for the mysterious tome that had laid abandoned in her purse for several days.

She flipped to the back cover, and her stomach dropped.

A black and white portrait of her father smiled back at her, taking all the blood from her face with it.

With a bolt of adrenaline, she abandoned the hardback on

the reception desk and rummaged through her purse for a much more interesting book. She traced the lettering on the front with a shaking fingertip.

Her father had written a manuscript involving vampires, that was shrouded in secrecy and stored in the the bowels of a community that had abandoned him.

Motivation renewed, Amelia tucked her feet underneath her as she sat in the reception chair and spun.

She skimmed the book, nodding along with all the information she already knew.

Not much is known about vampires within caster society, nocturnals choosing to separate themselves from those who walk in the sunlight.

To understand the vampire, one must first understand the ghoul. For after all, a vampire is simply a ghoul with fangs.

Ghouls are corpses that have been reanimated through the use of another's magic. They have no heartbeat or faculties to maintain life themselves, relying on the steady intake of magic to replenish the stores that animate them.

The presence of a soul is another discussion entirely, and well above the scope of this literature.

It is believed by some scholars that the original ghoul was an experiment gone awry. To this date, there has been no account of a ghoul being created, or the means of accomplishing it.

It can therefore be hypothesized that every ghoul seen was once a fallen soldier, risen after that famous battle nearly a hundred years ago, with 150,000 of his brethren.

Amelia skipped several lines, disinterested in ghouls. She had learned about the Great War in history class, a conflict between casters and seemingly everyone else. It only spanned a few years, and was ended abruptly by what the allied forces assumed to be a nuclear weapon. The crater left by the explosion remained so toxic, trespassing was strictly forbidden. Amelia wasn't particularly interested in matters of war, but she had been on enough dates with caster men to know that some still felt the sanctions placed on their society henceforth were an injustice.

She had her own sanctions to worry about, frankly.

Amelia did, however, find it curious that all of the fallen soldiers from that battle rose and began to wander the earth as undead. If this book was to be believed, whatever happened on that battlefield birthed every undead that had ever existed.

Interesting stuff, but not helpful to Amelia at the moment.

She needed to find out how to prevent an early death, and to remove herself from dependence on anyone else. She had deluded herself into believing she could trust Freddy enough to lower her guard, but it was time to refocus.

"The only one you can ever trust is yourself," the voice of her aunt echoed in her mind, and Amelia now knew it to be true.

Despite the way her mind tumbled, she had to trust it.

Though controversial, it is not only feasible but entirely likely that it was a caster who created and installed the dental modification responsible for magic harvesting onto the first undead. Unlike ghouls who simply feast on magic-infused flesh, the fangs of a vampire are a sophisticated piece of biomolecular engineering, too complex for a natural origin.

Amelia's gaze skipped over several paragraphs—impatient for information that would actually help her.

Without a steady intake of blood, both ghouls and their upgraded counterparts simply begin to decay again. The eyes cloud over, and the flesh shrinks around bone.

Amelia shut the book with a loud slam, heart pounding. It seemed that every time she was curious, she learned information that made her want to vomit.

None of this made any sense.

Freddy had a heart beat—she had listened to it as she laid on his chest. He looked malnourished when they met, but not like a corpse.

Despite the fact that the chair had been stationary for several minutes, Amelia's world spun wildly. As was common when control slipped from her, Amelia thought of Freddy.

She had to tell him, needed his input on the information.

His apartment was directly above the vampire bar down the street, she could just drop it off.

A stab of pain hit the place underneath her sternum, a small mourning for the romantic date she was promised. Amelia's stomach dropped when she realized that she didn't even want his bite or his dick. She wanted to protect him, to share what she had learned and provide him the truth—a privilege she had never had.

Mind decided, Amelia grabbed her purse and locked up the office.

The bar was busy, with a line extending down the side-walk–not surprising, for a Friday night. Amelia went up to the entrance, surprised when the bouncer stepped in her path.

"Hold your horses, lady. Just because humans are free to-night doesn't mean you don't have to wait in line."

"Can you tell Mo Amelia brought something for Freddy?"

The bouncer nodded his bald head and pointed to the line of suggestively dressed bodies. Amelia capitulated and set-tled behind the last human in line, only a few steps away from a group of young men.

The smell of their cigarettes both disgusted and excited her. Smoking was strictly prohibited by the rules, and the second-hand stench felt naughty. She shivered and cradled her torso in equally chilled hands. She hadn't been expect-ing to stand in the freezing night air, and her thin suit was not sufficient to keep the cold out of her bones.

"You look a little chilly, love," a heavily accented man slurred, breaking off from the group.

Amelia's skin prickled. "Oh, I'm fine really."

"Don't be cheeky, I could warm you up good."

"I'm waiting for someone, actually."

"Lemme guess, a big tough vampire boyfriend?" He leaned closer, his breath hot and stale. "Yeah, right. You're here looking for a nibble like the rest of us." The man reached forward, about to grab Amelia's arm.

The large and aggressive human man was waiting for a chance to get bitten, to feel the punishing pleasurable burn of venom.

Taking a page from Freddy's book, Amelia grabbed his outstretched hand and pulled down roughly, pausing when his ear was only a breath away from her lips.

"The one you should be scared of isn't my vampire boyfriend." She released his arm, a current of satisfaction rolling through her when she noticed a notable bulge in his stained jeans.

She had him, if she wanted him.

But she didn't.

"There you are, sweetheart."

Amelia was relieved to hear Freddy's voice calling out as he jogged down the cracked sidewalk.

It took her a moment to shake herself out of the cloud of sensual power in order to recognize his form.

He looked different.

Half of his usually floppy dark hair was pulled up in a bun, revealing a whole ensemble of ear piercings and the sharp lines of high cheekbones. Despite the disaster that was her mind and emotions, she wanted him.

"Thanks for keeping her company, but I'll take it from here," Freddy said, playing the perfect boyfriend. Instead of a tight black t-shirt, he was wearing a patterned button up. It was loose, rising up as he wrapped an arm around Amelia's shoulder. She caught a peak of the trail of hair that met his belly button, causing her center to ache.

"I don't think I was done actually." The man's grating voice interrupted her ogling.

"She's not interested," Freddy said firmly.

"Oh, come on, love," The man peered at Amelia, as if Freddy didn't exist.

"Hey, buddy." Freddy pushed the man's chest with both hands, causing him to stagger back. "Fuck off or you will be fucked off." Freddy's face was stretched in a snarl.

Amelia's heart raced, fear and arousal gripping her equally.

"And who the fuck do you think you are?"

"One second, baby." Freddy sighed and placed a quick kiss on Amelia's lips before leaving her side and striding closer to the man. "You want some action? Come get it," he snarled, fangs extended.

Despite Freddy being much smaller than the man, a mask of genuine horror flashed over his face.

The man backed away, palms up in surrender. "Hey, man, I was just trying to have some fun."

"What a coincidence, me too." Freddy launched forward and landed a punch in the man's distended gut. "Want some more?"

The man shook his head and backed up.

"Oh, come on, love." Freddy echoed his previous comment.

He turned and punched the obnoxious man in the jaw, knocking him to the ground.

Freddy crouched down next to the injured man. "You see? Consent is so important." His voice was a menacing hiss. "Stand up and tell the nice lady you're sorry." He grabbed the man's shirt, forcing him to his feet in front of Amelia.

"I'm sorry, nice lady," he croaked, nose bloodied and eyes swollen shut.

"Well done, now you better sleep on it." Freddy smiled and shoved his fist against the man's temple, rendering him unconscious. Amelia gaped at the altercation, heart and pussy pounding.

With the man incapacitated and his friends mysteriously absent from their spot against the wall, Freddy returned to Amelia's side.

"Thank you, baby." Amelia breathed, playing along with the earlier ruse. Freddy's lips pursed and head ducked in embarrassment.

"I'm sorry you had to see that," he said, regret clear in his dark eyes. Amelia certainly didn't regret watching Freddy unleash himself, but maybe she was missing something.

"Is he dead?" she asked, unsure which answer she hoped for.

"No, he's just taking a little nap to reconsider his choices." Amelia never thought she would see this side of Freddy considering how sweet and gentle he had been with her.

It made him even more intriguing and completely irresistible.

Amelia grabbed the waist of his pants as she pressed her

back against the brick wall, pulling his body flush against hers. He ground his pelvis against her as they kissed, his mouth opening for her tongue's intrusion.

"Ouch," She pulled away on instinct, sharp pain and warm blood filling her mouth.

Freddy blinked at the interruption, though his erection still dug into her middle.

"What happened?" he asked, frowning when she covered her mouth with the palm that was previously trailing up towards his hair.

"You cut me," Amelia smiled incredulously.

The flush that had been creeping onto his face drained. "I'm so sorry-"

"No, silly man. You cut me with your fangs, they responded to the threat of danger." Amelia laughed as she stuck her finger in the shocked vampire's wet mouth, hissing slightly when she pricked the tip on an extended fang.

The slight burn of his venom warmed her chilled digit. As if by instinct, Freddy licked the blood from her flesh. He sucked and laved her with his tongue, the desire that had waned from her discovery flooded back full force. Satisfaction and pride warmed her center, allowing her to momentarily forget about mysterious illnesses.

A gust of wind licked the backs of her legs, causing a shiver to ratchet up her body. Freddy frowned and wrapped his arm around her shoulder, leading her towards the entrance of the club.

"Let's get you out of the cold."

Amelia pulled back, causing him to look back at her with concern. She came here with a purpose.

"I have to tell you something."

Freddy's face dropped, and his lips pressed together.

"I know, you don't have to say it."

"You do?" Had Mo already told him the truth, and she was simply the last to know? Amelia couldn't discount the possibility, it seemed that she was always the last to discover the truth.

"I was late, and that's inexcusable. Will you take pity on me and let me make it up to you?" His dark eyes were tortured. They were almost black, too dark for a well-fed vampire.

"You look hungry."

Freddy ducked his head in embarrassment. "A little,"

"Why?"

"You're going to laugh at me."

441

"I'm not a judge, only an observer."

His forehead creased. "I don't think I believe that anymore."

"Why not?"

"You make about a hundred judgments every minute."

"But I'm nice about it so it doesn't count. Now, tell me why you're hungry." She held his face firmly in her hands.

"Ingesting blood that isn't yours feels...unfaithful," he admitted, gaze dropping with embarrassment.

The rational part of her brain wanted to laugh at the concept that she would feel entitled to how he sustained himself, but a darker, more primal fragment of her was decidedly pleased at his admission.

She acknowledged that it was wrong to feel a rush of pleasure from his self-denial.

Maybe that was just who Amelia was becoming—a predatory letch who was gluttonous for his sacrifice.

For some reason, she didn't care.

Instead of analyzing the future implications of her thoughts, Amelia lifted her vampire's chin and forced his eyes to meet hers.

"Your devotion pleases me," she said, earning a flash of silver from his eyes. "But there are consequences."

His face slackened with surprise. "Consequences?"

She let go of his face and began walking towards the open doors of the club.

"You've lost the privilege of arranging our date, and I think it's time for dinner."

BLOODY MESS

RULE 28

DON'T FORGET TO FEED YOUR VAMPIRE

AMELIA

The club was sweltering.

Amelia wasn't sure if it was simply due to her skin adjusting to the temperature change, or if the large number of humans increased the dance floor's median temperature. Regardless of the cause, a fine sheen of sweat covered her skin. By the time they reached the bar in the back, Amelia couldn't stand the heat any longer.

She peeled off the pastel pink blazer and placed it on a stool, leaving her in only a white collared shirt and high waisted pencil skirt.

Freddy's arms were wrapped tightly around her before she could even turn around.

"Don't do that." His mouth was mere centimeters from her ear, causing a cascade of shivers completely unrelated to temperature.

"Why? It's hot," she breathed, moaning slightly when his hands slipped underneath her shirt to cool her skin.

"Yeah, that's the problem. You don't want to make the wrong impression." He seemed genuinely unamused, making Amelia believe he wasn't referring to the temperature of the room.

"What impression am I making?" Her voice was somehow becoming breathier, and her skin getting hotter despite his touch.

"That you're available for taking." Freddy's mouth was deliciously sinful as it nibbled on her neck. He was pushing against the boundaries of their power-play—something about this situation made him uncomfortable, and he was seeking the comfort of a hard, predictable line.

Was it the anxiety of being expected to feed on another, or the competition of a room full of prowling vampires?

Amelia supposed it didn't matter—if he wanted to play, she would be his partner.

"Maybe I am," she teased, smirking when she heard a deep growl. "I was willing to turn a blind eye to your earlier transgression but I suggest you curb your hunger before I give you a punishment you don't like," she warned, turning around and nodding in gratitude as the smirking bartender handed her a glass. She didn't care what was in it at that point, her mouth was incredibly dry.

"But I've got such a delectable meal in my arms right now," Freddy murmured, grinding his erection into the small of her back.

Amelia spun and gripped his hair. "This is your last warning." As if on cue, his lips parted and fangs descended. He didn't attempt to free himself from her hold, though. He simply held her gaze, with his own—silver need and repressed desire.

"I'm sorry. May I redeem myself?"

Amelia nodded, regretfully releasing her hold on his hair. He carefully wrapped his arms under her buttocks and lifted, placing her on the bar top.

Freddy removed each shoe and stretched out her toes before leaning forward and placing the footwear behind the bar. The movement made his shirt ride up and Amelia couldn't help but clasp a hand over one firm buttock.

She couldn't be blamed, when the sexiest man alive was exposing himself in front of her and she was already a bit tipsy.

"Can you taste it when I'm drunk?" she asked, remembering the question she didn't get a chance to ask the last time she was inebriated around her undead lover.

Freddy paused before slowly pressing down onto one knee, the question already forgotten as she watched him.

He removed his black boots and tied them onto her own nyloned feet. They were heavy and large, weighing down her legs and pressing her thighs against the glossy acrylic bar. The space between those thighs grew hot and needy for his tender care and sacrifice.

"Thank you," she said, placing a palm on his face.

"My pleasure," he answered, raising a tall glass up to her lips.

Amelia swallowed deeply, pleased that the slight burn on her injured tongue meant it was alcoholic. Freddy's eyes remained glued to her mouth as she drank, his own lips twitching in tandem with hers—almost as if he was imagining it was him she was taking down her throat.

The top two buttons of his shirt were open, revealing the hollow between his collar bones. His fingers slowly crawled up the fabric of the boot and up the length of her shin, activating a cascade of pleasant tingles.

Suddenly, Freddy didn't look so young anymore. He looked like a wet dream, dripping with androgynous sexuality that hinted that no one was safe from desiring him.

Amelia certainly wasn't. Despite the hot hunger and throbbing arousal that was pooling in her core, curiosity nagged at the back of her mind.

Is this what he would be like if they came here as a real couple?

Were they here as a couple?

She supposed she had agreed to go on a date with him that night. Amelia couldn't overlook the possibility that there was some artifice to this version of Freddy, that it was just a bravado used to hide the quiet sensitive man he truly was.

Amelia still didn't quite understand why he felt the need to be an aggressive flavor of masculinity. Fortunately, Freddy was sexy regardless of the mask he chose to wear, and Amelia was in the mood to play.

After she made sure he was fed, of course.

The glass now empty, Freddy set it on the bar top and helped her back down to the floor. Threading their hands together, Amelia led him to an unoccupied section of brick wall near the staff area. She turned to scan the crowd for an appropriate target, acutely aware that his eyes hadn't left her face.

"Do you have a preference?"

"Are there any half-naked psychologists in the building?"

Amelia rolled her eyes. "I meant regarding gender." Freddy snapped out of his trance for a moment, eyes glimmering with something close to shame. Though it was only a small shake of his head, it held gravity.

He wasn't talking about biting, and that was clear.

Amelia observed the tables of club goers, looking for any interested glances. Though the room was a little blurry, Amelia zeroed in on two young women looking at Freddy and whispering.

Bingo.

Being a young hot vampire paid off, it appeared. Amelia plastered a wide drunk smile on her face and stepped towards the young women. During the walk to their table, she decided to go for the brunette, in case that made Freddy more comfortable.

"Ladies," Amelia said, reassured when the women smiled back. She reached forward and gripped the dark haired woman's hand.

Warm and human.

She leaned into her ear and pointed towards the back of the room.

"Do you see my friend over there?"

RULE 28

The woman squinted towards Freddy leaning against the back wall.

"The sad looking one?"

Amelia nodded. "He's sad because he's absolutely starving."

The woman looked puzzled for a moment before her friend mimed fangs with her pointer fingers. Her eyes widened with surprise or fear, it was too dark to be certain.

"Have you ever been bitten before?" she asked, glancing back at Amelia with hesitation.

Amelia nodded with and plastered what she hoped was a reassuring smile to her face. "Lots."

"Does it hurt?"

"A little, but the venom will numb you right up."

Her friend shook her shoulder. "You have too, I need to know what it's like."

Amelia looked to the blonde woman, shifting her strategy. "He's not picky, if you wanna give it a try."

The women traded guarded expressions. "How do I know he won't take too much?"

Amelia bit her lip in contemplation, she wasn't expecting this much resistance.

She was like a werewolf during a heat for Freddy's bite.

"I can stay, if it would make you feel safer."

The women traded looks again before the blonde one stood.

"Okay."

Amelia's heart raced as she led the woman to the patch of brick where Freddy was waiting. His fangs had retreated during her absence, a clear sign he had become nervous or doubtful.

"Freddy, this is..." She had never asked the woman's name.

"Emily," she squeaked, eyes trained on the floor.

Freddy pursed his lips for half a second and a mischievous glint replaced the tortured one. He reached down and grabbed Emily's hand, placing a chast kiss on the back of it.

"Nice to meet you, Emily," he murmured, pitching his voice to a low seductive lilt. The young woman's breath hitched and Amelia was struck at the complete lack of jealousy she felt. She knew, to the deepest pits of her soul, that Freddy was hers.

"Emily's a bit nervous, but I told her you would be gentle."

"I'm always a good boy," Freddy promised, pushing off the wall and stepping closer to the trembling woman.

To Amelia's surprise, Emily grabbed her arm and wrapped it around her small waist, clutching onto it with two sweaty palms.

"It's okay," Amelia soothed the small human, pressing a re-assuring kiss to the back of her head. The woman relaxed and tilted her head to the side, revealing her neck.

Freddy leaned in and paused when his mouth was only a breath away from the woman's jugular. Amelia's innards were a firestorm of desire, and something else too horrific to name.

"Tell me," Freddy mouthed, eyes pleading.

"Bite," she breathed, satisfaction rolling through her when Freddy's fangs extended and he punctured Emily's skin.

"Ow," she squealed, but melted into Amelia's grip with a sigh after only a moment.

Freddy's eyes didn't leave Amelia's as he gulped against the woman's neck and his eyes slowly returned to a medium emerald. Power and heat rolled through Amelia.

It was both erotic and strangely domestic, helping Freddy feed.

He detached and licked the remaining blood from Emily's neck. The woman sagged against Amelia's shoulder, panting wildly.

Amelia placed another kiss on the back of her head, "Good girl."

She shifted her arm from the woman's midsection to her hand, turning to lead her back to her table.

Amelia was surprised to see Mo standing with the other woman, eyes glowing silver. A bit on the young side, but she supposed immortality afforded vampire men that privilege.

Her father did only look to be in his early forties and he wasn't a bad looking guy.

When they arrived at the glossy black table, Mo turned and smiled at his daughter, eyes returning to the bright blue they shared.

"I take it this is Emily?" he asked, clutching the blonde woman's hand warmly.

She nodded, eyes skittish and lethargic. Mo's eyes glowed as he spoke directly to her.

"You had a rough hookup in the bar bathroom but you drank too much so you won't remember it in the morning." He licked the pad of his thumb and pressed down on the bite mark of the woman's neck. When he lifted his finger, the open wound was merely more than a faded scar.

Amelia's eyebrows raised, she would have to teach Freddy

how to do that.

"You mind controlled them," Amelia said as they walked back to the bar together.

Mo grimaced, "No, I just increased the likelihood that they will forget."

"Why?"

"To avoid unnecessary questions and complications."

Amelia considered her father's words.

Maybe there was a reason Freddy was so resistant to the idea of preying on human club goers. He must have watched the ordeal from behind the bar several times. Amelia's heart ached as the vampire in question came into her view, eyes closed and back leaning against the wall.

"It seems unethical," Amelia muttered, mostly to herself.

"Ethics and magic live in completely different worlds." Mo's voice rang with sadness. She turned back to ask him to elaborate but he was already gone.

Warmth and affection filled her chest as she gazed at Freddy. Her vampire seemed to have the best of both worlds.

Amelia opened her mouth to call out to him but was interrupted by a loud bird-like shriek.

"Dr. A?" A feminine voice screeched from the dance floor. A very familiar set of harpies waved their feathers at her. Amelia closed her eyes for a moment and took a deep breath.

It would be an inexcusable breach of professionalism, to join them on the dancefloor.

But it was Friday night and she was out on a date. Dates weren't bound to normal rules, Amelia decided.

She joined the group of writhing bodies, the music and crowd enveloping her.

"I'm Amelia right now, not Dr. A," she said to the tall woman, hoping to maintain a shred of professional integrity.

"Don't worry doctor, your secrets are safe with us," The other harpy said, hand placed on her chest in sincerity.

"What secret?"

"Your hot vampire boyfriend, although I don't think I would keep that fact to myself," Angela said. Or was it Jessica? Amelia supposed it didn't matter.

"Yeah, because you can't fucking keep anything to yourself, Jessica," the other harpy said.

"I'm just saying, props to her for pulling above her league."

"Jesus Christ, you can't say shit like that to people—we're

feminists now." She turned to Amelia with a reassuring smile. "You're hot too, in a cool mom sort of way."

"Thanks," Amelia laughed, choosing to take it as a compliment.

She tilted her head back and closed her eyes, letting the music fill her mind and move her body.

Amelia was glorious when she let loose.

Freddy watched her and the two women dance and grind together. Her eyes were closed and head thrown back, sweat running down her face and neck.

Freddy wanted to lick it off of her skin.

"It's the magic," Mo said, suddenly appearing next to Freddy against the brick wall. He was leaning back leisurely in the way he did when he wanted to say something important. Freddy shot him a lethal look, wishing he would go away so he could continue to guard his woman. "The reason you feel like that."

Freddy could have denied it but he didn't have the mental capacity for it at that moment. "Why?"

"I don't know, really. My best guess is it's just an addiction response, to protect your supply." That should have bothered Freddy, but all he could focus on was the sway of Amelia's hips.

Besides, he knew exactly why he felt like this, he didn't need Mo to tell him. Every molecule in his body begged for her, cried to worship her.

"What was it like for you?"

"Obsession."

Freddy nodded. That sounded accurate.

"All I could think about was taking, consuming, winning." Mo's voice was distant. Freddy didn't understand that part but he wasn't in a state to argue.

"Your wife?"

"My research." Mo's voice was a mix of pain and wonder. "She was just a casualty."

Freddy watched as Amelia swayed with a loose smile on her face. "I would rather die than hurt her."

"And yet you're not dancing with her on her birthday."

"It's her birthday?"

"It will be in a few hours."

Freddy watched closely as her usually brown hair began to glow a deep vibrant red.

She was magnificent.

Despite the adequate meal Freddy had just consumed, he was hungry again. Hungry for her skin, blood, body, and praise.

"She didn't ask me," Freddy answered the silent question , mesmerized by the way the light glinted off her skin.

"Maybe she shouldn't have to," Mo replied, mirroring Freddy's past words.

It wasn't permission but it felt like it.

AMELIA

The music changed, forcing Amelia to finally open her eyes.

Her dance partners were nowhere to be found, and just when she was going to turn around and look for her vampire, familiar cool arms wrapped around her.

She swiveled in his arms, smiling when she noticed his shirt was fully unbuttoned, revealing a smooth pale chest and abdomen.

Compared to the bulging muscles and tanned human skin that framed him Freddy looked slight and sleek.

Disinhibited from the alcohol and ambience, Amelia ran her palms down the newly exposed flesh. Freddy didn't stop moving, but lifted his arms above his head and tilted his head back in pleasure.

Previously, Amelia thought Freddy was handsome and soft from his age, since men didn't typically fill out until later in life, but on closer inspection his movements were seductive and almost feminine in quality. Perhaps there was more Freddy was running from in his human life than just poverty and crime.

Regardless, she wanted him, and she wasn't feeling patient.

In the cocoon of the nightclub she could believe he was hers, truly. She grabbed his belt loops and pulled him against her, smirking when she felt the hardness between his legs.

"How do you feel?" he asked, leaning down to make sure she could hear him over the music.

"Hot," she said, truthfully. Her skin and core were both dripping.

"Hmm," Freddy moaned against her shoulder, wrapping his arms around her back. "I think I can fix that."

Considering the husky lilt to his voice, Amelia doubted he was going to do anything to turn her off.

Before she could ask him any clarifying questions, he ran his mouth down her sternum and tore away the rest of her shirt when it got in his way. Amelia gasped, surprise and pleasure flooding into the space of her brain where rational thought once lived.

"Better?" Freddy asked, looking up at her with seductive green eyes.

"Not even a little," she whimpered, cradling the back of his head to steady herself. He nipped at the band of her black lace bralette. Despite the intense desire, Amelia's cognitive functions alerted her to the extended fangs that threatened to saw through the thin fabric. Amelia may be impaired with desire and alcohol, but an exhibitionist she was not.

"Kiss me," she said, relieved when he capitulated and pressed their mouths together.

His tongue was the one to breach her lips this time, working her over while keeping her tongue injury free. Amelia didn't have time to enjoy the pleasure of the kiss, because Freddy pulled back an inch to nibble on her lip.

"I can taste it," he groaned.

"What?" Her mind was hazy, but Amelia was sure his words didn't make any sense.

"Blood alcohol," he explained, soothing the bite with his tongue. Amelia opened her mouth to speak, but Freddy took the opportunity to deepen the kiss.

Amelia breaths escaped in pants, her mind only able to focus on his mouth and eyes as he spoke.

"Do you want some more?" she breathed.

"Not here, unless you want to give everyone a show."

"Having problems controlling your hunger?" she smirked, delighted at how he had changed.

"You've tortured me enough for one night."

"Tortured? Was my dancing so awful?"

Freddy moaned and nuzzled into the crook of her shoulder. He must be suffering if he didn't even chuckle at her joke.

"You are so fucking hot, and I am so fucking jealous I could kill someone," he panted against her collarbone.

Amelia scoffed at the compliment, "Hot in a mom way, apparently."

"I can call you mommy if you like."

"Please, don't." She didn't think he was kidding. "Why were you jealous?" If anyone should be jealous it was Amelia. She had to watch closely as he sunk his teeth into a much younger, sexier human.

"You called her a good girl." His fingertips dug into the flush of her hips, control slowly slipping.

"That bothers you." It was more of a statement than a question, but Freddy confirmed with a nod.

"I want to be your only good boy."

This was more than dirty talk, this was very dangerous territory.

But it would be her birthday in a few hours—there truly

was no better time to indulge.

"Good boys have to earn it."

He ground himself against her core. "Tell me what you need."

You, always.

"Privacy," she moaned when he palmed her ass. He detached himself from her body, hot air immediately replacing his cool flesh. He grabbed her hand and led her past a door in the back.

Amelia's mind was delightfully blank as her vampire escorted her into a supply closet, the pounding between her legs consuming her.

She yearned to disassemble Freddy's charismatic facade, to rip him open and gorge on his vulnerable insides. It's what he had done to her, after all.

As soon as the door shut, Freddy pushed her up against it and devoured her lips.

She pulled the elastic out of his hair and the shirt off his shoulders, deconstructing him back to the floppy haired Freddy she knew and loved.

"You've been a bad boy," she murmured in his ear.

"Make me good again." he whimpered, eyes closed. There

was heat in his eyes when they opened but also something darker and needier. She took the hair elastic and placed it around his wrists.

It was only the suggestion of a restraint but it would work.

"I don't want to make you good, baby," she murmured, lifting his arms over his head. She couldn't reach the entire distance, but he got the idea and plastered them against the door of the closet. "I want to make you mine."

She dropped to her knees and unbuttoned his pants.

"Doc-Amelia, please-" he began but cut off when she placed the tip of his cock in her mouth, swirling her tongue around the silver ball. "I don't want to come in your mouth."

"So, don't," she said, before taking the entire length of him down her throat. Amelia may be uptight but she was not a prude. She made love to his cock with her mouth, proving to him how much he belonged to her.

"Jesus, fuck," Freddy moaned, his hips bucking on instinct.

The barbel was cold and hard against her soft palate, making her gag and resurface. His whimper was pained, and a tight clenching in her chest made her stand.

"What do you want, baby?" she asked, pulling on his biceps so his arms lowered around her.

It wasn't so different from when his wrists were bound by silver handcuffs and yet the connection between them had amplified exponentially.

He wasn't a poor sickly client anymore, he was a man, desperately seeking permission to release himself.

Something told Amelia there was more than just sexual need in those silver eyes, something deeper that was seeking absolution.

There was something he needed to say, he just needed some help getting it out.

"To please you," he groaned out when she slowly stroked his shaft. It became clear to her then, that her need had never been to control him.

She wanted to free him.

From his guilt, his loneliness, and his self-imposed limitations. Her truest desire was to crack him open, and cherish whatever ugliness came flowing out.

She wanted to love him.

"Honesty would please me. I think there's something important you haven't told me." She bit her lip as she worked him and looked deep into his emerald eyes. She tried to pour every drop of compassion into her gaze, to wordlessly communicate that she would accept every part of him.

"I-I don't," he stuttered, face dripping with desire and suffering. Amelia was drunk on her power, on his submission.

She stopped stroking.

"Okay, okay, yes, just please don't stop." Freddy sighed when her movements restarted. He took a deep breath and swallowed before speaking again. "I-I love you."

Whatever Amelia was expecting him to say, that wasn't it.

She let go of his cock and slipped the elastic off his wrists. Freddy whimpered and his eyes filled with fear and frustration. She cradled his face in her hands and placed a soft kiss on his trembling lips. Despite the heavy surprise that sat in her chest, he was not in a mental place to have a serious conversation about the implications of their relationship.

She would have to take care of him first.

"Thank you." she whispered against his lips, rewarding his honesty. "Would you like to come now?"

Freddy whimpered and nodded, closing his eyes.

"Sit down," she murmured, unsurprised when his knees gave out and he slumped against the wood of the door.

She carefully straddled his hips and settled her pussy around his cock.

They both sighed in relief at the easy slide from her slickness. It had been only twenty four hours since he was inside her and yet it felt long overdue. He slid inside her easily, both of them more than ready.

When he was fully seated, Amelia let out a long exhale, she hadn't realized just how empty she had felt without him.

"Good boy," she whispered, earning a shudder from his body beneath her. Slowly, she rose and lowered, working him inside of her. She leaned forward, placing her forehead against his shoulder. He stretched her deliciously, the slow burn of pleasure shooting electric pulses to her womb.

"I-I can't-" he whimpered, squeezing his eyes shut. He was close.

"It's okay, baby," she cooed in his ear. "Come for me."

He squeezed her hips with his palms as he groaned and twitched between her walls.

Amelia didn't orgasm, but she hadn't planned to. This was his moment and for some reason it felt like it was her moment too.

RULE 29

TAME THE MONSTER

FREDDY

Freddy thought that his days of lamenting his death were over, but sitting there with Amelia collapsed on his lap, tracing lazy circles against his skin, was how he wanted to die.

The earth shattering orgasm was nice too.

"I like your idea of romance." she said, cheek pressed against his chest.

"Trust me, this was not my plan."

"No?"

He hesitated for a moment, in retrospect his version of that night was much cheesier and less sexy.

"Getting my brains fucked out in a storage closet was not originally on the itinerary."

"What was on it, then?"

He looked away from her, shame getting the best of him.

"Freddy, you know I don't judge."

His lips continued to press together in hesitation.

"If I have to ask again you won't enjoy the consequences." she warned. Freddy disagreed. He would give her at least one internal organ at that moment, bare minimum a kidney.

He sighed and shut his eyes, head leaning against the wood of the door.

"I was going to take you on a picnic. Feed you grapes under the moonlight and make love to you for hours."

There was a silence.

"Grapes make me nervous—they're one of the highest risk foods for choking."

Freddy laughed. "I guess it's a good thing I fucked it all up."

"What happened?"

"I took the challenge exam to get my highschool diploma,

but there was more traffic than I thought there would be. I even took the earliest test time I could-" She pressed her lips to his, effectively silencing him.

"Freddy, that's amazing. Why didn't you tell me?"

"In case I failed,"

She pulled back and inspected his face, hand tenderly cradling his cheek.

"What did you think I would do?" Her voice was small and self-conscious, worried that he saw her as someone to be feared.

Freddy didn't really think that far, couldn't even comprehend the idea of disappointing her.

"Nothing. You just have such high standards and I didn't want to be an embarrassment."

Didn't want to be your burden, too.

Her eyes softened.

"Those standards are for me, not you."

"Why should they be any different?" He deserved to be challenged, too.

"Because you're a much better person than I am."

Freddy coughed up a laugh.

"What the fuck are you talking about?"

Amelia rolled her eyes. "I did take advantage of you when you were near death."

"Are you talking about when I stalked you with every intention of stealing the blood from your body, because that would be a ludicrous misinterpretation of the situation."

"I think you're the one with a misrepresentation of me," she said into the skin of his chest, running her finger down the trail of hair that led to his cock. If she wasn't careful he would be standing for her again, not that Freddy would complain about another round.

He gripped her wandering hand in his. "What do you mean?"

"I don't live the way I do because I'm a good person." Her voice was small as she spoke, removing her hand from his and cradling his face again. He loved the feeling of her hands on his cheeks, the pressure was soft and reassuring. "I have to live with those rules to control my badness."

Freddy thought about her words for a moment, anger rising in his chest.

"Who told you that? That you were bad." Freddy would be happy to show that person what bad looked like.

Her eyes were soft and slightly sad as she ran her fingers through his hair.

"No one ever told me that I'm bad, but it just felt like it, I guess. If I was better I wouldn't need the strict schedule, the rules."

Freddy hated that answer more than not knowing, he decided. Maybe she wasn't ready to admit that others had wronged her, but she was ready for his challenge to her rules.

Hopefully he would walk away with only minor injuries.

"You know, for being so bossy, you're impressively obedient."

"What are you talking about?" There was a defiant edge to her voice that let Freddy know he was heading in the right direction.

"Your weird fascination with rules,"

"That's not obedience, that's discipline,"

"Is there a difference?"

Amelia didn't answer and the silence stretched.

"We're not so different you know," He ran a finger up her torso and up to her temple. "When I found you I was chasing punishment too. Yours simply happens in your own head."

"Is that why you got into that fight outside the bar? Were you hoping to get beat up because you were late?"

"I don't know, I wasn't really thinking rationally at the time."

"What were you thinking?"

Freddy considered the question, internally replaying the moment.

"I just needed to make sure you were safe."

"Hmm, I guess you were probably too weak to have any fight in you before." Her voice was eager in an academic way, the thirst for information was unrelenting—it made Freddy's chest burn painfully.

That wasn't the truth, but Freddy wasn't going to say it.

Amelia had changed him. His body acted before his brain could catch up when he saw the drunk guy step towards her.

Find Amelia, save Amelia, take Amelia.

Was that the primal instinct his uncle was talking about?

Or was it the magic worming into his brain and convincing him to take her despite logical sense?

Her hand paused its meandering, waiting for his response. He couldn't keep the thought in his head a moment longer, needed to thrust it out in the air for her to mull over.

"Mo said that the magic effects vampires too, so that might be part of it."

Her eyes lit up. "How?"

"He didn't know. Speculated it was similar to addiction."

Amelia's eyebrows pinched together. "Addiction?"

Freddy nodded. "Obsession."

A shy smile crept onto her face. "Are you obsessed with me?"

Undoubtedly, irrevocably, whole-heartedly.

"It's within the realm of possibility."

Her face sobered quickly. "You think it's just from the magic."

"Maybe,"

There was another pause—only the muffled thump of music filling the space of the small closet.

"But even if the tingles went away and I didn't feel this undeniable pull towards you, I don't think that would change anything. I respect you, doc. I like being your assistant, I like worshiping your body."

Her gaze was on her hands, fingers picking at tidy cuticles. "I don't get it."

"What do you mean, you don't get it?" Freddy couldn't have said it any more plainly.

"Why do you like me so much? I haven't really done anything that respectable. In fact, I think I've been a bit of a mess." The end of her sentence was distorted by a large yawn.

"Maybe that's precisely why I like you so much." He touched his finger to her nose. "It's getting late, I better get you home."

Amelia nodded and they stood, slowly righting their clothes and making their way outside the bar.

The walk to the vehicle was quiet, giving Freddy a chance to mull over his thoughts. He itched to offer to join her; they could watch a nature documentary and snuggle. He would watch her slumber and taste every inch of her skin, make her cry in ecstasy while she was still deep in sleep.

"Can you drive?" she asked.

"Of course, I can drive." Freddy scoffed.

"Don't look at me like that, I've never seen you with a car." She held up her hands in surrender.

"Let's remember until about a week ago I was half dead." He tilted his head in thought. "Half undead?"

"Freddy, I have to tell you-" she began, but he cut her off with a kiss. He wasn't ready for her rejection, for the fantasy of their relationship to disappear like a pumpkin carriage at midnight.

"Let me drive you home?"

She nodded, and smiled as he held open the passenger door.

The first few minutes of the ride were quiet.

"I have a question," she asked, finally turning her head to look at him.

"I can almost guarantee you have several."

"You won't like this one."

"Unless you're going to ask me to tuck and roll out of the car, I'm sure I'll like it just fine."

"It's about your father."

"Oh,"

"I just don't understand why you lived the way you did before. You seem to harbor deep seated resentment for your dad and yet you lived your life in a very similar way, almost like you were seeking his acceptance. The same goes for your peers. What you were trying to prove, if you hated them so much?"

Freddy's heart picked up into a gallop. Suddenly the cabin of the car seemed stiflingly small.

"I see why you don't have any friends now," he joked, though the tightness and nausea didn't recede.

She placed her hand on top of his in reassurance. It helped a little.

"I was a small kid, and I liked to read. That wasn't a thing boys did where I lived and they weren't nice about it. There's only so many times you can be called a fag before..." he trailed off, losing his nerve.

"You try to prove that you're not," she finished the sentence for him, clarity replacing the confusion on her face. She remained quiet as her mind tumbled, no doubt making connections between his need to prove himself a vampire to his developmental need to prove himself a man.

She leaned over and pressed a gentle kiss to his parted lips. "I like you just the way you are."

Freddy's heart threatened to burst into a fiery blaze, consuming them both with the amount of love and gratitude he felt for her in that moment.

"But you need to let go of the power your father has over you, or you'll never be able to really live for yourself. You can't break generational curses if you're still seeking approval from the generation that is cursed."

"Easier said than done."

"Why don't you just kill him, then?" There was a veil of impatience over the blue in her eyes.

"Pardon?"

Amelia shrugged. "He's a human and you're not. You're stronger than him now, and clearly he deserves it."

Freddy gaped, completely unable to believe those words had come out of his sweet Amelia's mouth. Had she suggested he kill his father? Commit murder?

They pulled into the driveway. Freddy leaned over and pressed a cool hand to her forehead.

"Maybe I was wrong and the sickness kicked in."

Amelia rolled her eyes and batted his hand away, but he captured her own palm in his and brought it to his mouth.

"I'm sorry," Freddy mumbled against her skin, pressing soft kisses against the warm flesh.

He could so easily pierce the artery that lay in space below her thumb, drink her spiced nectar.

Freddy didn't do that. Just inhaled deeply and ran his tongue over the sensitive area. "I ruined our date."

"You've never ruined anything, Freddy. It was easily the best date of my life and you are a very good boy."

Shutters racked up his spine, and before his cognition returned Amelia slipped out of the car and into her house.

RULE 30

ALWAYS TAKE OUT THE GARBAGE, EVEN ON YOUR BIRTHDAY

AMLIA

Amelia pressed her forehead to the door, the chilled wood hard against her forehead.

She didn't know if she wanted him to run after her, to demand to stay the night.

The alcohol had already burned out of her bloodstream and she stood on sober, shaky legs.

Freddy said that the effect of magic in his vampire body manifested as obsession, but it felt like Amelia was the one who was obsessed.

She begrudgingly peeled herself off of the door and followed her usual night time routine, trying not to stomp her feet like an annoyed child. There was no one here to watch her tantrum, unless she counted her pocketbook.

Penny stayed lifeless on the nightstand, not feeling called to remind her of anything.

She wished it would frantically scribble that she was being an idiot. That she should throw caution to the wind and spend every possible moment in Freddy's arms.

It didn't do any of that, and it never would.

Freddy was the embodiment of passion, desire, joy, and mystery, the complete opposite to the dull and predictable life she had lived.

How had she convinced herself that she was happy for so many years?

The cuckoo clock chimed from her bedroom, an unwanted reminder that it was midnight. The thing seemed to only function when she least wanted it to.

Happy birthday to her.

Unfortunately, she wasn't meeting her Aunt for a birthday dinner until the next evening so she had to manually take out the garbage one last time.

She pushed the bin to the corner of the driveway as she had hundreds of times, catching a faint hint of spicy cocoa, a fond smile rising to her lips. She closed her eyes and inhaled, letting her mind indulge in the memory of Freddy's body, and the freedom of enjoying a taboo moment with a sweet vampire man.

It had only been a week ago, and yet so much had changed for Amelia.

Sure, she had more questions than answers but her blood felt alive underneath her skin. Her fingers clutched the plastic cylinder of the handle, and if she were to let go they would surely be shaking. Her breath formed clouds in the chilly December air, but she didn't feel the cold.

Her skin was still warm from Freddy's touch, and her chest still burned hot from the depth of her affection for him.

She loved him.

It was fact, concrete and secure in her mind, even though nothing else seemed to be. It didn't make the possibility of a relationship between them any less unlikely, but the truth of it soothed her regardless.

"Thank god, I was worried you weren't going to show up."

Amelia jerked and turned her head, startled to see the object of her misery and affection sitting on the hood of her car.

"Show up for what?"

"Our date." He smiled and tapped the metal next to him.

Amelia laughed but joined him on the dark blue surface.

"Not much of a moonlight picnic without moon light or a picnic," she joked, touching her temple to his shoulder.

"Hold on, yee of little faith." He reached into his pocket and pulled out an apple and a pocket knife. She watched in rapt fascination as he expertly sliced the apple into tidy slices. Amelia recalled feeling jealous when watching her aunt slice things in a similar fashion—her hands were never reliable enough to attempt it.

He placed the tip of one slice on her lips.

"I don't have anything to feed you," she whispered, words muffled slightly as she chewed.

"I'm sure we can come up with something, but I need to say something first." He placed the remainder of apple on the roof of the car and tucked the knife back into his pocket.

"Freddy-"

"Please?" His bottom lip stuck out.

Amelia nodded and leaned back, pathetically weak to his pouting.

"I love you, Amelia," he said, grasping her face in his palms. "I don't need you to say it, or even feel it, but I can't play this game anymore. I will happily devote every minute of the rest of my life to you, but I need to know that there's a chance that eventually you would consider being mine, too."

She should lie and tell him that it was best to keep it platonic, to deny herself of the carnal pleasure and uncontrollable emotions. That would be the safest thing to do for her control, to maintain the status quo.

Amelia could handle the tortuous ache of denying her feelings, it was what she had done her entire life.

To break his heart seemed a fate worse than death, so Amelia did the only thing she could stomach—she was honest.

"I do love you." A lead weight lifted from her chest with the admission, though her fingers toiled nervously. "But I don't know how this would ever work."

Even if one ignored the societal taboo of a born caster dating a vampire, the logistics of a day-walker and a nocturnal would be hard to organize.

Freddy moved so fast all she registered was a dark blur and then his hard body was on top of hers.

"I think this is working quite well so far." She felt his happiness more than she heard it in her voice, the hum at the base of her skull dripping of overwhelming joy. Fangs scored the skin above her collar bone.

"That's not what I mean."

"What do you mean?"

"A relationship. I just don't see how it could possibly end well."

"Alright, well, we can just stay long term partners that fuck and are in love with each other." He nuzzled the skin between her breasts, and she was suddenly thankful she had chosen to wear only a sheer tank top to bed.

"That is a relationship, Freddy."

"Then by your own definition we're already in one so there is nothing to worry about."

"You are so annoying."

"I know, but how else will I get you to pull my hair?" She ran her fingers through said hair, pulling it back so she could watch the alluring way his lips pressed against each rib as he descended down her abdomen.

"Just for that I should shave it off in your sleep." Amelia gave it a good yank.

Freddy gasped, lifting his head to shoot her a horrified look.

"You wouldn't."

"No, I wouldn't," she laughed. She continued to comb her

fingers in the soft, dark, locks, admiring the soft mewls that left him. He was a very beautiful man. "A trim might not be a bad idea though, so people don't think I'm your mother."

"I guess you were serious about me not calling you mommy."

"Deathly."

To her surprise, he didn't continue nipping at her skin, but paused to lay his head on her chest. Her heart would likely be racing just beneath his decorated ear.

Could he hear how much he meant to her in it's bounding beats?

Reality settled into her pores slowly like a gentle rain, instead of an overwhelming sea. There was no threat of drowning, with Freddy's head keeping guard of her heart.

She admitted her feelings for a young, hot vampire with a serious case of daddy issues, and the world did not crumble around her. The deep lungfuls of night air were adulterated with Freddy's scent, and nothing could hurt her.

"Weren't you worried that I would hurt you the first time?" Freddy asked, his voice vibrating against her chest. It was an understandable question, she probably should have been. Amelia hummed thoughtfully and contemplated her intentions.

"Maybe I wouldn't have minded if you had." She remembered the rush of excitement at being taken by a handsome stranger. The feeling was so taboo, so novel, she would have accepted bodily harm to feel it again and again. "Maybe I wanted to be hurt to be reminded that I was still alive."

He reached down and ran his finger along the fading bruises on her inner thigh.

"Mission accomplished," he said, voice distant and subdued. She could not let him feel guilty for giving her the most intense pleasure she had ever experienced.

She pinched his chin in between two fingers, causing him to lift his head upwards to meet her eyes.

"You've never done anything I didn't want or need." She continued to pull him upwards, until their lips were pressing together in deep, meaningful kisses.

"Good, because you're stuck with me now."

Amelia sighed and pressed her forehead against his. "How is this going to work? I wouldn't even know how to make you fit into my life."

"Well, how do you eat a unicorn?" Mischief returned to his eyes.

"Eating an endangered species is highly illegal-"

Freddy placed a finger over her mouth, cutting her off.

"One bite at a time." His smile was heartbreakingly sweet and confident. He had no doubt in her capability, even when she had been slowly unravelling in front of his eyes.

The thought fueled her sensual power and consequently, her desire.

"Should I be nervous that my vampire boyfriend is talking about biting? "

She shifted to straddle him, taking the finger he had used to silence her and imprisoning it between her teeth.

Silver irises burned with restrained need, and Amelia knew what he wanted.

What they both needed.

She released his hand, only to plaster it beneath hers on the hood of the car. Instead of surrendering to her command, he adjusted her grip, threading his fingers with hers. He clasped onto her hand tightly, and cradled the back of her neck with the other.

She was the one in control, but his support was strong and intentional.

"Only if you object to an occasional nibble," he answered her question. His voice broke off when she ground her pelvis against his.

She hummed in faux contemplation. "I could get behind some recreational biting." Her back arched as needy hips gyrated in slow, sensual circles.

"Good, because I'm not going to ask," Freddy said, and it was more monumental than any confession of love.

RULE 31
HAVE A HAPPY BIRTHDAY
AMELIA

Amelia woke up with a smile on her face, despite only sleeping for a few hours.

Unlike the tiredness that stemmed from tossing and turning with fever and longing, Amelia's fatigue was the result of fucking her vampire boyfriend until she physically could not keep her eyes open.

Happy birthday to her.

A faint rhythmic beat thumped behind the walls of her bedroom.

Was that music?

She crept out of bed and into the kitchen, smiling when she

spotted Freddy swiveling his hips to the beat and pouring the coffee from the pot into her mug.

It was a sight she could get used to.

"Good morning," she said from her place against the door-frame.

Freddy turned and smiled, placing the coffee down to wrap her in his arms.

"Happy birthday, gorgeous. Any grand birthday plans?" He let go of her only to pass the steaming cup of heaven.

Amelia took a sip and groaned with pleasure. The amount of hot coffee she consumed had risen exponentially with Freddy around.

"I'm having a birthday dinner with my aunt this afternoon,"

Amelia felt a jab of sadness at her desire to involve her new boyfriend in her celebration, and the subsequent reality that she couldn't.

Her plans were for well before the sun came down, and Freddy would still be asleep.

Seeing the crestfallen look on her face, Freddy pulled her close again.

"Hey," Freddy said, tilting her chin up with two fingers. "You're not allowed to be sad on your birthday."

Amelia shot him a reassuring smile.

"I'm not sad, it's just going to take some getting used to."

"Good thing I've got some time. Now, you go get dressed and I will make you breakfast."

He placed a kiss on her forehead before pushing her towards her bedroom. She picked out a humble sweater dress, falling just above the knee. She wanted to have open access in case Freddy was keen for a nibble.

Amelia had taken longer than expected to shower and dress, mind wandering to Freddy and the prospects of their relationship. It would take some adjustments to her life, to make a Freddy-shaped space in her tight regulations. A deep anxiety gnawed at her back of her mind, self doubt creeping in despite the joy of having Freddy back in her bed permanently.

When she emerged from the bathroom, the sun had risen and her heart sank.

A full plate of what appeared to be bacon and eggs with toast sat on the kitchen table, with a sleeping Freddy slumped against the cheap wood composite.

"Come on, big boy," she murmured and led his sleepy frame to her bed, choosing to remove his shirt for comfort.

She also just enjoyed taking off his clothes.

Once he was tucked in and the dishes were rinsed, Amelia was left to decide what to do with her day. She had usually spent her birthday being luxurious and rebellious by sleeping in an extra hour but that seemed laughable now.

She decided to complete her usual chores first, since it was so early in the morning.

Several hours, half a season of a soap opera and four loads of laundry later, Amelia was out of chores to do.

Penny flew from her place on the nightstand and opened to her schedule with a usual mad scribble. Amelia sighed and rushed to put her shoes on, tucking the pocketbook into her purse.

Even with an abnormally long time to prepare, she still needed reminding.

Despite the fact that all she wanted to do was climb into bed with her vampire lover and snuggle until he awoke, she had made plans with aunt and Amelia always followed through on her promises.

The drive to the strip mall restaurant was quiet, and so was the wait for a table.

"Dr. Atkinson!" A familiar voice called. Judy and Richard were walking hand in hand, shopping bags clutched in their grip.

Amelia felt a pang of jealousy at their casual closeness. That would be something she and Freddy could never do, spend a saturday morning out and about walking hand in hand. Nonetheless, Amelia waved and shot a polite smile as they walked past.

"Amelia?" A vibrant green haired woman called out, looking around the parking lot. Amelia stood and followed the woman to the table, trying not to ruminate on all she would have to give up to be with Freddy.

"So, I came to drop off your birthday present," her aunt said, hanging up her purse on the chair as she joined Amelia at the table. "I was quite surprised to find a vampire sleeping in your bed."

Amelia cleared her throat, attempting to slow her racing heart.

"His name is Freddy."

Maggie's eyes widened but her smile remained plastered t o her face. "This wouldn't happen to be the friend you were talking about the other day?"

Amelia took a deep preparatory breath.

"It was, actually. He really was my friend at the time, though."

"And now?"

"He's my boyfriend." He was a lot more than that, truthfully.

A loud laugh burst from Maggie's lips.

Amelia ducked her head, trying to summon the right words.

"Oh dear god, you're serious."

Amelia nodded. Why was she so embarrassed? She was an adult woman, with a hot vampire boyfriend.

She hadn't done anything wrong, had she? When she got the nerve to lift her head, her aunt was a dusky lavender color.

"Yes, I love him."

"No, you don't."

Amelia shot her aunt an unamused look.

"You can't, I mean."

"Why not?" She crossed her arms, a familiar defensiveness rising to the surface.

"I thought I made it very clear that it would have a grave consequence."

"What consequence? That I would end up dead like my mother or a vampire like my father?"

Maggie stiffened and looked around, making sure nobody in the restaurant had heard her. Amelia couldn't care less if the Pope himself heard her. She was frustrated at her aunt's ignorance, and her nerves had been so stretched by the past week she couldn't hide it anymore.

"If Freddy drains every drop of blood from my veins I would thank him for it, because I've been more alive this past week than I have my entire life."

There was a tense silence as Maggie took a long sip from her beverage.

"If you turn, you would lose your caster status."

"And?"

"And then we wouldn't be able to meet like this anymore."

Stubborn pride shone from her eyes as Amelia's heart shattered.

Her aunt would choose her nonsense rules over a relationship with her niece. Amelia might have done the same, if it wasn't for her time with Freddy.

"Do I mean so little to you?"

"You're everything, Amelia. That's why I have to protect you."

"Protect me from a man you don't even know?"

"That's just the way things are. Just because you've been spending every night in a vampire fantasyland doesn't change who you are. Who we are."

Amelia froze at her aunt's words. "We? You've always tried to make it clear how different we are. I don't think I know who you are at all anymore."

And I don't know who I am either.

"I am a woman that keeps my promises. I don't try and ruin everything we've accomplished just because a weak little vampire asks for my help." Amelia's heart threatened to stop entirely.

How did she know so much about Freddy?

"You knew,"

"Of course I knew, I know everything about you."

"How?"

"I don't see why-"

"Tell me," Amelia demanded.

Maggie's jaw clenched.

"Your father," she said between tight lips.

Betrayal, hot and thick, oozed into every crevice of her chest.

"Don't pretend like you didn't need it. You've been so negligent since that vampire sunk his bloody teeth into you, you would have lost it all without me." Amelia shrank as her aunt spoke.

She felt so small, so inadequate.

Suddenly she was a child again, feeling the need to apologize for things she didn't do. Her tongue ached to pacify her aunt, to reconsider her relationship with Freddy and make everything okay again.

Amelia's heart flipped completely upside down with her aunt's dishonesty, and the world slowed.

It was like looking into a fortune-telling mirror, the quiet wildness of Maggie's eyes as her chest rose and fell in quick beats.

That was what Amelia would have been if she hadn't met Freddy. Bitter and spiteful, hardened to the exclusionary rules of a society that had rejected her.

Though her aunt was conventionally beautiful, it was an ugly thing to witness.

With the reveal of one fact, Amelia felt like a sunbeam moth, pinned to a display board of her aunt's making. It was painful and constricting and Amelia had the sudden inclination to run away and seek relief.

She didn't have to think twice about where to find comfort.

Freddy had been the only person to bring her true happiness that wasn't stained with pain of the past. She wasn't worried about being enough when she was laying on the hood of her car with him, wasn't concerned about anything but the pleading look in his eyes and the warm tingles he left on her skin.

Being with Freddy was easy.

Nothing in her life had ever been easy.

"Maybe I would have lost that life, because it wasn't meant for me to begin with." Amelia's eyes remained trained on her lap as she spoke, though her voice did not waver.

"Don't say that, you just needed some-"

"You don't get to decide what I need." She lifted her gaze, meeting her aunt's flickering orange irises with challenge. "I'm not a child anymore."

Maggie's eyes softened. "I just want to help you."

"You can help me by leaving me alone."

Amelia stood and turned towards the exit.

"Love isn't enough, Amelia." Maggie called out after her, voice quivering with unrestrained emotion. Amelia didn't care enough to analyze, deduce, or even ponder what emotion it was.

She hoped it was a painful one, so her aunt would understand that actions have consequences.

Amelia didn't let herself cry on the drive home, focusing on the future and what she still had left. Her mind centered on Freddy, the man she loved. A small bolt of happiness coaxed a smile to her face, a blessed distraction for her raw heart and whittling mind.

Amelia sighed as she parked in the driveway of her home, heartache now a dull throb in her chest.

So much had changed in the past few days, but Freddy's

arms were tangible and real.

She wouldn't come to find out that they were actually snakes this whole time and then proceed to swallow her alive.

She would come home to her reliably dull living room, with the sunshine of Freddy's love to bask in. Whatever life she chose, the choice would be exclusively hers.

Freddy was so good at this boyfriend thing.

His creation was complete and chilling in the fridge, though the kitchen looked worse for wear. He hadn't cooked or baked anything in several years, but it was the thought that counted anyways.

He needed to prove himself worthy of Amelia's love, to hear the words that would reassure him of his place in her life.

Despite her confession Freddy still felt the distance of their social and moral standing. Even if she loved him, he was still a twenty four year old bartender who didn't have anything to be proud of. He looked at the clock nervously, unsure he would have enough time to clean up before she got home.

He wanted it to be perfect, Amelia deserved that.

A horrified gasp made Freddy look up from the cluttered counter and his stomach dropped when Amelia's devastated frame filled the doorway.

"Surprise?" he smiled, hiding icing covered hands behind his back. "I was going to clean up but the cake took longer than I thought-" Freddy's voice cut off when Amelia hit the ground.

RULE 32
LOVE ISN'T ENOUGH

Amelia was very hungry and Mom wasn't answering the door.

They had run out of paper plates and burritos and Amelia thought she might starve to death if Mom didn't wake up soon.

"Hello, Amelia darling." Aunty said, stepping through the front door. "Oh, goodness, let's tidy up shall we?"

With a flick of her hand the full garbage bin began stumbling towards the side door and the brush and sponge animated to scrub the dishes that were spilling over the sink. Like an angel, her aunt had solved all of her problems.

Amelia hugged her aunt's legs, wishing she could transform herself and be a human sized sponge, wipe away everyone's worries. She wished she could transform into Aunty, to fix all the messes and bad feelings.

Amelia groaned as she opened her eyes, the back of her head throbbing.

For a blissful moment she forgot how she got on the floor, all she could see was Freddy's handsome concerned face smeared with white and hear the ringing in her ears. His pale cheekbones were surrounded by a backdrop of color and glitter, recentering Amelia on the carnage of birthday themed decorations.

Her house was a mess.

Although they were made from coloured paper and tinsel, they might as well have been atom bombs of karma. She had put all of her remaining faith in Freddy and where had that led her?

Chaos, dysfunction, and disorder.

Her aunt had been right, without strict guidance Amelia couldn't keep anything together.

She had no magic to clean up this mess—she was just plain useless Amelia, deluded into believing that she could belong in the supernatural world.

"Baby, are you okay?" Freddy's voice cleared the haze in her mind.

The smudge of powdered sugar on his cheek would be endearing if her entire life hadn't crumbled apart.

She should put on a calm front, explain to Freddy what had happened and how she felt but Amelia had not one spec of calm or logic left in her.

She was broken open, emotion bleeding out despite her brain's objection.

"No," she whispered, unable to collect enough air in her lungs for a stronger reply.

She couldn't breathe, couldn't think.

She needed to be alone, to pick up the pieces of herself she still recognized and put them in a sensible shape. Amelia needed to put distance between her vulnerable heart and Freddy's irresistible scent and adoring gaze.

"You need to leave," she said weakly, causing the vampire to furrow his brow. She hoped he would be obedient with this request, that she wouldn't have to hurt him.

Amelia didn't carefully consider her words and thoughtfully select the most appropriate or impactful. Her mouth carried the fears straight from the messy part of her soul. It was too easy to voice the words she had contemplated repeatedly, they had been etched deep like a tattoo into her subconscious.

"I need some space."

"No."

"What?" She wasn't expecting a refusal.

"No," he repeated and disappeared from her vision for a moment. "I thought I was pretty clear that you're stuck with me now," he called from her bedroom.

"But-" Suddenly he was back and a finger was on her lips to silence the objection. The pink comforter was wrapped around her shoulders and he carried her burritoed form to the bed.

"I'm going to clean up and when I get back you're going to tell me what happened."

"Freddy-"

"You don't get to sabotage your life because of a bad day, that's something I would do."

Amelia's lips pressed together and she nodded—he simply left no room for argument.

"Good girl," he patted her head gently and returned to the kitchen.

She would get him for that later.

The time alone and pressure from the tightly wrapped blanket centered Amelia and gave her a moment to collect her thoughts.

Slowly, her heart calmed and breaths returned to normal.

Her independence, the trust in herself, was a tentative stem budding through previously barren dirt, and much like the hard shell of a seed, some deep part of her was broken.

She surrendered to the pressure of the fabric that cocooned her, imagining it held together the cracked surface of her self control.

FREDDY

Freddy's hands shook as he wiped the white residue from the kitchen counter.

It was the first time she had looked at him like that, like he was a monster. He tried to make sense of her reaction, of the distance in her gaze.

Insecurity quickly replaced all curiosity, the reality that the first woman he had ever truly loved had tried to leave him not even a day after he claimed her. Freddy shook his head, willing the possessive term to wipe away like the etch a sketch he stole on boxing day in third grade.

He would have to get used to feral-vampire-brain, it was entirely too aggressive for his liking.

Amelia had claimed him, in all honesty; she had completely transformed both his relationship with his body, and the frame in which he saw himself. His time with her had changed him, had made him believe that he would be accepted even if he failed.

So, for the first time in his life he tried and succeeded.

His time with Amelia had also improved his critical think-ing skills, and he couldn't help but try and figure out what the fuck just happened.

The sound of her body hitting the ground echoed in Fred-dy's mind, horror following behind it. Something he had done was so dreadful that she completely shut down.

Well, he had a feeling she disliked messes with how tidy she kept her home, but to have that kind of reaction to a little icing was completely out of character.

 Amelia was focused and calculated, her actions guided by the acquisition of knowledge more than passing emotions. It reminded Freddy of the experiments she had used as an excuse to help him, and he began to think that maybe she used them as an excuse to take what she wanted.

It made Freddy sad for her, that wanting and taking didn't automatically go hand in hand.

Freddy's suggested experiment had definitely been for scientific good, since he would never willingly turn down even a drop of her blood. It had only been two days, but he missed the euphoria of her ambrosia filling his mouth.

He gasped with realization.

"Amelia!" He rushed into the bedroom.

Her startled face made him pause and remember himself.

She had just had a complete breakdown and now he was scaring her with his lunacy.

"Right, sorry, your thing first."

"My thing is stupid, what happened?"

"Nothing, it's just the weekend."

"Yes, it's also december." She didn't get it. It felt strange to know something Amelia didn't. Freddy would have savoured that feeling if he wasn't so excited.

"No, I meant it's the weekend and you're fine."

"If this is your definition of fine, we need to have a conversation about your standards."

"Doc, I haven't fed from you in two days."

"Oh."

"Yeah,"

"You were right."

"It appears I was." Mo was wrong, her illness had nothing to do with his bite.

They sat in silence for a moment, neither sure what to say next.

"I feel like I should apologize," he admitted.

"Why? This is great news." Her face didn't seem to agree with the words coming out of her mouth.

"Because your father lied to you. Isn't that at least a little bit upsetting?"

"It appears everyone has been lying to me."

"I haven't."

"No," her eyes softened. "You haven't."

Freddy was just about to unravel that blanket from her body (and follow it up with her clothes) but she closed her eyes and sighed.

"Besides, I've barely known the man a few days, and you said yourself he abandoned me. I'm not really expecting gold star behaviour."

Amelia nuzzled into the blanket, and Freddy suddenly felt jealous of the pink, quilted fabric.

"Regardless, we know it's not a magic withdrawal," he said, trying hard to resist the urge of tearing it to shreds with his teeth for having the audacity to bring her comfort. "He either didn't know what he was talking about or he wanted you to be sick."

Amelia shook her head, blessedly extracting herself from

the cocoon. "That's an assumption. Either he was wrong or he purposefully wanted you to bite me."

"Definitely not father of the year candidate, by any account"

"Well, he was never really a father to me at all." Her eyes zeroed in on Freddy, a tell tale concentrated frown blooming. "But what if it's not about me?"

"I'm pretty sure it has to be considering it's your magic we're talking about."

She laughed and stood, clutching the tops of his arms with excitement. "Freddy, you're forgetting a very important factor in this—You."

"Me?"

She released him and began to pace around the small bedroom.

"What if it's not about magic leaving my body, as much as it is magic entering yours."

"That can't be right, Mo was the one that told me how bad it was. That it would make me all feral, power hungry vampire." He waved his hands around his head.

"Maybe that was the point. Did he say anything else notable?"

Freddy sighed and crossed his arms.

"Not really. Just that you can't separate a caster from their magic."

Amelia bit her lip and sat back on the bed. "You should go ask him."

Freddy shook his head. "And leave you alone so you can convince yourself to break up with me again? I don't think so."

Amelia ducked her head in shame. "I'm sorry."

"It's okay, just tell Dr. Freddy what happened." He replaced the pressure of fabric with the firmness of his chest, wrapping her securely in his arms.

Much better.

Amelia recounted the conversation with her aunt and Freddy listened quietly until the moment she repeated the collaboration between her father and aunt.

"What a cunt," he breathed.

"Maggie or my dad?"

"Both."

"Well, I told her to stay out of my life. So, I guess it doesn't matter anymore."

"Good for you."

"Yeah, until even one little thing went wrong and I was convinced that I couldn't do it without her."

"What makes you think that you need her?"

"You're going to laugh at me."

"I really have no room to judge anything you do, doc."

"My brain is a siv, and I can't even keep track of the time."

Freddy motioned for her to continue.

"Um, doing things I don't want to feels physically torturous, I always stay up way later than I'm supposed to, and I've been masterbating and drinking way more than I should."

Freddy's face transformed from confusion to amusement before sobering.

"Hmm, I see," he said and stood, grabbing a random book from the nightstand and pretending to write in it.

"Patient exhibits signs of being human."

Amelia rolled her eyes. "I'm being serious. Without help my whole entire life would be a mess and then..."

"And then?"

Amelia didn't answer, simply looked at the ground.

Freddy closed the book with exaggerated finality.

"So, you believe that you are incapable, weak, pathetic, and bad?"

Amelia looked up and gave a small nod.

"I guess you're right."

"Wait, what?"

"You're a bad, terrible, girl."

Amelia gaped at him.

"Luckily, I have a solution for your predicament but you may find it unorthodox."

Her eyes lightened with intrigue. "An experiment?"

"Of sorts. Follow me to the treatment room."

She puttered after him, halting when they reached a familiar kitchen table.

"Freddy, this is my living room."

He continued to ignore her, and began rummaging through the refrigerator, pulling out baking ingredients and pulling off his shirt.

"I have to admit I like where this is going."

He scavenged through the drawers next, exclaiming happily when he found the silver handcuffs, and fastened them around her wrists behind the chair.

"Nevermind," she amended her previous statement.

"Trust me, it's necessary."

Freddy took the overflowing garbage bin from beside him and upturned it over his head. A sea of flour rained down, eggshells sliding down his abdomen.

Amelia's face distorted to something between shock and horror.

When he was sufficiently filthy, Freddy released her from the cuffs.

"What do you see?"

"About half a cake's worth of ingredients."

"That's right. Does the sky appear to be falling?"

"Well, no-"

"Do you still care about me?"

"Of course, but-"

"Good. Now, it's your turn."

"What, I can't-"

"No problem, I'll get you started."

He took an egg from the carton and cracked it directly on the crown of her head. It slid down her face and her neck, leaving a clear trail of slime in its path. He followed it up with two scoops of flower and about half a carton of milk. Her clothes stuck to her skin from the moisture and now Freddy's cock was hard.

Amelia's eyes were closed, and the rise and fall of her chest was slow.

He leaned towards her ear. "Will you look at me?"

Amelia's eyes opened but she was somewhere else entirely.

AMELIA

Amelia held a grilling fork in hand, swinging it around in an imaginary battle with a humongous tentacle monster that was going to abduct her mommy.

She ran forward, ready to deal the fatal blow when her weapon pierced through the abdomen of the alien and became lodged deep inside his evil heart.

Amelia pulled back and grunted when her small arms couldn't remove the blade from her enemy. She pulled off her orange bucket-shaped space helmet to find that she had sunk the winning blow into the bottom cushion of the leather loveseat.

Tears bubbled in her eyes and a scream exited her throat.

Amelia was certain that Mom would yell and she would never make it to the moon.

"Woah sweetheart, what happened?" Mom's calm voice appeared, and a warm arm enveloped her. Amelia continued to cry, pointing towards the buried utensil.

"Oh dear, that's no good," she said, easily removing the embedded sword with her superior mom strength.

"There, all better."

Amelia continued to scream, pointing at the large hole that now marred the surface.

"Hey, hey, it's okay." She rocked Amelia back and forth in a familiar soothing motion.

"Mess is just the residue that life leaves behind." Amelia didn't understand what mommy meant, but she wasn't yelling so Amelia decided she wasn't in trouble.

Freddy's face was a mask of concern, and Amelia couldn't blame him.

"You're going to make messes, doc. Big horrible ones, and little stupid ones, but that doesn't make you bad or irredeemable. If it did the earth would have swallowed me whole and I would be waving up at you from the fiery pits of hell."

"Just because you're worse doesn't mean I'm not bad."

"Never said it did."

"Then what were you saying?"

He pressed a kiss on her lips. "That I don't care either way."

Her ears were still ringing, but the love she felt for him was nearly painful in its intensity.

"I don't think I've ever had anyone on my team before."

"I'm sorry."

"Don't be, I should be the one apologizing for making you put up with this."

He didn't respond immediately, simply looked into her eyes with devastating seriousness.

"That wasn't what I meant. I'm sorry that everyone that was supposed to take care of you abused that power. I'm sorry that you thought it was your fault."

Amelia couldn't answer because she couldn't breathe.

Freddy thumbed the book he had been using during his faux-therapist role.

"I didn't know Mo gave you a book too."

Her eyebrows furrowed.

"He didn't, I got it from the library."

"Well, this is definitely his writing."

"I had a feeling, but why would he write a book about vampires?"

"Your guess is as good as mine, though it does seem a bit suspicious. We should pay him a visit."

"Maybe a shower first?"

Freddy's answering smile was silver-tinged. "Yes, doc."

He released the cuffs and hoisted her into his arms before she could object, sitting her dusty form on the counter of the master bathroom while he prepared the shower.

He placed her under the hot cascade of water, carefully washing every inch of her skin.

The flour combined with water to make an unsightly slurry that stuck in her hair.

Freddy carefully removed the globs before washing and conditioning it as per her instruction. He admired the re-action her skin had to the hot water, becoming red and in-flamed.

The freckles that littered her cheeks were a haphazard constellation, imperfect in size and arrangement.

Despite the mortal blood he had been taking from her veins since the beginning, she suddenly seemed very human.

A lost child that was abandoned, a girl who constantly had to mold herself into unnatural mental shapes just to find a semblance of normal and belonging.

Amelia had to try so hard to keep her life together, she was just a woman fighting to be good enough. He felt so selfish after all that he learned, disappointed that he too used her for his benefit.

She wasn't an angel sent from above to save him, and it was childish of him to ever think so.

It was only a matter of time before he let his thirst for validation overtake meeting her needs. Amelia was right, until he dealt with the source of his pain he would never be able to love her without the threat of insecurity looming over him.

Freddy needed to kill his father.

RULE 33
GET SOME PERSPECTIVE
AMELIA

"Freddy looks happy." Mo said, resting his elbows on the bar top and taking the glass from her hand.

It was the second one, and she had only drank the first to delay asking Mo what she really wanted to know. It was much harder to be brave without Freddy around, but he had gone to have a conversation with his father.

Every molecule in her body wanted to join him, but she knew it was something he had to do on his own.

She knew he wouldn't actually kill the man, but he needed her permission to feel his anger and hurt, to release the pain he had been running from.

They both needed to do that.

That was why she was here, intent on confronting her father. Without the full truth, she would never be free.

Amelia nodded but didn't say anything.

"So, what's holding you up?"

A complete lack of certainty and no appropriate coping skills.

She settled for a partial truth.

"I just don't know how to make it work with him, he's so young and we're so different." And Mo's misinformation wasn't helping the situation.

Her father pressed his lips together, and pulled a set of car keys from his pocket.

"You hungry?"

The hum of the car's engine soothed her, the streetlights passing in rhythmical predictability.

"How do you feel?" Mo asked, finally risking a glance at his daughter.

"Physically? Perfectly fine."

His shoulders relaxed a centimeter, giving her an opportunity she wasn't going to squander.

"Which is interesting because Freddy hasn't fed from me in several days."

The leather steering wheel cracked beneath Mo's palms. "Shit,"

"So, I'm left wondering if you were lying to us or just wrong."

"Lying, obviously," he defended, clearly offended at the jab aimed at his intellect.

"Why?" If there was information he wished to withhold, he could have easily claimed ignorance on the topic.

"It's complicated."

Amelia shot him a look overflowing with unamused expectation.

"Sometimes it's better not to know. When it comes to casters, asking questions can be dangerous."

"Neither of us are really casters, though, are we?" He lost his status when he became a nocturnal, and she...well, Amelia didn't really know who she was at all, anymore.

His eyebrows furrowed and Amelia could tell he was having an internal argument with himself. Finally, he sighed and spoke.

"I was doing research, before." He must be referring to his mortal life. "It was illegal, raising undead has been outlawed since the war and casters don't take kindly to anything that breaks their rules."

Amelia nodded, that she knew very well. Her aunt had shown her how important rules were. "I thought nobody has been able to create ghouls."

Mo's face relaxed, surprised at her knowledge. "Yeah, but I wasn't raising any undead, just giving them fangs."

The fangs of a vampire are a sophisticated piece of biomolecular engineering, too complex for a natural origin. Realization sparked deep in the recesses of her brain.

Dr. Atkinson, the dentist.

"You were writing a book about it, weren't you?"

Mo blinked.

"I'm surprised you know that, it was confiscated before I could publish it."

She mulled over the idea in her mind, slotting it into the known order of events. Her father had been doing forbidden research which involved putting fangs on ghouls. This meant he lost his job and was exiled from his family. His words were logical, but Amelia still couldn't understand his motivations.

"Why?"

"Retribution. My father was a bad man, it was part of the reason I chose the profession I did. I wanted the Atkinson name to be a signal of hope and good instead of the sick and twisted experiments of a mad-man."

Amelia pursed her lips to hold in a giggle. She could hear Freddy's snark in her mind, mumbling that dentists were not among the list of most trusted individuals.

"So, when did you become undead, then?" she asked, centering her focus back to the conversation at hand. She needed answers.

The car paused at an intersection, red light replacing the darkness. It bounced off her father's face, illuminating the flat expression.

"Why did you assume that I was?"

Her breath stalled.

"You have fangs-" she broke off, realizing that she had been making a big assumption. Being dead was not a prerequisite to having fangs, especially if you were the dentist that invented them.

"How else was I supposed to belong in the nocturnal world?"

A sense of wrongness filled her chest. He was lying again. She was on the outside of caster society but wasn't forced to prowl the streets at night.

"You didn't need to belong in the nocturnal world, it was a deliberate choice. If you didn't need fangs to survive, then there must have been some other advantage to having them."

The look he gave her as he pushed down the gas pedal was somewhere between annoyance and pride. It made an ember of rudimentary joy spark beneath her ribs.

"A caster's power is limited by the amount of magic they produce and a ghoul has no magic of their own at all, relying on harvesting it from others."

"Their bone marrow isn't alive to produce it." She parotted the information from his book. Mo nodded, a small smile on his lips.

"What if you could have the best of both worlds? What if casters could receive magic from others while still being alive?"

Amelia blinked, her heart beginning to race. It made sense, if one considered that vampire fangs were essentially just magic extractors. If he had never been an undead, that meant-

"You're not actually a vampire at all, are you?"

530

Mo shook his head.

"And neither is Freddy."

RULE 34
UNMASK THE MONSTER

Freddy always wondered what it would be like to face his father.

He had told himself he was too physically weak to find him, but likely it was bravery that he was lacking.

That was a different Freddy, a man who let his self-loathing rule every aspect of his life.

He stood outside the dilapidated shack, steps faltering when there were no mountains of abandoned scrap littering the perimeter. It was no different in structure than when he had been there last, and yet, it was nearly unrecognizable.

The grass was trimmed, and Freddy could swear there was

a lawn gnome sitting and reading a paper in the garden.

There was a fucking garden with a fucking garden gnome.

He walked up to the door and knocked, questioning whether he had come to the wrong house while he waited.

His worries were alleviated when his father answered the door. Clean shaven, well-dressed, and standing straight. There was no hint of the sagging, incoherent man he knew. Except for the cold green of his eyes, devoid of any warmth or recognition.

Surprise caught Freddy's tongue, but the man didn't say anything, just stared.

"Who is it, dad?" A high pitched voice called from inside the mobile home.

"Nobody," he answered. Freddy expected to feel angry, to want to rip apart the monster that plagued him for his entire life. To feel the burning need of revenge.

To his surprise, Freddy didn't see a beast looking at him; he saw a sad, sick man that was trying. Worst of all, he saw an acceptable life for the girl within the walls, a life he never got to have. This man didn't deserve another thought, let alone the mercy of death and that little girl didn't deserve to lose her father.

Freddy backed up, turning around to leave.

"You were always too good for this place, Freddy," his father said, voice weak and gravelled with age and poor choices.

"Yeah," Freddy nodded, turning to give him a final look."I was."

He didn't need revenge, he needed to move on and leave the monster behind. He was nearly at the car when a high-pitched voice made him pause and turn around.

"Sir, I have your book!" A girl no older than twelve ran up to him, dark hair swinging behind her. She held out a tattered copy of The Hound of Baskerville. Her eyes were green, a shared feature with his father. Their father, he supposed. "Your name is Freddy, right?"

"Yeah,"

"I think this book is yours, it has your name in it."

Freddy shifted the book in his hands, the weight and worn edges familiar in his grip. He had always wished to be a great detective, a source of truth and justice. Funny, how he had gotten what he wanted.

"What's your name?"

"Alex," she smiled.

He nodded towards the house. "Are they good to you?"

There was a strain to her smile, but it stayed firmly in place.

"They try."

A painful knot formed in his stomach.

They didn't try for me.

Though Freddy couldn't really be certain of that, as Amelia would say. She would tell him that it was an assumption and he had no way to know what battles his parents were fighting.

"Good, that's good," was all he said, though his throat was tight from emotion. He pulled out a pen and wrote a quick note inside the cover, just in case she needed it.

"Keep it, I've read it enough times." He had his own Sherlock at home, anyway.

"Thanks." She took the book back and clutched it firmly in both hands.

"You better go back inside, it's past your bedtime, young lady." He ruffled her hair, and watched as she ran back towards the house.

A strange sorrow settled into his bones on his walk back to Amelia's car. He almost wished he hadn't come, that he could gain back his ignorance.

The drive to the bar was quiet, not even the soft chatter of the radio was there to distract him from ruminating on his foolishness. He had been selfish, centering his dad's entire image on the hurt he caused him.

His father was more than his sins, more than his monsters.

Freddy was more than that too.

He was capable of good, of love, of learning and growing.

By the time he pressed down the parking brake, he knew that he would never return to the house that haunted him, physically or mentally.

He didn't need to prove his goodness, or earn retribution for his sins.

At that moment, he just needed her.

AMELIA

The pancake house was bustling with activity, despite the late hour.

Amelia tended to stick to the mixed parts of the city, so she had never ventured so deeply into the nocturnal part of town. Her aunt had only cautioned her to stay away from caster neighborhoods, so she wasn't entirely sure why. The thought of her aunt made Amelia's heart throb painfully again.

Her father's admission made his relationship with Freddy much clearer, and how it was possible that he nearly starved to death.

"You weren't worried about Freddy feeding because he didn't actually need to," she said, taking a bite of the omelet. It felt too vulnerable to order pancakes, now that she had reason to doubt her father's intentions.

He sipped on his coffee. "I gave him my blood at first, assuming he would start feeding on his own. I had a hypothesis that magic could slow down the metabolism of cells and replace the need for food. I just didn't expect him to have the troubles he did."

Freddy had been an experiment.

Something more feral than anger made Amelia's toes curl inside the comfortable sneakers she wore (Freddy hadn't allowed her to put heels on, so they compromised). She kept her face relaxed, a calm front that would ensure she received as much information as possible.

"That's why you said he needed to feed from me, wasn't it? He wouldn't ever do it for himself." It would be sort of sweet if it wasn't so horrible. "Why not just tell him?"

"Do you want the nice answer or the real one?"

"Both." If she could project his thoughts straight from his head, she would.

"At first I told myself that if I wanted to write about it, a blind study would be more accurate. In reality, I think his admiration was the only thing that made me feel redeemable."

She felt sad for her father, that he was living the consequences of his past actions. She was also living with those consequences, and suddenly she wasn't so sad for him any more.

"Why him?"

"He produces a bit of magic, but doesn't have the centuries of caster superiority to corrupt him. He doesn't have a thirst for power, he just..." Mo grappled, trying to find the right words.

"Wants to play." They both wanted that, and found it in each other. The truth that Freddy was a magic-less caster like herself was soothing, and confirmed an unspoken feeling she had.

They were the same.

Amelia watched the figures that ate and talked and laughed, seeing the world around her in a new light.

There were couples and families. Ghouls, goblins, vampires, and wraiths, having a meal, as if it were midday.

"I never even considered that we had so much in common."

Mo gave her a sympathetic smile. "You haven't seen much of the world, have you?"

Amelia bit her lip and shook her head.

She detested the unpredictability of travel. Her entire day was ruined when she couldn't use her favourite gas pump, she couldn't even fathom being stuck in a foreign place when she had to deal with a complication.

She wouldn't mind going on a vacation with Freddy, though.

He would undoubtedly find ways to make her laugh in the most uncomfortable situation.

"There's more than one way to live, Amelia."

FREDDY

It wasn't until Amelia had scrambled into the passenger seat that Freddy opened his eyes.

He didn't hide the sadness, didn't feel the need to put on a bravado.

His Amelia would see right through it, anyways.

"What happened?" Her voice was soft and sympathetic, though concern wrinkled her forehead.

"Nothing," he whispered. "Nothing at all. I have a sister, and she looks happy." His voice cracked on the last syllable and suddenly Amelia's arms and sweet scent wrapped around him.

"Oh, my sweet vampire." She held him as he sobbed and mourned the life he never had.

Why hadn't Freddy deserved that?

What had he done to be cursed with the shit parents he got?

"Was it my fault?"

"Of course, not."

He needed to hear that, needed to feel the pulse of her heartbeat against his forehead, the soft skin of her neck offering him safety.

"Then why? What did I do to deserve it?" He didn't expect her to answer the question, because it wasn't meant to be answered.

It was the sorrow of a hurt child, and Amelia treated it as such. She let him cry, stroking soothing circles on his back.

Eventually, the tears ran dry and his breaths calmed.

"Please tell me your father conversation went better."

"Well," She leaned back slightly. "Not exactly."

Amelia began to recount the conversation with Mo, but a rage-induced buzzing filled Freddy's head before she could get too far.

Her father, his former ally, had chosen supernatural dentistry over his fucking family. He had a loving home, and threw it all away.

Just because Freddy didn't feel called to hurt his biological father didn't mean his need for vengeance left him entirely.

A shitty father was a shitty father, after all.

Freddy launched himself from the driver's seat, rearing towards the entrance of the bar.

"Freddy, wait!" Amelia called after him, following closely on his heel.

They both stopped dead in their tracks when a familiar colourful caster opened the door.

"You have to save her, Mags." Her twin's voice echoed in her mind. *"Promise me you won't let him win, no matter what it takes."*

Maggie couldn't promise that, not anymore.

"Oh, good lord." Maurice said, undoubtedly unamused at her ambush. To be fair, she hadn't been expecting to see Amelia's car parked in front, or the despondent young vampire sitting inside.

She wasn't entirely sure why she came, to be honest.

"What have I done to deserve such a curse placed upon me?" He crossed his arms and leaned against the bar, leaving several feet between them. The establishment had been cleared of patrons as soon as she stepped foot through the door, so she wasn't sure who he was putting on the performance for.

"You stole my sister, and my niece."

"I certainly did not."

"Then why is she here in the middle of the night?"

"Why do you care, Mags? Ask her yourself."

Maggie stirred the ice around in the drink.

"Unless she's not talking to you." An irritating smirk crawled onto his angular face. It used to fill her with contempt but she suddenly felt entirely too old for this tired dance.

Nearly a century of life, and yet it wasn't until now that she felt the weight of the years past.

Without Amelia, what was the point, really?

There was nothing to fight for, no prize to claim.

Maggie placed a bill on the counter and stood.

"You're right, Maurice. She's not, and she likely never will again. You've won."

She turned and froze when a cool hand gripped her forearm.

"This isn't a game, Maggs."

Maggie let herself enjoy the physical touch for a split second before scoffing and ripping her arm from his grasp.

"It was always a game to you. All of it was just one sick experiment," she spat, opening the door only to run face first into a young, furious vampire.

RULE 35

BLOOD IS THICKER THAN WATER

The door slid closed, the sound echoing off of a suspicious-ly empty nightclub.

Freddy didn't have the capacity to question it at that moment.

"What the fuck, man?" He pushed forcefully against Mo's chest. "You had a wife and daughter, two living beings that needed you. And you chose helping fucking zombies eat a little easier?" He landed a punch to the side of Mo's face.

Just as earlier in the week, there were no defensive or retaliatory strikes. Mo stood with relaxed posture, a frustrating mask of calm diminishing any satisfaction in beating it.

"Why aren't you fighting back?" Freddy asked, pausing the wailing of his fists.

"Why don't you?"

Freddy's world spun, and he allowed one more uppercut before stepping back.

"I'm nothing like you."

"I wouldn't be so sure. What if you got the chance to be a hero? To show everyone that doubted you how wrong they were and earn a way back into the life that turned its back on you. Would you abandon your morals in pursuit of redemption?"

Freddy would have taken the chance, in fact that's exactly what he did with Amelia. He had been released from his ethical beliefs by her order to unleash the most primal part of himself, all in the hope of being worthy.

"Freddy," Amelia's voice startled him from his rage and spinning mind, like pulling a microwave from the outlet. "Stop."

Freddy stood, chest heaving as he helped Mo off the ground.

"Does he have to?" Maggie interjected, following behind her niece. "Oh, let the boy get some justice."

"Justice for what? A second chance at a life he clearly hated?" Mo replied, throwing Maggie a scathing look.

"Ripping away someone's humanity is typically something that requires consent, though your track record is poor in that regard," Maggie said.

"Oh, for Christ's sake, he's not even a real vampire." Mo fired back, a flush of anger reddening his cheeks.

"What?" Freddy's question was barely more than a breath.

"Shit," Mo muttered under his breath.

"Now look at who's withholding the truth." The smirk on Maggie's face was blinding in satisfaction. Mo turned from Freddy and pointed squarely at Magdaline.

"Don't even try to equate the way you've been lying to Amelia with this."

She rolled her eyes. "No, at least everything I did was for her protection."

Freddy cleared his throat. "Excuse me, can someone tell me what the fuck is going on?"

"Yeah, why don't you tell them, Mags? Since you're the crusader of truth now."

"Be careful what you wish for, Maurice," she said, voice muffled between bared teeth.

Maggie turned to Amelia, who was inching further and further away from the altercation.

"Once upon a time I was in love with your father."

The room went still.

"We were very close friends, and I think it was just assumed the children from two affluent families would marry. However, I was not amenable to aid him in his twisted ambitions. So, naturally, he married my twin sister."

Mo pressed his lips together but didn't interrupt.

Holy fuck.

"When I discovered what he had done, I was so twisted from the bitterness in my heart I thought it was a good thing. I thought she would leave him and I was going to get my reward for swallowing my misery, for being a good person. "

Holy fuck.

"I didn't get anything for my suffering. Her body couldn't handle being separated from his and she got weaker and weaker, until she was gone. And then all I had left was you." Maggie's voice shifted from righteousness to something soft and sad.

Amelia's face was a frozen mask of shock, and yet her eyes bounced between her father and aunt.

For once, Freddy's family was not the most fucked up.

Mo cleared his throat, urging Maggie to continue. She shifted uncomfortably.

"You asked so many questions, always talked about them. I don't know what came over me, but one minute I was just giving you a harmless kiss on the forehead and wishing that it could just be us and then your memories were gone."

Freddy understood wanting to keep that secret. He couldn't imagine losing so much, and living with the reminder of that grief. He probably would want to avoid thinking about it as much as possible.

"Happy now?" Maggie turned towards Mo, who's eyes had gone grim.

"No," he answered.

She huffed a broken laugh, "What more do you want from me?"

He stepped towards Amelia's frozen form, and pressed a kiss to her forehead. Her eyes were closed and brows furrowed.

He had done something to her mind, Freddy was certain of it.

"That's better."

Mo sighed and stepped back to his place beside Maggie.

"What did you do?" Freddy asked, a small growl rising to his chest. He would never let anyone harm his caster.

"He gave her a birthday present." Maggie's response broke the fog of protectiveness that had curled around his brain.

"I knew casters were cold, but saving physical affection for one day a year is a bit cruel, no?"

"Caster society is cruel, especially to those it values." Her whisper was distant.

"Doesn't that seem counter intuitive?" Surely, you would want to protect those who were most important.

Maggie shook her head. "It's logical. The best way to keep someone under your control is by making them need you. But you'd know all about that, wouldn't you, Maurice?"

Something hot sparked in Mo's gaze.

"If you're trying to imply something about my character, it's best to just spit it out."

"Fine. You lost your chance to recruit your child into your grand experiment so you found a replacement." She gestured towards Freddy. Before the vampire in question could open his mouth, his uncle stepped so close to his adversary, there was barely a breath's distance between them.

"If I hadn't found him, he would've died."

Maggie lifted her chin, unwilling to surrender to his intimidation. The tension in the room was thick, and Freddy had a feeling whatever it was that went on between them, went way beyond the current circumstances.

"So you take him to the hospital like a normal person, you don't implant him with bloody fangs and brainwash him into thinking he's a creature of the night."

Maggie's words threatened to cause bile to rise up and out of Freddy's throat but he pushed down the reaction, and the knowledge that he appeared he was not a vampire in the traditional sense of the word.

The two peculiar casters continued to bicker.

"I'd say it worked out pretty well for him, all things considered," Mo defended himself.

"The ends don't justify the means."

"It seems like nothing I do can ever be justified. No amount of greater good could ever make me a hero in your eyes."

"Oh good lord, I can't believe you're still obsessed with your twisted vow of moral retribution. Newsflash, Reece: you were a hero to that little girl, and your father was blown to smithereens on that battlefield."

"This has nothing to do with my father."

"What does this have to do with, then? Because I've been the only one with even a hint of interest for the girl's well-being."

"She's not a little girl any more! She doesn't need your twisted suffocating version of love."

"She also doesn't need whatever scraps of fatherly affection you can offer her." The air around them crackled, making the hairs on the back of Freddy's neck stand with unease.

He wasn't sure what happened when two extraordinarily powerful caster fought, but decided he didn't want to find out.

"I'm sorry to interrupt whatever this is, but has anyone bothered to ask Amelia what she wants?"

Three pairs of eyes shifted to Amelia, but found only empty space in the corner she used to be.

RULE 36
MESS IS THE RESIDUE OF LIFE

Amelia pressed her ear against the door of her mommy's bedroom, listening for the comforting voices.

It was wrong to stay up past her bedtime, but it was the only way she had a chance of seeing her daddy.

"I'm not going." Mommy said.

"What do you mean?"

"How do you think this ends, Maurice?

"We will go and start a new life together, where we're accepted."

"We?" Her voice was a tired hiss. "We are already accepted. It's your quackery that's the problem.

This isn't about us at all. This is about you being able to take your experiment with you where no one can see your horrors."

An invisible fist squeezed Amelia's tummy, and a stray gust pushed the door open an inch.

"They're not horrors, they're people. Don't you ever think about the thousands of ghouls out there, losing their humanity because they're forced to hack apart human flesh to survive?"

Amelia couldn't decide if mommy was angry or sad—somewhere in the middle, probably.

"I have spent decades trying to forget that bloody battle ever happened, so no, I haven't pondered the troubles of thousands of undead I will never meet. I have a much more important problem."

"She's getting stronger, isn't she?"

Mommy nodded and stepped up on the railing.

"She can pull water molecules from the air and force them to concentrate in her hand."

"Alice, what are you doing?" Daddy's voice was scared. Amelia didn't quite understand why, if anything it should be mommy who was scared. Amelia was afraid of heights, she could never walk on the railing of the balcony.

"What a mother is supposed to do, protect her child."

"Let's just take a pause and think about this."

"Maybe I could have kept them away before, but after all the negative attention you've brought..." She shook her head and a tear rimmed her eyes.

"Alice,"

"She's five, for Christ's sake. How can I stand by and let them take her? I can't, Reese."

"That's why we will go, far away where no one will find her."

Mommy shook her head. *"You must think me a fool."*

"Alice-"

"You must think I don't know my husband at all. That the pull of being a part of history is more important than the safety of his only daughter. That he knew what would happen if he continued playing with his little ghouls, and yet he did it any-way."

"It doesn't have to be like this."

"It does have to be like this, because someone has to protect her." Mommy turned, back facing towards the forest.

"I-I don't understand."

"Go be a hero, Maurice, but leave Amelia out of it."

Mommy's eyes shifted from daddy down to meet Amelia's, and a warm smile spread across her face.

"The only difference between a hero and villain is who tells the story."

And then she was gone. Swallowed by the wind.

The memory was hot and painful and Amelia could no longer stay still. She didn't know why she pushed past the doors of the bar, but once her lungs filled with the freezing night air, she needed to feel the wind in her hair.

She needed to run.

Her legs pumped with desperate strides, pushing her down the dark, empty streets. A sweet satisfaction of getting to do something she had only dreamed of doing.

She ran and remembered, mind focusing on the least painful parts.

She wouldn't think about the loss of her mother, or the betrayal of her father. Her mind centered on the fact that she had, apparently, been able to force water molecules to condense.

That meant she had done magic, at some point.

Amelia ran and tried to remember, her pace only stuttered

when a buzzing filled her head.

"You missed a spot, sweety." Mom said from the corner of the garden. Amelia rushed over, confused at the mistake. Amelia was very smart when she focused, that was what her Aunt said. She tried very hard to water every single plant, even when her palms became cold and sore.

"There's nothing there." she explained, pointing to the dark earth between the tulips. She wasn't going to waste her time watering dirt.

Mommy laughed, "Well, there won't be if you don't water it."

Amelia closed her eyes and focused, picturing the thirsty plant crying for some water. Liquid dripped from her open palms, soaking the dirt where the sleeping plant hid.

"Well done, honey."

The buzzing eased for a moment, before another wave of vertigo crashed over her.

"I saw my daddy last night," Amelia said, ice cream cone in hand.

"Did you?" Aunty asked, dipping her spoon in her cup of ice cream. She was pink today, Amelia was jealous as it was her favourite color. She wished she could do color magic like her aunt, all she ever did was fix stuff and water plants, completely lame in comparison.

Amelia nodded, taking a bite from the waffle cone. "I wasn't supposed to, I think."

"What was he doing?"

"Talking to Mommy," Amelia scrunched her nose, "and kissing."

Aunty pressed her lips together. "You'll tell me if he comes again, right?"

Amelia shrugged, absorbed in the mint chocolate chip ice cream. "Okay."

Slowly, the buzzing subsided and Amelia regained the use of her senses and limbs.

Guilt, shame, and disbelief pulsed through her at the resurfaced memories. She shook her head, determined not to get lost in the pain of the past.

She had to move forward, to fix her mistakes.

"Let's fix it, shall we?" Mommy said, looking at the tear in the couch with a kind determination.

Amelia nodded, lip still protruding in a display of overt sadness.

"Okay, put your hands on the booboo, honey," she instructed, nodding in encouragement when Amelia obeyed.

"Now, think about the thing that gives you the most joy and let it out." Mom placed her hand above Amelia's in support giving her the strength to imagine.

Amelia let her mind fill with images of pancakes with extra butter and dollops of whipped cream. She pictured the feeling of floating in the air when Daddy tossed her above his head.

She thought about the digging around in the garden, the cool dirt beneath her fingers and the vibrant flowers that rose from it.

Daisies and sunflowers, lilies and carnations. They were beautiful and never made anyone sad, just like Amelia wanted to make the couch happy again.

"Oh, well done!" Her mother cried, releasing the pressure from her hand. *Initially she was disappointed that the rip remained, but was dumbfounded to find that a single yellow-petaled daffodil stuck out from the foam.*

"But I didn't fix it."

"No, honey. You made it better."

BLOODY MESS

RULE 37
LOVE IS A DANCE

AMELIA

Amelia needed a new couch.

It sat before her in the dark office, a final to test for a class she didn't mean to sign up for. She knew down to the marrow of her bones that she could do it, that there was magic locked away somewhere that just needed to be released.

"Now, think about the thing that gives you the most joy and let it out," her mother had said.

Amelia closed her eyes and thought about all the things that brought her joy. She thought of her first cup of hot coffee in the morning, the feeling of taking off her high heels at the end of the day. She thought about Freddy taking off those heels and stretching each one of her toes individually. Amelia shook her head to clear it. Horny and happy were not the same emotion.

She thought about the look of relief on her client's faces as they made a breakthrough, the look of relief on Freddy's face when she finally let him come.

The couch did not stir underneath her palms. Amelia groaned—clearly, thinking about Freddy was distracting her from the goal.

Frustration simmered in her chest. Her mind's habit of getting distracted was the bane of her existence.

Why couldn't she do it?

Every critical word she'd ever heard whittled around her mind, weighing down her shoulders.

She clenched the foam in her fists, puncturing the leather that was intact.

Amelia was angry, and she let herself be.

None of this was fair. She had all this magic in her bloodstream causing her sickness, confusion, and she couldn't even fix a fucking couch.

She had tried so hard.

So fucking hard to do it all.

Hot, angry tears rolled down her cheeks, failure radiating through her.

A mechanical typing made her pause and rise to her feet.

Need some help?

"I don't know how to let the magic out."

How did you let it in?

"I haven't-" Except she had, hadn't she? Every second had been magic with Freddy, because she had let him in.

Because she opened the door.

Amelia stood and walked back to the couch, pausing to close her eyes and take a deep breath before kneeling before it again.

A gust of wind tossed her hair.

Amelia took no notice, simply furrowed her brows and pushed down into the foam, trying to will her mind to behave for once.

She needed to find the door that held her magic, but there was only one barrier in her mind.

It was the one that kept the mess inside, the place she put all of the parts of her that were too painful to live with.

Amelia's body stiffened as she carefully unlatched the first internal lock, and let herself remember the joy of her childhood.

It was uncomfortable, but tolerable.

She thought about her mother's smiling face and kind words, the way she softly encouraged Amelia through her problems.

The next lock was stiffer, and came with a rush of inner turbulence.

It was the pain of her childhood.

There was a dull throb and a release deep underneath her sternum. It radiated an icy ache, a mentholated burn replacing the weight she released.

Tears escaped as she clutched onto the foam stuffing.

Amelia cried for the little girl who had to pretend to be someone she wasn't, the girl who was so ashamed with who she was she tried her best to be nobody at all. That little girl didn't get to be a little girl at all, just a left over inconvenience in the downfall of her family.

There was the final latch.

Her desires.

The deepest door in her mind that she had unknowingly

opened when she let Freddy in. Her wants had been slow-ly leaking since then, and her magic with it. Her desire for companionship, for belonging, for love. She yanked it open with a triumphant cry, and suddenly the turbulence was gone.

Her mind was eerily silent.

Amelia opened her eyes, but all she could see was wind.

Freddy didn't have to think twice about where Amelia went. He knew, just as surely as he knew that she was in trouble.

Freddy turned the knob, grateful that it was unlocked.

His mouth gaped when it flew right off its hinges.

There was a literal tornado inside Amelia's office.

"Amelia!" Freddy yelled over the roaring wind.

AMELIA

Her mother's voice swirled around her, barely more than a whisper. She turned her head from side to side, trying desperately to locate the origin.

"Mom?"

Howling wind answered her, wrapping around her in a fierce cyclone.

"Where are you?" she called out, but all she could see was refuse and wind. "I can't find you."

The tears weren't angry any more.

Amelia felt scared, and she let herself drown in it.

In the eye of her storm there was no one to be strong for.

Amelia faced the couch once again, shocked to find that the wind and litter had shaped into the form of her mother. She knelt down on her knees and laid her head in the lap of the one she had lost so long ago.

"What am I supposed to do, momma?" The wind woman opened her mouth, but no noise came. A furious clicking followed and a piece of paper flew into Amelia's grasp.

What do you need, sweetheart?

Amelia shut her eyes, trying to summon the words to describe what she longed for.

To be enough.

To not have to fight against her own mind just to live.

"I need to fix it, but I don't know how to use my magic."

A series of papers flew from the typewriter, which stayed conveniently out of the path of the tornado.

Yes, you do.

"No, I don't. I wouldn't have landed up in this situation if I did."

Are you sure?

Amelia was always sure. Well, until now, at least. Surely, she would know if she was using her magic. She couldn't think of even one extraordinary thing that she had done, her life was so painfully ordinary.

Which was highly unusual, all things considered.

Realization made her heart sink.

She had been using her magic in order to be as ordinary as possible.

"I tried to fix it but it didn't work."

Is fixing it what you really wanted?

Being that plain, closed, hidden person had been her goal for so long.

"I don't know what I want anymore."

Don't you?

"Amelia!" The voice she once assumed was her mother's now grew in volume above the roar of wind, and it was definitely male.

Freddy.

"You think I did this too?" she asked. Had she willed him to knock on her door, to free her from the life that was slowly destroying her?

When she turned her head back, the form of her mother was gone.

One last paper flew into her hands.

Indulge in the fruits of your labor, my little storm.

"Amelia!" Freddy shouted again, his form now visible through the turbulent wind.

"What are you doing?" he yelled, barely able to makeout her silhouette inside the curtain of flying office supplies.

"Do I look like I know what I'm doing?" she yelled back.

"Have you tried stopping the tornado currently surrounding you?"

"Thanks, Sherlock."

"No, I'm Watson. Which means you have to do the thinking."

"I don't know what to do." Her voice was shaky. Freddy had to change tactics.

"Sure you do, doc." He smiled at her, despite a nervous tremor to his own voice. "You just have to relax."

"Thanks, Freddy. All fixed," she hissed at him, ducking when a stapler flew past her head.

"Okay, okay, try thinking nice thoughts," he suggested.

"That's what started this whole mess."

"Clearly they weren't that nice."

A tape dispenser hit him in the shoulder. He grimaced and rubbed the injured skin, determined to forsake his personal safety to save her.

His lightningbird was beautiful and now she was ready to be free.

"Fuck this, I'm coming in."

"No!" A gust of wind pushed him backwards. "I can't control it, I don't want to hurt you." She was pushing him away—literally—for his own protection.

Unfortunately for her, Freddy knew how to slip between the spaces of her ribs, knew how to speak directly to her heart.

She had prepared him for this moment.

He stepped forward confidently, and the tightness of fear relaxed when the wind parted.

"You have,"

"What?" The roar quieted by a few decibels.

A reassuring sign.

"You've hurt me." He repeated several more steps. "Demeaned me." Two steps. "Made me beg on my knees and crawl at your feet." Three steps. "And yet I worship you all the same. Do you know why?"

"Because the only love you know is painful."

He ignored her quip, correct as it may be.

"Because my place in your life isn't conditional. I don't care how messy it gets or how much it hurts, Amelia. I'm not going anywhere."

"You're only saying that because of the storm threatening our lives." He had never seen her this insecure, so broken open.

"I thought I made it very clear that I love you."

"Love isn't enough, Freddy." Her face was buried in her palms.

"Says who?" he whispered, taking one last step and leaning down to cover her palms with his own. "It seems to have gotten me pretty far."

The floating objects dropped to the floor with an ocean of soft taps, the larger items making a louder thump, and she looked up at him with surprise and relief. She wasn't Amelia the genius, repressed, clinical psychologist; she was a hurt child, lost and vulnerable.

They had ventured from her expertise to his.

"Come here, baby," he cooed, wrapping her in his arms.

"Oh, Freddy. I was so scared." She wept into his chest, the tears from her eyes mixing with droplets that were falling from the ceiling.

It was raining in her office.

"It's gonna be okay, now. Tell me how I can help."

"I tried to fix it, but all I did was make everything worse," she sobbed into his shoulder.

"What were you trying to fix?"

Amelia pointed to a pile of leather and foam.

"Why don't we do it together?"

She swallowed thickly but nodded, turning to the remains of the couch and kneeled, placing her hands on the material. Freddy went down with her, his chest plastered to her back. He covered her arms and hands with his, enveloping her frame with his weight.

"Okay, good," he whispered in her ear, pleased when her

body relaxed into his chest."Now walk me through what to do."

"I thought I was supposed to close my eyes and think about things that bring me joy, but obviously that didn't work."

"Come on, doc. It's obvious."

She was silent for a moment, and he had a feeling she was gnawing on her lip.

"Just imagine what you want it to be."

"What if I don't know?"

"Then there's your problem."

"How do I decide? I don't have any rules to live by anymore."

"You don't need anyone else's rules to know what's right."

"But what if it's the wrong choice?"

"Then you try again. What's the worst that could happen?"

"Nothing," she breathed and Freddy understood. He understood that was her greatest fear, that all of this magic meant nothing and she would be forced to return to the life she was living.

"And if that happens, I'll be here. You're allowed to fail Amelia, but you have to try."

AMELIA

What did Amelia want?

Freddy's voice was low, the vibrations soothing against her back. There was a confidence to his words, a calmness that didn't exist when they met.

He was so pale and weak, barely even alive.

She too was barely alive, in hindsight. She didn't laugh, didn't look forward to six o'clock every night. She didn't feel the hum of his venom under her skin.

"The rain stopped, doc. Whatever you're doing, it's working."

She barely registered his voice, the words on the piece of paper flashed in her mind.

Indulge in the fruits of your labor, my little storm.

She let herself feel pride, wiping away the shame that constructed the blockade in her mind.

She pictured the feeling of Freddy's lips against hers, the sound of his voice when he said her name.

Amelia imagined the way he smiled and the way his body felt when he was inside of her.

She thought about Freddy, over and over again until she could no longer feel the torn leather underneath her palms. She wanted him—a young, imperfect, impulsive vampire that loved her.

His grip drifted from her arms to her torso, holding her tight against him. She was acutely aware of his mouth on the side of her neck, of his breath against the sensitive skin there. Desire bloomed in her core at his touch, a familiar craving growing steadily.

"Bite me, Freddy," she breathed. He complied, sinking his teeth into her with a learned efficiency. There was no hesitancy, no anxiety in his bite.

Amelia had done that.

She gave herself to the pleasure of his venom but also allowed herself to celebrate her success, with no hint of regret or guilt.

"The flowers take the nutrients from the dirt and use them to bloom. They cannot give us their beauty without taking as well." Her mother's voice was gentle as she sprinkled the fertilizer into the dirt beneath the roses. Amelia wrinkled her

small nose.

"Does it have to be so stinky?"

Mommy laughed, picking Amelia off the ground and helping her lean in to smell the delicate pink petals.

"Not so stinky now, is it?"

"Why not just poof the flowers so we don't get dirty?"

Mommy sandwiched Amelia's hands with dirt, making her giggle. "How does that feel?"

"Silly," Amelia answered truthfully; hands were supposed to stay clean.

"What does it teach you?"

Amelia thought about all the describing words she knew, how to explain the cold, gritty feeling of the dirt and what it could possibly show her. "That dirt is cold and scratchy."

"If we poof the flowers, we would never know what the dirt feels like on our hands, or what the fertilizer smells like."

Amelia's eyebrows scrunched.

"Why would I want to know how stinky the dirt is?"

"Because then you wouldn't appreciate how good the flowers smell."

"I'd rather be a flower than stinky dirt, I think."

"I wouldn't be so sure."

Amelia gave her a skeptical look.

"The dirt can grow hundreds and thousands of flowers, but what can the flower do?"

"Make you sneeze, and look pretty in a vase," Amelia answered, she was always very good at answering questions.

"But it cannot live without its roots, without the ground that nourishes it."

"So, the stinky dirt is the boss?"

"Exactly. Power can't really be taken, only borrowed. But everything has a consequence, little breeze. Every flower takes nutrients out of the dirt as well. That's what love is, a dance between giving and taking."

The buzzing subsided enough for Amelia to hear Freddy's voice behind her.

"Amelia, open your eyes."

BLOODY MESS

RULE 38
STOP AND SMELL THE FLOWERS

NOBODY CAN SAY WHAT BROUGHT THE FIRST VAMPIRE INTO EXISTENCE, THOUGH SOME BELIEVE THAT LOVE HAD SOMETHING TO DO WITH IT.

- VAMPIRES: SECRETS OF A FORBIDDEN MAGIC BY DR. ATKINSON

The entire office was completely restored to its previous plain appearance, ripped couch and all.

"What-" Freddy began.

"I don't want perfect," Amelia explained, standing and turning in his arms.

She wanted this vampire that couldn't hunt, the prey who held all the power in the world.

"I just want you," Amelia sighed, the aftereffects of adrenaline leaving her bones heavy. "And maybe a proper vacation."

"Amelia!" Her aunt's breathless voice called from the doorway. "Are you alright? What happened to the door?"

"Must have blown off in the storm," Mo answered, stopping just behind Maggie's form.

"What are you doing here?" Freddy asked, voice merely a hostile hiss. "Both of you."

"Apologizing," Mo said, stepping into the room.

"For?"

"A lot. More than any person could ever be forgiven for. Even though I was so close to finding my retribution, it wasn't worth the cost. "

"You weren't close," Amelia interrupted.

Mo looked like he was going to object, but Maggie pressed a hand to his chest.

"You were trying to find a way to increase a caster's magic past the natural set-point, correct?"

Mo nodded, though there was a flush of shame to his skin.

"And you figured that stolen magic would have no consequence, that slapping fangs on a caster would lead to infinite power and put an end to arranged marriages and careful breeding?"

"The possibility was certainly there."

"So, why haven't you become the most powerful caster in the world?" Freddy's eyes narrowed, picking up his love's thought process.

"He's made himself into a flower." Amelia explained.

There was a silence. Likely because Mo was not, in fact, a plant. He was a caster and a vampire, sort of.

"I mean his perspective is wrong. His focus was always on how much power he could take, how big he could grow. Of course, a man would assume in order to gain power he would need to become the predator," she continued.

A hint of understanding began to bloom on Freddy's face.

Power can't be taken, only borrowed.

"He grew up in a place with only one caster-flavoured perspective. The pedigree and privilege that made him so superior was his greatest hindrance." He hadn't been forced to grow up straddling two worlds where he did not belong, he never grew the capacity to understand other people's point of view, too clouded by his own ambition.

Enjoy the fruits of your labor.

Amelia had never felt more grateful for the life she had lived.

At first she was so blind sided by the truth about Freddy she couldn't even think, let alone ask questions. She never questioned why she was so surprised in the first place.

How is it possible that she had studied hundreds of different species of supernatural creatures and yet never met a vampire?

If taking caster blood was a feasible way to gain power, you'd hear of kidnappings or violent attacks. If the vampires were licking their lips at the thought of caster blood, she wouldn't have been able to make it half way down the street without becoming a magical snack, and yet when she was in a vampire bar looking for trouble Freddy was the only one that would go near her.

Amelia didn't know how she didn't see it sooner.

When Maggie came to visit the other night, the bar cleared out like there was a bomb threat. She thought it was prejudice at the time, but that wasn't it at all.

Where are the vampires?

"Well, are you going to share what I was missing?" Mo's voice was displeased and his eyes expectant.

"No," Amelia answered, making her father's eyebrows knit together.

"Why not?"

"Because I don't want to." And several other reasons, none of which were as important. "I have a question though, if you don't mind."

Mo's jaw clenched but he nodded.

"If you went through the effort of fanging yourself to attain more magic, why haven't you been using it?"

"That seems like an assumption." He glanced between Freddy and Amelia, face tensed with shame. Her own face crinkled in a thoughtful frown—how could he have been using his magic in regards to Amelia and Freddy?

Realization hit her with a wash of anger.

"Oh,"

"Oh?" Freddy echoed.

Amelia turned her face into Freddy's. "Magic is limited by distance, usually. But let's say somebody has been slowly using borrowed magic to expand the range a little bit. It's feasible that it could extend half a kilometer, far enough to reach where your daughter's office was conveniently locat-ed."

"Yeah, I've still got nothing, doc."

"Doesn't it seem a bit convenient that you would end up in my office, on the same day that my entire life began falling apart?"

"Oh,"

"And you," she pointed to her aunt. "You fed me little bits of the truth, just enough that I would be too scared to choose him." She reared back towards her father. "Your plan backfired. You gave me my memories back so I would remember you, but there was nothing to remember. You were never there, even when you were, so obsessed with your own ambition you discounted the earth that grew you. *She* was there, and she was messy, and imperfect, and she loved me unconditionally, enough to forfeit her life just to give me a choice." Amelia stepped back, shaking her head. "Thank you, for giving me back my memories, and I'm sorry."

"Sorry for what?" Mo asked.

"Choosing myself."

A large gale blew towards Mo and Maggie, pushing them backwards and past the doorway.

Despite the rejection, her aunt smiled and whispered, "Sway righteous," before the door closed behind them.

Silence bathed the room, and Amelia had the strangest feeling she had passed some sort of silent test.

"So, do we not care about discovering the cause of your illness anymore?"

His words reminded her that she still needed to fill him in.

"Oh, I figured that out when they were bickering at the bar. Mo actually told you the answer a while ago."

Freddy looked at her expectantly.

"You can't separate magic from the caster," she quoted.

"I thought he meant that a caster was only as powerful as their intention."

"He did, but two things can be true. A caster's magic is intrinsically linked to their desires. It can be borrowed but that intention doesn't change just because it's in another vessel."

589

"So, you were sick because…" Freddy's lips were pursed and there was not one drop of understanding in his eyes. Amelia closed the distance between them, wrapping two fatigued arms around his neck.

"I tried to seperate myself from the hot vampire holding my magic hostage," she purred. The corner of Freddy's lip turned up.

"That would explain why you're in such good health now." He trailed his nose down the side of her neck. "Though, I can get a little closer if you'd like."

She would like that very much, but guilt caused her to pull away.

"There's more," She gripped the hair on the back of his neck, committing the texture of the strands to memory. There was a chance the truth would cause him to reconsider their relationship. "When I went to the library, the only information I found was one line: Tragedy follows a caster and her vampire."

His face went grim, eyes losing the sensual fire that had sparked. "Do you think it'll cause you permanent damage?"

Amelia took a deep breath. "I don't think tragedy means death. I think it's indentured servitude."

Freddy blinked.

"Oh, you mean for me?"

Amelia nodded.

"I think you're always going to respond to my desires."

"And?"

"And I wouldn't blame you if you didn't want to continue on with a romantic relationship."

"Why the fuck would that change anything?"

"Because I can literally control you against your will."

"Yeah, obviously. I know you won't take advantage of me, if that's what you're worried about." There was dumbfounded amusement on his face, which irked Amelia for some reason.

"How do you know that?" They had just confirmed that she was not a morally righteous, perfect person. In fact, she had essentially just proclaimed to her entire family that she was choosing to be purposely selfish. He should not be looking at her like she was the one not understanding. She had been the one to solve the case, after all.

"You gave your typewriter a name."

The indignation washed from her, and then she was one who was incredulous.

"What?" Amelia resisted the urge to laugh.

"The night we met, you introduced me to your typewriter as if you were old friends. That's when I knew,"

"Knew that I was a basket case, no doubt."

He cupped the back of her neck in his palm, and a faint glow returned to his eyes.

"That everyone is a person to you, even if they're not."

All Amelia wanted was to feel like a person, the one thing that evaded her.

Until now.

"Aren't you worried I'll use my magic to hurt you?"

"Would it be any different than if we were two humans? A man could easily hurt a woman, but she trusts him not to." He demonstrated by squeezing the circumference of her neck gently.

He had a point, she had to admit. There was never a perfect balance of power in any relationship, but there had to be trust.

"God, can you stop being so smart and sweet?"

Freddy laughed, releasing her throat and trailing his hands down to the small of her back. "Only when you do."

She held the sides of his face tenderly, admiring the features that now undoubtedly belonged to her.

"Don't you have any desire to retain your free will?" She couldn't believe that such a beautiful man would find it acceptable to be under her command permanently.

"Didn't do much with it when I had it, honestly. I meant what I said, doc. My love is unconditional, and even if it wasn't, I like who I am when we're together." The smell of sweet cinnamon enveloped her, and her skin tingled where he grasped it. Still, there was a tight hollowness in her chest, one that no amount of sweet words could fill. She still had work to do, to heal from all she had lived through.

"I'm so lost right now, I don't even know if I can be what you need."

He tilted her chin up and all she could see was the silver of his eyes.

"I don't need you to save me, doc. I want to earn a place in your life, to stand side by side with you. If I had known you were out there-" his speech was cut off by the desperate press of her lips against his. She meant it as an act to silence his oncoming guilt train, but quickly became distracted by the heat in her core and the softness of his mouth.

By the time they parted for air, her head spun and breath left her lungs with laboured puffs.

ABLY MESS

"You would have come to me before I was ready," she said with deep assurity.

There was no doubt he would have been banging down her door if he knew that it was possible to feel this way, because that's precisely what she would have done.

"Are you ready now?"

Amelia took a deep stabilizing breath and rested her forehead on the center of his chest. She didn't know anything about herself anymore, except for who she wanted by her side while she figured it out.

"Being with me won't be comfortable."

"I guess it's a good thing I'm a glutton for punishment."

Amelia lifted her head, unable to resist meeting his gaze. Silver flashed in his eyes at the thought of the other ways she could make him deeply uncomfortable, no doubt.

"There's nothing I could say that would make you leave, is there?"

"Nope," The glow of his eyes didn't wane, but his grin was proud and slightly goofy.

Amelia rested her cheek against his heartbeat and sighed, finally focusing on the plain interior of her office.

"Then, I guess we're both starting over."

RULE 38

He placed a kiss on the top of her head. "Together?"

"Together."

Freddy cleared his throat, making her head raise to meet his eyes again. "Can I finish what I was saying, before you rudely interrupted?"

Amelia giggled and flushed slightly, making his heart melt.

"Sorry,"

"Listen, I know I'm not enough right now, but this is a start." He removed the paper from his pocket, and held it out for her to read.

"What is it?" Amelia snatched it out of his hand, making him smile. She always needed to know everything.

"I passed the challenge exam." He tried to make the smile on his face somewhat humble, but was pretty certain he failed.

The pride that shone in her eyes twisted into something smaller and sadder. "Did you do this for me?"

Freddy hated the way she always had to make sure her presence in his life wasn't harmful, like she was just waiting for him to make her the villain in his story. It would take time to heal her from that, but he wasn't going anywhere.

"No, doc. I should've done this years ago, I was just too scared to believe I was worth the effort. I know you've already done me a lifetime full of favours but do you think you could give me some time to get there?"

Amelia nodded somberly, folding the paper and placing it back in his pocket. He almost began purring from the sign of ownership. His pocket was her pocket, his body was her body.

"It'll be tough breaking the news to my large roster of sexy young vampire lovers."

Freddy's purr turned into a growl which made Amelia roll her eyes. "Of course I will, Freddy. It's been established that I'm not very good at staying away from you."

And the bizarre vampire-caster connection they had prevented it. Her tone drifted from annoyance to deep thought, and he was almost certain he knew what she was pondering.

Why had any of this happened if he wasn't a real vampire?

What did it mean for their future?

The orange glow of morning sunlight filtered through frosted windows, and Freddy pulled away to step in front of one.

He unlatched the lock and popped it open, allowing the full light to fill the room and crisp morning air to fill his lungs.

Mortal lungs, of a man that had never died.

Warm arms circled his waist.

"I wasted so much time," he said, knowing she would understand.

"Have you?"

Freddy didn't answer at first, just watched as an elderly goblin hopped off a garbage truck and rolled the bin from the curb.

"I could have slept beside you every night, could have taken you for proper dinner dates."

Amelia hummed against his back, lazily running her hands on the skin below his belly button.

"I could have been entrenched in caster society, if I knew then what I know now."

And they never would have met. He sighed and covered her hands with his.

"Thank God we didn't know." He supposed he should thank

Mo, as well. Even if his intentions were questionable in their morality, his desire to finish his research and reconnect with his daughter was the reason Freddy was here.

Though his body had never died, the man had revived him.

"So, what do we do now?" Amelia asked, rounding his side and tucking herself in the crook of his arm.

She had no plan, no framework to guide her future.

Freddy squeezed her body tightly against him, looking out onto the sunrise of a new day he had never seen before. His master, his love, his Amelia standing beside him, under the safe protection of his arm.

"Live."

BLOODY MESS

ABOUT THE AUTHOR

S. Nasonov is an independent romance author with a firm belief that everyone needs to relax.

She writes stories that allow men to relinquish their power, and simp unabashedly about women who are definitely overthinking the situation.

Her personal goal is to have you laughing on the first page and crying by the last.

She lives in a world where straight people don't exist and neither does normal. It's a neurodivergent realm, where nice guys finish first but sometimes don't finish at all.

When not writing she can be found chronically ill at large (so probably in bed, doomscrolling.)

If you have something to say about her book, she encourages the good, bad, and ugly. (She's just very bad at initiating conversations.)

www.ingramcontent.com/pod-product-compliance
Lightning Source LLC
Chambersburg PA
CBHW060209030726
47499CB00004B/980